MW00964344

New Canadian Speculative Writing

Tesseracts 8

edited by

John Clute

and

Candas Jane Dorsey

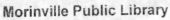

TESSERACT BOOKS

an imprint of

THE BOOKS COLLECTIVE

EDMONTON

The translations in this book were made possible by a generous grant from the Canada Council for the Arts. Thanks to the Canada Council Block Grant program and Alberta Foundation for the Arts for overall publishing support. Thanks to Gerry Dotto of Screaming Colour Inc., David Macpherson at Advance Graphic Art Services Ltd., and Bill Williams at Alpine Press Ltd.

Cover design by Gerry Dotto.
Typesetting by Jena Snyder of Clear Lake Ltd. (Publishing) in Goudy, Template Gothic, and Officina fonts in PageMaker 6.5.
Printed at Alpine Press Ltd. on 60-pound #2 offset stock with softcovers of 10-point Cornwall and hardcovers in buckram with Luna Gloss dustjackets.

Published in Canada by Tesseract Books, an imprint of the Books Collective, 214-21, 10405 Jasper Avenue, Edmonton, Alberta, Canada T5J 3S2. Telephone (780) 448-0590. Tesseract Books are distributed in Canada by General Distribution Services, 325 Humber College Boulevard, Etobicoke ON M9W 7C3, phone: (416) 213-1919. Trade sales representation is handled by Literary Press Group, 110 Eglinton Avenue West, Suite 401, Toronto ON M4R 1A3, phone (416) 483-2908. Mail US orders to press.

Canadian Cataloguing in Publication Data

Tesseracts[8]: new Canadian speculative fiction

ISBN (bound) 1-895836-62-X (paperback) 1-895836-61-1

1. Science fiction, Canadian (English) 2. Canadian fiction (English)–20th century. I. Clute, John, 1940- II. Dorsey, Candas Jane III. Title: Tesseracts eight.

PS8323.S3T499 1999 C813'.08762008054 C99-901234-7 PR9197.35.S33T499 1999

∞ Table of Contents ∞

Foreword	v	*John Clute*
Strategic Dog Patterning	1	*Hugh A.D. Spencer*
Umfrey's Head	21	*Daniel Sernine (translated by Jane Brierley)*
Holes in the Night	52	*Jean-Louis Trudel*
Viking	53	*John Park*
The Sea Below	73	*Francine Pelletier (translated by Sheryl Curtis)*
Gone With the Sea	101	*Ursula Pflug*
Speaking Sea	125	*Sally McBride*
Games of Sea	143	*Sandra Kasturi*
The Edge of the World	145	*Sara Simmons*
The Oceanographers	155	M. Arnott
Chaff	156	M. Arnott
The Dark Hour	157	A.M. *Dellamonica*
Why Starships Should Be Named For Moths	180	*Peter Bloch-Hansen*
Home Again, Home Again	181	*Cory Doctorow*
Nightfall	206	*Susan A. Manchester*
Rice Lake	207	*Ursula Pflug*
Smokestack in the Desert	219	*J. Michael Yates*
Within the Mechanism	221	*Yves Meynard*
The Dragon of Pripyat	235	*Karl Schroeder*
The Energy of Slaves	275	*René Beaulieu (translated by Yves Meynard)*
Extispicy	291	*David Nickle*
Afterward?	307	*Candas Jane Dorsey*
Biographies	309	*About the authors*

Foreword

∞ John Clute ∞

HERE IS A PUZZLE. Most of us have faced something of the sort. I am at Readercon, an sf convention held in the heart of New England, at the hot bitter northern end of the Boston-Baltimore megalopolis, in the United States of America, in July, in a forbiddingly modern global-village hotel overlooking Interstate 95. How can I tell that I am not in an exactly similar hotel overlooking Highway 401 at the hot bitter northern end of Edge City (the megalopolis formerly known as Toronto), in Canada, in a summer month?

The puzzle continues. Here at Readercon I meet certain fellow writers, some of them Canadian like me, some not. How can I tell the difference? I meet Terence Green, I meet Gene Wolfe, I meet Rob Sawyer, I meet John Crowley, I meet Jean-Louis Trudel, I meet Barry Malzberg, I meet Yves Menard—who brilliantly fronts a panel I'm lucky enough to be on. I meet Candas Jane Dorsey in the antarctic chill of the hotel atrium, where budgie-like we exchange gravel with the easy affection that has made our co-editorship of *Tesseracts*[8] a legend throughout the Western World, and in the following several seconds agree upon the shape and contents and permitted maximum sale of the anthology you are now holding.

Two days later I am in a car, which may be of Canadian or American manufacture, driving west through Massachusetts with two fellow Canadians, Peter Halasz and Robert Knowlton, whom a Martian anthropologist might not immediately recognize as exiles spelunking the sulphurous depths of America. The speed limit is 65 mph (in Canada the speed limit will be 100 kph). We drive on the right, as we soon will in Canada. We stop at a Thruway service centre which, thirty years ago, might have housed a Howard Johnson's, but now gives off the stale stomach-churning stink of fast food stuck to cardboard cartons: in Canada we will inhale the same stink, but will read the menu in two languages. We drive on into the night northwards, and reach the Ganonoque Bridge. Peter, as usual, exhales with relief when we reach the border.

Could a Martian anthropologist say why?

A few hours later we reach Toronto. We stick to the lunar Edge defined by Highway 401, skimming the rim of the Old City, which does still exist downhill lakewards in the dark, an enclave of urban theodicy traversed by streetcars, with small houses dreaming under big trees 500 yards from 70-storey skyscrapers owned by one or another of the ubiquitous Canadian banks; and I thought: Here is something for a Martian to notice, maybe.

We all know that Toronto is a favourite location for American film makers, who shoot there not only because it's cheaper to do so, but because the inner heart of Toronto is time-warp country. (Recently I see Bob Clark's *A Christmas Story* [1983] without knowing at first that, though it's set in 1940s Cincinnati, it has in fact been filmed 40 years later in Toronto. Two children are looking into a department store window at a Christmas display, noses pressed against the clean glass. The camera pans slightly, revealing an embossed metal window frame, my ears prickle, I fall through: it's Toronto, it's 1948, my nose is pressing against clean glass, I'm staring at Eaton's Christmas display.) Toronto is a polder which protects an urban life that Americans tend to think resembles the urban life of their own inner cities half a century ago.

They can wish.

Wise Canadians know different. We know that the highways and atriums, that the fast food and the internet glums, that Edge City and all the megalopoles of the world make the same dazzle, pock the same pocks in our souls: now we know how many holes it takes to fill the Albert Hall. We know that Canada, in so far as it is a "modern" country, is a mirror of America as a whole, is almost imperceptibly nuanced from the larger moiety below the belt, south of the undefended border. But we also know that the "backwaters" of the Canadian soul and the Canadian city and the Canadian landscape, just like the "backwaters" of Canadian literature which this anthology proudly manifests, are not naive continuations of a vision of life no longer tenable down there, but a *preserve*.

The inner Toronto of 1999 is not the Cincinnati of 1949 but a kind of pun on that disappeared world: a knowing artifact, a small scruffy sacred grove in the late century. Canadian writing in particular has retained an anticipatory hush, an island solitude, a willingness to queue for the epiphany to come, that signals a difference we must cherish from the world net we will, more and more, be inhabiting for the rest of our span here.

We are competent within the net of the world, but as wise Canadians we are exiles there. Wherever wise Canadians happen to meet, in whatever atrium in the burn of the world, exiles meet. It is, sometimes, hard to detect; it would take a particularly competent Martian anthropologist to distinguish most of the Canadians I meet at Readercon from their fellows. And yet. And yet, sometimes, I see a flash of the cunning of the exile in the soothing gaze of even the pleasantest of Canucks.

Good. I drove back to Toronto with two spies, semblables, frères. The world, which is burning, needs a cunning eye to perceive it. Not all the stories originally submitted to *Tesseracts*^{8} showed that cunning; some of the rejects displayed a sensitivity to adolescent loneliness, as iconogrified by tropes out of the lumberyard of sf and fantasy, that might have been more moving had they not so closely resembled each other. What came through in many of the stories we eventually selected, what excited my own exilic nerve-endings, was not loneliness (loneliness is the lowest form of exile) but solitude: the solitude of the prairie gaze upon multitudinousness, the solitude of the bullet bit, the task of seeing undertaken.

There are two or three stories here which I think may one day be understood to be great; but I won't load the deck by pointing them out. In her afterword, Candas may talk about the contents of *Tesseracts*^{8} in some detail. She may give her own take on the large number of stories involving bodies of water, as though seen through a gauze of polder; or upon the landscapes sometimes in evidence here, the kind of landscape—it's always a water margin petering into the unknown, never a borderland—that Canadians are justly famous for creating. Here, at the beginning, it may be enough to thank our contributors for continuing to perceive, continuing to preserve, continuing to remake the world. ∞

Strategic Dog Patterning

∞ Hugh A.D. Spencer ∞

Ogilvy's Notes: *The Sacrifice Principle: behaviour that appears non-adaptive, even self-destructive, when found in individual organisms. However, when viewed in a more dynamic, collective context, the same actions are revealed to be a decoy—giving up a few lives to expand the pack community.*

Monday

IT WAS A BAD TRANSMISSION: the dead skyscrapers and old streetcar lines were breaking up the signal from Animal Control.

"Bring us the Alpha Dog," the ghost voice on his helmet speakers whispered.

Morrow looked over at Fixx; his partner's blue-crystal eyes were tracking the last of the pack disappearing into the decaying parking garage.

"Stop here," said Fixx.

Morrow braked the van and Fixx kicked open the door. The gothic tattoos on Fixx's forearms twisted into flesh baroque as he hauled out stained metal tanks and black tubing from below the front seat.

"We'll do well here." Fixx pulled a helmet over his pony tail and ran toward the concrete building.

More of that freak intuition, thought Morrow. Then he noticed Fixx clamping a chrome nozzle onto the tubing as he approached the entrance.

Fixx was going to use a wide-angle flame thrower.

Shit! thought Morrow. He wasn't going to give up on a good commission. Morrow released two multi-pistols from the dashboard gun rack. The pistols could get messy, but if he aimed properly he could keep the cranium and upper spinal column intact.

"Do you have the Alpha in sight?" the voice in his head asked.

"Fucking, eh," replied Morrow and clicked off the signal. AC didn't need to know his problems.

Morrow knew the drill on building infestations, so he headed for the far end of the first level basement. Packs liked to be underground, but not so from the surface that it was hard to scout and forage.

Inside there were some truly unusual smells. The building reeked of dog urine from where the pack had marked its territory and of the smell of many dead things. Kills brought in to feed the pack.

Morrow saw bursts of bright blue and orange at the opposite end of the level and then there was a new smell: napalm and live meat cooking.

Now Morrow was really pissed off. Fixx claimed he was some kind of mystic, really he was just a goddamned peasant. The jerk had just charged in, burnt out everything and would be collecting minimum bounty on everything he could salvage.

No style at all.

When Morrow reached his partner there was another smell. Fixx was smoking an enormous reefer as he contemplated the concrete-bound fireball. Contact with cannabis would have meant immediate termination for Morrow—but Fixx was a Registered Functional Head and so was excused from drug fee regulations on religious grounds.

"Did you get them all?" asked Morrow. The fumes from the napalm and the reefer were making his eyes tear up. "Did you see the Alpha?"

Fixx inhaled deeply and kept on staring at the burning bones. "No A-Dog in there. Just puppies and bitches."

Morrow knocked one of the tanks of the flame thrower with his gauntlet. "For god's sake don't use that thing anymore!"

"Whatever, man," replied Fixx as he extended the spring on his specimen-scooper. "Got my quota."

Morrow was already running up the main ramp leading to the ground floor.

It was back to his basic training in animal behaviour now. If the Alpha Dog and his elite guard weren't back there defending the pack, they'd be on the upper levels of the garage: checking out potential new territories and packs, working out escape routes.

Don't give the leaders time to think, the manuals said. Hit them hard, hit them fast. Before you end up reacting to whatever they are going to do to you.

The rampways had dozens of dark corners and abandoned doorways. The elite guard were spread out along these spaces on each floor—leaping out at him as he passed by. He took out the first four with standard slugs through the brain. Nothing to worry about: big muscles, small heads, enormous teeth. Definitely E-Dogs but no sign of the Alpha.

Number five leapt out from a washroom and Morrow used an explosive charge to transform it into a wet red cloud.

This is too easy, Morrow concluded. These E-Dogs are too stupid, they must be expendable. He figured that the Alpha Dog wanted him to come up the main ramp.

Ah, well. The risks are part of the fun, Morrow thought.

Morrow humped over to the far corner of floor eight and found the fire escape ladder on an outside wall. Climbing with 150 pounds of field gear on your back was not easy.

These dogs were starting to be a real pain in the ass.

Six floors later, Morrow hauled his body over the edge of the rooftop. As quietly as possible, he staggered behind an air conditioning unit and looked around. On the other side of the rooftop, right next to the main ramp access, was another cadre of Elite Guards. They had big heads and bigger teeth. These were the ones the A-Dog valued.

They were waiting for Morrow to appear on the main ramp, but they were facing the wrong way. Maybe these dogs weren't so smart after all.

Another dog pushed its head around the corner of a huge old air conditioner, it was only six feet away from Morrow. This one had a really big head and absolutely huge ears. The body was smaller than the others. This was probably an Alpha-Minor, a smart runt, or maybe the A-Dog's pup.

Morrow surprised the A-Minor. It reacted to Morrow with a classic fear-threat snarl instead of barking loud to alert the others.

Almost reflexively, Morrow kicked the animal full in the body. The A-Minor went flying off the roof. It didn't have time to yelp before it hit the pavement.

The up side to this, thought Morrow, is that I'm still alive. The down side is that the inside of that dog is now the consistency of strawberry Jello. He wouldn't be collecting much on that one.

Where was the real thing? *Where was the damned Alpha Dog?*

It was crouched on another air conditioner unit next to the main ramp.

Morrow did a head count: there were ten dogs on the roof. Even with the utility pistols, Morrow wasn't sure he'd make it. The Elite Guard could swarm him before he could get off a single shot.

Stop thinking like a dog, Morrow thought. Don't fight your way up the pack hierarchy.

He selected a .303 calibre setting on one of the pistols and aimed at the Alpha Dog. Cut off the head and worry about the limbs later.

The bullet severed the Alpha Dog's spinal column. The animal collapsed, paralyzed but still breathing.

The Elite Guard panicked, barking at their fallen leader, leaping around in frenzied fear-attack-defence postures.

They noticed Morrow as he clicked in an explosive charge and aimed.

After one ear-splitting sound, there was no more barking. Just a ragged edge where there used to be the corner of the rooftop.

Not much to collect on there, Morrow realized. He would have done better if he'd torched them like Fixx. But direct action was so satisfying.

But the Alpha Dog was still intact. Its frantic eyes tracked Morrow as he walked over to its side.

"Stay," Morrow whispered as he took out the spring-clippers and the doggie bag.

∞

On the way back to AC Central Morrow did some mental arithmetic. He was still going to do well at the bounty counter. And he didn't mind too much that his partner was going to make more than him on this kill. Fixx would probably just use the extra money for dope, Morrow decided.

"We should give thanks for this bounteous harvest," muttered Fixx as he slid a chrome pellet into the van's entertainment system. "Do you mind if I worship now?"

Morrow shrugged, knowing that he could be facing disciplinary action if he said that he did.

The van vibrated to the sound of vintage Hawkwind as they rolled into human-occupied territory.

What a jerk, thought Morrow. Fixx was wasting his time with religion. Not like me, thought Morrow. I'm on a fast-track. Gonna be the world's greatest dog-killer.

∞

Morrow cornered his shop steward in the locker room. "Got a minute?" Morrow asked.

McDermitt unfastened his armoured vest, releasing a wave of beer-fed flab. Some of the younger DKs believed that the union man was lazy and stupid, but Morrow had noticed that Animal Control's most senior non-management employee seemed to know a few things. Sometimes it was good idea to talk to the dinosaurs.

McDermitt squinted at Morrow. "Aren't you supposed to be over at the Vet-Section lecture?"

Morrow opened his locker and shed his gauntlets. "When I'm getting screwed, I make time to adjust my priorities."

McDermitt struggled to put on his duty shirt. "What's the problem?"

"They pulled me off the Sweep," Morrow replied. "And I figure I was in for at least forty klicks in bonus kills."

"You know what they say," McDermitt grimaced as he bent over to pull on his runners. "A bonus is a bonus. You shouldn't count on them as part of your take-home pay."

"Puppies couldn't live on regular take-home," said Morrow. "Besides, it's not money I'm pissed about, it's career path. How can I get promoted if I can't score on the Sweeps?"

McDermitt looked thoughtful. "What's your new assignment?"

"Some research project," said Morrow. "Management is burying me!"

McDermitt sighed. "So what can your union do for you?"

∞

Ogilvy's Notes: *Skills Transferability: the adaptive capacity of new organisms to assume the roles and responsibilities of older, or deceased, organisms.*

Tuesday

"Did you bring the dog's brain?" The man in the jeans and faded lumberjack shirt looked up from a screen of psychedelic patterns.

Morrow held up the aluminum cylinder. "Hope it didn't go bad on you," he said. "It took me a while to find your lab."

The man took the cylinder in both hands and strode over to a rusting sink. "We're a bit off the beaten track but we have great co-axial connections."

There was a moan of cheap tortured metal as the man turned the tap and a trickle of brown water ran out of the goose-necked faucet.

"But perhaps AC management just feels more comfortable with us out of the way," the man muttered as he unscrewed the cylinder.

Morrow noticed racks of TV monitors and computers stacked against the concrete walls. There were lots of cables, a sleeping bag and a half-deflated air mattress.

"So do you get a lot of TV channels here?" Morrow thought it was probably safe to joke with a weird guy who wore jeans and lived in a sub-basement.

"We use that gear to process our satellite and sensor transmissions," the man said as he slid the brain out onto his open palm.

"Shouldn't you wash your hands before you hold the brain?" Morrow asked.

"I wish I knew," the man replied and nodded to some stools by a folding table. "Make yourself at home."

Morrow sat and watched as the man removed an exacto knife from his shirt pocket and started to scrape the surface of the brain. Layer after layer of grey matter curled above the blade and disappeared down the drain.

"Arthur!" the man shouted. "Get over here, please!"

An overweight young man emerged from behind one of the TV racks. He was also wearing jeans with a *Land of the Giants* T-shirt.

"Take a look at this, Arthur." The older man lifted the remains of the brain out of the sink. "How enlarged would say the auditory lobes are?"

"Maybe twenty-six, twenty-seven percent bigger than the last specimen we had," replied Arthur.

"Big even for an Alpha." The man sighed. "Amazing. I just wish I had the slightest idea of what it means." The man slid the rest of the brain back into the cylinder. "We'll deal with it later."

Then he turned to face Morrow and extended a slimy hand: "Hi, I'm Ogilvy. Welcome to my team."

∞

Ogilvy's Notes: *Reproductive Behaviour: Most observers seem to think that sex is quite important in the lives of most organisms. But from the altitudes I have available, the meaning and significance of sex is not always apparent.*

Wednesday

Morrow steered the van down a crumpled strip of asphalt that used to be Royal York Road.

He was wasted. Last night, around 10:00, Sheila accessed his computer. A friend of hers who worked at the Barnes & Noble at the mall had dropped off some old paperbacks about a wild fantasy planet .

"Bring your handcuffs, dog-killer," she said. "Not the play ones—the ones you use on the dogs."

"Hurry."

Morrow put away the fact sheets on weekly area kills and hurried.

Things got a little rough when Sheila started strapping on appliances and proclaiming herself to be the "Master Tarnsman."

At breakfast, Sheila asked about his new assignment but Morrow didn't feel like talking. Job titles like "delivery boy" or "radio repairman" didn't sound as exciting as dog-killer.

Ogilvy showed him the drop-off point on a print out from one of the Global Information System satellites.

"There's some good open space there…it's a mini-park," Ogilvy explained. "You can connect the sensor to the climbing structure at the west end." The scientist pointed to something that looked like a bird dropping on the shiny paper. "The metal frame will make an excellent antenna."

The van rolled past burned-out residential blocks; Symons

Street...Mimico...Wheatfield Road... Sure, from thirty miles up, I'll bet this looks real easy, he thought.

To his left Morrow saw the remains of a red-brick church. Ahead he saw a stretch of tangled weeds and large piles of dog shit. This must be the mini-park. There was the climbing structure, right next to some rusting poles and dangling chains where the swings used to be.

The monkey bars were set in the shape of a domed cylinder. They reminded Morrow of the nuclear reactor buildings he saw when he took his nephews to the Atomic Park Attraction over at Pickering. He laughed as he turned off the ignition and pulled on the parking brake. Yeah, let's play melt-down and watch all your budgies and house plants mutate.

"I'm here." Morrow spoke into his wire mike and began connecting the air nozzles in his EVA suit.

"Wonderful." It was Arthur's voice on the helmet speakers. Everything that guy said sounded like sarcasm.

A few minutes later, Morrow was outside, lumbering around in his EVA suit. Two years ago, these suits were guaranteed to protect you from bites for at least five minutes. Last year, a memo from the supplier adjusted the time frame.

Morrow sealed off two more air vents in his helmet. The damned faceplate was fogging up every time he breathed. He walked to the back of the van and swung open the doors.

It was very difficult to move around in a full EVA suit. But it was his best bet out here. Every few months, each time a new generation of litters was pumped out, their teeth seemed to be a little sharper, the jaws a little stronger. Last month, another memo from the supplier said that the suit's armour "would resist canine dental penetration until an officer has time to take retaliatory action."

I.e., no guarantees.

Morrow grunted and hefted a metal carrier case onto the curb. These sensor components were goddamned heavy.

"I don't see anything moving," Morrow said. Maybe he was just being optimistic.

"We do," Arthur replied. "Our satellite is picking up a pack lying in the weeds over at the far side of the park."

Shit! Thanks for telling me ahead of time!

"Don't worry," Arthur chided. "They're just mutts and mongrels. Little guys."

Fine, let them bite your ass, Morrow thought. He dragged the carrier case over to the climbing structure as fast as he could.

"And they appear dormant," Arthur added. "They're probably taking a nap right now."

Fortunately, it didn't take long to set up the sensor unit. Most of the components were heavily insulated plug-in-play-on stuff and the rest were big ceramics. Impervious to extreme weather and chew-resistant.

"That ought to do it," Morrow reported as he clipped the cables from the solar panels into the base of the sensor. With the solar panels in place at the top and the sensor assembled inside, the climbing structure looked like a very badly designed Mars probe.

Ogilvy spoke: "Treat the unit before you start transmitting."

Morrow cursed softly and removed a long aerosol canister from his backpack. He started spraying mist on the climbing structure. Morrow worked as fast as possible—the mist contained Canine Erotic Stimulation Pheromones and nobody in AC ever wanted to work with the stuff. C.E.S.P was dangerous; if you got any of it on you, all male dogs within fifty miles would seek you out with serious amorous intent.

C.E.S.P. was developed to trick hyper-horny dogs into fighting with each other over non-existent mates—but it just didn't seem to work out that way. The alphas and the betas would just have sex with each other, while the deltas, gammas and subs would just engage the nearest inanimate object.

"Give the structure a really good dose," Ogilvy said. "If we're going to get good readings we need to attract as many subjects as possible."

There was movement just outside Morrow's field of vision. Something impacted the back of his leg.

"*Ouch!*" he cried. "The pack is here!"

"Sorry," Arthur said. "They must be too small for us to pick up."

Before Morrow could move, another dog gripped his other leg. The small animal was frantically gyrating its mid-section onto his calf.

"*Fuck!*" screamed Morrow as a curtain of randomly coloured fur pushed him to the ground. His body shook as a chorus of determined panting almost deafened him.

Morrow slowly bent one arm, shook off the animal that was trying to mount the crook of his elbow, and grasped the release of his multi-pistol.

"*Don't shoot!*" commanded Ogilvy. "*You might damage the sensor!*"

"*So, what am I supposed to do?!*" Morrow gasped in exasperation.

"Remain calm, stay still," insisted Ogilvy. "These are small specimens, probably some kind of terrier variant. They aren't strong enough to penetrate your suit."

"Stay still ?" Morrow could feel at least a dozen little reproductive engines hammering away at his back and legs.

"That's right," said Ogilvy. "Once the specimens have ejaculated, they will probably become docile and apathetic. You can get to the van once they're finished."

Morrow laughed bitterly. "Sure, fine, I'll just lie here and think of Toronto."

The hot huffing and humping continued. Morrow was definitely not going to tell Sheila about this.

∞

Ogilvy's Notes: *Leadership Hierarchy: Pack movement patterns often identify the location of the Alpha Dog and his elite guard. This is strong evidence of stable social organization with effective lines of communication. It also differentiates them from the human species.*

Thursday

"I think everyone's here," Edwards, the Assistant Supervisor, looked around the meeting room. "Anyone who isn't here, please raise your hand."

Petrie, the Administrative Assistant, laughed at his boss' joke. Morrow and McDermitt sat at the other side of the table. They didn't have to smile.

McDermitt opened a plastic folder bearing the eagle and gun logo of the International Brotherhood of American Infestation Workers. He removed a three-inch thick computer printout from the folder.

"This is our first addendum to our Grievance Application." McDermitt pushed the slab of print at Edwards and Petrie. "These are selected abstracts of labour law precedents."

Petrie picked up the folder and flipped through the pages: "Starting with 1967, I see."

"I'll bet it's absolutely fascinating reading," Edwards added.

Petrie opened a leather satchel embossed with the crest of the North American Association of Urban Control and Reclamation Professionals. He slipped the printout inside and moved the satchel under the table.

"Speaking of which," Edwards continued, "I haven't had a chance to review your application in detail…"

"Which, considering your schedule, is very understandable." Petrie nodded to his superior.

"…so let's cut to the chase," said Edwards. "Officer Morrow feels that he's being hard done by in some way?"

By now McDermitt had produced a copy of the Collective Agreement from his shirt pocket. It had gold binding and onion-skin pages, reminding Morrow of a Gideon Bible that somebody had actually read. He smiled tightly. McDermitt wasn't going to let Edwards throw them off due process.

The shop steward turned to a page and started reading: "This grievance addresses a violation of Article 7.2.1.5, stipulating the right of all bargaining unit members to reasonable expectations of career advancement."

Edwards shrugged: "How can you say that Officer Morrow is being denied career advancement? My understanding is that his current assignment is with an advanced research group directly funded by the Mega-Municipality. Very challenging, I would imagine."

"I'm working with two loons in a sub-basement," growled Morrow. Something dug into his shin and he noticed that McDermitt was looking at him. Message: *Shut the hell up and stick to established procedure!*

"But Officer Morrow has no vocational interest in this research," replied McDermitt. "His long-term career goal is to become highly skilled in the use of the Department's latest weapons systems."

"I was counting on the training and experience for the upcoming Sweeps," added Morrow. He was pretty sure that was what he was supposed to say.

Edwards nodded and looked carefully at Morrow. "So this is all about wanting to be assigned to the Sweeps?"

"No," McDermitt said. "It's about placing a promising young officer in a dead-end assignment."

"Don't you mean a less profitable one?" asked Petrie.

McDermitt looked offended. "Officer Morrow resents what you're implying," he said. "I'm sure," he added after a few seconds of silence.

Petrie sneered at the union men. "I'll bet he also resents losing the kill-bonuses, too."

McDermitt sighed and returned his attention to the Collective Agreement. "If you look at the language of Article 7.2.1.5..."

"...Then we will also have to look at the wording of Article 2.10.8." Now Petrie was looking at his copy of the Collective Agreement. "Where you will note that Management retains the right to make work assignments at its discretion, and without needing to consult the staff involved...or any union representatives."

"Even so, Management must still respect the spirit of the other clauses of the Agreement." McDermitt looked at Petrie—not the Collective Agreement.

Spirit of the clauses? Morrow didn't think this sounded very promising.

"*This is bullshit!*" barked Petrie.

I was right, thought Morrow. This is not very promising.

"It is Management's responsibility to assign the best people to the job," continued Petrie. "And we aren't going to take chances with some moron who blows up half a parking garage to get a bonus for a lousy Alpha Dog."

Edwards coughed and looked at the table top.

McDermitt flipped to another section of the Collective Agreement. "If you're now admitting that there were punitive motives involved in Officer Morrow's re-assignment, then we will be filing another grievance under Article 9.8.7.8…"

"*That's bullshit, too!*" Without another word, Petrie put his copy of the Collective Agreement into his satchel and left the room.

A moment of silence followed. Morrow wondered if Petrie might cool down and come back to the meeting. The Administrative Assistant did not return.

Edwards sighed and smiled wistfully. "Well," he said and left.

∞

Ogilvy's Notes: *Boundary Maintenance: Maintaining the appearance of territorial control is essential. For that reason guards and scouts are often more active within the heart of claimed territory than at the frontiers.*

Friday

A sparrow was trapped in the food court. It darted crazily between the canvas geodesic folds of the mall ceiling.

"We'll see some ACs in a minute," Morrow said.

Sheila put down her plastic fork and tracked the bird's frantic movements with her newly-violet eyes.

"Just to get a tiny little bird?" she asked.

Morrow nodded as he poked at the diced tofu on his Styrofoam plate. "This is the border between 905-land and the Reclamation zones. AC has to show the taxpayers that we take the protection of Sherway Mall seriously."

"God, yes," Sheila replied earnestly. "We have the only decent Benettons left."

"Gotta keep The Wild in check."

Morrow's prediction was right; two mall security guards and three people in AC coveralls came racing up the escalator leading to the food court.

"Here's the cavalry."

The ACs were definitely small-timers. Morrow noticed that only one of them was armed, and she was just carrying a kind of pellet gun.

Rookies, he decided. Maybe even trainees.

"Shouldn't you help?" asked Sheila.

"No," replied Morrow. "I worked hard to be a dog-killer, I don't have to do birds anymore."

The rookies and the security guards climbed onto some empty tables, and waved their arms, whistling and calling at the bird.

"They're scaring the poor thing," said Sheila.

"They're just trying to look effective."

Sheila sighed and returned her attention to her salad. "How was your day?" she asked.

"Pointless," he said. "I got my orientation from my new boss."

"Was that a problem?" Sheila asked as she peeled off the top of something labelled low-fat. "Did they have lousy training videos?"

"No videos at all, not even disks or printouts," he replied. "Just some sci-fi burn-out case, raving about dog communication, movement patterns and computer images."

"Well, it can't be so bad if you get to use computers." Sheila was a good 905er; she devoutly believed in the upwardly mobile potential of digital technology.

"I'm not so sure," Morrow sighed. "He kept on going on about really old computers, one called UNIVAC and how it couldn't predict the weather."

"So what's his point?" Sheila pushed the edge of her plastic spoon through the surface of her colourless food.

"My new boss says that now his computer can predict the patterns—but these are dog patterns, not weather patterns."

"Dog patterns?"

Morrow shrugged. "Yeah, he says that with his computers and the right information from satellites and these sensors—he can determine what the dogs are going to do next."

Sheila sucked the food off the bowl of her spoon. "Sounds like that might be useful."

"Only if it works," said Morrow. "And I kinda doubt that it will—this guy runs his operation like the House of Frankenstein."

By now the AC with the pellet gun had drawn her weapon and started shooting. After about ten puffs of air, she finally connected and a little ball of grey feathers plummeted to the tiles just in front of the frozen yogurt concession.

The ACs put on rubber gloves and carefully placed the dead bird in a small aluminum case.

"Pitiful," said Sheila. "You could have taken that bird out with one shot."

"I could have removed both its eyes and pinned back its tail feathers with one shot. But as long as I'm sidelined I won't be shooting anything."

Sheila looked at Morrow carefully: "Sidelined?"

Morrow noticed that he had broken his plastic fork.

"It means that I won't even be doing sweeps for a while," he said. "I might be experiencing some cash-flow problems."

The ACs and security guards shook hands and walked towards the down escalator.

Sheila took a few sips from her Styrofoam cup of herbal tea.

"I forgot to tell you," she said finally. "I've got a training seminar this weekend. I won't be able to go out."

Later, when they drove to her apartment, Sheila explained that she had to get up early the next morning.

Morrow was not invited in.

∞

Ogilvy's Notes: *Sacrifice Principle, An Elaboration: Some entities seem to trail off from the pack and then go silent...after a time we are unable to pick up any life readings. It is as though these individuals know they are now a liability to the community, so they isolate themselves and prepare to die.*

Saturday

At 07:00, Morrow woke up, drank a power shake and put on his exercise sweats. Then he started listening to tapes on professional assertiveness while doing sit-ups.

At 08:37, Morrow noticed that the air conditioner wasn't working right, so he decided to bend a rule and have a cold beer before starting in on the free-weights work-out.

By 11:18, Morrow was drunk, but still coherent enough to know that if he timed the drinks properly he would be able to stay that way for the next twelve or so hours.

He wasn't sure of the exact time when he threw up and passed out.

∞

Ogilvy's Notes: *Defence Options: Politically, it would help this project if I could develop some. But my real passion is studying the pack behaviour—regardless.*

Sunday

The high frequency buzzing seemed burn through Morrow's eardrums and make his eyes bulge into throbbing balloons of pain.

He lay there for what seemed like an hour but the buzzing didn't stop. An idea slowly assembled itself in his murky consciousness:

I…think…therefore…I…may…vomit…soon…

But the buzzing would not stop.

I really am going to vomit if I don't do something about this, Morrow realized.

Heaving and wheezing, like some kind of diesel-powered mechanical man, Morrow forced his body to move. He gripped the telephone receiver.

"*Ugh-lo,*" Morrow stammered into the speaker.

"Get over here right away."

Arthur.

"Y-you c-crazy?" Morrow half-squeaked, half-whispered into the receiver. "It's Sunday morning."

"Are you getting dressed for Church?" Morrow wasn't sure if Arthur was serious or not.

"That isn't the point…" began Morrow, then Ogilvy's voice came on the line: "There have been some developments overnight, Officer Morrow. We need you to do some repairs."

"Can't this wait until Monday?" Morrow tried to say something else but he started coughing and the only words that got out were "regular working hours."

"You are on call to this project, Officer," Ogilvy replied. "And I believe you will be paid time and a half for working today."

How the hell did Ogilvy get a copy of the Collective Agreement? wondered Morrow.

∞

An hour later, Morrow was driving the service van towards Lakeshore, approaching the scene of the grand humping.

My mistake, thought Morrow as he turned up Royal York Road, was that I didn't lie and tell Arthur that I was going to church. The exercise of religious freedom and/or ethnic identity had paramount language in the Collective Agreement. No way they could have made him work then. But then maybe he'd have to get a note from a minister. Fixx never had those kinds of problems.

"Is the unit still in place?" Ogilvy's voice fuzzed a little over the van's speaker.

Morrow peered through the windscreen.

"Yeah, but it doesn't look too good," he said. "The main dish is on the ground and there's no sign of the secondary antennae."

"That would explain the signal interruption. Let me see it."

Morrow clipped a cam-caster onto the side of his helmet and stepped out onto the cracked asphalt.

That's one giant leap for an under-employed dog-killer, Morrow thought. He started walking toward the unit.

"No sign of any packs," Morrow said into the helmet mike. So, maybe I won't have to wash off any embarrassing stains , he thought.

"Take your time," said Ogilvy. "I want to get a good look at the damage."

Up close, Morrow saw ragged points sticking out of the unit, as though the antennae had been snapped off by a high wind. There was a tangle of utility-coloured fibre curling of the socket-connector that had once held the dish.

"Doesn't look like equipment failure to me," Morrow said. "Unless it was some kind of weird metal fatigue."

"Repair it." Ogilvy signed off.

About two hours later, Morrow had plugged in a newer, smaller dish and tapped in some copper wire to serve as makeshift secondaries. He used a remote control to power up the system and then he called the lab.

Arthur answered. "We've got good signal."

"What are you trying to pick up with these things anyway?" asked Morrow. With nothing else to do, he decided that he might as well learn something about his job.

"Ultra-high frequency sound." Arthur yawned. "Kind of noise that only dogs and radar can pick up."

∞

The unit by the old museum was a problem. It was set in between the loading bay and the dome of the planetarium. When Morrow had set the unit up last Wednesday this seemed like a good idea, but in the meantime a pack had moved onto the grounds.

Morrow estimated that over fifty betas and deltas were hanging around. At least twice that many pups and bitches, too—but you'd never see them out in the open. Morrow couldn't see the Alpha but he wouldn't be surprised if the Alpha could see him.

"Don't worry so much," Arthur said. "The heat signatures from the GIS say the pack is in passive mode."

"Modes and moods change," Morrow replied. He wasn't going any closer than the abandoned GAP outlet over 500 metres away.

"I thought you were the Great White Mutt-Blaster," Arthur said. "You're afraid to take on some sleeping dogs?"

"Not if I can burn them out or blow them up," replied Morrow. "But that wouldn't be very good for your sensor."

"You're right." Ogilvy's voice clicked in before Arthur could say anything.

They agreed on a compromise.

Morrow would set up a powered antenna by using a crossbow and a grappling hook to string a wire between the planetarium dome and a nearby lamp post.

Ogilvy wasn't too happy, but he agreed this would be enough to pick up louder sounds in the region.

∞

It was after eleven at night when Morrow came to the last problem site—an old teleconferencing array on one of the bank skyscrapers around University and Front Street. Morrow was feeling impatient. He'd shot two gamma dogs in the elevator lobby and didn't even bother to pull their teeth. Wouldn't get me beer money, he thought.

And there was no power for the elevators.

Not a surprise, Morrow thought. But irritating anyway.

He fired a bolt from his crossbow and hauled himself up the main shaft using the motorized pulley connected to his suit's torso harness. Unfortunately the lifting gear wasn't fitted properly. Morrow realized this too late, and it felt like he was getting a sixty-storey wedgie from God.

Typical of this stupid-ass job.

Morrow grunted into his helmet mike and hoped it annoyed Ogilvy and Arthur.

At the top of the shaft, Morrow kicked through a ventilation grill and pulled himself up onto the roof, where he encountered about twenty betas and gammas pushing at the base of a sensor unit with their backs and front paws. They had moved the unit over ten meters, right to the edge of the roof.

Morrow had a sudden headache. He blinked and he noticed that his eyes were streaming with tears.

"You're breaking up at little," Arthur's voice crackled over the helmet speakers. "There's some kind of ultrasonic interference."

Morrow turned his head and noticed three alphas crouched behind what remained of the central antenna array. The short snouts were pointing at the labouring betas and gammas.

There was hardly any sound as the dish went over the edge; just a faint tinkling sound as the high-tech artefact finally hit the pavement, like the sound of a house cat knocking an ornament off your grandmother's Christmas tree.

The panting shapes of the pack stood at the roof's edge for a moment and Morrow felt the pressure in his temples ease a little. His old instincts kicked in:

Do an inventory, he thought. Access your kill zone:

Twenty-two betas...no gamma...four alphas...

Four is too many, Morrow realized. The more alphas, the more competition—the alphas should be tearing each other apart.

They're not acting like alphas at all.

Morrow reached for his multi-pistols. On top of the time-and-a-half and four alpha-kill fees, he was looking at some extremely serious money. The beauty of it was that if it was self-protection in the line of duty, Edwards and Petrie couldn't say a thing.

He would be able to afford to take a couple of weeks off, take Sheila to an executive chalet in Huntsville for assertiveness training and rough sex.

Morrow lightly touched the holster release...the pressure in his temple started up again and...*he noticed the eyes*.

Red slits, pulsing behind the chill clouds of wild breath.

If he had paused to think about it, Morrow would probably have been dead. Instead, he just moved his hands away from the pistols and toward the harness controls.

Slowly, quietly, he descended into the shaft.

∞

Ogilvy's Notes: *Extinction Context: This is not a catastrophic event. This is a gradual process of environmental change whereby one species replaces another. Therefore, the prognosis for the city, for the human race, is not particularly good. I wonder if the dinosaurs had an uneasy feeling as the Cretaceous Era approached its conclusion...the situation was very serious but there was damned all they could do about it...*

Monday, 12:10 A.M.

"I don't think I'll be able to fix the unit," Morrow said softly as they drove into 905 territory.

"No, I guess not," replied Arthur. "If the area clears up any time soon we can go in and clean up."

"Sorry."

Morrow didn't know why he was apologizing to these morons. Maybe he was just embarrassed about backing down from the pack. But those dogs were doing weird shit. Maybe he ought to make a report or something.

"Don't blame yourself," Ogilvy's voice echoed over the speakers. "We still have enough sensors in operation to generate an operational composite map."

They already have enough sensors?!

Morrow felt like putting his fist through the dashboard. So why did these fuckwits risk his life and waste his Sunday?

Arthur's voice came on: "Yeah, RADARSAT 18's signal is coming through great. Do you want to see it?"

"Sure." That was all Morrow could say without screaming.

But the images were striking, even with the cheap vid-screen. It reminded Morrow of those old 3-D illusion posters.

He could make out the edge of the Lake…the main intersections at the City centre…the 905 barrier…

"That's really interesting," Morrow said as he turned his attention back to the road. What the fuck is it, he thought?

"The composite pattern," replied Ogilvy. "It shows the movements of hundreds of packs at once."

"So it's easier to locate them?"

"That's part of it." Ogilvy sounded irritated. "More importantly it's the way they move—" Then Ogilvy stopped short. "Look at that!" he cried.

Morrow saw two red and purple blotches of near-identical size slowly move across the top and the middle of the screen.

"That's perfect parallel movement." Arthur whispered.

"They're massing," said Ogilvy.

Massing?

"What do you mean?" asked Morrow

"The packs seem to be coordinating their movements over long distances," explained Ogilvy.

"That's impossible!" Morrow said. "They're just dogs!"

"More than just dogs," replied Ogilvy. "At the macro-level, the dogs are working as a single organism."

"We're tracking the thoughts of the giant doggie brain." Arthur giggled nervously.

Ogilvy sighed. "Just keep tracking, Arthur."

∞

Ogilvy's Notes: *Extinction Inevitability: Honestly, I'm not sure if any of this information will do us any good. Perhaps we can delay the inevitable for a time, but there will be no deviation from the long-term projections.* As I stated be-*fore, the situation is serious but there is very little we can do about it. Even so, I remain cheerful; the research itself is absolutely fascinating*.

By the time he parked the van at Control, Morrow was starting to see some benefits to his situation.

Yes, the money was lousy. Yes, he had zero prestige and negative promotion opportunities—but at least he had some inside track. Whenever the packs started doing some new weird shit, Morrow would be the first to know.

And as a service man he didn't have to take on the alphas if he didn't want to.

No more bonus money, no more Sheila, but he got to live a little while longer.

By the time he reached the cafeteria, Morrow decided that he could handle the losses.

McDermitt was sitting at a table talking to some guy just off night shift patrol.

"We have to go for more danger pay," McDermitt said. "Hayward and Jang are going to be in hospital for over a week."

"Accident?" the other man asked.

McDermitt shook his head. "Gurney says the dogs were waiting for them; and they got through the body armour before anyone could get a shot off."

"Wow, shit," the other man murmured.

McDermitt looked up and called over to Morrow: "Brother! Go home and get some sleep, you're going to need it!"

"What are you talking about?" Morrow's voice croaked with tiredness. I just pulled a Sunday shift, he thought. I'm taking the day off, you cretin.

McDermitt looked surprised. "You didn't get the message I left on your machine? You're supposed to report to Arsenal at 08:00 today."

"What for?" There was no way the grievance could have gone through so fast.

McDermitt smiled. "Officer Fixx has volunteered to replace you on the research assignment. You're taking his place on the front line Sweep."

Morrow sat there with a stupid grin on his face, wondering if this was a good time to start banging his head on the table top.

McDermitt smiled back at him. "Huge bonus money, massive opportunity. You're a rising star again, boy."

Oh yeah, I'm heading right up the goddamned evolutionary ladder, Morrow thought.

But he had a feeling that on his way up he'd find something with flaming red eyes and razor sharp teeth.

Just waiting for him. ∞

Umfrey's Head

∞ Daniel Sernine ∞

Translation by Jane Brierley

IN A FEVER OF IMPATIENCE, Walt Umfrey swears at the antediluvian truck rumbling in front of his rickshaw and slowing it down. Characters are escorting the truck, wearing beige or khaki shirts and shorts, and pith helmets. Explorers no doubt of the African desert or jungle, bringing back treasure from their journey.

Umfrey turns to Necca for corroboration. His assistant's eyes are already sparkling. The truck and its escort are part of a scenario.

The scene explodes into action before their eyes as a dozen black-robed Arabs with faces muffled in crimson scarves leap out of two porches like so many Jack-in-the-Boxes, the coppery glint of their sabres flashing in the torchlight.

"Temple guardians," says Necca with quick understanding. "The explorers must have robbed some desert shrine or tomb, and the guardians have just caught up with them."

The rickshaw driver edges gingerly around the scene while the head guard harangues the white explorers, calling down the wrath of some offended deity upon their heads.

The whites are outnumbered and only a few of their weapons still work. They try to barricade themselves behind the truck, but the Arabs quickly encircle them. Shots ring out amid shrieks and cries of hate as sabres clang against rifles. Necca has instructed the rickshaw driver to go slower still as she and Umfrey watch the unfolding scenario over the heads of the onlookers.

"Did you see that? They're actually hitting each other!" says Walt Umfrey in alarm at the sight of blood seeping from a neck and the sound of a rifle butt cracking against a skull above the uproar.

"Sometimes the scenarios get a little—out of hand."

Another vociferous band streams out of an alley—baggy trousers and saffron turbans—perhaps some heretic sect trying to snatch the stolen idols. They use their torches as cudgels, and Umfrey's last glimpse of the tumult over the heads of the milling crowd is a whirlwind of sparks in the middle of the square.

It's been—what?—five or six years since Walt Umfrey's last trip back to Earth. The fad for scenarios wasn't so widespread then, and the Carnival wasn't the centre of the planet's cultural life as it is today. In those days Rome and the Empire were all the rage. Umfrey wonders if they still hold those troubling orgies that scared him off.

Six years beneath the domes of Erymede. Six years of research, interspersed by brief holidays at his doctor's insistence, indifferent holidays spent among the tame amusements of the crater-parks.

This evening he finds the Earth's crushing gravity a definite trial, despite the myostims injected at the orbital station. From the shuttle port, he and Necca took a rickshaw to Stardust Boulevard. A costumed automaton goes through the motions of pulling it, but the real motor must be in the axle.

As soon as they crossed the bridge from the orbiport island to the riverbank, invisible loudspeakers recreated the hubbub of an overpopulated Oriental city. The real traffic is far less heavy.

"Did you know that in French this contraption is called a *pousse-pousse*, even though it's meant to be pulled?" says Umfrey professorially. But his research assistant is accustomed to his pedantry and also to ignoring it. Instead, she looks raptly at this year's Carnival theme, that of a souk somewhere in the Middle East selling every possible sort of junk.

"It's an anomaly," says Umfrey, still quibbling. "Rickshaws were used in the Far East—Japan, China, Indo-China, and India—whereas those terraced white houses were typical of the Near East."

But the Carnival is a mass of contradictions. The city is constantly changing, and the flotsam and jetsam from various fads have slowly accumulated into a motley amalgam. Umfrey is right, however; from the bridge just now they could see a floating village of feluccas, single-masted Mediterranean tartans, and houseboats along the shoreline. The golden reflections of dozens of paper lanterns bobbed on the black surface of the river. Did Cairo or Alexandria have floating villages?

But the pyramids and the Sphinx are a long way away from Stardust Boulevard.

∞

Twin suns, one bluish in its electric glare, the other blinding white with a hint of yellow. A third sun—an imaginary one—orbits the very fringe of Barnard A's corona. Every once in a while, for the briefest of instants, it radiates invisible beams, the spokes of an unseen wheel. Only the cylindrical hub and the outer tips of the spokes are material. At each tip a thin but gigantic metal corolla robs the star of a little of its energy, just out of reach of the titanic, arcing flames soaring from the surface below. From the corollas, the energy shoots toward the centre of the wheel—a symbol of liberation, as was once the spinning wheel of India.

For in the centre lies the threshold, the threshold of the stargate by which mankind at last escapes to the stars.

∞

It isn't as though Umfrey were some young greenhorn, brought up on one of Neptune's moons and landing in the Carnival for the first time. Among a masked group met on Tomcat Street, he easily recognizes traditional bogeymen—the Ogre, the Reagan, the Saddamussein, and the fearsome Syndrome with his rubber trench coat and evil look.

On Stardust Boulevard, Necca and Umfrey meet a string of caricreatures. Necca stops the rickshaw to watch them parade past: a two-legged zebra arched backward like a chess knight; flowers with human faces smiling out of their petals, wavering on supple stalks; an authentimorph giraffe—for Nature has shaped her own caricreatures and the mere copy of some species is enough to make the crowd laugh. But the Carnival creatures ring false. For the most part they are imitations, parodies—animated travesties like this two-headed white ostrich, that plush-winged tyrannosaurus; or again this fat sheep, round spectacles perched on its small head above a downy pink fleece that looks like a gigantic puff of cotton candy… In passing, Necca pats a big bear cub gobbling like a turkey. As the bear moves away, the imprint of her hand on the russet fur widens in concentric circles, showing up in tawny undulations on the velvety fur. Umfrey forgets to hide his surprise for a moment.

"I thought they were all automatons."

"That's exactly what they are," Necca explains. A chameleon-like moss that reacts to the slightest variation in heat grows on their biosynthetic skin, gorged with nutrients. The basic colour is fixed in the culture stage, and the range is infinite: that placid-looking moose, for instance, with its blue and mauve peacock markings, or that haughty smooth-haired camel whose coat changes from apple green to turquoise as Umfrey watches.

It strikes him as funny and he begins to chuckle, until he sees a truncated, two-headed cow munching the grass nibbled from her own flanks.

He shakes his head and looks away, ordering the cooliematic to move on.

Two white-faced Pierrots stare quizzically at Umfrey, each mouth a thin wound, red and cruel. A midget court jester bursts into laughter, thrusting his face at Umfrey's and jingling the bells on his cap. He follows the rickshaw, capering about and rattling his bauble as he mocks Umfrey in a rasping voice, waxing sarcastic about the Erymean—omniscient and omnipotent, but alarmed by the playthings of the Carnival.

But Umfrey is no Erymean: he is an Earthman. He has only made Erymede his home because of the huge computing power available at its research facilities. It is Necca, born an Erymean, who seems utterly at ease with Carnival vagaries.

The Carnival lives within ourselves… Who said that?

Necca has acquired a vermilion wig and a powdered face, courtesy of some reveler attracted by her sparkling eyes.

Umfrey scowls. Quick! Let's move on to the Caliph's Vaults!

∞

A white-walled café with fans hanging from the ceiling, the back room separated from the front by a clicking bead-curtain. Bright light slants through two windows in the side walls, hot and dazzling though it is evening.

This is the Limping Jew, sunk in the gloom of an unending late tropical afternoon, languorous and stifling. The low, husky voice of a woman sings softly in German. Sometimes the blues singer is there in person, leaning nonchalantly against the old upright.

The customers at the battered little tables are mostly men, some real, others automatons or transvestites. Women, too, in long, tight dresses. Small-time crooks, soldiers of fortune, adventuresses, a few parole-jumpers and deserters from the Foreign Legion.

In a smoke-filled corner, three characters speak in low tones, a slow exchange of weary rejoinders punctuated by morose silences. One is fat, sweating a little beneath his short, slicked down hair. Rings on his fingers, immaculate suit, narrow little mustache. The other, young and tall, displays a little more energy, but its source is revealed by pink-rimmed, watery eyes. The third is a thin, fairly short man, a grey man dressed in a pale grey suit—ageless or else prematurely aged, with a trim body that belies his fifty-year-old face.

"Are you sure she's coming?" asks Slim, the youngest.

"*He*. She'll be a he. Called just now—will be here any minute."

"We don't need her."

"Who's calling the shots around here? She'll get a piece of the action, period."

"He."

"He."

∞

The Caliph's Vaults. "You'll find what you're looking for," Necca said, "or someone to take you to it." What one finds here are mainly drugs, and Umfrey never touches them. His neurones are too precious to risk even sucking on a munchie. Yet what fireworks would light up his brain amid the gold and azure of these surroundings!

Necca has been to the Wardrobe Master next door, and now returns in drag. She's even had her hair cut short. It's been an hour, in fact, although time passed quickly for Umfrey as he watched the belly dancers.

"What outfit is that?" he asks, his good humour restored.

"Mid-twentieth-century, Mediterranean area."

A sandy-coloured suit, worn with two-toned patent-leather shoes, broad-brimmed fedora, tie, pocket-handkerchief, Malacca cane and cigarillo. The short hair makes her face look different, roughening the features, though they're still too fine for a man's.

"And what are you supposed to be?"

"A gangster. Or maybe a detective. I'll soon find out."

"Are you meeting friends?"

"At the Limping Jew. But I don't know everybody—people come and go, you know. Yes, I've got friends there."

She gets up to leave, her expression a mixture of haste and anxious expectancy.

"And what about me?" he grouches.

"Here's your guide."

With a wave of the cigarillo she points to a narrow staircase leading to the Vaults. A little man is standing there, Persian or Arab, ageless, heavily wrinkled. Necca slips out of the smoke-filled room by some other exit.

Achmed comes over to where Umfrey sits sipping his drink in one of the alcoves surrounding the room. Achmed, or Selim, or Raschid.

"The Caliph's Vaults don't have everything," he rasps in a low voice.

Umfrey leans back, putting space between himself and Achmed, whose face is a perfect caricature of lewd complicity. *Does he have to have bad breath?* thinks Umfrey irritably. Even his teeth are rotten!

"Get to the point," he snaps. He's not here for playacting.

But the little man goes on whispering, thrusting his chin at the dancers in the middle of the room.

"Here, one can only look. At the Sultan's Gardens, one can…one can do everything."

Everything? Even play Jack the Ripper? But Umfrey doesn't ask that much.

"I'll follow you," he says curtly, getting ready to stand up.

Achmed hurries on ahead.

"But I want them younger," warns the visitor. "Much younger."

"I know," whispers the guide, although Umfrey has spoken loud and clear. "I know your tastes."

Umfrey nods, satisfied. Things are going according to plan. Before going he takes another dose of myostim: this is no time to falter under the Earth's weight.

∞

A hollow cylinder, wide enough to swallow a small asteroid and three times as long.

Pivoting on an imaginary axis, the threshold reorients itself as it diaphragms open. The brilliance of Barnard A shoots through the cylinder, becoming an ellipse akin to an eye of blinding intensity, then narrowing to a mere slit of light. In its new alignment, the axis of the cylinder cuts a tangent across the nearest stellar surface, aimed at a precise point in the galaxy.

A vessel heading into the threshold and passing through it in real space would only brush by the sun, not hurtle into it, as it came out the other end. But it is not meant to come out at all, in fact.

Simultaneously, the receivers on the circumference of the threshold also reorient themselves in perfect alignment with a corresponding number of capting arrays whose delicate corollas shine like metal flowers facing the sun.

Then the whole system stabilizes, with the hub now slanting in relation to its rim, diaphragm open, the gaping cylinder pointing to the Orion nebula. At some distance floats the threshold's control station. Much farther away, gathering momentum as it rushes inward from the edge of the planetary system, a vessel gains speed each passing second with a little help from the suns' gravity. Matter and antimatter, magnetically confined in its reaction chambers, annihilate each other as in the first moments of the universe. By the time it crosses the control station's orbit at nearly lightspeed, the vessel has become an aberration, a moving point in space where time slows down and where the laws of physics are pushed to their very limits.

The universe shrieks like a blackboard scratched by a nail.

The surface of the star quivers and plasma lashes up toward the capting arrays. For a brief instant the spokes of the imaginary wheel become visible, formidable beams converging on the threshold's receivers. Faster than the eye can see, the vessel is engulfed in the silence of the gigantic cylinder…

...and does not emerge at the other end.

∞

So many games going on at the same time, muses Umfrey as an incoming shuttle lights up the Sultan's Gardens briefly. The gardens, enclosed within high white walls, run down to the river and offer a view of the busy orbiport. So many games going on at once. His own, without any real scenario. Necca's, glimpsed just now as she and her group of stooges climbed into ancient cars in front of the Limping Jew. That of Achmed (or Selim, or Raschid)—possibly a metapse lord from Psyche assuming some incredibly farfetched role. Umfrey caught sight of him again, smoking kif in a tiny courtyard with other servants of the Gardens, old sages telling tales to the masseuses in their off hours. This is certainly pushing the Carnival spirit to the limit, choosing such a menial role for the mere pleasure of playacting.

The night is mild and heavy with the fragrances of the garden. How tropical and subtropical plants can survive here is hard to imagine. The whole garden must surely be covered over in cold weather, even if winters aren't as long and harsh as they used to be.

So many games being played... At least two distinct scenarios are being acted out at this moment in the Gardens, amid flaming torches and illuminated fountains. No doubt they are drawn from the *Thousand and One Nights*. It's all the rage at Carnival this spring. Janissaries with huge sabres have just caught a fleeing houri; a vizier in brocaded silk is gesticulating dramatically and threatening her with Allah knows what dire fate. A little farther on, a genie has just burst out of a magic lamp in a highly effective display of pyrotechnics. Unfortunately for Aladdin, the hologram flickers in the cloud of steam and the spectators jeer at his discomfiture.

The tinkling of a bell catches Umfrey's attention. He leaves the lanceolated arcades of the balcony and goes back into the sitting room of the apartment. A hostess, the same who presided over his bath and served him a light meal, signals him to follow. She, too, plays a role—they all do. Perhaps it's the important people, the ones with responsibilities and worries, who satisfy their taste for change by performing the duties of valets and servants. This woman may well be in charge of some Argus service. Recycling, Renaturation, Public Order. Fatma is her name; she speaks perfect Erymean to Umfrey and attends to his slightest wish.

He follows her through corridors, down staircases, and along galleries, all lined with rich mosaics and marble, gold leaf and silk draperies. The Carnival can afford its most extravagant whims.

So much energy, so many resources, ponders Umfrey, all wasted in vacuous amusements while space beckons mutely, waiting for humans and their ships. The distant stars, their unknown moons and planets, the Galaxy—all wait for the gates to open. Humanity needs new goals, new challenges—not lunacies.

But now for the Pink Moon Pavilion.

From his palace balcony just now, Umfrey could see the Pavilion at the end of the Gardens, connected to a wing of the main building by a covered walkway. A few round windows with pink-lighted curtains give the place its name.

Inside, only draperies separate the rooms from the central court and its mezzanines. Groans and gasping cries set up an erotic feedback of sounds from one alcove to another. The curtains are translucent, and some are left unabashedly open. In the amber light of shaded lamps, Umfrey glimpses curves of flesh as he passes by, movements among the cushions. His sexagenarian breathing becomes a hint more audible.

"For you, it's downstairs," murmurs Sybla, her face a mask.

Below. At the end of a dark tunnel. At one time the sort of thing he's looking for used to be associated with secrecy—something clandestine. Without that, even today, the fantasy would be incomplete.

He feels the carpeted floor sway slightly beneath his feet, is he having a dizzy spell? The floor seems less solid somehow, unstable. The rooms are low-ceilinged and the drapes cover varnished wood rather than marble. Beneath the perfume of incense the air is cooler.

But what does it matter? *They* are there: the girls—the little girls.

Tonight the moons glow white and ochre for Walt Umfrey, and they are so very near.

Walt Umfrey, astrophysicist. The Carnival is within ourselves…

∞

Slim and Necca, in a century-old car that slows down to a prescribed crawl at an intersection. The marketplace, cluttered with stalls despite the late hour and buzzing with activity that is half real, half artificial, like the whole Carnival. A modern Samarkand, a tinsel Samarkand,

where one finds every possible costume of the periods and areas that are fashionable this season.

Dromedaries prance around in a circle, a dance that soon turns into burlesque, and only then does Necca notice they are mechanical. For a moment she was taken in—but only for a moment.

"Who do I ask?"

Slim leans out the car window and searches the colourful crowd.

"That veiled woman all in white."

"And for you?"

"I've got what I need."

Necca steps nimbly out of the moving car and goes over to the white figure.

"Truetense?" she murmurs in the woman's ear.

The other turns around and lowers her yashmak, gazing intently at Necca with an amiable, almost conniving look—taking in the elegance of her impeccably tailored suit.

"Have you ever taken any?"

"A few times."

The figure in white gives her what she craves and Necca walks away, only now realizing it was probably a man.

She catches up with the car as it reaches the other side of the square. She takes off her jacket and rolls up her shirtsleeves.

∞

A time for somnolence, their heads resting on his chest, his fingers in the satin of their hair. The holovision is switched on, and between its horizontal plates one of the Garden scenarios is being broadcast for the benefit of the guests. Other channels feature the sex play going on in some of the Pavilion's rooms, with the consent of the partners—as may have been the sexual antics of Umfrey and his nymphets, to grant some voyeur his thrill. One is always someone else's Carnival.

In the ceiling mirror, Umfrey contemplates the slender bodies of his little girls entwined with his. After this, how can he ever go back to the prattling teens of Erymede, moody and prone to running commentaries of their pleasure?

Can he even go back to his work? *Earth has debauched me!* He laughs silently and makes a mental note of a point of Smalean topology to discuss with Iptor.

Couldn't he take one back with him? No. What matters is the moment. The hour is precious in its uniqueness.

His attention is suddenly drawn back to the holovision. Something new is happening up there in the Gardens. Now he's looking at a bird's eye view of the palace and its grounds, where shapes in light-coloured uniforms are converging. A police raid! The gendarmes bypass the main building. They surround the Pink Moon Pavilion instead. Umfrey smiles at their képis and little mustaches. Then his face clouds: so many games going on at the same time... It's all very well to play cops and robbers, but will they interrupt his own game? He doesn't really have the Carnival spirit. He'd be annoyed if he had to enter into someone else's game.

The place isn't completely surrounded: three cars are tearing up a little alley that ends on the other side of the wall against which the Pavilion stands. Judging by their streamlined curves, the cars are probably mid-twentieth-century—the ones Umfrey saw in front of the Limping Jew. An entire mob led by a short, grey-suited man spills out of the cars and falls on the flank of the police through a hidden door. Bursts of machine-gun fire. Pandemonium in the Pavilion: shots rattle in the little courtyard.

The gangsters are driven back into the alley, leaving their leader sprawled on the tiles. But a handful have managed to slip unnoticed into the secret tunnel.

Soon Umfrey hears them galloping over the floorboards of the bordello. It sways again, quite noticeably this time. A floating brothel!

He dresses hastily and the little girls giggle at his hurried movements. In the hallway he finds other patrons, men, women, cuties. Umfrey notices a steep staircase that is more like a ship's ladder. Through the open hatchway he can see a vaulted roof of cement or stone, lit by the glare of torches. He climbs on deck.

The gangsters are there—so it was gangsters, not detectives—and Necca is among them, directing the operation. Their eyes meet, but she doesn't seem to recognize him.

On the narrow cement quay, Fatma has just been tied up with strips of silk curtain. She is gagged and Umfrey can't understand what she is trying to yell as she struggles against her attackers.

"Move it, old nigger," raps out a gangster who is running from port to starboard with a boat hook while Achmed ships the mooring cables.

Driven by an almost silent motor, the boathouse emerges from its underground mooring slightly downstream from the wall of the Gardens. Exclamations, shouted orders, and the occasional scream can still be heard from the Pink Moon. But the most secret rooms of the Pavilion are safely afloat, slipping quiety down the river.

"Our reputations are safe!" exclaims a patron dressed as a nineteenth-century aristocrat, acting out his fantasy in an atmosphere of clandestine sin. "What's it worth to you to keep quiet?"

"You catch on quick," replies the chief mobster, paying no attention to the clashing costumes from different eras.

Necca is in charge now. She may have been second in command, but her leader, the small grey man, was killed in the initial attack.

She's taken something, Umfrey realizes. Her eyes are open too wide, as though watching something larger than life and twice as real. Greendelight, truetense, cokeplus? He knows too little about drugs—nothing, in fact—to differentiate among symptoms.

"Your ransom will be set by the Boss. If you refuse to pay you'll be handed over to the gendarmerie—or executed: the Master has no use for your kind."

A sudden uneasiness sweeps over Umfrey: that tone of voice, almost metallic, is it really Necca? The poised Erymean who so efficiently coordinates the data processing for his research?

But Achmed, who has just finished winching in the mooring cables, gives him a benevolent wink. Achmed? Didn't he last see him in one of the palace lobbies? But in his role of tout he must be a Pavilion employee, someone Umfrey can trust.

A small hitch, that's all. Not unforeseen. Umfrey resigns himself to the role assigned to him. He'll go back to his little girls, as the shamefaced aristocrat has already done.

∞

The ride is almost over. Along the riverbank junks, sampans, and dhows make up a little-known floating village nestled in the bay formed by a peninsula projecting into the river. The pleasure boat edges its way along the canals lined with rickety wharves, lighted only by lanterns, their reflection shattered by the wavelets. Here is a landing-stage at the foot of a trellised terrace. "Casablanca," breathes a gangster to the fierce-looking men guarding the wharf.

The "patrons" climb down—or rather, climb up, as the wharf is higher than the boat. They are shunted roughly toward the staircase to the terrace. A large white villa, with a decidedly Moorish cast to its architecture, overlooks the riverbank and the floating village. It is the only building on the narrow spit of land.

The villa is more soberly decorated than the Sultan's Gardens. The inside is almost severe in its lack of ornamentation—a few rare carpets on the white walls and some lamps of openwork metal hanging from the vaulted ceiling.

"The dogs who wallow in the mud must pay!"

It is the Master welcoming them with a stinging rebuke. Umfrey takes one look at his fanatic expression and decides that this scenario is definitely not funny.

∞

The threshold is crossed.

Far away, in the Barnard binary system, the primary spins a fraction less quickly than before, a minute fraction, imperceptibly dimmer since the capting arrays drank in the lashing energy.

For a nanosecond, space turned inside out like a glove, between Barnard and Rigel.

From the giant cylinder that is the second threshold of the stargate, the ship bursts out into real space, greeted by Rigel's radiance. For the voyagers, time, suspended for a moment, resumes its course.

The wheel spokes vanish. Beneath the arrays, the solar flames subside. The eye of the threshold closes once more. The universe, contracted for an instant, now relaxes.

Little by little the ship slows, seeking an orbit among scattered asteroids and never-to-be planets. Light-years away, but now visible to the naked eye as a spot of pinkish light, the Orion nebula awaits the next quiver of space.

∞

"Walt Umfrey. I'm a resident of Erymede."

"Erymede, eh?"

"And an important man, if I may say so."

The gangsters greet this remark with a roar of laughter and a chorus of catcalls.

"I'm an astrophysicist. My research...my research is crucial."

They torment him with gentle ferocity, jabbing his sides with the barrels of their machine guns. Nothing brutal—more like a tickling session. Umfrey squirms breathlessly, like someone winded by laughter.

"Cut out the funny stuff," interrupts Necca. "Everyone into the main courtyard."

This is not as bad as Umfrey feared. The guys and molls are mostly young and lighthearted. The henchmen, the fanatic guards he saw on arrival, looked fierce because of their makeup. The "Boss" himself, fat and a little flabby in his immaculate white suit, is cynical and good-humoured, although he seems to blow hot and cold about his role, sometimes playing it with bored indifference, sometimes with the intensity of a greendelight junkie.

Who is the real master? That disquieting, motionless, almost speechless mullah? He looks as though he's swallowed a poker, standing absolutely rigid on the sill of a little room, like a statue in a niche. Despite his lack of movement, he is not impassive: his nostrils flare, his eyebrows sometimes frown more deeply, his folded hands tighten over each other. From time to time his eyes, his dark eyes, seem to flash in anger.

Each of the victims of this kidnapping-rescue has been identified and interrogated separately. The Boss now tots up the ransoms, stroking his little mustache with his forefinger.

"You've been imprudent, Baron Danfoire. If this scandal got out, the ministry would fall. The Emperor agrees to pay twenty million if he has your signed note."

"Twenty million!" chokes the nobleman.

"You're worth more than you thought, aren't you?"

The baron calls for pen and pad, his face alight with enthusiasm.

"Reverend Paley," continues the Boss, "shame on you!"

The pastor's face is white as chalk above the severe black coat and breeches of an eighteenth-century parson.

"You thunder against the sins of the flesh from the pulpit, you breathe innuendo on your adversaries, and we find you playing around kids' bottoms!"

The reverend trembles, unable to utter more than a strangled gasp. His face has turned almost as grey as his eyes. *How does he do that?* Umfrey wonders, dumbfounded. Do some of them slip into their parts so deeply that they end up believing?

"The archbishop pretended not to understand our message, but he'll pay: a gold casket in exchange for your ring—and I've a hankering to leave your finger in it for good measure."

Seated nonchalantly on a sofa on his patio, the Boss goes on, case by case. He calls out to an improbably attired queen, more or less Elizabethan.

"And you, Majesty, getting yourself laid by young darkies, are you still worthy of reigning over Sorovia? Your son-in-law doesn't think so. He's ready to hand over your throne's weight in gold in return for the video of your fornications."

The sovereign leans toward one of the gangsters and protests that videos didn't exist in her period. Slim whispers the message to the Boss, who shrugs.

"The evidence of three clerks will do. They were posted behind the two-way mirror."

A kangaroo court, a Star Chamber in the shade of a trellis, amid garden tables loaded with cocktail glasses.

"And you, Walt Umfrey, astrophysicist of Erymede."

"In fact, I'm an Earthman by bir…"

"I don't give a shit. We haven't found anyone to pay your ransom."

"I don't know many people here. The only woman who…"

"The only *man*. And Necca won't answer for you: it's as though he'd never seen you."

Necca seems to look right through Umfrey when she glances his way. Occasionally her upper lip widens in an involuntary tic, baring her teeth, but not in a smile. *Drugged to the gills*, Umfrey realizes. This is no longer his research assistant, but a ruthless female gangster—a gangster, period, with that haircut and those men's clothes.

The Boss goes on. "The mullah, our Master, doesn't want us to hand anyone over to the police. All the Pavilion's patrons are rich and influential, and they'd get off lightly. The Master wants to punish you himself—those of you who aren't ransomed."

The fanatic moves forward a step, emerging from his arch. Behind him, two henchmen stand profiled against the reddish-orange light. His face is brown, the skin like parchment stretched over a bony skull. He wears a whispy grey beard and his eyes have Necca's fixed stare, but they are twice as bright, bulging even more from time to time, so that the white shows around the iris.

"Perversion!" he hisses. "Licentiousness and vice!"

"He'll slit your throat," says the Boss helpfully, smoothing his brilliantined hair.

One of the prisoners bursts into loud, skeptical laughter—an effeminate young man Umfrey hadn't noticed on the pleasure boat. He could even pass for one of the mob if it weren't for his fanciful outfit—pale yellow suit, silk Ascot tucked into his shirt collar, and boater on his head.

"Your Master is nothing but a bogeyman," he snorts scornfully. "A showroom dummy, that's what he is."

But the Master, without removing his gaze from the man, turns his head to the side. At his signal, the sabre-carrying guards move forward and pass on either side of him to converge on the dandy.

"Leo Gurnief," the Boss calls out, "did you think I wouldn't recognize you under that phoney goatee and wig?"

Two gangsters grab the man by the wrists, twisting his arms behind his back and forcing him to kneel. He struggles clumsily.

"I'm going to send your head to your father. Perhaps he'll get the message. This city is my territory and I don't want anyone horning in."

The anguished scream of the young man is cut off as one of the guards shears the air with his sabre, and only when the other guard brandishes the head does Umfrey take it all in: the spurting red fountain decreasing in its pulsations, the body tumbling forward, the feet jerking spasmodically, the head held by one ear, the blood running down the fanatic's arm…

"Sodomite!" croaks the mullah between clenched teeth. He looks scornfully at the prisoners. "Now you know who's master here." Umfrey doubles up in painful nausea.

∞

Expelled by a contraction of the universe, the ship again bursts forth from nothingness. The Kaifu-Orionis threshold closes like a flower and folds back its capting arrays.

The nebula, although still far away, fills half the sky with its pleated veils, pink, salmon, crimson, a glorious splash of gaudy plasma on the fabric of the Galaxy.

With this view of the ship floating against a background of frozen aurora borealis, the holovideo comes to an end.

"An excellent job," remarks Umfrey. "They're artists."

The team seconds him eagerly. Presented this way, the project acquires an aesthetic, almost mystical dimension. But in fact it already had this mystical dimension in the minds of Umfrey and several of his coworkers.

Only Necca appears to harbour reservations.

"You find it too pretty?" Umfrey asks.

She shrugs. "Too pretty? Perhaps. We won't be seeing it, in any case. Orion—it would take two thousand years to set up a threshold that far away."

"But just think: by that time, they'll have invented ships that will be their own stargate. The thresholds are only a stepping stone."

"We won't even see the thresholds."

"There I find you a pessimist, Necca," protests another physicist.

Necca smiles, unwilling to make an issue of it. "Okay, okay. The Barnard A threshold, the Sol-Barnard stargate, we'll live long enough to see built. Anyway, we'll show the video at the symposium the day after tomorrow, and everyone will be bowled over."

What is the use of harping on the old arguments? If a genius like Walt Umfrey is prepared to be a mere link in the chain, a mere stage, and never see the concrete application of his theories, why should she, Necca, be more demanding of Time? As a child wasn't she able to watch the Exodus ships leaving the shores of the solar system? The first antimatter researchers didn't get to see this sight, didn't watch the first relativistic vessels sail away, could only dream of achieving near-lightspeed. They lived by their hopes and dreams, like Walt Umfrey lives by his extravagant dream and makes the whole Asgard team live.

Soon, all of Erymede may dream of the stars.

∞

"That beheading was marvelously realistic, don't you think?"

Umfrey raises his head. His face is still ashen. He looks at the queen, his companion in misfortune. The effect of the myostims is wearing off, and Earth's gravity is becoming an intolerable burden. If only that were all… He and the queen are in one of the little rooms where the hostages have been shut up, two by two. The window with its ornamental yet unyielding bars gives onto the interior courtyard, where the confrontation took place. The body of Leo Gurnief is still lying on the pavement, half-soaked in a purple spill.

"Marvelously realistic?" asks Umfrey in bewildered tones.

"The blood spurting and everything. It was very effective."

"You think that…"

He gets up painfully from the divan where he'd collapsed, and goes over to the bars. The way the body is lying looks distressingly natural.

"So it's an automaton?"

"But what did you think it was, my poor man? They play rough, all right, but not that rough!"

"He seemed…"

"Did you see him in the pleasure boat? Did you see him walking back here? You didn't, did you? He was probably here already when we were marched into the courtyard, and he didn't move or say much."

Umfrey begins to understand, or at least to hope.

"Even the most advanced automatons—"

"—can't keep up the illusion if you see them walking through a fairly complex course."

"And all that blood?"

"But that's just it: there isn't that much. That puddle should be a pool of blood. That dribble from his head amounts to one or two litres at most. A pump, a couple of tanks, a little meat—why do you think they took the head away so quickly?"

"To send it to his father, the rival gangster boss."

"That's the scenario. But where've you been, my dear man?"

He must look pretty provincial in front of this opera queen with her resonant, musical voice, her extravagant costume, her histrionic gestures and intonations.

He'd like to believe the queen, but he remembers his last glimpse of the "scenario" that Necca and he met as they arrived at the Carnival. Those blows weren't entirely fake, he thinks, recalling the sabres, the rifle butts, and the torches used in combat. Necca herself admitted that the scenes sometimes got out of hand. Umfrey had already heard rumours to that effect, although they were fairly vague.

Is the queen fooling herself? Is she *being fooled*? Is she just a player in a drama that she thinks she's co-authored? Maybe they're letting her think the victims are just automatons. Maybe the gamemaster and a few of his accomplices are the only ones who know there are real victims, and that one of these victims could just as easily be young Gurnief, the queen, or Umfrey.

And anyway, who knows for sure whether anyone has ever been killed in one of these scenarios, accidentally or even deliberately? Carnival derelicts nobody ever reported missing? People can take off on a whim for another city, another continent, and be gone for weeks or even months at a time. Who'd think someone dead because he's no longer to be seen prancing about the streets of Carnival?

"I've got to speak to the gamemaster. There's been some misunderstanding. This has gone far enough. I *must* speak to him."

By pushing his head against the bars of the open window, Umfrey can get a side view of one of the gangsters seated against the outside wall of the little rooms. He is near a door, and probably has the keys to the cells.

On the far side of the little quadrangle, the Boss and his acolytes have retired to a sitting room separated from the patio by an arch draped with a transparent curtain. The interior beyond seems richly furnished and brightly lit. State-of-the-art hardware provides a sharp contrast with the décor. Umfrey can't identify the silhouettes through the curtain at this distance, but most of them are dressed in light-coloured suits.

"Which one is the gamemaster?"

"The Master, of course!" replies Her Majesty. "The terrible mullah. He's the one in charge. That fat man who thinks he's the Boss is certainly under his thumb. Have you noticed the old man's magnetic glare?"

The Master. A silent but powerful presence, allowing his acolyte to do the talking with the scum captured by the mob, and only opening his mouth to order them executed… Is that it?

Beside the arch leading into the sitting room, Umfrey can see another, smaller arch opening onto the tiny room with the reddish light where the Master must have retired when the hostages were marched off. The two faithful guards are still waiting there, watching for the Master's slightest move to signal another beheading.

Speak to him…but how to make him see reason? Like Necca, he must be soaked in truetense, letting the most secret emotions of the subconscious rise and take over.

Despite the mild and not particularly humid night, Umfrey wipes away beads of sweat that have formed on his brow.

A rattle in the lock. Umfrey swings around as the queen stifles a shriek. The wrought-iron handle is turning… At this moment Umfrey wishes he were a man of action and knew instinctively what to do. Should he hide behind the door, jump the man and pin him down? But he's given no time for such heroics.

It's Achmed, a finger on his lips cautioning silence. His acting is less exaggerated than earlier, as if his role as rescuer were a more serious one. He beckons Umfrey to follow him, and the queen delightedly moves after them, but the little old man shuts the door in her face.

They move in silence a short way down the corridor until they reach the passage leading to the inner courtyard. The guard sags in his chair as though asleep. Achmed has probably put him out of commission with the anaesthetic dart gun he's wearing. The darts take effect instantaneously. The gun is completely anachronous in the present scenario, and what's more, the Arab has lost his stoop and displays surprising agility.

Achmed is about to continue down the corridor, perhaps toward some exit leading directly to the outside, when suddenly the noise of a door opening and closing comes from that direction. The little Arab pushes Umfrey into the passage to the courtyard. The only way out now is through the main gate, and they must cross the courtyard at the risk of being seen.

Gurnief's body isn't really in their way, but Umfrey makes a detour: he has to check, to make sure. Is it an automaton or a real victim? That large puddle of blood… Umfrey doesn't really know whether there ought to be more, whether all the blood should drain out of a decapitated body lying horizontal, or whether the gaps between the tiles have soaked up a good deal of it. Umfrey feels sick to his stomach as he looks at the gash, the hideous gash. Is it real or faked? It seems to be flesh, severed muscle and conduits—trachea, esophagus, arteries… Should he feel them and see how deep they go? Ugh! Never. He gags and spits out a mouthful of bile, grimacing. *Oh my God,* he whines to himself. *Why have I come…*

"What's the matter, Master Umfrey? Haven't you ever seen a corpse before?"

He freezes. So does Achmed, a few metres off. The Master has sprung from his fiery chamber and is standing there in front of them, the ghost of a smile on his thin lips.

Umfrey's mouth is dry with fear, but he manages to ask, almost to shout, "It's not true, is it? It's an automaton! You're just playing stupid games!"

"I can ask one of the faithful to cut him up for you," replies the old man. "Then you'll see for yourself."

Beside him now, stands a fanatic, sabre-wielding killer—an assassin in the original sense of the word. Achmed raises his weapon in his fist. The four of them form a square, the Master and his guard facing Umfrey and Achmed.

"Or we can chop the head off this spy from Argus who's come to get you. That should convince you our 'games' are real enough. Unless you think that Argus uses automatons for agents?"

The old man's voice is mesmerizing in its calm sarcasm. Achmed an Argus agent? Sent by Necca to protect him amid the Carnival turmoil? Is that why he followed Umfrey from the palace to the Pavilion, from the pleasure boat to the villa? Achmed remains cool. His pistol jerks with a hiccup: the guard staggers and falls as the anaesthetic dart dissolves in his veins.

"The gamemaster!" shouts Umfrey in a frenzy. "Shoot the Master, he's got them all in his power!"

A second burst of compressed gas, then a third. One dart hits the Master in the chest, the other grazes his neck, tearing off a fragment. The skin is lacerated and the muscle grazed raw, but the Master doesn't bleed.

He continues to walk forward with short steps, his mouth barely open in a sardonic leer.

Achmed swings around, possibly alerted by a rustle, at the very instant that Umfrey catches something moving, out of the corner of his eye. A sabre swirls through the air as Achmed turns, and his head sheers off in another direction, describing an arc toward the ground while his body continues its spin and crumples like an unstrung puppet.

The second guard, of course. He crept up from behind. Umfrey clasps his hands to his head in dismay at having forgotten about him and failing to warn his rescuer. A paralyzing chill floods up his legs and he collapses. Achmed's dying hand tightened on the trigger and swept the courtyard with a few stray darts.

Umfrey sees the Master toss a small device on the agent's body.

"This belongs to him, I believe. He won't have been able to contact his friends in Public Order."

Total darkness fills Walt Umfrey's head.

∞

Asgard's annual symposium is in full swing, buzzing with rumours about the theories of Umfrey and his team. Of course, it's no secret, but everyone is eager to hear the details, to see the development formulas and examine the calculations.

"We worked as a team, and now we're going to give you the results," says Umfrey after being introduced. "This report is therefore a collective effort..."

Necca is there as one of the few collaborators picked to take part in the presentation. "We've worked as a team." He can afford to be modest. He needed the team, clearly; but the team could never have functioned without him. Potentially, he's even indispensable to humanity. His is a mind capable of synthesis, of comprehending all aspects of a problem, even the most minor. And he has the intuition that is perhaps the only true sign of genius. That's what keeps him ahead of the most competent team of intellects or the most efficient computer system. That's it: Walt Umfrey is always one step ahead of his team. Always ready with some new idea, some new synthesis or vision, while the rest of the team is still assimilating and exploring the previous one. He is the cutting edge, the inspiration.

"...a reminder of how things stood at the beginning of our work..."

The rest of the group only exists through Umfrey, in fact. Individually, each would only give a little push to the advancement of knowledge, probably without ever making it leap forward. But Walt Umfrey... The name will go down in the history of science: "Walt Umfrey and his team of researchers," or "Walt Umfrey and the Asgard group." By the same token, people in the next century will speak of the "Asgard symposium" and mean one in particular—this year's.

"...the differences inherent in our premises..."

In the hall, each seat has an armrest equipped with a monitor on which the participants can follow the paper on a documentary cassette. Every spot is taken, and among Umfrey's team, seated in a semicircle in front, there are a few rather tense members. Not Necca, though. Like Walt Umfrey, she could talk for hours without notes, her mind clear and her sentences articulate. Perhaps people will even take special notice of her, sitting immediately beside the genius at this table of physicists.

But what they're waiting for is Umfrey's elucidation.

"...the metamathematical tools and the complex models used in our calculations..."

The lighting dims gradually as Umfrey finishes his introduction to the team report.

"...the Alcubierre hypothesis of time-space warps and its theoretical application to what we call 'stargates'..."

The holovideo is already flickering in the dark space above the panelists' table.

Walt Umfrey, father of the stargates.

He'll be very careful to make it clear, when all's said and done, that the whole thing is still hypothetical and requires considerable development before a sound theory can be proven. What he won't say, either from modesty or prudence, and what his colleagues surmise, is that the next stage is already in his head in the form of actual theories or potentially as slowly-ripening intuitions. He will formulate them in due course, when he himself is sufficiently sure of his ground.

Above his precious head, the twin suns of Barnard shine for Walt Umfrey's audience.

∞

Umfrey recovers consciousness long before he regains control of his muscles. The dart just nicked his hip, explains the Boss. It only penetrated the derm, so the drug spread very slowly. He took several seconds to lose consciousness and was only out for two hours.

They are inside now, in the large sitting room that Umfrey glimpsed through the curtain in the arch. The Boss, who seems fond of divans, is half sitting, half lying among the cushions.

"Our 'Master' is only there for effect," he confides, pointing to the immobile mullah beside him.

The figure is still standing, now mute, its eyes lifeless. The neckline of its robe is soiled by an oily liquid that has spread from its wound, possibly incapacitating the hydraulic mechanism in the neck and jaw. On a table within arm's reach of the Boss sits a flat little device with a keyboard that is almost certainly the automaton's remote control.

Umfrey is in a state of collapse. He can't tell whether it's the result of the crushing gravity, the anaesthetic, or the emotion. The Boss, with his new, honeyed tone and mock courtesy, now seems as fearsome as the Master. But *he* is very real. How could Umfrey let himself be duped by a mechanical figure whose movements were so restricted? Perhaps it was the voice—the transmission was perfect—or possibly the powerful expression of the face during its occasional animation in its restrained range of mimicry. It was the eyes, mainly; probably full of minute lights that made them literally shine or sparkle, or that created barely perceptible spinning effects.

"Two of my men out of commission, and the Master especially... You're causing us a lot of trouble, Umfrey."

The physicist feels sick. Is it the drug? With such radical strength it must have unpleasant side effects. Perhaps he is simply ill with fright? Through the transparent dividing curtain he can make out Achmed's cadaver still lying where it fell. So much for the Argus agent watching over the pleasures of VIPs who venture into the madness of Carnival.

For it is sinking into madness, this Carnival, and Umfrey isn't sure that Erymede fully realizes it. Or perhaps it does, and chooses to ignore the fact while making sure that visitors of any importance don't get killed during their leaves.

"I should've had your head cut off right away. The guard wouldn't have had to wipe his blade a second time."

"No!" protests Umfrey, raising his hands. "No!" Part of him refuses to believe that all this is real.

"Give me just one good reason why I should let you off the hook."

Umfrey looks at his assistant, terrified. She twitched when the Boss uttered his threat of execution, but now she is frozen again, not impassive, but apparently entranced by an inward spectacle where the same scene is being played out with twice the intensity.

Necca, young Slim, and a sabre-carrying guard are the only members of the gang left in the room. They are armed, and so is the Boss, probably. Anyway, their captive is still weak.

"My work…my work is too important for me to be killed just for the fun of it! It would be insane!"

"You have a high opinion of yourself, don't you?"

"But it's true! Necca could explain it all. We're on the verge of a…"

"Necca isn't on your side. Do I have to draw you a picture?"

"A picture!" exclaims Umfrey, leaping to his feet.

He has to grope for a table to recover his tottering balance.

"May I? Do you mind?"

He points to a holovision with a graphic console that he'd noticed in the corner of the room.

"Our work will enable mankind to escape the Solar System! It will bring back adventure, discovery! Interstellar voyages…" He points to his forehead. "It's all in here. You can't cut off this head!" He switches on the apparatus. "If you'll just let me explain."

The Boss watches him without getting up. Slim goes over to Umfrey, pretending to take it all very coolly. Necca hardly moves.

Umfrey rattles feverishly on the keyboard, cursing the drug that still scrambles his brain and hampers his muscular coordination. Just when he really needs nimble fingers and a razor-sharp mind.

"Think of space as a three-dimensional grid."

Between the holovision plates, a network of luminous lines springs into view. He tightens the threads.

"Since Saavlik and Einstein, we know that space-time is warped, curved around massive objects such as stars."

He produces three luminous marbles. To bend the three-dimensional network around these little suns is no small task. He gives a mistaken command, then another, before finding the right configuration.

The result is good: horizontal and vertical lines curve toward the luminous spots, as though they were solid and undergoing a real attraction.

Umfrey allows his audience time to absorb the picture, while on the preparatory screen he conjures up the image of a hand and chooses three movements from the too-vast range offered.

"Well, what else?" says the Boss with offhand impatience.

"Just a minute."

He deletes the suns, and the grid resumes its rectilinear form.

"We'll build what we call 'thresholds,' gigantic devices that will draw their energy directly from the suns."

Two rings appear, each halfway from the centre of a line bisecting the angles of the gridded cube of "space." He doesn't even try to show the capting arrays or the suns. Forget the details. A bright dot will do for the ship that is to make the journey.

"We still can't get past the theoretical barrier of lightspeed. Space is still infinitely big, and distances are … well, astronomical! The ship—that bright spot—would take, say, a hundred years to get from point A to point B."

Where is the eloquence that made him such a fascinating speaker? It seems years since the Asgard symposium, although it was barely two weeks ago.

"So we look at the problem from the other angle: we shrink the distances, we shrink space locally."

Slim no longer hides his interest and his eyes widen as he watches the phantom hand that appears in the holovised space grid.

"Imagine—I should have started with this!—Imagine space as a piece of loosely woven material, like a hairnet. And imagine this material, this net, going in every direction: it's three-dimensional. Now, imagine a hand taking a tuck in this net, as you might crumple a piece of material by pinching it between your fingers."

The translucent hand has inserted its index finger and thumb, spread wide apart, into the rings representing the thresholds.

"Well, that's what we're going to do. We're going to 'pinch' the space between the thresholds."

Thumb and index finger draws closer to one another as the imaginary fist revolves slightly. The bright spot remains near one of the thresholds.

"There will be a torsion of space between the two thresholds…"

The threads in the three-dimensional network bend as though attached to the rings, drawing tighter between the thresholds, and stretching elsewhere.

"Between the two thresholds that are momentarily drawn closer a passage of virtually zero space-time is created, which does not exist in real space..."

Passing through phantom fingers, the bright spot leaps the gap between the two threshold rings.

"Those are what we call stargates. And here's our ship, already at point B."

Space quickly relaxes, the three-dimensional network resumes its normal shape, and the bright spot follows the second ring back to its original place.

"You see?" asks Umfrey, his eyes moist, his lip trembling. His voice breaks as he asks again, his tone at once fervent and suppliant, "You see?"

The Boss, eyelids heavy, lips curled disdainfully, examines the rings on his left hand instead of looking at the holovision.

"And all this," adds Umfrey, "all this is mostly in my head. It would be a crime...a crime against mankind!"

The Boss chuckles, genuinely amused.

"Really, Umfrey..."

Then his expression hardens. "I've never heard such a lot of hooey. And I'm supposed to let you live so you can keep on drawing cartoons like that?"

Necca, leaning against a wall, seems to be watching the scene a little less intensely than before. The Boss claps his hands for his henchman, who advances with sabre held high.

"No. In the courtyard. I don't want my lounge messed up."

He signals to Slim to take the prisoner into the courtyard. Umfrey's blood freezes in his veins and he breaks out in a sudden sweat. *No, it's not true, it's not true! Not like this, it would be too stupid!* His body goes rigid against any attempt to drag him away. Perhaps they think he's going to make a break for it: the Boss reaches for his shoulder holster.

Slim drops his sten gun—a noisy, spark-shooting toy used during the assault on the Pink Moon Pavilion. He plunges his hand into his jacket and pulls out a revolver. A shot rings out. Only the Boss's hand and the butt of the pistol in his holster saves him from a bullet through the heart, and he howls in pain as his right hand is pierced. He tries to pick up his weapon with the left hand, but Slim's revolver barks twice more, breaking the Boss's left arm.

"That was for Leo," says the young gangster in a boy's voice on the verge of breaking down.

Two further shots ring out. Umfrey ducks in panic, thinking he must have wandered into a shooting range. But the target is the henchman. He sways in his sabre-brandishing charge toward Slim. Two spreading purple holes appear in his chest at the base of his neck. He knocks over a little table and collapses on the thick carpet that the Boss was so eager to keep spotless, drenching it in blood.

With one accord, Umfrey and Slim look at Necca. She seems indecisive, unable to react, her useless sten gun pointed in their general direction. But another weapon speaks before Slim can make up his mind to kill her as well—not a shot, but a brief and intense hum, very loud, like the sound of a live wire. Slim is thrown violently backward, landing spreadeagled on a wood and leather chest that collapses beneath his weight.

Everything stops for an instant, as though the scene were a movie still: Umfrey huddled in a heap as though to offer a smaller target for stray bullets, Necca mute, trying to grap a scenario run amok, the Master rigid in his mechanical paralysis, the henchman dead, Slim inert and unconscious, and the Boss grimacing in an unsuccessful attempt to stifle his groans, dapper suit soaked with red—six different stillnesses.

Enter a seventh man, hidden until now behind a louvred screen at the end of the room. In his fist is a modern pistol like Achmed's, but one that shoots electrical charges instead of anaesthetic darts.

It's the grey man Umfrey saw climbing into a car in front of the Limping Jew and later leading the attack on the Pink Pavilion. But that isn't what strikes Umfrey.

The man is Necca's brother.

The face is the same, although older and textured with fine lines. The resemblance is all the more striking because Necca is in male drag. The features are regular and rather fine-drawn, but otherwise quite ordinary, although the man has a certain presence, despite being shorter and slighter than average. Perhaps it's the effect of his agile physique—that of a man in his fifties who has stayed in shape.

He and Umfrey stare at each other for a moment, one with interest, the other with astonishment mingled with fear and incomprehension.

A stooge totters in from the courtyard. It's the guard that Achmed took the keys from. He's been trying to fight off his lethargy for the past hour. The shots must have helped.

"Mickane!" he gasps thickly. "You were killed in the attack on the Pink Pavilion! You've no right to keep on playing in this scenario!"

"Shut up, you moron," snaps the grey man. "I've every right."

So this Mickane was behind the louvres the whole time. Now Umfrey remembers the Boss and Necca glancing furtively in that direction every once in a while.

"Gamemaster," says Umfrey softly. "You're the one controlling the game!"

"That's right, old nigger."

"No!" exclaims the tottering gangster. "The Boss was controlling the dummy."

As though in reply, the automaton comes to life. "There's only one gamemaster here," says the voice, "and he holds the power of life and death." The head movements are unnatural because of the damaged neck, but otherwise the mullah glides easily toward the little table. He leans over and picks up the little device with which the Boss supposedly controlled his functions. With one hand he crushes it like an empty beer can and tosses it carelessly at the gangster, who catches it gingerly, as though it were a hot coal.

"But how…?"

The automaton raises his hand, and touches his head with his index finger while rolling his eyes in Mickane's direction. Only then does Umfrey notice the interfaces on the grey man's temples: two flat protrusions almost hidden by the hair.

A metapse playing God among the Carnival movie sets? Or perhaps he isn't a metapse. Almost anyone can get an interface now and establish a simple mental link between a human being and a system.

Umfrey sits down limply on a hassock. A wave of nausea sweeps over him and he feels the acrid bile rising in his gorge as he holds his head between his hands, prostrate. All that blood, all those deaths—it's just beginning to hit him. Gratuitous beheadings, savage, coldblooded, pointblank murders, the Boss bleeding helplessly in a state of shock, perhaps on the point of hemorrhaging to death. The divan cushions are like sodden sponges. The bullets must have severed the main arteries in the arm.

The gamemaster dismisses his henchman with an order to remove the bodies sprawled in the sitting room and the courtyard.

"You saw everything," Umfrey manages to utter, "watched everything…and you let these murders, this massacre happen."

"Those are the rules of the game, Umfrey. My game."

The physicist says nothing. Necca sags; only the wall keeps her from falling, and she seems to be fighting off an overwhelming fatigue. The truetense has scoured her of energy in a few hours; she'll need a full two days' sleep to recover.

"Let's pick up from where we left off with you and the Boss. You'd just shown him a pretty cartoon, but he was going to hand you over to the mullah's zealots anyway, because he considered you worthless. You know, the mullah could've beheaded you himself. Only he might have needed two tries. He isn't as nimble as his servants."

Anger, a desperate anger, restores Umfrey's energy.

"You're sick!" he bursts out. "All of you. Sick!"

He wipes his mouth with a clean corner of his handkerchief and struggles to his feet.

"Is that what your Carnival is all about? Killing people for pleasure?"

"Murder provides a thrill, an emotion you can't imagine, Umfrey. No, you can't imagine."

Despite the superficial detachment of Mickane's words, Umfrey senses a suppressed excitement behind them, an exaltation.

The Carnival is within ourselves.

For Umfrey, it's little girls. For Slim, action, a brawl. For the Boss, the illusion of power and domination. For Mickane, it's murder.

"But it's a dead-end road!" exclaims Umfrey. "A few years ago these scenarios were reconstitutions of period atmosphere and scenery—it was theatre!"

"Well, we got bored with playacting and pretending. At first there were accidents. Little slips…"

"But you're *still* playacting! It'll never be anything but games. There's a limit, if only because there aren't all that many people to kill! And everyone isn't ready to let himself be massacred for the sake of your realistic scenarios! What thrills will you find after that?"

The gamemaster makes no reply, irritated at being contradicted in this fashion. He hasn't sat down since entering the scene, and only his enormous self-control stops him from striding up and down the room to vent his anger.

"You're getting on my nerves, Umfrey. Who are you to preach, you who come to live it up at the Carnival then go back to Erymede and pose as the dedicated scientist?"

"I'm the future, that's who I am! The future is there!" he shouts, pointing to the holovision. "It's there, gamemaster, and not in the movie sets of Carnival!"

"If you could just hear yourself, you megalomaniac windbag! I ought to put a few bullets through you just to let out the hot air."

The two men glare at each other like fighting cocks, almost screeching, ready to claw each other in their anger. Mickane grabs the Boss's gun and shoots it almost at random, blowing away urns and tinted glass vases, filling the sitting room with a thunderous volley, brief but deafening. Then he hurls the weapon at Walt Umfrey's head. But Umfrey has thrown himself to the ground, his arms over his face.

The gamemaster, his rage spent, looks around the room for a moment then goes over to Slim, who is lying semiconscious amid the debris of the trunk. Mickane feels his pulse and examines one of the half-open eyes. With surprising strength, he lifts the young man in his arms and seats him in a wicker chair that creaks beneath the weight.

A stifled sob makes Mickane turn around to find Umfrey, sitting on his heels, his back hunched and a thread of blood dripping down one side of his face from a cut where the pistol hit his balding skull.

Mickane shrugs with an impatient snort. The physicist falls silent in an effort to pull himself together. For a long moment he sits motionless, as though drained of all energy, of all possible reaction. When he finally does get up, he sees Mickane standing near the holovision, running through the projection composed by Umfrey just now.

"Necca mentioned something about your work," says Mickane conversationally. "I didn't think it had such potential applications."

Umfrey moves toward him. He speaks in an undertone, as though he had no voice left. A slight whine reveals his broken state.

"You see," he murmurs, "there's no future in the Carnival. It's a dead end. Earth is a dead end. The Solar System no longer fascinates anyone. The Exodus ships are long gone and nobody's preparing new ones."

Behind him, the mechanical mullah leans over carefully, bending his knees to pick up the sabre still resting against the little table.

"These thresholds," Umfrey goes on, "these stargates are our only hope. They are—they are a renaissance for all mankind. So that our descendants can have something better to do than…this," he finishes, sweeping his eyes around the pseudo-Moorish décor of the sitting room.

"And all that is in your precious head?" asks the gamemaster, looking over the physicist's skull meditatively.

Behind Umfrey, the mullah smiles cruelly, baring yellow teeth. His eyes are shining again.

"There's so much to do: the whole conception still has to be worked out. In my head…yes, there are still theories that I'm allowing to ripen, just the germs of ideas. I don't talk to my colleagues about them until I'm sure of being able to state them clearly."

"You should have come here disguised as an inventor from some Jules Verne novel."

"Oh, no," Umfrey demurs. He smiles timidly, his confidence somewhat restored by the gamemaster's affable tone.

"Look behind you," says Mickane softly.

Umfrey turns around slowly. His face becomes ashen. The mullah is two metres away, sabre raised above the shoulder ready to slice through the air, eyes sparkling as they never would have done when the automaton was meant to be realistic.

And no one's left to come to the rescue. *Is this how it ends for me, among madmen and junkies? Dumped in the river with the rest of the dismembered carcasses?*

Necca seems literally asleep on her feet. The gamemaster moves back into Umfrey's field of vision, walking unhurriedly, pensively, towards the chair where Slim is lying. He has now regained consciousness, although one side of his body is still paralyzed by the electrical shock. The other side, however, is recovering slowly: fingers bend and stretch, the foot jerks, the eyelid blinks.

Mickane steps behind Slim and lays his hand on the shoulders of the youth, as though to massage the numbed muscles. He does it mechanically as he gazes absently around the devastated room.

"During your little lecture just now…"

He is addressing Umfrey, but seems to be talking equally to himself.

"I was looking at Slim. Did you notice his eyes at that moment? No, of course you didn't."

He touches lightly Slim's almost beardless cheek.

"His eyes shone as you were talking. You were showing suns, stargates, the twinkling little ship. His eyes…they seemed like a child's."

Umfrey listens in silence, every muscle in his neck sensitive to the sabre blade hanging just two metres away.

"I hadn't seen his eyes light up like that in…in years."

He seeks Umfrey's eye and catches it.

"The night is over, Umfrey. The Carnival and its theatrics are done. This corridor leads outside. You'll find a launch moored at the foot of the lawn; you can take it to the orbiport."

The physicist moves slowly, hesitantly, his glance wavering between the gamemaster and the mullah. He steps cautiously backward, like a mouse moving away from a trap that by some miracle has failed to snap shut, although the spring could be triggered at the slightest clumsy movement.

What about Necca? He looks in her direction, wondering whether she'll remember anything about this night, about his humiliation, his grovelling. How will she get back? Her life isn't in danger; she'll manage somehow. It's Umfrey who'd better get out, and quick, before the gamemaster changes his mind once more.

The curtained doorway indicated by Mickane gives onto a bare white corridor. There is no lamp, but at the end of it Umfrey can see a grey gleam. Something tightens in his chest.

Umfrey hears the faint throb of engines die away.

The wide expanse of garden before him is in shadow, the alleys of white gravel and the flowerbeds still monochrome, the trees etched against the colourless sky like a Chinese ink drawing.

A troop of figures is running purposefully toward Umfrey, but before he has time to lose heart he recognizes the speedhovers of the Watch who've just landed, as well as the uniforms of the men and women now fanning out over the terrain. A woman is leading them. The physicist identifies her in the chiaroscuro of first light. Her long skirt is rumpled, her blouse ripped. It's Fatma, the hostess from the Sultan's Gardens, the one who escorted him to the Pavilion. She has a bruise on her cheek and a puffy eye, but as she runs her energy and agility reveal the body of an athlete. Earlier, only her height had struck Umfrey; the rest was hidden beneath the hostess's graceful reserve.

"I'm Officer Sybla."

She carries an automatic like Achmed's, but larger, able to shoot rounds of darts. She grabs the physicist by the arm and examines his head wound.

"Are you all right?"

He nods with a bitter smile: he wasn't aware that he was so well protected, and yet this protection has failed; his elegant guardian has materialized too late.

The Watch complete closing their noose, but the physicist is already walking away between the still-warm engines of the speedhovers. He keeps on walking until he reaches the garden gate.

Singing voices float toward him, slightly nasal tones. Beneath his feet the grass is wet with dew. Shakily, he removes his shoes and socks.

He is standing behind the villa, on the other side of the peninsula from the floating village that the pleasure boat passed earlier. Here the lawn descends in tiers to the river. At the inner end of the cove, on a wide-stepped stone terrace overhung with exotic trees, a small crowd of worshippers is bathing in the river water and chanting prayers. All these people, adults, boys and girls, wear pink or lilac saris pulled up and knotted at the waist. Umfrey feels dizzy, and momentarily thinks he has been transported beneath the skies of ancient India to the shores of the holy Ganges. He makes a vague mental note that the oriental flavour of the Carnival is decidedly eclectic.

The sky is colourless, except for a faint glow of pearly rose in the east. The sun has not yet risen, and deep shadows lie beneath the trees and fountains.

A puff of cool wind brings with it the echoes of a barrel-organ piping the last notes of the night. Carnival is going to bed. It is also rising, with these worshippers of the day calling to the sun with their chants. They turn to the east, in silence now, watching for the blinding arc of the rising sun.

Umfrey lumbers down toward the pontoon dock where a launch is moored away from the faithful.

Dozens of birds fly up from their branch at the sound of a whistling rush in the air. Umfrey turns around. A large private speedhover has just taken off from the villa roof, leaving a vapour trail tinted pink by the dawn. He watches it wing low and disappear rapidly from view.

Umfrey looks back at the shore where the worshippers stand on the submerged steps, saluting the rising sun with their prayers. They seem to be talking to the light that makes them squint.

Their voices meld in a monotone hum as Umfrey sinks heavily to the ground, overcome with fatigue.

"I'm going to sleep for a while," he tells the sun, and lies down, his face buried in the damp grass. ∞

Holes in the Night

∞ Jean-Louis Trudel ∞

The squares of the city are hollow,
Outlines of elemental light
        aglow with neon, sodium, mercury

Perched atop a bluff of moonbright snow
Overlooking the streets stitched with electric glare
I see not the frame but the square, empty and dark,
        save for icy glints and starry candles,
As if pieces of the night had come unstuck
        landing in the city's midst
        never to leave again

And, sitting in front of darkened sets,
Of inert phosphorus waiting to be reborn,
What sudden aliens look at each other,
And jabber,
In languages old beyond their reckoning,
Yet new to their tongues?

What messages pass in the cold and the night?
What coded yearnings, what star-whispered thoughts?

We never thought first contact would be here,
        among us, inside our homes, inside our heads,
        and that infinite night would call to unending dark
But the gates are opened
When I walk down the pristine slope
        through the shivery powder,
will I dare to empty myself
        and cross the line,
and be filled with shadow voices?

The snow will remember my tracks. ∞

Viking

∞ John Park ∞

"THIS MEANS WE'RE GOING TO HAVE TO DIG IN."

Beside the estuary, in the shadow of the tower of the wrecked suspension bridge, a man in a patched leather coat peered into the west where the brown river lost itself inland. Then he looked down again at the corpse the water had cast up on the mud. "You heard it last night, didn't you, Sammy? Gunfire up the river."

Beside him a man with a red beard, his bodyguard, lifted a repeating shotgun and scanned the river and the ruined city behind them. Dumb, he nodded.

The first man sighed. Three hundred metres away, under the dank grey sky, the roadway slumped into the river, still reaching for the abandoned town on the southern shore. The wind whipped at the brown water and sent waves slapping over the crumpled bridge railings. The man pulled his coat tighter against the chill. He turned to check that the unloading gang, the least damaged of his group of survivors, was on the jetty downstream from the bridge.

"The barge is late." Gulls glided above the bridge tower and shrieked. "If it's all starting again, I don't know where to begin. Sandbags, roadblocks..."

His hands were hidden by leather gloves, his face bore the scars of old burns, imperfectly hidden by false flesh, and he limped when he walked. Stearns he had called himself for several years now, a name no more real to him than the ruined mask he saw in the mirror.

He looked back at the crew on the jetty. They were more animated than they had been a few years ago, but now Werner, his second-in-command, was letting them stand easy and they looked as though a switch had been turned off. "And how many can I trust with weapons, even now?"

He was interrupted by Sammy waving his arms and mouthing silently.

Stearns turned towards the mouth of the estuary. Red sails glimmered. "Finally," he muttered. "Thanks, Sammy."

He peered at the ruined body again. His shrivelled cheek and mouth twisted. "In the wrong place at the wrong time, were you? We'll get you lain to rest soon." He straightened up. "Come on, Sammy. Let's get him out of sight. Then we'll see what Marlowe's sent us."

∞

When the old barge was tied up, Marlowe himself lumbered down the gangplank. He was a red-faced man, with a bush of grey beard and a shining crown of weather-beaten skin.

"An unexpected pleasure," Stearns said. "I was looking for your associate."

The planks thumped as the sacks of coal and potatoes Stearns had bartered for were unloaded.

"Pleasure be damned," said Marlowe. "I've found the replacement module for your device, and it's the last we're likely to get. But it's serious business I'm here for. Let's go where we can talk, shall we?"

At the landward end of the jetty, a man was sitting engrossed, his long-fingered hands running like spiders over the booty he had been collecting—rusty pipes, lengths of driftwood, pieces of circuit board and whitened seashells, incandescent light bulbs and a lead-acid battery. His wispy blond hair stirred in the wind.

Marlowe raised his eyebrows as they passed him. "Harrison's not getting any better?"

"Not lately," Stearns muttered. "I think this one's a time machine." When had he given up trying to talk to Harrison in these phases? Or even to find a treatment for him? "He wants to go back."

"Don't we all?"

Stearns looked at him quickly without replying. They started along the street towards Stearns's office. For a few moments sunlight gleamed on the building ahead of them. "Glass in the windows now," Marlowe commented.

"You say that as though you think it's been a waste of effort," said Stearns. His leg was stiffening.

Marlowe shrugged.

They went into the office building where Stearns had his quarters. Sammy flicked a light switch several times without result, turned and shook his head.

"We had battery power in this block—enough for lights anyway," said Stearns. Then Sammy tried another switch, and dim orange light filled the far end of the corridor. "Damn it. That light bulb Harrison was playing with, back there… I ought to keep him out of here."

He unlocked a door. "There's still daylight in my office."

Inside, while Sammy poured parsnip wine into enamel cups, Marlowe took an old film canister from his pocket and handed it to Stearns, then pulled out a hip-flask and spiked the cups with potato vodka. "That what you wanted?"

Stearns had opened the canister and was peering at the black domino of circuitry nested in yellowed cotton wool. "Yes," he whispered. "Yes, it was." His fingers quivered.

He sat up quickly and began pulling grey boxes from the desk drawer where he kept his Beretta. "Let's get this end of the deal over with. Got your cube?"

Marlowe nodded and handed him a black rectangular box with interface sockets. He watched impassively as Stearns pulled away his hairpiece and uncovered the socket into the interface in his skull.

As Stearns slotted Marlowe's memory cube into his recorder, he said, "It was harder to get all the specs than I thought." He plugged the optical cable from his recorder into his skull. "I had to read some of it myself from hard copy and upload it." He tapped his head. "The interfaces in here still work after a fashion, but it's getting harder to keep the synthetics apart from the natural software. I won't ask why you want that sort of information."

He pressed the power switch and closed his eyes, and the data streamed from the memory chips in his skull into the recorder and onto Marlowe's cube.

When the transfer was complete, Stearns allowed himself five seconds for the muscle spasms to ease. Then he fumblingly uncoupled the cable and switched off the recorder. He wiped sweat from his forehead. Marlowe and Sammy were sitting stiffly, as usual, as though ignoring his sudden nakedness. Stearns's fingers trembled in their gloves as he replaced his hairpiece and smoothed the covering for his scarred cheek, but were steady again when he handed Marlowe the cube.

"Thanks." Marlowe lifted his cup and drank. He shook his head. "Not getting younger, any of us. I'll tell you what you weren't going to ask me. I'm interested in that equipment because it can be used for defence. And it's not only me. This is what I wanted to talk to you about. I had an offer a couple of days ago. Man looking for weaponry—something special he'd heard about. Not shotguns or assault rifles, either. Something bigger."

"That burned-out tank we found here a few years back?" Stearns asked, looking at the film canister.

"Don't think so. He couldn't say what it was—or he wouldn't—but he had the name. Viking."

Stearns said nothing, did not move.

"Mean anything to you?" Marlowe asked, watching him, the lip of the blue mug held motionless beside his mouth. "Well, whatever. The reason I mentioned it is it seemed clear he wasn't looking to start a museum. There's been gunfire heard these last weeks, and stories. You've heard some of it yourself, I don't doubt, even here."

"What's your friend expecting to find then?" Stearns asked. "A tank, a gunship? A Harrier squadron? It doesn't make sense: even if there was machinery like that still around, you'd need fuel, lubricants, spares, ammunition, and someone to fix it when it breaks down." He was watching Marlowe intently.

"Maybe there's a military base—underground bunkers or whatever, full of supplies."

"Not around here," said Stearns. "I think your friend's on the wrong track."

"He doesn't. And he's not my friend. That's why I'm here—to warn you. He's hunting this Viking thing, and he's pretty well narrowed it down to your neck of the woods. If you find anything that looks like what he wants, you may need help."

"You're assuming I wouldn't just hand it over to him."

"Yes," said Marlowe. "I do know you that well. But he's getting impatient, and the clock's running."

"Yes, isn't it?" said Stearns. He glanced at the windowless buildings across the square. "I just wonder in which direction."

∞

As the red sails vanished upriver, Stearns led Sammy and Werner to the hut where they had left the corpse. The air was clean and cold and the wind was opening blue gaps in the cloud.

"Give me the light," he said swinging the door open. "Something Marlowe said."

Ten minutes later he came out. He inhaled and breathed out raggedly.

Werner glanced at his hands.

Stearns winced and clenched them together. He shook his head. "The armour's unusable and there are no electronics I can find. Better put him to rest before he suffers any more indignity."

"Burn it?"

"No!" Stearns had flung up his hand. He drew a breath. "No. Bury him. Get four men and we'll do it now."

They dug a grave, only the third in the plot, and Stearns spoke to the burial party and the shadows about how even the most obscure life had its own meaning and secrets. By sunset, there was just a low mound and a concrete fencepost as a marker.

On the way from the burial ground Stearns, limping beside Sammy, glanced ahead at Werner, then muttered, "He'd been shot through the body several times—different angles, different weapons. And his lungs were full of water... There might be other explanations, but to me it looks as though he drowned after taking enough small arms fire— O Lord."

They were passing the jetty. Harrison was still there. Reality had returned and he was smashing his creation. His thin face was scarlet as he swung an oar from over his head, and his cheeks were wet. One of Stearns's men gave a thin giggle that stopped when Stearns faced him. Stearns hesitated, then walked past.

"Defences," he said heavily. "Lookout posts. Use the bridge tower as a support. We'll have to re-invent weapons. Make gun barrels out of metal pipes—blunderbusses. Even if they're only good for one shot."

"Molotov cocktails," Werner said.

Stearns swallowed. "Yes. Molotov cocktails. With luck it won't come to that. But we'll never defend our current perimeter. We're going to have to create a citadel, fortified and supplied, where we can withdraw and weather a siege. We'll centre it on the square and the town hall..."

When they reached the corner he glanced back. Harrison had dropped his oar and was staring blankly into the sunset. His boat rocked on the muddy water, ready for the next bout of collecting. Stearns sighed and turned the corner.

∞

The module Marlowe had brought snapped into the vacant slot in the circuit-board, and Stearns closed the case of the easy-out. Methodically he stripped off his hair-piece, the false skin and the gloves, and placed them in a wooden tray on the side of his desk. He stiffened his shoulders and breathed deeply for two minutes, as though preparing for a long free-dive. Then he set up the easy-out and fitted the adapter into the socket in his skull.

Once his lost memories had seemed almost a joke, and he had invented identities for himself, out of old laminated passes, plastic fiches, EU passports. In the last few years, his search had become more urgent; he spent evenings and sleepless nights with this machine, trying to find which memories were real, and which had been poured into him through the interface as the fire seared his body—trying to get back to the fire, to find out what he had been before it.

Now, "Viking," he whispered and pressed the button that plunged him into the depths.

His awareness swam through a void, where shadows loomed and threads of light vanished into gloom. Caves promised wealths of gold; rock faces hid secret doors, behind one of which lay the mirror that would show his real face.

While he swam there, his body wrenched and twisted as the voltages fluctuated, and the pain threatened to drag him back to the surface world, or open his mouth to the hard, crushing pressure.

Twice, in that upper world, his teeth parted and a gasp of pain forced itself out. But in the depths where he searched, there was only a shiver as though he had passed through a rush of cold water.

After an hour, an interruption came that he could not put aside.

He unplugged himself from the easy-out and slumped across the desk, trying to make his eyes focus. Werner took his hand from Stearns's shoulder and said, "Arrivals. From the West. I have them held at the gate."

"Are they armed? Can't you handle it, Werner? We'll have no room for anyone else in the citadel."

"They have just two shotguns, as far as I can see. But they insisted they talk to you. And they have medical equipment."

"Tell them we can't take them in."

"I don't think that's what they want. And they look as though they will camp at the gate if need be."

"Damn." Stearns pushed himself to his feet. "All right then. Let's go."

He hurried, limping, to the checkpoint, Sammy and Werner at his side. Beside the burned-out Leopard tank that blocked off half the road stood a moving van painted white with red crosses. Steam hissed from the safety valve of a bulky, unhooded engine mounted on an extra axle in front of the cab. At the rear of the vehicle, half a dozen of Stearns's men clustered around the lowered tailgate.

The woman in the cab frowned as she plied steel knitting needles and some greyish yarn. As he walked past, Stearns noted the shotgun clipped to the dashboard.

Two other women stood side-by-side in the back of the van. One looked up and peered shortsightedly at him from dark eyes in a narrow, inquisitive face. She was holding a blood-analysis probe like a slim silver pistol. Behind her, grey cabinets with glowing indicator lights were ranked along an inside wall of the van. At her side, a taller, fair-haired woman stared around blandly, not quite casual in the way she held her shotgun.

Stearns pushed his way to the woman with the probe. "Passing through?" he asked.

She looked at him, then turned and glanced ahead, in the direction of the river. "Not exactly: this thing won't stay afloat long enough. We heard about you, and we thought you might need some help."

"Did you? So what are you offering? Morphine and bandages in exchange for a shelter from the storm? Because, I have to tell you—"

She slapped the side of the van. "Room for three dozen at a squeeze. Hold tight please and have your tickets ready. Standing room only; no smoking inside."

"I don't think we need a day at the seaside."

"By the look of you, you could do worse. But that's not what I meant. In case you hadn't heard, this part of the world isn't going to be very healthy in a couple of weeks. Unless you and your army of invalids are planning to imitate the last days of the Roman empire, you'd best head south. There's a new community across the river."

Stearns shook his head and gestured at the analyzer, the electronics in the van. "And you're trying to buy recruits with all this?"

She put down the instrument then turned and pointed to Durkheim, fidgeting in the group beside the van like a spring-loaded scarecrow. "I examined that man; he has epilepsy, hasn't he? What are you giving him for it?"

Stearns said curtly, "Phenobarbitol when I can get it. Phenytoin otherwise."

"I can let you have a stock of phenobarb, at less than you're probably paying now. But I've also got instrumentation for tracing brain lesions. There's a good chance I could find a permanent cure."

"You take a lot on yourself."

"You mean you've got a medical certificate on your wall?" she said. "Do you really want to debate this here?"

He clenched and opened his fist. "Come to my office. Werner will show you where to leave the van."

"We'll finish what we've started here first, thanks," she said. "And my name's Moira Norman."

"You can call me Stearns. Good day." He turned and limped off.

∞

Stearns watched with Sammy and Werner as concrete was mixed in oil drums at the ruined end of the town hall. Scaffolding was going up the sides of the bridge tower. After few minutes, the moving van rolled from the checkpoint and parked in the square.

"Water," said Stearns. "We'll need better storage and purification measures. Food. More effort into cultivating within the city limits. Dig the weeds out of gardens, start on the football field. Let's think about those. But now we've got to plan how we shut the door. Let's get the tank towed down to the river, patch up the holes, make it look as though the gun still works. Put both machine guns in the watch towers on the bridge. And as soon as you've got those towers up, take your crew to the north end and scuttle the overpass. I know what you've put into it, but the other road is easier to cut at short notice. All this may turn out to be a good thing if it makes us more self-contained. Now, weapons..."

When the others had dispersed, he met Sammy's gaze and said, "Yes, I've been remembering. That what I'm afraid of. Marlowe's ultimate weapon, Viking. I think we just buried one of them. Enhanced soldiers. A special state—jacked up metabolism that could be triggered by a command phrase. Augmented muscles and reinforced bone. Faster reflexes than anything alive when the state was triggered. They could put a fist through a brick wall, hurdle a three-metre fence, practically run across a river. Where there's one, there'll soon be more; they'll call each other. Give them whatever weapons are still around and... I'm just hoping Marlowe was wrong."

∞

"You've done a remarkable job here," Moira Norman said in Stearns's office that afternoon.

"But?" Stearns asked. "But now the past's coming back? The sand's climbing out of the hourglass, the dead are crawling from their graves?"

"If you want to put it that way. We have hopes for the new group across the river."

"Then you'd be advised to move on there, now. There's something dangerous in these parts. From the old days."

"I've seen enough to know what's a reasonable risk."

"This is something you haven't seen. Human."

"Most dangerous things are."

Stearns sighed. "And what happens to my people when your new order arrives?"

She met his eyes. "There's several of them I'm sure we could help. Your guard—Sammy? He doesn't talk? I examined him. A strange case: I'm sure there's nothing organically wrong."

"And that means it's trivial?" Stearns asked. "Something you can cure with a magic wand?"

"What about you then—those scars? They're physical enough."

"Burns," he said carefully. He looked down, drew a breath, made his hands unclench. "Nothing to be done."

Looking at his face, she swallowed, then dropped her gaze. "Still," she said after a moment. "You can't stay here—not you or your group."

"You're good at telling people what they can do."

"You said you'd heard stories of fighting," she said. "I've seen some of the results. The fighting's coming this way, from the west, and maybe the north. We're pulling back, and you're a fool if you don't come with us."

"I'd be a fool to uproot my community on the words of a stranger."

"Listen. You're clinging to your little empire because you've spent years building it. It's natural. But even small empires are brought down in the end. And they burn too," she said, then bit her lip.

Stearns's hands were clenched together, his wrists quivering. "Don't tell me what's natural," he snapped. "I'll give you my decision tomorrow."

∞

Stearns watched her cross the square. Werner approached her, short and strong, but oddly hesitant, followed by Harrison, carrying a coil of wire, a multimeter and a telephone handset. Harrison spoke to her; she nodded and fished something from her pocket and gave it to him. Then she walked on, talking to Werner as they turned the corner.

Stearns drew the curtain and coupled himself to the easy-out.

∞

At sunset he went to check progress on the fortifications. A low wall of rubble and concrete blocked the road between the town hall and the department store where most of his community slept. Stearns told the sentry to keep his eyes open and his nerves steady, and went on.

His shadow stretched away to the side as he neared the river. In the sunset the water shimmered; motes of red gold danced across it, and the shadow of the bridge was black.

The sentry called to him. He tested the rungs of the ladder to the nearest watch tower, and hauled himself up.

On the far shore were four steady sparks of orange and faint plumes of smoke. Campfires.

Then he turned to look upriver, where the sentry pointed, towards the sunset. Shading his eyes he saw another glow, and a trail of smoke oozing upwards. Straining, he thought he heard faint popping sounds, and imagined the shouts, the screams for help, the crackle and hiss of burning. He felt the icy bite of flame in his bones.

Then his gaze was caught by the mudflats on this side of the river, and a black hulk that had not been there before. He squinted until he was sure what it was. One of its masts was down and the other canted at a crazy angle. Rags of sail swayed in the evening air. It was impossible to be certain in the twilight, but Stearns thought the sails were red and he knew them.

∞

Outside his own quarters he watched the moon scud through ragged clouds. He doubted he would be able to sleep, but there were still plans to make, and he would have to be alert in the morning.

His hand was on his door when he heard the sounds from Sammy's room. He went across and eased the door open.

With a band of moonlight slashed across him, Sammy was spreadeagled on his bed, his back arched and his face contorted as though he were being crucified.

Stearns knelt beside him. Sammy hadn't been like this for years. Stearns put his hands on the man's temples, massaged with his fingers, pressed with his palms. Sammy groaned and shivered. His eyes darted back and forth; the tendons in his neck stood out like cords.

Hold on, Stearns prayed silently. He tried to think of his hands as lightning rods, willed the tension to discharge through them. *There's no one else to help us. And I'm afraid.* Perhaps Sammy would ease into sleep and he would never know what had happened. *Marlowe's weapon, Viking. I know what it is. But I don't know how I know.*

Finally Sammy rolled onto his side, his breathing quiet, and Stearns slipped from the room.

∞

A fire of oily rags and wood was laid in his fireplace, but when Stearns went to light it his mouth dried, his hands started to shake. "Stupid!" he whispered as the match flipped out of his fingers, and he groped for another. Sweat chilled his face, his armpits.

The second match broke.

"*Light the damned fire!*" He clenched his teeth, then fumbled with another match, braced it with a finger—scraped once, twice.

Flame spat. Yellow light flared at his face. His guts tensed. His teeth ground; his jaw began to throb.

He hissed and dropped the match on the hearth. With his back pressed against the door he watched until the flame had burned itself out. Then he took three long, ragged breaths and returned to his office and the easy-out.

∞

Dimly he was aware of the day brightening, shadows shifting. He groped among overgrown shapes, wrecks and pinnacles, hidden chasms.

Somewhere his body ached and sweated, whimpered. He reached up into it, steadied its breathing, continued.

Then a slab moved, light spilled out, and he fell into the fire.

The shock threw him back into the room.

He had ripped the connector from his skull. Shuddering, he slumped in his chair and fought for breath.

The morning sun slanted along the wall of his room and showed pale hills and shadowed valleys where the plaster bulged. Slowly the shadows shifted, grew, covered the wall. *Another five minutes*, he told himself, *and you'll know*. And he could not move.

It wasn't just the pain. It was the fear of the mirror and what it might show.

He pushed himself to his feet, stumbled out of the door. Through thin cloud the low, coppery sun gave little warmth and threw no shadows. Mist clung to the water and hid the far shore; it would obscure whatever lay abandoned upriver.

Harrison was looking around the construction site until Werner, arriving with the morning shift, shooed him away and sent him wandering across the square. The moving van was still parked there; a couple of Stearns's people waited outside.

As he turned, he noticed the weight in his pocket. He must have picked up the Beretta when he left his rooms. He shook his head and watched the morning's work begin.

Moira Norman appeared at his side with Werner fidgeting a metre behind her. "You'll never pour enough concrete to wall it out," she said.

"We'll have a chance if we keep quiet and don't hold much that anyone else wants," Stearns answered. "If we're prickly enough we won't be worth the trouble."

"As long as whoever finds you is rational."

He looked at her. "You've seen something on your way here."

"Too much. I've seen things that I could only call inhuman. Appalling things. Impossible things." She shifted her gaze away. "But I've also seen a man stand in a doorway and support half the weight of a burning house while his family escaped. I've seen a fifty-year-old woman lift a haycart off her grandchild. The effort probably broke both of them." She met his eyes. "The human body is capable of extraordinary responses, for good and evil. But if I want to sleep at night, those sacrifices are the ones I try to remember."

"If you're trying to tell me something, it's not coming through."

"I think I'm telling you not to be afraid of surprises," she said. "No, I'm stalling. You'd better see this." She handed him a sheet of paper. "A secret ballot," she said. "Or the best we could manage. Werner helped us. *Yes* for leaving. *No* for staying here."

Stearns read the tally. His teeth ground together. He looked at Werner, who nodded and avoided his eyes.

"Well then," Stearns said tonelessly, "they'd all better go. Six of us couldn't keep this place running." Between two buildings the hidden sun shimmered on a stretch of river. He found he had wadded the paper up and was trying to push it into his pocket.

"Are you all right?" asked Moira Norman. "I didn't want—"

"I'm all right. Go. Leave as soon as you can."

"Tomorrow. First thing."

He was alone in the square. The sun had come out and the shadow of a dead tree stretched towards him. The barricade was deserted.

Then he was outside his quarters. The wind was cold. A couple of metres away, a pigeon cocked its head at him then went back to pecking at the ground. He put his hand to his scalp, pressed until his wrist shook, then lowered his arm. He took a long breath. *Five more minutes*, he told himself, and went in.

He had forgotten to lock his door. Inside, Sammy was crouching over Harrison. In the corner, spread out on the floorboards, beside a dead lithium battery and four ceramic insulators, was the easy-out, reduced to an array of square black fragments, like geometrical cockroaches.

Without an interval Stearns was kneeling in the corner, with Sammy's hurricane lamp glaring into his eyes. The shadows were hard-edged and empty. His mouth was making choking sounds.

Against the far wall, Harrison cowered as though he had already been hit. Sammy watched him without blinking, his breathing fast and harsh, his face a mask of tension.

Stearns picked up fragments in fingers that would not hold them, scraped them together, felt their broken edges, and swept them into the corner.

He lurched to his feet. He closed his eyes and covered his face with his hands and made himself breathe. After a while, he looked again, into the corner. His hands fell and clenched into fists.

"Get him out, Sammy," he whispered. "Get him out of here now."

∞

He was in his bedroom, the door at his back, the room full of shadow. He closed his eyes and sank into the dark.

The dark pressed on his eyelids, filled his mouth. He clawed and kicked and spat his way out of it. Earth flew from him and the sky glared down. And then he was running. He ducked his head forward so that the wind cleared his sight, and his lungs drew like furnaces.

He ran onto a bright yielding surface that clogged his steps, and kept going. The surface rose up in hills like metallic glass. He was poised over a green glittering valley with wisps of white smoke streaming from its outcroppings. Pearls and flecks of brown were caught in its sides. The walls of the valley moved; they steepened and swayed beneath him.

Far ahead of him, the others stood like a copse of stunted trees. Then he knew he was in hell, because he could not stop what was going to happen.

He slid down the side of the valley as the opposite wall toppled towards him. It turned white and broke into a torrent of gravel and pearls that battered his body. His arms and legs churned. He scrambled up the side of the hill as it slumped, and up the next—balanced on the crest, and plunged—and then up the next, and on, and on, until he was on flat ground again, and running, skimming the ground, and the end was close.

The others stood half-turned—hands lifted, eyes fixed and staring, mouths opening to cry. He flung himself among them.

There was the crazed inventor, hammer poised in mid-stroke. And he was flimsy as paper, folding over, crumpling.

There was the epileptic, the shock cases, all sucking life from the air, all reaching to pull him down. And they crimsoned at the first touch. They twisted and fell, one by one, in screaming silence. All of them.

∞

Light, dim through his eyelids. Wetness, chilling his body. An ache in his hands. And sounds: someone in his room.

What had he dreamed?

He opened his eyes.

Sammy tugged at his arm, his eyes staring.

Stearns tried to sit up. Blood roared through his head, and pain spiked his elbows, his shoulders, hacked into his guts. He retched and fell back.

"Let me—get my breath." He levered himself up and followed Sammy outside.

Fog hung low to the ground. Out of it the bridge rose into a pale, clear sky. The river rippled quietly and faded into a false horizon thirty metres out.

Something lay between them and the water. It was a moment before Stearns could focus on it. Then he limped forward and dropped to his knees.

"Harrison," he whispered. "O Christ. Sammy, what happened to him?"

Sammy shrugged desperately, turned and pointed, gestured to Stearns.

"Are trying to say he fell from the bridge and hit the cable? No, you're not. Sammy—"

Stearns looked at his bruised hands, saw the stains and tears in his clothing.

"Sammy, I can't remember."

∞

In the square, the van was building up steam. Fog hung over the group when he and Sammy approached. They all had small bundles, the few memories they wanted to take from this limbo. There was little emotion, but of course there never had been among them.

Stearns stood with Sammy in the doorway of his building, then took a couple of steps into the square, turned and came back. He moistened his lips.

He whispered, "We both know, don't we? Harrison . . ." He flexed his fingers. Across the square, steam hissed from the safety valve. "You'd better go with them, Sammy."

∞

One or two of them looked at him with dim curiosity or concern as they passed, then pushed into the van and out of sight. Werner went last, head lowered, with a only a glance in Stearns's direction.

"We're ready to go," said Moira Norman. "The red cross will help us, and so will the fog, but I want to be at the ferry before dusk. Are you sure?"

"I'll follow you. Later. I want to think for a while here. I have some goodbyes to say, and I don't know how to say them yet."

"If you want my advice, you'll think less and move on, now."

"No," he said. "It's best that I stay."

She shrugged, then asked, "You're armed—in case?"

He showed her his Beretta, slipped it back into his coat pocket.

"Ammo?"

"Enough," he said, and smiled.

∞

The van hissed and creaked into motion. By the time it had crossed the square it had built up a respectable speed. It turned onto the old road west, lurched over a pothole, and drew away into the ground fog. A pair of starlings chattered.

Stearns stood for a while, not looking at anything, then walked back to his quarters. He collected his ID cards, the passports, and piled them in the box with his false hair and flesh. He carried the box outside and placed it beside a stack of firewood from one of the ruined buildings and a brazier the work crews would have used in the winter. He thought for a moment, then took out his pistol, with its single clip. He weighed it in his hand, then put it on the firewood near the brazier. For later.

He hauled Harrison's body to the graveyard in a wheelbarrow, and laboured with a shovel until he had dug a place for it. When he had tamped the earth down, he knelt and stayed motionless until his shadow reached the chipped concrete of the fencepost he had set up as a marker. *Never again*, he thought. *Never again. Never again*.

Then he walked. He paced the empty streets, and listened to the quiet. He noted where grass had begun forcing its way through cracks in the road, where windows still glittered with fragments of glass, where pigeon droppings had whitened the gilded statue of a horseman.

He came to the bridge. He climbed to the watch tower, and leaned out so that the water glittered and swayed below him. The sun was starting downward, and it stung his eyes when he turned to look upriver. Not that he would have seen the van on the sheltered road in any case.

Rising from the far shore were the pale streams of smoke. Eight of them now. He looked at the water again, and the shadow of the tower rippling over it. He could imagine he was a tiny blur on its edge. Under the scatter of reflected sunlight, the water was brown, but from this height he would make a white splash. Harrison's boat lay on its side in the mud.

Stearns sighed and began to climb down.

∞

When he came back to the square, the sun was setting and only the top storeys of the buildings were still lit. Soon the van would be across the river, heading south.

He stacked wood in the brazier, then put his box of possessions on top. He opened Sammy's hurricane lamp and splashed half the oil into the brazier. Then he struck a match and dropped it in.

There was a muted puff and a burst of orange flame. Smoke rose. The box began to burn.

The flames glinted on his Beretta. He stepped away from the fire, backed up until he was against one of the dead lamp standards. His flesh felt loose as ashes.

The air darkened; embers fluttered up like crimson-winged moths, and were lost in the dusk. He stared after them as the last sunlight faded and only the fire lit the square. He leaned against the lamp standard and did not move.

"I see we're too late for the others," said Marlowe from the shadows.

Slowly Stearns turned his head to face him.

"I was hoping you'd stay." Marlowe stepped forward until the light from the brazier gleamed on his face. He was holding an automatic pistol.

Stearns moistened his lips. "I thought you'd be out trying to find your ultimate weapon, for your client."

"I was. I think I've found it."

"I don't know what you mean." Stearns started to push himself away from the lamp post.

Someone came out of the dark behind him and grabbed his elbows. His arms were wrenched behind him and his wrists shackled around the concrete pillar.

"Thank you, Joe," said Marlowe. "You can help the others search the main buildings, and then come back here." He turned back to Stearns. "That's the main thing that makes me wonder—how could such a pathetic liar ever have made his way in the security services?"

Stearns shook his head.

"All right," Marlowe said. "Why don't you tell me what you know about the Viking project?"

"The Mars landing? Back in…"

"Better, but now you're too eager." Marlowe jerked the muzzle of his gun. "The Viking project."

"If you know, why are you asking me?"

"Because I want to. Come on: once upon a time…"

Stearns looked at him and said nothing.

Marlowe came around the fire. "At least you're not asking why I'm coming to you with this. You know why. Don't you?"

Stearns whispered.

Marlowe shouted, "I've lost my barge and two men this week. I'm not very patient. I can't hear you."

"I said, I can't be certain."

"Ah yes." Marlowe looked him and nodded. "Which frightens you more—that there's really a monster inside you, or that you're just the empty shell of one?"

"I'm no use to you, whichever it is."

"Oh, but you are," Marlowe said. "If you're not what I'm looking for, then the real one went with the others, and you can tell me where. But if you are what I want, everything's a bit easier. I've got the control phrases now—they were the same for the whole cadre. But the trigger phrases were special. The Vikings were supposed to be bodyguards; only a few of the chosen could call them up. I'll have to bypass the trigger phrase."

"It mightn't work any more, any of it," Stearns said thickly. "Things like that in the brain, they get corrupted—mixed up with what's already there."

"Exactly. So I'm betting I can trigger the state indirectly."

Marlowe threw wood into the brazier. It crackled. Flames quivered up, yellow and feverish. "Fire," he said. "The ancient terror. Pain. And the fear of burning." He looked at Stearns. "Yes. In your case the fear may be enough."

∞

The concrete pillar grated along Stearns's back as his knees buckled, and he sank into a black familiar void. He sank until he was far away from pain, from Marlowe, far down in a dark space filled with numbers, abstract sounds, memories—far from fear, far from the fire.

"Where did they go?" Marlowe shouted. Flames hissed between them.

Stearns writhed, was dragged back into the world. The concrete scraped his wrists; the chain gouged them. His eyes would not turn from the fire. "They went to the coast," he whispered. "Then north."

"Don't lie to me."

And then he was not Stearns or any nameable thing, but only a mote of terror, shrinking away into the dark, away from the flames and the flesh that cowered from them—that twisted and howled and tore itself to get away from them, and burned.

Come back, something screamed. *Wipe me away*, *make me a monster*. *Just make it stop*.

After a long time, the mote at the centre began to return. It came back to where the pain waited.

"You've just about convinced me you're not the one," said the voice from outside. "So tell me where the others went. You gave your life to them, and there's none of them around when you need them. Who is there to help you? In the whole world?"

"No one."

"What is there to keep you going?" asked the voice, and now he could not tell whether it was inside or outside. "Look inside yourself—what is there? What?"

The body was shivering and wet. Its eyes were screwed shut. Its mouth gasped and drooled.

"Nothing. There's nothing there."

The mote at the centre closed the mouth. The shivering went on.

The mote waited in the place it had always known of, where there was no safety, no light, and no hope. Then, because there was no hope, it made the mouth open and croak again.

"They went north."

∞

The world changed a little. The flames moved away. The pain still nagged, but remotely, as though in a dream.

He lifted his head.

Marlowe had stepped back and was peering into the shadows. "Joe?" he called. "Is that you?"

Footsteps clattered behind Marlowe. He spun, snatched out his pistol and fired. But Sammy had already slipped to one side.

Marlowe shouted a short phrase. And Sammy jerked as though struck, but came on. Marlowe shouted once more, and fired a long burst.

Sammy's body shuddered. Dark spray drifted from his chest.

Stearns drew a breath to scream.

Sammy's mouth was wide, his eyes fixed. A cluster of droplets slid in front of his face. An eye began to blink.

Then Stearns was crouched where Marlowe had been standing. Broken chain swung from his wrists. Sammy was still stumbling forward. And five metres away, sprawled on the ground, Marlowe stared back at him over his shoulder. His eyes gleamed like chips of glass in the firelight. Somewhere in the dark, the gun rattled to the ground. Marlowe's body twitched once and was still.

Inside Stearns a piston was battering his ribs. He dropped to his knees and retched and choked for air until Sammy's fingers clamped on his arm and dragged him away.

They found Harrison's boat a couple of metres above the rising tide. Sammy pushed him into the bow and shoved the boat into the water, then tumbled in and picked up the oars. In the dim light Stearns could see the dark stain spreading across Sammy's chest where his body armour had failed. He could not tell if Sammy was still in the Viking mode. Feebly he reached for an oar, and Sammy pushed him away.

Stearns fell sideways, and found he was shivering or trembling too much to sit up. His head rolled against the gunnel, so that he had a view of three stars among the clouds.

The creak of the oars and the sounds of the river filled his ears.

Come back, he thought tentatively, and could not tell if there was anything to hear him.

Once he thought Sammy's face floated before him, like the scarred circle of the moon; he thought Sammy's mouth opened, and slowly croaked out: "We are still men. While we live, we change." Then Stearns's eyes closed.

∞

He awoke into dim moonlight. The boat was beached, with the oars lying across one gunnel, and he was alone. He thought he could see stains on the oars and the gunnel, but he could find no tracks in the mud.

While we live…

On the opposite shore lay the ruins where the man known as Stearns had lived his life. Slowly he sat up and looked around. A little way upriver there were fires on the beach, and two guards talking together with rifles slung on their shoulders.

Come back?

Nothing.

Then the wind brought the sounds of laughter and a snatch of song. He crawled from the boat, pushed himself to his feet, and, limping, ran towards the fires. ∞

The Sea Below

∞ Francine Pelletier ∞

Translated by Sheryl Curtis

FOR VIRGIL OGAN EVERYTHING STARTED to fall apart the day Domi first felt nauseated. More specifically, it was the day Alex received his summons to Asterman.

Virgil was an environist—what busy people called an *enviro.* (He liked that word, it rhymed with *dynamo.*) *Environism* was the perfect art for humans confined to the limited area of an orbital station. To imagine a setting, reminiscent of Earth, mould it, model it in three dimensions, give it life, and then project it. He could transform the white walls of any room into an oasis, create a restful environment, conducive to dreaming and internal peace. Virgil wasn't a master enviro yet. That's why he worked on the small, distant Relay stations. One day, he'd be invited to Asterman, where he'd show the petty bureaucrats who managed the world just how talented he was. Or, looking down his nose at the worn-out scenery of Earth, boring old Earth, he'd head off to yet more distant sites, on Ganymede, Madox Mines, to dazzle the plant workers. Or, better yet, he'd go to Titan, and perform for the miners working in the complex there, or the colonists of Antarctis.

That day, after debarking at Relay II, he headed straight to the cytogenetics laboratory. Dominella Gaitanis and Alexander Malan worked there. Domi and Alex.

Virgil's entrance in the laboratory went almost unnoticed at first. Virgil was back from Relay I. The trip had been a short one, there and back, but he'd still been gone for eight weeks. Had his friends even noticed?

Alex and Domi were hunched over the long white counter, examining a series of equipment. Their heads, the one blond, the other brunette, bent over in the same position. As Virgil hesitated at the doorstep, Alex stood up and waved at him nonchalantly.

"Well, well, well. Our great creative genius has come home to the roost!"

Virgil lowered his eyes. He felt the heat rising, his face reddening. He was never really sure whether he should take Alex's sallies as insults or simple teasing.

Domi came over to him. She went to embrace him, then stopped.

"Hi Virgil. Did you have a good trip?"

Her face looked drawn, her eyes weary. Had they partied? Or fought? You could never tell with Domi and Alex.

Alex suddenly turned away from the counter, towards Virgil. "Hey there, old buddy, your stuff was really smoking. Did you think of me?"

Alex really went for the synthetic drugs so fashionable in the mining complexes on Titan and Ganymede. Every time Virgil went to Relay I, he went out of his way to get the latest creation. And when he got back, the three would get party for a night.

He smiled and handed Alex the small package he'd brought back just for him. "So, how about celebrating my return?"

He watched Domi as she paled. She gave a strange little hiccup, then rushed to the washroom. Virgil looked at Alex, worried, but Malan just shrugged. He perched on a stool and pretended to return to work. Virgil leaned on the counter near him.

"Alex, what's wrong with her?"

Malan shook his head, irritated. "It's nothing. It started this morning. I have a lot of other things to worry about…"

"What's wrong with you?"

Faced with Alex's silence, he insisted. "Was it the last batch of chemicals I brought you? The formula wasn't stable. The salesman told me as much."

Domi came back out of the washroom, a little unsteadily. He went over to help her, but she pushed him aside. She spoke to Alex, her voice pinched. "I'm going to see Roberta. I need her to examine me."

Once again, Malan shrugged. Domi turned on her heal and left the laboratory, her footsteps tapping on the floor. Virgil went back over to Alex.

"What's going on here?"

Malan didn't answer right away. He drummed his fingers on the counter, then sighed. "I've received a call from Asterman. From Schreiber, at the G.R.C."

The Asterman G.R.C.—the Genetic Research Centre—supervised the cytogenetic department that operated on the two Relay stations. Alex frequently complained to the central administrative offices about how work was organized on Relay II. He considered himself a research scientist above all, and yet he had to fight with a thousand administrative details every day. He accepted his situation only because he hoped to obtain research credits. In fact, the Relay II lab was a simple business unit. Malan, Domi and the genetechnicians manufactured babies, nothing more, nothing less, for the civil servants posted to the station. They stocked the "cabbage patch," as Alex liked to say. Virgil was well aware of his complaints. He'd heard them a hundred times.

Malan went on. "Old Schreiber was grey with fear. With the change in government, it's housecleaning time for the civil service."

"So?"

Alex clenched his fist, as if he were having trouble controlling himself. Virgil found this upsetting.

"So? He's calling me back to Asterman. Did you hear me? I'm being forced to go back there."

Alex was trembling slightly. Virgil placed his hand on Malan's arm.

"Calm down. I don't understand why you're getting so worked up over this. I'd love to be called back to Asterman."

Alex stepped back, abruptly.

"You! You're just a pitiful little artist. How would you understand? While the entire space development program is focussed outwards, towards Saturn, while everyone's talking about building a third Relay station, you still dream of Asterman! What an idiot! The future is out there, ahead of us, and not on that old scrap heap! Asterman!"

Virgil shook his head, unable to respond. Alex's disdain did not hurt him. He was used to it. But why was he so angry? So Alex had been called back to Asterman. Would it really harm his career?

"Alex, what do they want from you? What did they tell you?"

Malan waved his hand. "A few meaningless words. That's all old Schreiber was up to. *A position with responsibility, dear Alex*. Responsibility! I'll probably be carting around automatrix equipment!"

He bent forward, leaning his forehead on Virgil's shoulder. "I'll never amount to anything, Virg."

Distraught, Virgil hugged Alex tenderly. But Malan immediately moved away from his embrace.

"If old Schreiber thinks he can impress me…"

He burst out laughing and Virgil backed away.

Just then, the lab door slid open and Alex's laugh broke off immediately. One of the genetechnicians had just come in. Alex eyed her contemptuously, but she simply said, "Roberta just called. She said she sent Domi home to lie down." Then the young woman went on into the next room.

"I'm going to see Domi," said Virgil.

Malan let him go without a word.

Domi and Alex lived in a two-room unit arranged to make it look a lot larger. The apartment occupied two levels. There was a living room nook, by the entrance, dominated by the meal nook in the mezzanine, with the bedroom set back in a recess. The tables looked like marble, the knick-knacks pewter. Malan owed this comfortable little nest to his situation as an administrator. Obviously, a couple enjoyed more space than a single person. Virgil didn't rate more than a studio.

He waited a few moments in front of the closed door. When the panel slid open, Virgil took a few steps, then the door closed behind him. The only lighting in the room came from the feeble light that the bluish glass located above the mezzanine gave off. As his eyes adjusted, he could make out a white spot on the sofa. Domi lay there, motionless.

Virgil sat down next to her.

"Domi…"

She moved her hand, gently.

"It's nothing."

"Alex isn't well, Domi. This recall situation has made him completely…"

He felt her tense and hurriedly whispered. "Why do you stay with him? You don't have to."

She sat up, leaning on one elbow, her face very close to his. "Listen to me, Virgil Ogan. When Alex is transferred to Asterman, I'll go with him."

He turned away, embarrassed. What right did he have to talk to Domi like that? He'd thought about her so much—dreamed about her—during his long, long trip.

The room suddenly lit up. Blinded, Virgil heard Alex laugh. "So, you've started the party without me?"

Domi stood up, shading her eyes with the back of her hand.

"I don't enjoy your jokes much anymore."

Alex embraced her. "A thousand apologies, sweetheart. For a moment there, I thought I'd surprise you in bed with my best friend."

Best friend. Virgil had never been all that sure that Alex felt any friendship for him… He searched for something intelligent to say, but came up empty. Domi gently freed herself from Alex's grasp.

"You don't want to hear Roberta's conclusions about my sickness?"

"You want to hear mine?"

Domi gave him a severe look that gradually softened. She burst out, "I'm pregnant."

Alex remained silent for a few minutes, dumbfounded, before bursting into an astonished laugh.

"Dominella! Pregnant! The baby maker got caught! That's the best one I've heard in a long while."

Virgil just stared at Domi, speechless, completely stupefied. She turned to Alex, who bustled about, laughing.

"Alex, it's not a joke!"

He suddenly stopped laughing, fell back onto the couch, and looked at Domi.

"Do you know who the father is, at least?"

"No."

Alex jumped back up.

"That doesn't seem to worry you a whole lot."

"I asked Roberta to get rid of it as quickly as possible. She suggested that I speak to you first."

Alex embraced her again, his supple body moving sinuously against hers.

"Darling, Roberta's right. We make our decisions together, don't we?"

Virgil felt somewhat disgusted. He found himself standing there, a voyeur despite himself. He wanted to leave, yet stood there, paralyzed, frozen in place.

Domi tried to free herself, but Alex clasped her firmly against him.

"So, you don't know who the father is? It could be just about anyone?"

"You're exaggerating."

Virgil felt Alex's eyes directly on him, mocking.

Malan nodded at him. "It couldn't be out dear friend Virgil now could it, Domi?"

"I don't think so."

She seemed to be having trouble controlling herself.

"In any case, there's no problem. I told you I wanted to get rid of it. Tomorrow."

"But, sweetheart, that's completely out of the question!"

Domi's efforts to free herself were becoming more and more frantic. Alex remained unruffled. Virgil could have stepped in, but what right did he have to do that? He didn't feel like being reminded about the possibility—the infinitely small possibility—that he was the baby's father. He wasn't even sure he'd had an erection the last time all three of them had made love. But what exactly did he remember about that night?

Alex watched Domi as she struggled.

"Sweetheart, it's a unique opportunity. An extraordinary chance! Do you realize what's happening inside you? That small little creature is wriggling about, is going to grow, will feed off your very flesh, is going to push itself out of your body!"

Domi paled. She stuttered, "Alex, please...I'm going to throw up."

Abruptly, he released her. She collapsed, on the verge of nausea. Virgil took a step towards her, but Alex got there ahead of him and helped her to the couch.

"Excuse me. I'm sorry. I didn't mean to upset you..."

She shook her head. Alex helped her settle on the couch, then kneeled next to her.

"Domi, listen to me. I mean what I'm saying. I really believe you've got a unique chance here. Think of all the sterile women, all of those failures who come to us so that we can make babies for them. You're a hundred times better than they are. Your belly is your laboratory. Don't you think that's amazing?"

She hesitated a fragment of a moment then nodded her head slowly. Alex grabbed her hands, gripping them enthusiastically.

"Sweetheart, listen to me... I don't want you to stay ill. We'll go back to the laboratory and transfer the embryo to an automatrix. Then we can follow its development in peace and you won't have any discomfort. What do you think?"

Domi seemed to hesitate. Just for a second, Virgil almost ran to her, cried out to her to refuse. Alex dominated her, his slender silhouette standing in front of her like a superb statue. She agreed, with a pale smile.

"You know... I couldn't bear to...to carry it."

"I understand, sweetheart. I'm only trying to help you."

He bent over her and kissed her gently, one hand caressing her abdomen. Virgil slowly backed towards the door, blood pounding in his temples.

∞

Virgil was working in his "studio." In front of him, in the three-dimensional image cube, a scale representation of his latest creation turned slowly on itself. In silence, Virgil observed the small corner of green and pink jungle from all angles. The wild flowers formed a light patch on the leaves, with their thousand shades of green. A small waterfall rose in a silent mist, pearling on the leaves. It was alive, happy. But it still lacked a certain something. A body of water, a pond, perhaps, at the foot of the waterfall?

The door chimed, forcing him to abandon the cube. He stepped over the modeller keyboard standing on the floor near the small console that controlled the projection in the image cube.

He didn't open the door immediately, preferring to view his visitor through the screen first. Alex's face bore an unusually friendly expression.

"Hey, there, Virg! Do you know it's been days since we last saw you?"

"I'm working."

He could see from Alex's face what was going to happen next. Alex would try to make him feel guilty—and succeed, of course. Virgil couldn't do anything but yield. Return to the fold.

"He's been working! So, it's that easy to forget all about us? Have you forgotten about Domi's birthday? It's in three days. Don't tell me you forgot about it?"

He hadn't forgotten about it, of course, but he had hoped to get out of it. Domi would have never allowed herself to remind him about it.

"Alex, I've got work…"

Alex raised his hand to interrupt him.

"All right, already. I didn't say a word. I'll give your message to Domi. No little celebration. No birthday, either."

Virgil sighed.

Alex watched the door slide closed with a small smile of intense satisfaction. He walked into the studio with an ostentatious nonchalance.

"So, then, you've been working?"

Virgil pointed to the image cube. Alex walked over to it, assessing the scene with a connoisseur's eye.

"Well, not bad… A little old-fashioned, don't you think? All that's missing is a few parrots and an ape man swinging from the trees, you know…"

He ran across the room, shouting, beating his chest with his fists.

Virgil allowed him to complete his little show. Alex had never had one good word to say about any of his works.

Out of breath, Malan threw himself to the ground, then, eyeing Virgil with a searching look, decreed, "Well, you work too much."

As long as Alex was in the studio, in any case, no one ran the risk of working too much. Virgil bent over the image cube to save the jungle corner before turning his equipment off. A simple precaution in case Alex decided to erase something he considered outdated.

Leaning against the partition, Alex crossed the legs that lay stretched out in front of him. He made himself comfortable. It looked like this was going to take a while.

"My dear Virgil…"

Virgil grimaced. Alex frowned.

"Old buddy, this is all very serious. You haven't seen Domi recently, have you?"

Domi? Yes, her submissiveness the other day was not normal. She was hiding something. Maybe she had decided to get rid of the baby on her own? Virgil couldn't feel more relieved.

"Domi's been acting strangely," Alex continued. "Did you know that she finally decided to keep the child. In vivo, I mean."

Virgil's face must have revealed his stupefaction, since Alex continued on, his tone serious.

"She almost begged me to allow her to get rid of it… And now she wants to keep it. For the experience, or so she says. I think she's just doing it to annoy me. She's trying to delay my departure."

Sighing, Virgil sat down next to Alex. "When do you have to leave?"

"In six weeks. I'd really like to get this whole thing settled before then…"

And just how did he plan to settle it? Of course, if Domi showed the least little interest in the child, you could fully expect Alex to suggest an abortion. And what if Domi were counting on his contrariness to get what she wanted? That would be just like her.

"Alex, you're the one who asked her to keep it."

Malan glanced at him, a look full of offended dignity. "I didn't think she'd take me seriously. It was only an experiment after all."

"Why don't you talk about it with Domi, calmly?"

Alex shrugged. "She won't listen to me. Virgil, you have to talk with her. After all…"

He didn't finish what he had to say, settling instead for a suggestive smile.

"We'll have a little party. OK? For Domi's birthday…"

Virgil had swung back and forth in recent days. His desire to see Dominella again was not as strong as his repugnance towards Alex's attitude. Alex seemed to exaggerate everything he did out of the sheer pleasure of angering those around him. How could anyone know what he really thought?

But he gave in gently. "OK. For Domi's birthday. I'll speak with her."

"Good shot, old buddy. Now that's what I call a friend."

He stood up, in one sinuous movement, stretching like a cat. He gave Virgil a wicked wink before leaving, nodding at the image cube.

"Honestly, old buddy, the jungle of space…"

Virgil locked the door behind him.

∞

Domi had a very gracious laugh, her head thrown back, her brown curls tumbling in studied disarray on her shoulders in their light blue wrap. Virgil didn't want to stare at her with such intensity. At the start, she'd looked completely normal to him, maybe even a little too normal. Then, that constant laughing… Sensual, provocative, she never left Christopher, one of the genetechnicians, alone for a second. In one corner, Roberta, draped in an orange creation, stood alone, reflecting flames onto a dark wall. Roberta, who looked about her in surprise. Even Alex looked too natural.

As soon as he had arrived, Virgil wanted to leave. And what about his birthday gift? Yes, he'd even be willing to give that up. But Alex hadn't left him any initiative. He had stuck him with one of his close girl friends. Not before whispering to him that he should wait for the right time to speak with Domi, however.

That time would never come. He would have to create it.

The package Virgil had brought a few days earlier lay open on a low table. The chem was already circulating, a soft, sweet-tasting paste. As it made the rounds, passed from hand to hand, people would take a piece, roll it gently in their hands, and then slip it under their tongues where it would slowly melt. Virgil didn't want to get high. Not tonight. Not like this. He got up, staggering a little under the influence of the alcohol fumes as they went to his head.

He headed over to Domi, politely pushed Christopher aside, and leaned down towards her. "I've got a surprise for you and I'd like to show it to you."

Domi looked up at him, her eyes astonished. "A surprise?"

"If you want to see it, come with me."

Nearby, Christopher shrugged. Was he the father? Him or anyone else… What did it matter to him? To Virgil?

Domi stood up. She was waiting for him, smiling, a far-off look on her face. Virgil dragged her outside the apartment. Alex followed them with his eyes for a moment. Too bad for Alex! Virgil had to speak with Domi and he had no intention of doing it in that small room with its unsavoury atmosphere.

As they left that level of the station, he slowed his pace, Domi hanging onto his arm. She looked at him with a mocking smile.

"What's with you, Virgil? You're acting very strange."

"You're the one who's acting strange. Don't you agree? You changed your mind about the baby so quickly."

Her smile froze on her lips. "Virgil, don't get involved with this. And don't listen to Alex. You're not the father."

You're not the father. Should he be happy or upset?

He lowered his head, hesitated for a moment. "Why did you change your mind?"

"I was afraid. That's why I wanted to get rid of the baby."

Afraid of what? He looked at her, astonished.

She sighed. "Afraid of the monstrous child that can't be controlled, afraid of the creature who would devour me from within, I don't know. I tried to look at things differently. *It is* a child, you know. It's not an experiment. It's not some foetus you can watch in an automatrix. It's a *child*. And now, it's Alex who's afraid."

He smiled. Alex? Afraid? Jealous of the pleasure Domi might enjoy as a result of her condition, maybe. Frightened at the thought of losing his privileged position as a pampered baby. Of course. But *afraid*?

Domi closed her eyelids for just a second.

"Virgil, I never intended to continue this pregnancy in vivo. Do you believe me? It's more frightening than amusing. I swear. But Alex is so unpredictable… If I transfer the embryo to an automatrix, the child will get away from me. I won't be able to protect it any more."

"Do you think Alex would…"

"I can well imagine the type of accident he might arrange. It wouldn't be so serious, if it were a baby we'd manufactured ourselves. We could always start over and make another one. But I don't know if I can ever get pregnant again. It's an act of nature. Uncontrolled. Unplanned. I don't want to risk losing the baby."

The baby. He tried to visualize the thing. To call up an image that wouldn't be some sort of fantasy. A concrete image. A child. In Domi's belly. How could she stand it? Maybe Alex was right. Maybe she was just trying to annoy him. What was the real point of this situation? *An act of nature*. An act of chance, yes. One that could only result in a shapeless, deformed creature.

He shook his head. Domi drew away from him as they arrived at his studio. His hand trembled as he gave the command to open the door. Domi entered ahead of him, unhesitating. The studio was brightly lit. The enviro keyboard stood in the centre of the room.

"Your surprise, Virgil. A work? A projection that you've made for me?"

"Only for you. It's a unique recording. There's only one copy. You can either keep it or destroy it. It's up to you."

She stared at him brightly, laughing, attentive to his slightest movement. He dimmed the lighting, gradually plunging the studio into shadow.

"Close your eyes, Domi."

She obeyed. He turned the projector on.

"You can look now."

She didn't make a sound, barely a sigh. She remained perfectly still, frozen in an interrupted gesture.

It was night, a hot, scent-filled night, bustling with the noisy chirping of crickets. The air was somewhat heavy, humid, salty. The heavens extended over their heads forever, brilliant starlight illuminating the scene. Around them, nothing, dunes stretching as far as the eye can see, their gentle curves forming a wall of sand, hiding everything from sight. Beyond the dunes, however, they could just make out a regular murmur calling to them, captivating them. Ebb and flow, rise and fall. The ocean lay beyond the dunes. It could not be seen and yet filled the air with its presence, imposing its own rhythm on every beating heart. Ebb and flow, rise and fall.

Domi's nostrils flared slightly, her body swayed slowly, keeping time with the invisible waves.

"The sea."

"For you, Domi."

She remained silent, totally absorbed in the landscape. Virgil smiled. He'd been waiting so very long for this moment.

The door chimed in the humid air, like a ship's siren. Domi jumped. Virgil shook himself.

Alex stood impatiently on the other side of the screen. "What are you two up to in there. Why are the lights off in your studio?"

Domi went over to the screen. "We're looking at a projection."

She turned to Virgil. "Let him in."

"Let him in!" mimicked Alex. "The little lady is far too generous!"

He stopped at the threshold, contemplating the scene. "Well, not bad, for something you scratched together in three days!"

Virgil forced himself to remain calm. He counted slowly, stringing the numbers out in his head, where they echoed about as in an empty crate. No, he would not humiliate himself by tallying up the endless hours he'd spent "scratching together" the scene. He would not tell Alex that the idea had come to him a year earlier, that he'd spent months making sketches, skeletons of the final scene, unfettered by any landscape. He wouldn't mention the ideas that remained buried in the depths of his memory.

He simply reached his arm out—slowly—satisfied to note that he wasn't shaking, and turned the projector off.

Domi fumed, "Don't listen to him Virgil. It's the best projection I've ever seen in my life. I'll come back to see it."

She headed over to the door, then added, "Later."

Before following her, Alex turned quickly towards him. "Say old buddy, are you in love with my wife?"

Virgil remained alone, petrified, in the centre of his studio.

∞

He jumped out of bed, his face haggard. The studio was completely dark, apart from the blue halo of the com control. He stood still, listening to his ragged breathing, the only sound to break the silence of the night. Something must have wakened him, though. What was it? What had drawn him out of his nightmare? It was already fading from his memory. He was locked up in a deep, viscous gorge, where the slightest movement caused him to sink even further…

He shook his head, and stood stock still once again. He could hear something, a feeble sound, far-off. Like a very gentle scratching. He slipped out of bed and walked over to the door. Had the chime wakened him?

Domi stood there, in the white light of the hallway. A nervous Domi, her face a little puffy. Virgil rushed to her as soon as the door slid open.

"Domi…"

Hesitantly, she placed her hand on his lips, interrupting him. She walked away from him, stumbled in the dark, bent over the enviro keyboard standing on the floor. Suddenly the studio disappeared, transformed into dunes, calm, gently moving shadow, the beach a bed of sand.

In a silky rustle, Domi came back towards him, reached out to hold him. Arms dangling by his side, he didn't dare touch her. Deliberately, she undid her robe. She pressed her body against his and his hands slowly slid up the length of her naked body of their own volition.

They lay down together on the fine sand beach. Stars sparkled at them from the ceiling, a brilliant multitude of lights, twinkling knowingly. The ebb and flow, the rise and fall of gentle waves…

Later, much later, he woke to find himself abandoned, fleshy flotsam on the studio carpet. In his fists, he gripped the programming plate that Domi had removed from the projector before leaving. Snapped in two, cleanly, by a firm hand that knew no regrets.

∞

He woke up, his entire being hoping that the night before had been nothing but a dream. Domi slipping into his bed in the middle of the night, famished, mute, blind, as if she wanted to know nothing at all about her partner…

He walked down the corridor, his steps beating a staccato rhythm. He had to see her, to face Alex. As if nothing had happened that night.

He found them in the laboratory. Domi was not wearing the white coveralls she usually wore to work. She was standing in the doorway when Virgil came in and stepped back a little when she saw him. Alex didn't even notice his arrival. He was bent over an automatrix and Christopher was handing him a series of slender instruments, connected by wires to an analyzer. Alex grumbled, without looking up from his work, "You're always changing your mind. How an I supposed to know what you want?"

Since Domi did not answer, he stood up, and noticed Virgil.

"Well, hey there, buddy."

He gave the plate he was holding to Christopher and indicated that the technician was to keep on working. Christopher tried to look absorbed in his work, but Virgil saw him glance at them several times, disapproval on his face.

Alex came over to Virgil, and tapped him vigorously on the shoulder.. "You're just in time to convince my wife."

"Convince her of what?"

Alex paced about the lab. "She's finally decided to transfer the foetus in vitro."

Virgil turned to Domi, who nodded.

Alex continued, "Everything would be perfect if the little woman wasn't still being so temperamental. She doesn't trust *me*. Get it?"

Domi looked up at the ceiling, and sighed. "That's not it. No doctor treats his own family. Why should you be an exception? Besides, you're not a doctor, you're a geneticist."

"How irrefutably logical of you!"

"Alex…"

Virgil looked at the two of them, questioningly.

Domi explained, "I don't want Alex to be responsible for the transfer. I've asked Roberta to supervise the surgical unit programmed for the operation."

Virgil spread his arms. "But that's perfect! So what's the problem?"

Alex spun around to face him, accusation written on his face. "What? You don't trust me either? You've got a few doubts about my competence?"

Virgil almost replied that he did. Just for once, to treat Alex as he himself had been treated. But he sighed, "You know that's not true. Domi's right. You can't mix your personal and your professional life. No surgeon would operate on his own wife."

"I won't be operating on her. I'll be supervising a robot. I'm not capable of doing that?"

Domi walked over to him and grabbed him by the shoulders.

"Alex, be reasonable. You've got work to do. You said so yourself. You're going to wait here while Roberta takes care of me. It will take a few hours. Virgil will stay with you, won't you Virg?"

He agreed, uncomfortable. Why had he come here today? To show Domi that everything was the same—or hoping that everything had changed? Domi begged him with her eyes. But she couldn't be thinking about the night before. All that counted was the present, Alex's bad mood, Roberta who was waiting in the medical section, the operation to be performed... Domi pressed his arm affectionately as she walked past him, nothing more.

Alex watched the door close and started in on a surly tone, "You poor stupid husband, wait in your lab. Go on, little woman. Above all, don't put yourself out."

He kicked a metal stool, and noticed Christopher who was watching him. Christopher wiped the smile off his face too late and wound up being the target of the abuse Alex intended for the stool.

Virgil sighed and crossed his arms. When it came down to it, Alex was right. Domi was imposing another whim on him. That child. She could have got rid of it days ago, and much more discretely. Maybe that was the purpose of the child, to draw attention to the mother.

Oh, why had Domi come to him during the night?

He turned around, took a step towards the door, then hesitated. Alex was already on his case. "Virgil, don't leave me! We'll go home together, eh? We'll wait for news about Domi at home. All right?"

Anyone looking at his face would have thought Domi was having a tumour removed. Virgil shrugged, before agreeing. He followed Alex, while Christopher, standing near the automatrix, smiled at him, full of commiseration.

As they entered the apartment, Alex brought his hand to his forehead in a melodramatic gesture.

"I think I'll lie down..."

Virgil headed towards the couch.

Alex held him back "Come with me. Don't leave me alone."

Virgil accompanied him into the bedroom, with its perfectly made double bed. Not a single wrinkle in the bedspread. Perhaps Alex hadn't slept there either. Had Domi come to him out of spite? To take revenge on Alex?

He chased the questions away as he watched Alex stretch out languidly, then tap the covers next to him.

"Come…"

Virgil lay down beside Alex, his back against the partition. Alex grabbed his hand, entwining their fingers, caressing. Virgil forced himself not to pull back.

"Alex, you're not the least bit worried."

Alex grinned, catlike.

"You're not comfortable there, beside me?"

Virgil sighed. Alex turned on his side to get a better look at him.

"Do you know why Domi refused to allow me to supervise the transfer?"

"She told you why, didn't she? It wouldn't be prudent, it wouldn't be professional."

Alex gave a mocking laugh.

"Virgil, poor old Virgil… Are you as stupid as you look? Domi refused to allow me near the transfer because she's afraid I'll take advantage of the opportunity to destroy her precious embryo."

He smiled. "An accident can happen so quickly…"

Abruptly, Virgil pushed him away. In a clumsy effort to get out of the bunk, he fell to the floor, Alex's arms wrapped around his legs. Malan burst out laughing. Virgil tried to roll out of his grasp, but Alex flattened him against the carpet.

"Afraid of me, Virg?"

Alex was excited, twisting about like a serpent on the sand, before coming to rest, eyes bright.

"Do you remember our nights together, before Domi? You and me. Just the two of us…"

Virgil nodded his head, slowly, submissively. Alex moved away. Virgil took his time to get up, sluggish, his body heavy. Alex had jumped onto the bed. Sitting with his back straight, his legs crossed under him, he watched Virgil, full of contempt.

"You've got old. Poor old Virgil."

Virgil stood up. For just a second, he dominated Alex, his breathing hoarse. All he had to do was stretch his arms out, grab the slender swan-like neck and squeeze it hard, harder yet, until the laughing face turned white, all its ugliness revealed. That body, so skilled in giving pleasure, with its movements that could sometimes be so gentle, was so very fragile. Too vulnerable. Strong in its weakness.

Virgil closed his eyes, and took a deep breath. He could never hurt him. Alex could skin him alive and he would still be unable to lift a finger to defend himself. And it wasn't out of affection for Domi.

∞

He was running through the corridors of Relay II. Well, they looked like the corridors at Asterman, but he knew, with an amazing sense of detachment, that he was on Relay II. He was running. Occasionally he turned his head, to see only the deserted hallway behind him. He ran with long strides, slowly, ever so slowly. Ahead of him, he saw the entrance to the laboratory, like an open, laughing face. He would have liked to stop his race, to head off in another direction. Wasn't this the place he was fleeing from? The lab loomed inexorably closer. Inside, it looked like the apartment where Domi and Alex lived. There, in the middle of the living room, was the long white counter with its instruments. Alex was leaning against the counter, smiling, welcoming, arms open. Virgil dove left to avoid him. Alex jumped, grabbed him by the legs and Virgil rolled into a ball. He fought without any strength. Alex roared with laughter, lifted him up and threw him like some inert package onto the tool-laden counter. Unable to move, Virgil watched Alex as he climbed onto the counter and stretched out on him. Virgil grabbed the body that covered him. He had the strange sensation that he was penetrating a woman. Abruptly, he pushed the body that had wrapped itself around him, convinced that he would see Domi's face. But it was still Alex, languid, provocative. Virgil screamed, but no sound came out of his mouth. Alex tore the delicate arm off a surgical unit. Virgil could make out a sharp instrument, a blade. Alex bent over him, smiling. He repeated the same words over and over—Virgil could read his lips—*to slit your belly*.

Virgil closed his eyes, eyelids clenched, waiting for the pain…

He woke up suddenly, brutally. Smothering a cry, he rolled onto his side in the damp sheets. Sweat trickled down his shaking body. Eyes wide open in the dark, he waited for the heavy pounding of his heart to slow.

∞

"So, you see, the probes maintain the vital functions of the automatrix."

Looking very serious, Alex pointed to the delicate web of wires that connected the equipment to the laboratory analyzers. This entire section of the cytogenetics department was filled with one cubicle after another, lined up along the corridor. Inside the tiny rooms, which were about the size of a closet, automatrices perpetuated the cycle of life. Invisible embryos grew there, enveloped in dark-colored flesh. Technicians came and went in the corridor, walking past the robots with their articulated limbs that maintained constant surveillance over the automatrices. Every now and then cubicles were closed, some because they were unused, others because the experiments being attempted required specific security measures.

Alex played his role as tour guide with a light touch.

"Here, we create life, here we give birth to the future generation…"

Virgil followed him, without a word, a polite smile pasted on his lips, all the while experiencing the confused sensation that he was drunkenly clattering down some metal ladder. The sound echoed, bouncing around.

Since coming back to Relay II, reality had become less and less tangible, escaping from him every time he tried to grasp it. And reality wasn't the only thing slipping away. Alex and Domi were becoming blurred as well. Before, everything had seemed so simple. Their evening get-togethers. The chem that sent them soaring. Brief pleasure in a short instant of lucidity as all three of them made love with vague gestures, disconnected from real time… They could no longer meld, as if their temporality were suddenly out of tune, dissonant. Domi cast to one side with that being in her that wanted to take over the entire place—*in her?* Yet the transfer operation had been successful. Why *in her?* An unwelcome thought that he could not drive out. Then there was Alex… Alex who was headed off in another direction, pulled between Asterman, the seat of power that demanded his presence, and the future Relay III, a project, a hope—something inside him that only wanted to grow, to push, to go even further yet. And what about himself? What about Virgil? Here, for now—a moment without consideration. Alex and Domi were each running a race that certainly had some meaning, some purpose, for them. He watched them as they ran, drawn and quartered, not knowing which one to follow, not understanding where they were headed.

"Virgil?"

Alex had stopped and was smiling insistently, somewhat mockingly.

"Are you listening to me?"

Alex lowered his head, contrite. Alex sighed.

"Invite tourists in and this is what you get! Guess where we are?"

Virgil glanced around himself, a little confused. They were standing in front of the closed door of a cubicle, as equipment came and went around them. Alex was holding a small white plastic card, a key that he waved under his visitor's nose. It was just like him to draw attention to such a banal object in order to steer it away from the main item.

With a dramatic gesture, he inserted the key in the slot in the control panel of the door. The door slid open, revealing a cubicle that was absolutely identical to those they had visited earlier. Maybe Alex and his genetechnicians could tell the difference by the type of equipment that watched over the automatrix, by identifying features specific to the cubicle. But Virgil only saw an automatrix, connected to a supervisor. And just like everywhere else, there was no way to make out anything at all from the clutter that floated in the amniotic fluid. Virgil cleared his throat. Alex pointed, "There she is. I say *she* because it's a girl."

He smiled ecstatically.

Virgil probably should have been less moderate in his enthusiasm, but all he said was "Oh, well," before glancing back out into the corridor.

"That's all you have to say? After all, it could be your daughter. What would you like to call her?"

Virgil shot him a pained glance, "Look Alex, if you intend to…"

"Calm down, old buddy. I was just teasing. Domi doesn't want any paternity tests. And she's already chosen a name. It's registered somewhere…"

He walked out of the cubicle and Virgil rushed out behind him, giving the automatrix a disgusted glance. Knowing that he had come from there one day made it no less repugnant. As an adult, he was a defined, palpable, controlled being, whereas that little thing, there, had been totally unexpected. She could not be anything but monstrous. *She*?

Alex had just been stopped in the corridor by another visitor. Virgil took advantage of the opportunity to put a little distance between them. He ran into Domi, who arrived suddenly. She frowned at him, and rushed into the cubicle that had remained open. Alex watched her rush past, without reacting. She gave the command to close the door, removed the key that slid out of the slot and held it out to Alex, cutting the visitor off in mid-sentence.

"Take this, Alex. And try not to leave specially controlled cubicles open!"

The visitor looked dumbfounded. Alex smiled gently and Domi added, her voice quavering, "I hold you responsible for *that* human life, Alex. Don't forget it."

She abruptly turned on her heel and Virgil raced to catch up with her. He finally did in the large corridor that linked the laboratories.

"Domi, I have to talk with you…"

She stopped, looked him up and down for a minute, then looked away.

"I don't have time, Virgil."

"It's important. Why are you trying to avoid me?"

"I'm not trying to avoid you. I'm very busy."

He stared at her in silence, a sceptical smile on his lips. She sighed, "All right. I'll see you, but not now."

"When?"

"I'll come to your place tonight."

She freed herself from his grasp and hurried into the laboratory. He let her escape, disturbed. He had no hold over her. But he would be there that evening, waiting for her.

∞

She arrived late, hesitating on the doorstep.

"I shouldn't have come. If Alex catches me here, he'll be furious."

He had given up waiting for her, and was preparing for bed. His bunk took up most of the free space. Quickly, he pushed it back into its nook, stood up, aware of his embarrassment, and pointed to the armchair in the corner.

"Would you like to sit down?"

Domi looked around, before sitting in the easy chair.

"You've put your projector away… Too bad."

He nodded.

She sighed. "You wanted to speak with me?"

I want to speak to you about us. I want to speak to you about love. He turned away for a moment. He wanted her so much it hurt…"Domi, I want to talk to you about Alex."

"Alex?"

"You have to leave him."

She looked up at him, exasperated. "You're not starting that all over again, are you?"

"And why not? I just don't understand why you insist on staying with him."

"I don't have to justify my private life to you, Virgil Ogan."

"But Alex is ill. For months now…he's not been the same. You never know what to expect from him. Who knows what he's capable of?"

She jumped up, furious. "How can you say that. You're the one who gives him his chems, all that synthetic filth that he's been taking for months!"

He looked at her, eyes wide. She snarled, "Don't look at me like that! Of course, Alex is ill. I am too. You probably are as well! We're all going crazy!"

He stammered her name.

She shook her head violently. "I want to leave him, if you only knew how much I want to leave him!"

He stood there, motionless, flabbergasted.

She spread her arms, allowing her anger to dissipate, powerless. "Virgil, if you only knew..."

He went over to her, gently, and stood beside her, without touching her, and leaned his head on her shoulder. "I don't feel...I mean, if I hadn't given it to him, he would have got it elsewhere, I think."

"Forgive me, Virgil. It's too easy to make you take the blame for everything. It's my fault. I made him jealous. But recently, our sexual encounters...have all been so pitiful."

He trembled. Had he been such a terrible lover?

"You must not blame yourself, Domi. Neither of us is responsible for what Alex is becoming. I only want you to be free, without me if that's what you want."

She stepped away from him, angrily.

"Free! Do you really think you can get 'free' from Alex that easily?"

"I don't know. I don't understand anything anymore. That's what worries me. What's happening to you and Alex, Domi? What's happening to *us*? I don't know who you are anymore."

"You should worry about yourself, Virgil."

He shrugged, ready to face her mocking. "I know who I am, I know what I'm worth, no matter what you and Alex think of me. I'm a master enviro, already fairly skilled, and I'm proud of my work."

Totally unexpectedly, she relaxed. And smiled a t him, strangely compassionate. "You're not just a 'fairly skilled' master, Virgil. You're a great artist. But you're still sitting on the fence, hesitating between going ahead, and going back, between the past and the future. You came to Relay II because Alex told you over and over again that this is where the future is at, here at the edge of the solar system. But you just spend your time looking back, towards Asterman, because you feel that's where you could achieve your full potential. Why can't you choose, Virg?"

"For the same reasons you can't, I guess. Which of us is the worst?"

She replied immediately, her tone abrupt, "What do you know about my reasons, about my failings? What do you know about me, Virgil?"

He opened his mouth, unable to speak, raised a hand, then let it fall back. He'd always allowed Alex to treat him poorly, but Domi... To see himself pushed aside with the back of her hand...

What exactly had he hoped for? What had he been foolish enough to hope for? He didn't mean anything, not to her. He'd just been a body that she had desired, like Christopher, like anyone.

She watched him a moment, in silence, heartbroken, and finally sighed.

"I didn't come here to fight with you."

As he remained silent, she took a small package, wrapped in white paper, from her pocket.

"I came to give you this."

He reached out his hand, felt the package through the wrapping. But all he felt was the box. Nothing rattled inside.

"What is it?"

"It's something very important to me, but I can't keep it with me. You're the only one I can trust it to."

So, he was to be the faithful friend. He nodded his head slightly.

"Thanks for your trust."

She touched the package one last time, then quickly drew back her hand.

"Listen. Don't open it. I'm only leaving it with you in case something happens."

He wanted to protest—what could happen to her—but she stopped him.

"If I leave before I get it back from you, then you can open it. Understood?"

"But what does that mean?"

"Please, no questions. I'm asking you to keep something important. That's all."

He agreed, unwillingly. What could be so important? For a second, he imagined that he would find a tape in the box, a letter of some kind. *Dearest Virgil*… He blushed.

"All right, don't worry about it."

She grasped his arm and embraced him very gently, before being swallowed up by the door.

He looked at the package from all angles, sniffed it, shook it gently before giving up. Really now, a love letter? Why not a bomb? And what if it was just the last batch of chem, or whatever was left of it, that she had confiscated from Alex? It wasn't a very large package.

The thought invaded his mind with exasperating slowness. What if it was the key to the cubicle? The package was almost exactly the right size. A little thicker, perhaps. But the object had to be wrapped in paper so it wouldn't rattle about.

He started towards the door, then stopped himself. Rushing off to the lab wouldn't be all that great an idea. The technicians on duty would ask questions, particularly since he never went there without either Alex or Domi. He could go there and sniff around, pretending nothing was up, when the couple was on duty, but not before. Should he open the package? Wouldn't that make him look good, when Domi came back for it!

He pulled the bunk out of its nook, sat on it, lost in thought. The package weighed on him. He lay it on his thigh, and gave it a slightly vindictive glance. If Domi had dared leave the key with him… She had no right to involve him in their quarrel. It was none of his business. He'd never interfered in their spats. He'd always remained a spectator. Attentive, yet impartial. Yes, that was it, he was an *observer*. He wasn't going to get involved in their affairs now. Domi would have to listen to him.

He would give her a chance to explain. He would not call the apartment. He'd see her discreetly, when Alex wasn't around. He'd take Domi aside, wave the package under her nose, and this time she wouldn't get off so easily.

He sighed deeply, and buried the package under his pillow. At least no one could say that he wasn't keeping good care of the "precious object." Then he drew the covers up, determined not to give it another thought. He would sleep.

I don't appreciate being used like this, particularly by a friend. You must be honest with Alex. No. Too direct. He might wind up involved in their dispute. Nonchalant, then. *Here's your precious package. I'm not a babysitter.*

He punched his pillow, then buried his face in it. *Shut up!*

∞

An eternity later, he was barely drowsing when the communicator sounded, waking him. He jumped out of bed, stumbled over to the control. He blinked with the brightness of the screen. Alex's face filled the screen, his features distorted with anger. His voice high, Alex shouted: "Well, well, well, here's our good friend, dear, dear Virgil."

He saw Domi, as Alex held her by the wrists and shook her. She didn't look frightened, but beseeched him with her eyes. He drew closer to the screen.

"Domi, what's happening? What's up with him?"

Alex laughed, wickedly. "What's up is that my wife wants to leave me. Get that, Virgil? I'm going to leave without her, so she says, after all those damned promises she made to me! 'No, sweetheart, I'll never leave you!' What do you think I should do, Virgil?"

Domi fought in silence. Alex shook her violently.

"Should I hit her? Should I fuck her like the whore she is, until she begs for mercy? Hey Virgil, what about that?"

"Alex, stop!"

Virgil had placed his hands on either side of the screen, as if he hoped to be able to reach the couple through it. "Calm down, Alex. Calm down."

Alex jerked his chin in Virgil's direction. "Get your filthy paws away from there. Do you think I don't understand anything? Do you think I'm blind? You're wrong, dear old Virgil, if you think you can get away with it like that!"

Virgil stepped back, palms up, gasping. "I'm not trying to get away with anything, Alex. I want to come over. If you want to fight with someone, then take me on. But let her go. I'm begging you!"

"He's afraid!" Alex was jubilant. "He's afraid for you, sweetie. Did you hear that?"

Suddenly, he punched her right in the face. Domi cried out, briefly. Virgil leapt.

He ran until he ran out of breath, roughly pushing aside those who got in his way. He sped down corridors. A distant memory spurred his discomfort, a feeling of déjà vu. As if in a dream, his legs felt like lead. Yet he raced on. He raged against the elevator. Too slow. He struck it with his fists. The elevator arrived. He drove the shouting, protesting passengers out. Eyes fixed on the display panel, he raged as the elevator slowly moved up, level by level.

He stumbled in the hallway, breathing suspended, heart ready to burst. He activated the com signal, pounded against the door panel with all his strength.

"Alex! Open up! You want to fight, here I am!"

Passersby came up to him, as he shouted himself hoarse. He glared at them venomously. "What are you waiting for? Go get Security!"

A few people slipped away. He attacked the communicator. The screen remained blank. Virgil steped back, flailed about for a second, looking for passage, looking for a way to get in. If he only had a weapon, a tool, he'd have torn the door down with ferocious joy.

How stupid of him! To let Domi go home like that. She knew Alex was ill. She must have thought about leaving him for a long time, without daring to tell him. Why hadn't she told him, earlier tonight? She wanted to handle things on her own. She had refused his help and now…

He screamed out Alex's name and once again attacked the door, before leaning against it, exhausted.

"Alex! Open up!"

He turned at the sound of footsteps in the corridor. Two officers were on their way.

"What's going on here?"

They wanted explanations.

"He's beating her. You have to open up. You have to stop him."

He trembled.

The officers looked at him, their faces serious. Finally, one of them inserted a black card in the locking mechanism of the door. The panel slid open, docilely. Virgil leapt forward, stopped as one of the officers grabbed him.

"Wait here."

His colleague walked in, carefully, his weapon in his hand. Inside, nothing moved. Tables were overturned, knick knacks strewn everywhere. The officers turned towards Virgil, who stared. All this time…

"The lab!"

He raced down the hallway, followed by the two officers. Why hadn't he thought of it earlier? Alex obviously wanted to destroy the automatrix…

They didn't even have to knock the door of the lab down. Jodi, the technician on duty, was standing neat the cubicle section, looking shook up. There was a large bruise on his cheek. Alex must have struck him before throwing him out.

The two officers stopped suddenly, when they noticed the open panel. So did Virgil. They started walking ahead, slowly—with Virgil following right behind. Mechanically, he pressed Jodi's arm as he walked past, in an unconvincing attempt to reassure him. Jodi tried to hold him back, but seemed to have no strength left.

The officers hesitated for a fraction of a second on the doorstep, as if petrified. Alex was seated on the floor, idiotically, in front of the open cubicle, in a pool of bloody liquid, eyes closed, hands plunged in a heap of viscous flesh that spread over the white tiles.

Virgil walked on, mechanically. He bent down near Alex, touched him on the shoulder. Alex opened his eyes, smiled.

"Hey there, Virgil!"

He looked around him, surprised, gave a brief bark of laughter, then raised his fist, clasping a piece of purple flesh.

"All for nothing!"

The officers finally entered the room. Virgil heard them approach. He stammered, "Domi…"

Alex gave a vague wave of his hand.

Virgil stood up slowly. The officers were bent over behind a piece of equipment, busy. Virgil headed over towards them. Detached, he recognized Domi sprawled on the floor. One of the officers was examining her. The other spoke quickly into his portable communicator. He looked up, saw Virgil. Virgil would never forget that look.

He took another step, then stopped. Domi looked straight at him, staring, barely astonished. A ring of red marks circled her neck. The expression on her face was strange, almost triumphant.

The officer stood up, shaking his head. The officer with the communicator did the same, then came towards Virgil to push him gently aside.

"Go on. Don't stay here."

Virgil stumbled over to the door. He heard Alex repeat, in his high-pitched voice, "All for nothing, I'm telling you. For nothing!"

His eyes met Jodi's horrified eyes, and he smiled. The officer looked at him, insistently. "Are you all right?"

Virgil nodded, carefully. The officer left him. He leaned against the wall. His fingers were red. He examined his hands, stupidly. It couldn't be blood. Oh yes, the amniotic fluid. What a mess!

∞

In the medical department, everything was white, an immaculate white, like in the laboratory. Roberta sobbed in one corner, consoled by a young colleague who glanced at Virgil, as he sat on a plastic chair, over and over, a concerned look on his face. A man entered the room, well dressed, wearing a dark suit. He headed over to the young doctor and asked, "What did you do with him?"

The man nodded towards the corridor. "He's been sedated. I feel his case is more a matter for a psychiatrist than the justice system."

He walked over to Virgil, and sat down on the edge of an examining table. He cleared his throat, and looked Virgil up and down, circumspectly. "They told me you were Ms. Gaitains' friend."

Virgil stared at him, unblinking.

"Yes."

The man turned his face away. "Viau, of Security. If you'd come with me for a few minutes, we have some questions we'd like to ask..."

Virgil stammered, "They argued. I think she wanted to leave him."

The other nodded, soothingly.

Virgil insisted, "He was afraid of the child." He sighed, "It was a girl, a little girl."

∞

He looked about his studio, uncertainly. The room looked completely foreign to him, as if from some other time, some other universe. The unmade bed, the wrinkled sheets...someone had leapt out of that bed a century earlier. Unless he was still sleeping there, in some happy sleep.

But he was wide awake. He felt that pain in his chest. His heart was trying to burst. He took a few steps, then sat on the edge of the bed, looked at his red fingers. He hadn't had time to wash them.

Domi and Alex, relegated to the bottom of some drawer.

He stood up from the bed, headed over to the small door that hid the washroom. He washed his hands for a long time, carefully, rubbing his fingernails, much longer than he needed to. Then he dried them carefully and returned to his bed.

The pillow was a shapeless heap. He lifted it up. The white package was still there. Hands shaking, Virgil picked it up. His fingers caressed the smooth paper, soft to the touch. He started to rip the paper off. It crackled under his touch. The small plastic box opened easily, a piece of white cloth floated out, unrolled, and the key to the cubicle fell to the floor.

He bent down to pick it up, and held the now useless plate in his hand. His tears formed a dark stain on the carpet.

∞

Christopher fidgeted about on the doorstep to the studio, his eyes cast down, his hands jammed into the pockets of his pants. Virgil waited silently for him to finally decide to explain the reasons for his visit.

He hadn't seen anyone for weeks. He had remained locked up in his stuffy room, modelling nightmare scenes, caves whose walls oozed scarlet. He paced back and forth in the middle of these horrors, then destroyed the recordings. He had thought about destroying himself as well, but he couldn't find the courage to do it. All he wanted was to stay locked up in his dirty, messy studio.

And then Christopher appeared to pull him out of his retirement. The young technician stood a little straighter.

"Someone from the family has come, to settle the estate…"

Virgil didn't ask whose family. He didn't even know if Alex had been transferred elsewhere. It didn't matter. Christopher was getting worked up, "I'd like to ask them… I'd like to have something that belonged to Domi, you know? But I'm a little embarrassed, so I thought maybe you'd like to come with me."

Virgil didn't respond. Christopher insisted, "I want something to remember Domi by. Don't you?"

Something to remember Domi by! All he had was memories of her. A smile, a word, the caress of her fingertips. The odds and ends of existence. What more could Christopher want?

"I don't want anything."

He noticed the key on his bed, the plastic key that opened the cubicle in the lab... He picked it up, showed it to Christopher.

The young technician drew closer.

"What is that?"

"The key. The key for the cubicle."

Christopher stared, wide eyed.

"You mean...the cubicle where Alex broke the automatrix?"

Virgil nodded, already regretting having shown Christopher the key. He didn't want any of his controlled curiosity. But Christopher shook his head.

"That's impossible, Virgil. The cubicle...they found the key in the lock. You remember? Domi had given it to Alex."

Virgil backed up against the bed, groped his way along it and sat down, completely dumbfounded, as if caught in the beam of a bright light. He remained there, minute after minute, blinded, his muscles taut. Little by little, he was able to make out Christopher's face, as he bent anxiously over him, Christopher who was shaking his arm.

"Virgil?"

He pushed Christopher away, his hand grasping the plastic plate. The young technician must have been forced to back off, since he disappeared from Virgil's field of vision. Virgil inhaled deeply. Then he stretched out his hand, palm up.

"Are you certain that this key..."

The technician picked up the plate and examined it. "It's from our department in any case. It must belong to another cubicle. We'd have to check the terminal."

Virgil shivered. He wasn't going to...he couldn't go back there. Could he give the key to Christopher? No way. He might well keep it to remember Domi by. He stood up, painfully.

"Let's go."

Christopher took him to the large lab first, the lab where Alex and Domi usually worked. Virgil had regained his vision, but walked unsteadily. When they entered the lab, he almost expected to see Domi, leaning against the bench, Domi who would turn to him and smile, *Virgil!*

Jodi was alone in the lab and turned as he saw them come in. Christopher sat down at the terminal and inserted the key in the coding slot. Behind him, Virgil forced himself to stand straight, and not stoop over with the pain.

Christopher motioned to him.

"Here it is. It's clearly indicated. Here's the number of the cubicle. A special order. Reserved access."

He turned to Virgil, "Since you have the key…"

He held the plastic plate out to him. Virgil picked it up, without thinking. Christopher added, "Are you going to open it up?"

He walked slowly down the hall, surprised that he felt no pain as he returned to the scene, that he felt almost no emotion. Domi was no longer there. It was nothing more than some cold place, walls without meaning.

Christopher pointed out a door to him. Virgil slipped the key into the lock slot. The panel slid open, soundlessly. He walked into the cubicle, his fingertips caressing the glass wall of the automatrix. *Dominella…*

Obviously, it was impossible to see anything. But he didn't need to. He knew what was there.

∞

The shuttle to Asterman is a little behind schedule, but Virgil waits patiently. A passenger service employee is moving from seat to seat, soothing the less patient travellers. Virgil, his head titled back against his seat, watches the young man move about, distractedly.

Nearby, the baby wriggles about in her baby seat on the seat next to his. She gurgles as she shakes a toy. Virgil sits up, looks at her, then smiles. At 6 months old, she's already very cute.

He didn't try to find out. The questions he might have asked would have raised other questions. Alex did not destroy an empty automatrix, or there would have been an investigation. Domi did everything she could to protect her child. So Virgil prepared for his trip as discreetly as he could. It was as simple as that.

He has no idea what lies ahead of the two of them, but it's not really important. It doesn't matter to him that the future lies ahead and not behind and that some of his colleagues think he's taking a step back by moving to Asterman. Virgil isn't worried. He's found his inner peace in this small, wriggling, babbling creature who cries sometimes, laughs others. She is not named Dominella, of course. Virgil never gave her that name. But when asked, he says she's his daughter. It doesn't matter whether it's true or not. She was a gift from Domi. ∞

Gone With the Sea

∞ Ursula Pflug ∞

"WE GO IN. WE'RE IN ANYWAY. We go in; our virtual bodies eat the virtual fish."

"Yes, but how does that provide nourishment, how does the fish protein enter your meat bag?"

"We don't have meat bags anymore." Snicker.

"Seriously, Jake."

"Seriously, Mum, I can come down and check out your computer tonight."

"Thanks, son. I'll make you dinner. You people still eat dinner, right?"

"Sometimes," Jake said, with just a hint of wistfulness. "But eating is so much trouble. You have to de-gear to eat."

"I know. You live on shrimp pills and Jolt Cola. I'll give you a case of pills to take home with you. I can't afford to pay. For you and your friends. So you don't have to go out, go to the store."

"How come you're so broke?"

"The shrimp are sick. I haven't been able to fill the last two orders. I'm cash strapped."

"Ship sick shrimp," Jake suggested.

"Ship sick shrimp, she said, shelling shrimp by the seashore. I know a lot of people do it, Jake, but I just can't."

"Ethical as ever, Ellen. I take it fixing the computer would expedite a medical diagnosis?"

"You got it."

"You should've said they were sick. I'd have come last week."

"Seems to me I did."

"Oh. See you at four then?"

"Thanks. Bye."

"Bye."

∞

OpaeCorp had been built sixty years before, in the last years of the previous century, in approximately the same location as an ancient Hawaiian fish farm, on the north shore near Haena. Much easier and less expensive to excavate and reline the 500-year-old ponds than to dig new, a tribute, Ellen supposed, to ancient aboriginal engineering. Ellen had wanted to expand last year, cut down the mangroves, put in two extra ponds. Her local neighbour Maui had discouraged that, instead talking her into hand building a small outrigger canoe according to traditional design. "You wouldn't cut them down if you knew them," he'd said, and Ellen had replied they were unknowable. A mangrove forest wasn't the kind of thing you could walk through.

She'd given in mostly because Maui had been so stubborn, and found he'd been right: now she loved the mangroves surrounding her farm. Their fantastic other-worldliness rarely failed to refresh her when she was feeling fraught and burdened, as now. After hanging up on Jake she got her little boat out of the decommissioned outtake canal that was its driveway, sailed it, just for a couple of hours up the coast, through mangroves. All trees of course, are more or less vertically symmetrical, Ellen thought, it's just that with most we can't see the roots. Not so with mangroves. The roots rise up out of the water, a wickerwork tripod suspending the trunk, the dense, fragrant interwoven branches. The shade, the quiet of the mangrove swamps. It seemed the only peace. And then back to work.

She checked the inlet and the discharge canals, the pump intakes, the sediment traps. While she knew enough to see whether engines were working smoothly, she wasn't happy repairing them. Her mechanic had moved to Alaska the previous winter and she hadn't found a reliable replacement, even though she kept offering Maui the job. And now the pump was coughing. Had it been coughing all week? Was e-coli the cause of her shrimps' illness? She should've checked the pump sooner. She visited the nauplii in their pond, the postlarvae in the adjacent one. They were seemingly still healthy, which was a relief, but they didn't solve her business problem. You couldn't ship babies.

The shrimp themselves had been genetically engineered, a hybrid between Penaeus monodon, japonicus, and a freshwater Macrobrachium species that was extremely disease resistant. The ancient Hawaiians hadn't thought of biotech. Too bad for them. They could've been the ones who made millions in the first years of the new century, as Ellen's great-grandmother Eileen had, feeding farmed shrimp to a starving world. Of course, they could've made millions too if they'd owned the big resort hotels on the southern beaches. But they hadn't. They'd just worked in them.

It was only biotech that had made it possible to replicate the entire life cycle, from egg to market-sized, in ponds, and that hadn't happened till the nineties. So while Maui had been the one to insist she not raze the remaining mangroves to build more ponds, but rather to plant more to enlarge the final stage filter system, as was traditional, he wasn't really up on modern methods. But he was good with pumps and so she called him, left a message on his machine, resisting the temptation to call him Sun-God, as she occasionally did, to tease. Did Maui really mean Sun-God? Ellen couldn't remember. Did it help him to have a god's name? Probably not. He was very poor. At one time he'd worked as a unionized hotel janitor, but tourism had plummeted, as ozone depletion worsened. No one wanted to lie in the sun anymore, catch cancer. But the world was starving, worse than ever, and bioengineered shrimp culturing methods seemed one of many cures. Those with foresight scrapped their south shore beachfront hotels in the first decade of the new millennium, razing them to make room for shrimp farms. And so the rainy little volcanic island began to resemble its earlier self, a forested place, the coastal waters farmed. Irony.

Maui often claimed his family had done a little shrimp farming, now and again. They'd practised the traditional method, allowing juvenile shrimp to be carried by the tides into hand built coastal ponds where they were grown to market size. Otherwise they caught gravid females at sea and allowed them to spawn in ponds. Or so she assumed. Animal husbandry, and not true science.

And here he was already, come to look at her pump. "Where were you?" she asked, stress making her blunt. Or perhaps she'd been blunt for years, just hadn't noticed.

"Bodysurfing," he grinned, already disassembling the motor. "Come with me tomorrow? The weather'll be perfect."

"Bodysurfing is dangerous. I've lost three friends to it."

"I know. They were stoned out of their gourds on mushrooms," he reminded her. "They took stupid risks. They swam in an undertow. The rip tides were posted. They were too stoned to read."

"True. You sure you don't want a job?"

"What's wrong with your employees, Ellen?"

"They're doorknobs by and large. Everything they do, I have to check and double check to make sure they've gotten it right. There isn't that much room for error in shrimp farming."

"You're telling me. But I don't need a job," he said.

"What do you do, now?" She asked. She never had been able to figure. He moved in and out of her life, appearing and disappearing. Alternately friendly and a little distant.

"Huh?" he asked.

"Where d'you work, now?"

"Don't need to work really. My grandmother, she left me a few acres on the coast near Hanalei. I got avocado, mango, banana. I grow a few greens. There's a bit of old terracing there, I repaired it, put in taro."

"Ugh," she said. She still thought poi was disgusting, in spite of having grown up just outside Lihue. She'd never been a mainlander. Kamaainas, the Hawaiian born whites called themselves. It translated, roughly, as locals. As if.

"You raise a few pigs. You fish," she continued for Maui. "What about money for gas?"

"Oh there's always things. Trade and barter and it's not I don't work. I put in a few weeks each year on one thing or another. What about you, Ellen?"

"I run the farm. Somebody has to or what would the world eat?"

"Is that what you want?"

"It's okay. I'd like to travel, go to the mainland, way up north maybe, Alaska. I've never been to the mainland. A lot of my friends did that."

"I know."

"How d'you know?"

"Kauai is a small island. You hear everything."

"True." He was standing there looking pretty well done, like he wanted to leave now.

"Pump okay now?" Ellen asked.

"Pump's fine. I think what you're facing here, Ellen, is a monoculture problem."

"But the wild varieties aren't disease resistant. These are stronger and healthier; you can raise three harvests a year in a much smaller acreage than from traditional methods." She sounded like the OpaeCorp promotional material, she knew.

Maui looked uncertain. "Maybe for a few years."

"It's been sixty," Ellen laughed.

"That is a few, really, if you think about it. What you figure their problem is today?"

"A new brand of e-coli, resistant to antibiotics."

"What you plan on doing then?"

"Search the Web, see if there's a stronger antibiotic I can order," Ellen said.

"You can't eat them if they're all dead."

"But they won't be, you see. And I should've gotten to you sooner about the pump."

"I don't think the pump is the problem, really. Like I said," Maui insisted, stubborn as ever.

"But of course it is. That and the computer. Jake's coming tonight to fix that."

Maui said nothing, crouched down and scooped a handful of wriggling adult shrimp out of the water, examined them closely.

"What d'you know about shrimp?" she asked defensively. "I thought you were a janitor." Now she'd done it. While without a ticket, Maui was the best mechanic she knew. And now he'd never come back, and who could blame him?

"Oh, I've done a little shrimp farming in my day," he reminded her. "Traditional methods, largely."

"So I've heard. That'll never feed a world." Now who was stubborn?

"Maybe. Maybe not. I'm not entirely against gene-splicing and all the rest of your high tech, anyway. It's just a matter of how it's done. You put money ahead of fish, ahead of people, you'll never come out ahead, not in the long run. Nature doesn't care about dollars."

"I always thought so too, actually."

"I'd hope so, or I don't think I'd be standing here talking to you. And on that count I should tell you these fish won't make the week, no matter what new-fangled tetracyclines you dose them with. Not a one."

"I've been in this business all my life Maui, don't tell me how to farm."

"Suit yourself, *haole*," he said. With derision. It was amazing how much derision a local could fit into that one little word. Irony-free derision. Watching him leave, she had never felt less a *kamaaina*. *Haole* meant white, foreigner.

∞

Ellen wanted to travel, but she had to stay because she was the last one who knew how to look after the farm. The old people knew too, of course, in fact had taught her, but were now themselves too old. Most of them lived in Seaview, a senior's home on a Princeville cliff, overlooking the Pacific. The place had been sold to them for its huge plate glass windowed common room, where they could sit in their recliners, sipping morning coffee and watching whales. But of course, there were very few whales. They'd moved away, resisting their genetic predisposition to return to this same spot, year after year, and raise their children. There had been too many tourist Zodiacs at the turn of the century, frightening them. Their age-old reproductive behaviour had been altered. Ellen wondered whether it was a conscious decision to move away from the whale watchers who'd come too close, too often, and too many. If the whales could decide to move north, Ellen thought, alter their instinctive, transgenerational routes and trails through water, as well marked to them as highway maps are to us, then perhaps humans could do the same. As of course they had, in different ways, her own generation and her children's. As with the whales, it was too soon to see what the results would be.

Ellen wondered whether to go to Seaview to ask for advice or wait for Jake. She decided to stay, check the manual systems. It was already two o' clock and she wouldn't have time to make the return trip and prepare food for her son, trial as she knew the dinner conversation would be. She dumped extra tetracycline into the adult ponds, even though, without her computer running properly, she couldn't pinpoint the bacterial problem. But Jake would fix that, hopefully. And it was better than having all the shrimp die overnight.

She'd tried to find an assistant manager to train among the younger people, but they all worked in computers at the industrial park up in the valley behind Kapaa. They created virtual shrimp, longing for the day when they'd discover the interface, an alteration in either the cyber-Penaeus or their own bodies which would enable them to eat information shrimp, and no longer need flesh.

Ellen thought they lived in a world of their own making, had been hexed by the cyber-witch, spellbound. It would never happen. They'd depend on her for their fleshly needs, to feed the meat bag which they so abhorred, which, goggled and gloved in most of their waking hours, they had only a passing intimacy with.

∞

"We're getting closer," Jake said by way of conversation as he rebooted her hard drive, wanting her encouragement as he had as a child. He was still a child, she thought, only nineteen, a cyber-wizard of the highest order yet knowing nothing of life. What had they raised, she and her peers but a generation of little demons? When the ancient silicon based IBM she used to monitor the conditions at the farm crashed, as it had now, her son could be depended upon to come down, reboot the O/S, reinstall all her applications, check that the IO ports were all working, and the sensors they linked up to still effective. Checking the saline levels, the nitrogen levels, the pH and the e-coli count of the water in the ponds. Yet how to raise the year's shrimp, how to provide optimum breeding conditions, how to cull only so many shrimp for the shipments as well as Kauai's winter food supply so that there'd be enough remaining to breed the following year, of all this he knew nothing, and wanted to know nothing, looking a little bemused when she tried to teach him, finding it odd she found it so important.

"The new transistors are all biotech anyway," he explained earnestly, "living tissue is a much faster transmitter."

"Well, duhhh," she said, as though it was only to someone from the next generation, the one she'd so foolishly allowed to be raised by computers, that would find this surprising, an unobvious piece of information that required sharing.

She remembered them sitting in the huge blue and green living room, he and his friends, talking about dreams and computer games as though their narratives were interchangeable. They hadn't even noticed they were facing the sea. Prime real estate and what did they care? She should've shipped them all off to some urban ghetto, in the same containers she filled with frozen shrimp. At the time she'd found it fascinating, their exploring, had tried to keep up, even pretending an interest in computer games whose narratives she found dull, compared to the life cycle of Penaeus. Encouraging them to learn to program. She wasn't stupid, she too could have learned, she was even yet perhaps not too old, but then what would they all eat? It was a time sink, this wire head business. Sixteen hours a day; all the shrimp would've died without anyone to look after them. They didn't have children either, not one of them, because of course, they never had anything other than virtual sex, a break in the day's endless code crunching which didn't even require the removal of their gloves and head sets. Which was perhaps a wise decision in light of the continuing AIDS pandemic and yet self-chosen infertility was putting an even faster dent in the population than the AIDS deaths, which had, in the last twenty years, reached sixteen per cent, never mind having taken both her parents and her husband. It was like wartime, you couldn't really complain; it had happened to so many. And in spite of her heavy personal loss she'd catch herself thinking the widespread deaths were a good thing. If there's less people spewing toxic sludge into the water the oceans will have time to clean themselves, she'd think, the fish populations a chance to make a come-back. Not that they deserved it, any of them. To have cared so little for the fish meant in the end that they cared equally little for themselves. What was destroying one's own food supply but a form of death wish, a slow suicide?

No wonder her son and his friends were trying to find a way to make digital fish edible. It was a search, however doomed, born of desperation. It wasn't they who'd poisoned the waters but her generation, her parents and grandparents and great-grandparents, right back to the very beginning of the industrial era. Hurtling proudly into the information age, too busy to think about fish populations. And of course, it had taken more than four generations for the effects to show so dramatically, to become something one couldn't ignore. And by then it was too late. By now, Ellen thought, it's really too late. I'm just whistling in the dark, trying year after year to save my family farm. The children have already left, thrown too quickly into a half grown brave new world, not grown enough yet to shelter them. So many of my family, my friends and lovers have died but we'll all be dead before it's over. Of course this was always true, but in those days we didn't care; just like the fish we'd done our job, made grandchildren.

She cried often although no one saw. She cried because she was getting older. She cried because she had no man, no grandchildren and no company. For company she talked with the old people at Seaview. She enjoyed their stories and paid a close and calculated attention to the information they passed on, the tiniest most subtle nuances in the methodology of shrimp farming: a lifetime's experience. It was only a lifetime of attention closely paid that could garner anyone what could truly be called a skill. A skill was worth passing on. The most basic skill of all is my own, husbanding life which is the source of our own life, Ellen thought. Yet her son and his friends didn't want it. It was old fashioned, it made them squeamish; eating cooked fish off a plate made some of them gag, even retch. Jake was one of the few who could still do it.

Strange alien beings. Post alien beings. She'd thought them aliens at twelve, now, at twenty they were beyond flesh, even alien flesh. She missed her friends, but the ones who hadn't died had moved to the Arctic.

"Heard from Lucinda?" Jake asked, her machine reliably repaired. She could count on him in that area, at least. This mention of her best friend, on the other hand, was highly unusual. Keeping track of your mother's life, even in the most cursory fashion, asking occasional personal questions had gone the way of thank-you notes and now dinner plates.

Lucinda had moved to the northern mainland, was, in spite of being a GIS programmer, a hippiesque biological Luddite who believed the air and water were cleaner there, that it was necessary to move north for the sake of her family DNA. She'd moved her son Patrick with her.

"She e-mailed last week," Ellen replied, and added pointedly, "Patrick got married and had children, and the children, so far at least, seem fine. Physically perfect, handsome and clever even."

Jake nodded sympathetically. "It's so rare." A risk not worth taking, he appeared to think but did not say. Up north children still had children. Up north you could be a grandparent. How she longed to go, join Lucinda in her tree-line community. Bring Jake. Perhaps he'd still mate, breed. Years of studying marine biology at Hilo, coming back after graduating to take over OpaeCorp, and she was using animal terms to describe human behaviour. But what was the difference after all?

"Soon we'll be able to eat them," Jake said, eagerly switching the subject back to his favourite. "Living proteins, strands of DNA now process information; the cyber world, as you know, is no longer exclusively silicon based. Soon we'll be able to eat virtual shrimp and then we won't need you anymore."

He said this as though it should please her, and not entirely as though it was a joke. She cried but he didn't notice. When had she learned to do that, cry in such a way that it was unnoticeable? Probably around the same time she became so blunt.

"But they always did process information," Ellen said bluntly and Jake seemed surprised, not getting it.

"They were just reproducing meat bags, Mum; now they do something useful."

She listened even though it drove her mad. After all he'd just spent hours debugging her software. And he was still her son, still company; she wanted him to just to stay a little longer. They'd go back to the house; she'd fry him real shrimp and make a salad to go with; he'd eat it with something like distaste, as though it was gore. Real food made him squeamish; he did it to please her, he still needed that. They'd always been close.

He wanted to show her the cyber fish, the collective pet project they worked on feverishly, in their time off from paid programming. He'd brought his own laptop anyway to run the diagnostics on her system because of course it had a larger memory than her old machine; he could run more sophisticated debugging software. Jake laughed, calling it her clockwork computer. "It's just wooden gears and spindles in there isn't it, Mum? Positively medieval; I'll get you a new one."

"I'd have to learn all the systems then," she sighed.

"But you have to some day anyway, or someone does; your machine won't last forever and whoever takes the farm over will have to be younger." Jake looked at her sternly, reminding her of her age as though it was some kind of vice she secretly cultivated just to offend him. "The person you train will be my age, they won't understand your clockwork system any better than you understand my biotech laptop."

"So show me the damn cyber fish."

It looked like a shrimp of course, swimming around its little aquarium sized screen. That much he'd learned from her, thought it important. The new fish must still look like a fish. Not that it mattered. He could just as easily have wire-framed a swimming potato.

"But how do you eat it?" she persisted. "How does it provide nourishment?"

"The code it's built out of, it's living code. The information is living, it isn't dead. We'll eat the living information."

Living Information; it sounded like a new god, or a new nickname for Jake. "That should be your web name," she quipped, "Living Information."

"It is," he replied.

With a crazy futurist for a son and an anachronistic aboriginal for a neighbour no wonder she felt stumped. Where had all the normal people gone?

To the mainland. North.

"The same was true when you ate a carrot that grew in dirt," she snapped. Living Information looked completely puzzled then and she had to wonder: had he actually ever done that? She couldn't remember. It was likely he'd only ever eaten hydroponic.

"What I meant is, how do you get the fish out of the machine to put it on your plate and eat it?"

"Oh Mum, we don't bother with plates anymore, you know that, we just use the pills." He looked at her blankly. Not getting it. So smart and so dumb. Cyber-hexed, that's what they were. She cried, she said, "Come north with me."

"I'd like to, Mum," Jake said, seemingly meaning it. "But we're so close, that's what you have to understand. We're so close, it'll pay so well; we're almost there. And once we're there we can close OpaeCorp; you can retire up north, be with your friend, you'll be so old by then you won't be needed anymore anyway. And you'll be rich; I'll make sure of that. Now, I need a month's supply of fish pills to take back to the park with me, are they ready?"

They went to the warehouse; she gave him a box. Laughing, looking at the size of the box, Jake suggested she just e-mail him the shrimp pills, send them as an attachment. She hoped it was a joke but she wasn't sure. She stared at him, said it again: "The material body requires material food; you can't download it, you can't e-mail it, it won't pass through a modem." He suggested she send the chemical composition of the fish pills.

"That's the code," she said, "not the actual food."

"There's no nutritional value in code?" he asked, startled. "But that gives me an idea, something to work on." And off he went on his ATV, the carton of fish pills lashed on back, back to the park. He called it the park, as though it was somewhere to play. And perhaps it was.

She watched him lurch up the road, jamming the gears. She was surprised he could still drive. They so rarely left, any of them. They'd chosen to live in dorms at the park; they no longer had homes. They no longer walked on the beach at sunset. They could make better beaches, better sunsets.

Most likely I'll die here, Ellen thought, never get north. And maybe they're right. Maybe they'll make cyber fish with nutritional value, or else they'll remake their bodies so that digital information does provide nourishment.

∞

In spite of heavy doses of antibiotics, the shrimp were dying the next morning, in a pandemic of infectious disease. She'd seen it before, of course. Once yearly a mutated virus or bacterium attacked her shrimp, and she, trying to adjust their environment if not to the original one, for who even knew what that was anymore, then to one which would mitigate, offset the effects of disease.

And so she rode her dirt bike up the highway to Seaview, to visit Grandfather Frank and his wife Dora. They, of course, wouldn't know how to deal with the new conditions either, but she'd found their wealth of experience more useful than all the fish farming Usenet groups. She sat and drank tea, prodded their brains, watched for nonexistent whales. She had to listen, yet again, to the history of OpaeCorp, the history of Seaview, their family history going back four generations. The Copelands had apparently hailed from Iowa. Who even cared? Ellen yawned, exhausted, worried. Dora smiled, said, "You're not as old as we are yet."

No. Although she surely felt like it. But in the middle of one of Dora's stories about how Harry Copeland married Eileen Drinkwater the year before he took a loan out to buy the original OpaeCorp property, five miles up the coast, Frank interjected and said, "Eileen was the science head; Harry did the money. They started the shrimp farm together, in the beginning the research was government funded. All the mangroves had died, she kept having to dose the nauplii with antibiotics because it seems the mangroves release something into the water which neutralises the effects of the bacterium in the shrimp habitat. We never did isolate what it was, although we had people work on it for years; we just kept doing it because it worked. They're more adaptive when the intake runs through mangroves."

Dora interrupted, continuing, "And then Eileen had to grow mangroves, not just a fish farm but a mangrove farm, seedlings of it to be planted, she got the boy scouts to help her; Harry said they looked like Chinese planting rice paddies, all forty of them."

And Ellen, who was Eileen's great-granddaughter raised her eyebrows and said, "All our mangroves were grown from seed? You never told me about the damn mangroves before. I learned that from Maui. And he only said the part about them being the best final-stage filter system for effluent, he never mentioned the resistance thing."

"But neither had anyone else," Dora said, excited now, her eyes shining. "There'd been no mangrove on Kauai for years and no one had ever mentioned that it was an important part of the shrimps' ecosystem, and Eileen said to her local friend, "But where can I get any mangrove to replant—if they all died we've changed the water so much they wouldn't grow anyhow," and her friend said "but they've been breeding a naturally resistant variety on Molokai," and so off Eileen flew to Kaunakakai…"

And then Dora lost her thread, looking momentarily blank, saying, "Remember Martha's wedding? You were there too, Ellen, only you wouldn't remember, you were two."

"The locals breed things?" Ellen asked, shocked. "But that's science. What was this local guy's name, anyway, Eileen's friend?"

"The cake was six feet tall," Dora murmured.

"Finish the story about the mangroves," Ellen said, leaning over to jab Dora with her elbow. Dora's tea spilled on her lap; it seemed to snap her back.

"Off Eileen went to find the resistant mangrove, gone wild on Molokai, just enough reestablishing itself each year for her to gather an armful of seed, dig up a few boxes of saplings. The locals had been babysitting them for years; it was some little pet project they had going. Eileen replanted it in the shallows of her farm, and now it's spread up and down the coast. But each year there was some new such challenge, and some years Eileen, or now you, Ellen, found a solution and other years…"

And other years the old peoples' information was useless and she'd have to wing it, and mostly, Ellen thought, most of all, I miss the friendship of people my own age. At least Eileen still had that. And the shrimp were sick again, and her visit to Frank and Dora was doing no good. We did our bit, their eyes seemed to say. It's your turn now. Her grandfather sighed, as though, behind his memory loss he knew exactly what kind of a failure they were facing this time. He shrugged, he sighed. "More antibiotics, kid, that's all I can think of. Or go ask Maui."

"He's a local," Ellen said derisively.

"All the better," Frank said. "They've been here thousands of years, we've been here a few generations. Information."

"Information fish," Ellen said, getting up to kiss him on the cheek. Thin thin skin, transparent and dry as paper. And that smell. She wondered whether Anita had them washed every day. "You should have told me sooner," she whispered, feeling terribly sad. She'd lose him, she'd lose the farm. She'd hunkered down under the weight of her previous losses but this was starting to push it, even for someone as blunt and stubborn as she.

"Tell you sooner what?"

"To go to the locals for advice. I thought you thought they were backwards idiots."

"I thought I thought so too. I'd forgotten they were the ones who'd told Eileen to replant the mangroves. Until Dora told that part of the story."

"And so they're responsible for all our millions," Ellen said.

"In a way. But there was always something new. The mangroves were only a part of the solution."

"How's Harry doing?"

"He's okay. He's older than we are, he forgets more. Why?"

"I want to ask him the name of Eileen's local friend. See if he remembers."

"Well, go see him, he's upstairs in 204. He doesn't get out of bed anymore. But he'd love to see you. He might even be having a good day, remember who you are. Just say you're his and Eileen's—"

"Great-granddaughter," Ellen said, running for the elevator.

∞

But Harry was dead. Ellen could tell by the lingering smell, although the bed was empty. Seaview's manager Anita stood at the window, looking at the sea. Ellen had known Anita since kindergarten. They were the same age, but they were no longer friends. "Surf's up," Ellen said, and Anita turned, a vacant look on her face. Ellen couldn't help herself, she rushed forward and took Anita by the shoulders, shaking her. She stepped back, appalled by what she'd done.

"I'm sorry, Anita. But I felt like doing much worse. I wanted to throttle you."

"He was a hundred and two. He did good."

"If you'd kept him alive just three more weeks I would've finished taping him. Put it in the OpaeCorp archives. You don't know what you're letting die here, Anita. It's like destroying crucial survival information."

"So you come work here then, Ellen," Anita snapped.

"But I run the farm," Ellen replied, exasperated.

"The rich bitch. You inherited OpaeCorp or you will. Your family owns Seaview too. You own half the damn island. I'm the manager of an old folk's home."

"Jesus Christ, is that what you think?" Ellen sat down heavily in an overstuffed chair overlooking the rising tide. "The money's all in the ponds, the processing plants, the payroll. I take a salary. A hundred measly thousand K per year."

"You want to know what I make? And what about that local mechanic of yours? I heard you don't pay him a cent. He fixes the pumps for nothing, because you're screwing him."

"Is that what people say? It isn't true, Ellen. You have to believe me. We've known each other for thirty-five years, that should count for something. I keep trying to hire him, but he won't condescend to work for me. He's much too superior for that. And we're not sleeping together."

"Why not? He's cute. Or d'you think you're too good for locals? You're just like Eileen."

"What?"

"You don't know that story? I can't believe it. Everyone knows that story."

"I don't."

"Well, I won't be the one to tell you. You can ask someone else. If you paid a little more attention to what goes on around you and a little less to the Penaeus life cycle you might even have a life."

"The farm's going down, Anita. My salary won't count for much when I declare bankruptcy."

And Anita sat down beside her in the second chair that matched the first, the one Ellen had meant to sit in while Harry sat in hers, telling her the name of Eileen's local friend. Anita took her hand and said, "I'm sorry, Ellen, and you'll think of something. I know you will. You've faced problems before at OpaeCorp, you've always fixed them. For generations."

"I got a real bad feeling this time, Anita."

"I've always envied you, Ellen. You're so lucky you're a scientist, it's much better than gerontology; you should listen to them go on and on and on, and how they scream when you forget to change their bedpans on time once, just the once."

"I'd scream too," Ellen said, annoyed all over again, thinking of Harry, of dirty bedpans, of pathogenic bacteria.

"You only studied marine biology because you knew you had the farm job waiting for you."

"What's it matter, Anita? Any of it. We shouldn't fight, you and I. We're the only ones left from our kindergarten class. The rest have all died or moved away."

"You've still got Jake. I never had children."

"Yes, I have. Although to tell you the truth, sometimes I'm not sure Jake counts."

∞

When she got home it seemed Maui had forgiven her unspeakable rudeness because he was busy touring the farm, checking all her mechanicals. It was thoughtful of him, and he was pretty good about showing up to do it regularly, but she wished she could just put him on the payroll and know he'd be there every day. But that wasn't his way, he always said, and so she was grateful and invited him for dinner.

"How are your shrimp today?" he asked.

"Not well. And how come you're asking me? You're the one who said they wouldn't last the week. You've got me in a panic."

"I'm just a simple mechanic without a license," he said opaquely. "You went up to Seaview today to ask the old people for advice."

"You know everything, don't you?"

He shrugged. "It's not hard." It was funny but she'd never noticed before how cute he was, not until Anita mentioned it. Maybe Anita was right and she hadn't seen his beauty because he was Hawaiian. Maybe she was horribly racist and had no clue. Maybe all the Copelands were. He was born handsome, and all that bodysurfing seemed to do wonders. There was something to be said for looking after the meat bag, in spite of what Jake thought.

"How's Harry doing?" Maui asked.

"Harry died this morning. Did you know, Maui, that if people don't die of AIDS or cancer or industrial accidents, some of them live to a hundred and two?"

"So I've heard," he said ironically. "How old are you, Ellen?" he asked, walking beside her on the path back to the house.

"Forty-two, just like you," she said.

"Rhymes, doesn't it? You gone through menopause yet, Ellen?"

"Is that your business?"

"Not really. I'm just curious. What are you going to feed me, Ellen? Let me guess. It starts with s-h."

It was shrimp, but real shrimp and not pills with the powdered Chitosan included, which the children preferred. Chitosan, basically powdered shrimp shells, worked as a fat absorber, a fibre which collected dietary fat on its way through the body. Being sedentary wire-heads, her children's' generation shared a propensity towards obesity. Ellen would tell Jake and his friends to exercise. They'd laugh, think her old-fashioned.

And even she found Maui old fashioned. Didn't he eat fruit and vegetables grown in soil? No one else she knew did that. Worse, he opened a Tupperware container of poi to eat beside the shrimp. She gulped it down, not wanting to appear rude. Purple glue. It was their traditional starchy staple, a tuber. If you didn't cook it for seventeen hours until the hard white taro root turned to mauve paste your throat would scratch for weeks. Like eating fibreglass. Ellen knew she was exaggerating, even in her thoughts.

"Tell me about your family," she said. "Did they convert?"

"They converted to Homo Sapiens," Maui said. "My great-grandmother was actually a fish. Or she could turn into one, some full moon nights."

"Really? What kind?"

"Technically not a fish but a dolphin. Bottle-nose."

"I see."

"We all converted," he went on. "We had to. Some passed on the old ways, though. In secret."

"Kahuna magic?"

"Yes." He looked uncomfortable, as though he wanted to avoid that subject. Was afraid she'd make fun of him. He looked around the room, its muted blues and greens, the acres of picture windows overlooking the sea. "Nice place. I've never been inside."

She felt uncomfortable then. Said, "It needs repairs. The windows leak when it rains, even when there's trade winds. I can't afford to redo them, and it's too big for one person, now that Jake and all his buddies have moved to Kapaa. What's your house like?"

"It's a tin roofed shack on the beach," he said. Ellen looked away. They'd finished eating and she didn't know what to do with her hands. She wished she hadn't given up smoking. "You don't have to apologise," he said. "I like hearing the sea, I can't sleep if I don't hear rain on the roof. I can reach out the window and pick apple bananas for breakfast, and I can clean it in half an hour. This place is spooky, and I don't envy you living here."

"Just asking."

"Just answering."

"So, does it heal?" she asked.

"Does what heal?"

"Kahuna magic?"

"It's science and religion in one. If you want to call that magic, so be it, and maybe it even is. And indeed it does heal, perhaps because of that. The methodology of science was never removed from reverence for all life, and its poetry."

"Rain on a tin roof at night?"

"Precisely."

"Women who turn into dolphins at the full moon?"

He raised an eyebrow. "Don't make fun of what you don't understand, fish-killer. I never saw her do it, but my grandmother did, and told me, and I have no reason to disbelieve her. But have you ever noticed the irony?"

"Which irony in particular?"

"You come for wisdom, for spiritual healing, to a culture you set out systematically to destroy. Christianity didn't work out for you or what?"

"But I'm not, Maui. I think you're old-fashioned, not any kind of saviour. I'm not a religious person, I'm a scientist. I'm just being nosy."

"That could be part of your problem, did it ever occur to you? No respect for biodiveristy in the science. I'm repeating myself, I know. Although I didn't mean you in particular, Ellen. I was talking about your race's short memory. It's because your grandparents didn't tell you enough stories."

"Seems not. There's hardly any wild shrimp left, in the whole world." It was true. Each year she released a few nauplii and postlarvae, hoping to repopulate the wild, but as the e-coli had gotten stronger, the released fish never survived; they weren't fed antibiotics with their food as the farmed fish were.

"Who's surprised?"

"Although today Frank and Dora told me an interesting story about mangroves. You know anything about that one?"

"Could be."

"You know who Eileen's local friend was, by any chance?"

"Yes I do. They fell in love. I'm his great-grandnephew. She wouldn't divorce Harry because her lover, my ancestral uncle, was only a local. In spite of having saved the farm during its first big crisis, making her millions."

"I never heard that."

"Like I said, your old people didn't tell you the right stories. The true ones."

"Today, Frank said I should ask you for advice."

"Thatso? About a hundred years too late, you ask me. Come bodysurfing tomorrow?"

"I would, Maui, but I got a little bacterium problem in my ponds."

"But that's why you should come," he said.

"Bodysurfing. My son and his friends would find you hopelessly out of date. Exercising the meat bag."

"You might yet have grandchildren, you look after your body."

"Jake will never breed."

"I meant you're not too old to start a second set."

Whatever that meant. "You have kids, Maui?"

"Yeah. Two girls. They live on the mainland with their mother."

"She local?" It was funny how local meant Hawaiian, while *kamaaina* ostensibly translated as local but usually referred to whites who'd grown up in the islands. *Haoles*. It didn't really make sense.

"No. She's a *haole*, like you. Seems we never learn."

∞

The next day all the shrimp were dead. Maui phoned, asked her to go bodysurfing. "I got orders to fill," Ellen said, bluntly turning him down. "There's no shrimp to go to the processing plant. I have to pay the workers regardless. It's in their contract."

"Rightly so. It's not their fault you killed the fish."

"A little support might be nice, here."

"Come bodysurfing," Maui repeated. "If your shrimp are dead anyway."

"Maui, this is serious."

"Sounds like."

"Okay. What the hell. I'm coming."

∞

They went every day for a week. He taught her to dive under the waves. The mainland supermarket chains were suing her. Seventeen messages on her voice mail and another fourteen on e-mail. She cross-posted her reply: "All shrimp are dead." She'd have to sell OpaeCorp to pay her legal bills, never mind the suits.

"Let it go down," Maui said. "Go down with it. Just as the wave is about to crest you take a deep breath and dive underneath, deep."

She missed it of course, dove too late. The wave caught her and smashed her onto the beach. When it receded her hair was full of grit, her knees bloody. She spat out sand.

"Feels bad, doesn't it?" Maui said, scraping her off the sand.

"Yeah. I'm trying to remember why I came."

"To Earth or with me, today?"

"Both."

"To feed a starving world, Ellen. You said so yourself. It's the one thing I like about you."

"Well, you can stop liking it 'cause I've failed big time."

"That's the problem with you *haoles*. You never learned to do what feels good. You always go the other way, as though there wasn't a choice, and then you're surprised when your world crashes around you."

"Like the wave?"

He nodded severely. He took this bodysurfing business seriously. He considered it a metaphor. She should've known. She should've stayed in bed. Or shot herself. She had an old hang glider in an equipment shed, she could still gobble three grams of mushrooms; jump off the Na Pali cliffs some full moon night, turn into a bat, or a squash. Ought to work.

"Is that Kahuna magic?"

He just looked at her. Derisively. "We'll go out again, next set. When I say dive, dive. Okay? You have to trust me." It didn't sound ironic at all. It scared the shit out of her, his lack of irony. Scarier than her farm going down, scarier than being thrown by the ocean.

She got it the next time, and the time after that missed it but swam under the bone crushing surf, and a little later in the afternoon she caught another short ride.

She went home and cross-posted again, without reading her messages. They all received the same reply: "All shrimp are dead." She defrosted a pound of frozen shrimp for dinner instead of going to the pond, dipping out a net full of fresh like she usually did. She ate the whole pound. She took the phone off the hook. She went to bed. She was so sore the next morning she wanted to sleep all day but Maui appeared at her bedroom door, take-out coffee and microwaveable saimin in hand. "Wake up, *wahine*; we got work to do."

∞

A deep cool tunnel propelling her. Across the entire bay. It had its own momentum. Weightless, both supported and propelled by its power. Being picked up by the ocean rather than thrown by it. Its pleasure and its arc were so joyful and required such a similar surrender she couldn't help but think of sex. And she'd thought of it so rarely since Jake's father had died of AIDS, ten years earlier.

All the shrimp are dead. Who cares?

Trust. She saw him not twenty yards away. What was he? An American, like herself. That's what he'd answer. And: my great-grandmother was a fish.

No kidding.

The wave they were riding was hurtling towards a breakwater made of piled stones, looked to be old, real old. It was funny how much time there was to think in split seconds. Nano seconds, Jake would've corrected her. How old?

Oh, say, five hundred years old.

Jesus Christ, we'll be killed. How could she not have seen it sooner? He meant to kill her, in revenge for all her family's generations of *haole* nastiness, and himself too, except he probably knew some fishy trick to save himself. The wave had carried them so far so fast she hadn't seen the wall coming. Entranced by the ride. Tubular, man.

"Swim like hell," he was yelling. "Follow me." And she did, grateful for her fins. The ancient Hawaiians, his predecessors, hadn't had those. Or genetically engineered shrimp. It was all fine to engineer them to be resistant to disease but the little problem was the diseases, which had shorter life spans, also grew resistant to the endless antibiotics dumped into the water, mixed into the food. Because the food was spoiling. Because the water was filthy. Because the shrimp were crowded. Surprising, really, they'd made it this long. That was about the extent of all their big science, really. Not very farsighted, she had to admit. You couldn't beat a bug. Not really, not in the end. They had more grandchildren, and they had them faster, much faster. Grandchildren won.

Simple, really.

She swam like hell, solving her problem as she swam. She'd never swum so hard in her life. She'd never done anything so hard in her life. And then they were in it, a four foot wide channel in the piled stone breakwater. Through the channel a clear still pond, many of them linked together.

She treaded water, winded, barely able to breathe. But alive. Unlike her shrimp. It seemed a miracle.

∞

She got home. There was a message from Jake.

"We're experimenting with synthetic stomachs that process digital information," his recorded voice explained earnestly as though the answer was just around the corner and not a hundred years away. "It's not much different from a pacemaker."

"Well," she left a return message, "your implanted cyber stomach, if the body doesn't reject it, might be able to eat a digital data flow but that still doesn't give your cells the proteins they need to keep rebuilding themselves." Just in case he'd overlooked that one little problem. Spending sixteen hours a day plugged in might make you a genius of a programmer but it also had a small tendency, she'd noticed, to impair your sense of reality.

And maybe he'd turn out to be right, one day. Who could blame him for trying? All the wild shrimp were dead after all, and now all the farmed shrimp too. Still, he was her son and she noticed she'd spared him the bad news, of all her correspondents. She hadn't gone far enough, her message should've read: All food gone. She should've posted it all over the net. No food left. Then maybe they'd wake up. The tribe faces famine. It had been awhile. They'd forgotten what it was like.

It could happen, but not in their lifetime. The children had gone too far ahead, they didn't know the way back; they were visionaries in the worst possible way. They couldn't find their way back now, and in fact they thought back was bad. They wanted nothing to do with their parents' old fashioned notions about the body requiring food. And I never said it's impossible, Ellen thought. But it's too big a leap. They have no idea how far from its realisation they are. They don't realise they need grandchildren.

She listened for Maui, hoping he'd come, she hadn't read him wrong. It was funny, she couldn't remember what he drove, a dirt bike or an ATV or a pick-up, couldn't remember the sound of him parking his vehicle, couldn't visualise him walking in the door, a fine coating of Kauai's red road dust on his skin.

But he usually came silently she realised, dripping, out of the sea. Having swum around the Haena point. Who could do that but a dolphin or a whale?

"Wild shrimp," he said, carrying a lidded bucket. She could hear it sloshing. "Postlarvae. Twelve different species. Nine marine, and three Machrobrachiums. You need to convert one of the ponds for the freshwater. They're important, resistant to certain bacteria the Penaeus aren't. For hybridization."

"I know." She said. "Eileen and Harry did that too."

"And who told them to do it?"

"Let me guess."

He shrugged. "We'll clean out your ponds, restock. They're much stronger, you know. There's much more chance of adaptation, because the gene pool's larger."

"You can swim with buckets?"

"You mean you can't?"

"Is that what you do with yourself," she asked. "Is collect and breed heirloom shrimp species?"

"It's what we do," he said "for five hundred years."

"But how did you know it was going to be so important?"

He just looked at her, dripping. "*Haoles*," he said, shaking his head. There was a little less derision in it, a little more humour.

"I'm still going broke."

"So take out another loan. Isn't that what you people are good at, is financing? You're a good swimmer, Ellen, you just don't know it yet. You can't let your great-grandmother down."

"So what's your big interest, Maui? You got your own little ancestral shrimp farm to look after, round the point, just like I got mine. You showed it to me yesterday, remember? What possible interest you got in saving OpaeCorp from the great white sharks?"

"Yours is bigger. On account of you people being better at money, buying more land. Grow more shrimp, feed more of the starving world. It's not for you Ellen, but for the grandchildren."

"Why didn't you help before?"

"Seems to me I tried, you weren't listening. And you had to let it go down, so you could start over, do it right."

She looked him up and down, assessing the potential of his DNA in the production of grandchildren. He was in great shape, better than she was, and his science seemed to have proved a little better too. Although all the data wasn't in yet.

She touched his arm but he pulled away. "I didn't say our grandchildren," he said. "I said the grandchildren."

"Oh."

He smiled just a little. "Well anyway, we'll just have to see. I've always liked you, Ellen, but we've got to take it slow. One more thing."

"What's that?"

"You got to write me over half your shares."

"I beg your pardon? Half?"

He picked up his bucket of shrimp, headed back towards the sea, to his invisible road. "Remember the mangroves?" he called back. "You people might never learn, but we do, eventually. Think of it as a retroactive share of profits."

Think of Harry and Eileen, of Maui's still nameless ancestral uncle, of the small scary fact which had just occurred to her, that she and Maui might be a little bit related, on that count. She watched him go, carrying his bucket. Those heirloom shrimp were worth millions, even on a chance. Nobody else had them; if they were hers she really could refinance. She'd do it too, she'd sign over half of her OpaeCorp shares, she didn't care what the old people said. After all, they were old. And they should have told her sooner, about all of it. You can only pretend to forget for so long before it catches up with you. ∞

M.STUART 99

Speaking Sea

∞ Sally McBride ∞

SURF DOESN'T POUND, at least on Long Beach. It's a constant deep roar, each wave following the last in such close succession that there's no time for the predatory silence that ends in a crash on other shores.

It was just after six in the morning. Ron and I were alone on the wide expanse of hard-biscuit sand that is Vancouver Island's Long Beach. Out on the water, a few early surfers bobbed up and down, wearing wetsuits against the cold Pacific. Mist like smoke whipped shoreward ahead of the waves; the surfers turned their boards in unison when the perfect ride came, preparing to catch it like commuters. Two of them rode it in, the third fell immediately into the breaker's froth, and the fourth let the wave go by.

Ron dawdled, binoculars at his eyes. He'd already been for a dawn dip, and was proud of himself for it; I could tell by the way he walked. The cat waving his wild tail, carefully not looking at me. Oh, Ron. I'll always be fond of him, but not as a wife should love her husband. This trip was meant to clarify things for both of us, and it seems to be doing so. Neither of us is unhappy about deciding to call an end to the marriage.

The wet sand was hard enough to drive a Winnebego on. When it's dry it's as soft as powder on your feet. Broken shells litter it, glyphs of white and purple. A knot of kelp ahead of me seemed laden with significance; it was wound around something, clinging as if the seaweed and what it held had dragged each other to shore before dying.

I walked up and prodded it with the toe of my shoe. A lump of plastic or exceptionally smooth metal, it was as brown as the kelp and hardly noticeable except for the artificial curve that had caught my eye.

On it lay rows and swirls of an intricate pattern, a pale shimmering grey against the darker background. Flotsam or jetsam? I couldn't remember which was which.

I looked back for Ron, who was ambling my way, his big bony toes digging the sand.

The problem with Ron, I had come to realise, was that he'd never really been my type. Nor I his, despite our eight years of marriage.

He's good-looking in a professorial sort of way, as angular and old fashioned as a slide rule; at one time I found that utterly charming. I think he'd liked my blond thinness, the way I could do my hair in a dancer's sleek chignon. Trivialities mean so much at the start of a relationship, just as at the end. We both looked like what we were: an academic couple on the dry side of forty. I think both of us knew setting out that this last grasp at a relationship wouldn't work.

"It's a great day," he said, his wet toes whitened with a dusting of dry sand. "I'm glad we came, Celia." When he looks directly at me I know he's being honest, if not completely forthcoming. He really was glad, but not because we're together.

"Yeah. It's beautiful." I could appreciate the qualities that captured me in the first place: his logical mind, for instance. "Have you heard anything about a wreck lately?" I gestured at the kelp-bound stuff.

He frowned. Had a newsworthy event escaped his notice?

"How lately?" he temporized, crouching by the knot.

"I don't know." I ran my finger along a smoky swirl. "What does this look like to you?"

"Huh." He began gingerly to tug the kelp away, afraid of jellyfish lurking squashed among the fronds. "Are you thinking it's from a boat? A lifeboat?"

The surf roared like a train, a never-ending train going hell-for-leather; like a fire consuming everything in its path. Shells and kelp and lifeboats stand no chance in it. The ocean swells and spews things out, jetsam.

"I don't know."

The piece was like a section cut out of a hard brown bubble, a thin partial sphere made of some plastic-like material. It was about a quarter inch thick. I could see that the grey pattern was an integral part of the material, more like a weave in cloth than anything painted on. It wasn't hard to interpret the piece as eggshell. A container? For what? Ron turned it over. Its curve could have held something the size of a TV set.

"Look at this." The stuff bent in his hands, slowly, and when he let go it slowly bent back to its original shape.

"Here's more of it." The piece I picked up felt completely rigid until I saw my fingers sinking in. When I hurriedly dropped it, impressions of my fingertips stayed in the material for a few seconds, then filled in.

"It smells funny—like some kind of chemical." A pungent, artificial reek that stung my nose. "I don't think we should touch it. Maybe someone's been dumping toxic waste."

We both stood up and wiped our hands on our shorts in unison.

"Let's walk on, see what there is to see."

I nodded and we made south towards a headland, black rock bounding out of the sand to form a barrier topped with stunted fir and blossoming devil's club.

Ron started to climb, using his hands, his toes searching for barnacle-free footholds. I followed him.

Above the tide line there were strange little plants striving for life, some looking like unripe raspberries stuffed into cracks in the rock, some like miniature perfect daisies, their wiry roots taking sustenance from minuscule pockets of silt. Life seeking a niche anywhere it can.

On the other side was a beach almost identical to this one, and on it were a lot more pieces of whatever-it-was.

As Ron and I hesitated at the top, planning a route down, a jeep bounced out of the fringe of thin scrub pines to the east and drove onto the beach. A man dressed in a park ranger's khakis and tie hopped out, holding a mobile phone to his ear, and began to stride along the beach. He noticed us when he turned back, and immediately waved us down.

"How long have you folks been here?" he asked, eyeing us.

"We just arrived," said Ron. "What's going on? What's all this stuff?" He gestured with one hand. The other was in his pocket, a Ron habit when encountering something or someone new: project a casual indifference.

The ranger squinted at us. "I'd like to suggest you folks stay off the beach until we can get an expert's opinion on this stuff." An expert in what? Plastics? Some asshole from an oil company to cover up an ecological crime? I felt a thousand questions bubble up, but the ranger was talking on his phone again. I heard only his side of a terse interchange, something about schedules and what time it was on the East Coast.

He snapped the unit shut and faced us. "Visiting the area?"

"We're staying at Silver Sands." Ron frowned. "What exactly—"

The ranger held up his hand. "Just stay off the beach for the next day or so. It's probably nothing, but Environment Canada has been called in to do some testing of the water. Till then, it's best to stay inland." He flashed a grin, as if to say, *Well, you know those Chicken Littles over at Environment—but duty is duty*. "Okay?"

"But—"

We all heard the helicopter at the same time. It approached fast and low, swinging down over the pine trees and sending a blast of sand up as it landed. When the grit had settled and the blades stopped, a couple of armed soldiers jumped out, followed by five assorted men and women dressed in civilian clothes. One of them looked very much like someone I knew, Jack Toszak from Simon Fraser University. What could he be doing here?

"Look," said Ron, frowning now. "just what the hell's going on?"

But the ranger had trotted off to join the newcomers. I took Ron by the arm. "I see someone I know. Remember Jack? I told you about him, you know, that inorganic chemistry conference where he hit on me." Telling Ron about Jack's pass at me had been a deliberate testing-of-the-water, a phrase most appropriate in this circumstance. I liked Jack Toszak. Perhaps I could worm our way into his group and find out the score.

"He sounded like a bit of a fool to me," replied Ron. "Sorry."

I snorted. Too late to be jealous now, dear. "Fool or not, he's in on this, and I'm going to use whatever female wiles I still have to get in on it too."

He smiled thinly. "Charming twist to our little vacation, isn't it?"

It's difficult to hate someone you've never really loved. And I know Ron too well, know the way he likes to get his meaning across; for him it would be embarrassing to be open and up front. Too easy. So he felt threatened and tense; well, fine.

Ignoring the ranger's suggestion to leave, we headed for the scientists, who were crouched staring at the eggshell-like bits just as we had been earlier.

A strong reek of plastic came off the shards.

A woman in mask and rubber gloves was putting some the stuff into a thick plastic bag. We stood outside the circle till Jack noticed us, or rather me.

He looked astounded for a second, then bounced to his feet and came over, holding out his hand.

"Celia Muir! And you must be Ron." He shook hands enthusiastically. Jack was almost buzzing with excitement, a stocky, bearded man with salt-and-pepper hair and big shoulders, looking more like a lumberjack than a scientist.

"What the hell are you guys doing here?" he asked, looking deeply into my eyes. I found myself blushing. "How did you manage to get here so fast?"

Ron and I looked at each other. "We were already here," I said. "At the resort down the beach. So what's going on?"

"I don't have a clue," he said, grinning. "Apparently this material started washing up about two o'clock this morning when the tide came in. No one has any idea where it came from, or maybe they're just not telling us."

"Guess which," said Ron sarcastically, his hands jammed down hard into the pockets of his shorts.

"You were brought in?" I asked Jack.

"Yeah. I was hoping to call you later, when we had some idea of what we have here. I was impressed by the work you were doing with lithium ions in that calcium carbonate crystal experiment. Good stuff. Lots of applications."

"Well, thanks." I blushed again, damn it.

He looked uncomfortable. "Actually, you probably shouldn't be here, although considering the circumstances..."

"Quite a coincidence."

"You're on the list to be in on this, at least what we've been able to put together so far, but I'm afraid you're fairly far down. It all depends on what we find."

"Oh. I see." I nodded. My ego is small, for a scientist; I congratulated myself on the good luck to be here now.

A couple more vehicles drove onto the beach, olive drab army trucks. They disgorged a dozen or so armed soldiers, who stood listening to orders, then deployed themselves along the beach. I was starting to feel downright worried.

A member of the group of scientists caught Jack's eye and beckoned.

"Gotta go...listen, Celia, Ron, I'll try to let you know what's happening, but no promises. This thing's gonna slam down tight very soon." He trotted away.

Frowning, I turned back to Ron, who was watching the soldiers with a paranoid gleam in his eye.

"They're going to cover this up so fast our heads will spin," he stated. "We'll be locked up before we know it."

"Locked up? Well, you may be right." I've learned over the years that this is a good thing to say when you disagree on a basic philosophical level with someone, even though you may actually suspect that, in this particular case, they're right.

He loped off towards the officers. The Americans were sure to be here soon if they weren't already; there was no way they'd stay away from this. I didn't know enough about the military to tell whether the ship I'd just spotted about a kilometre out was Canadian or American.

I looked around for Jack and joined his little group, one of which was the woman in rubber gloves, still stuffing bits into bags.

"My fingers sank into it," I remarked.

Everyone swivelled to look at me, then their eyes snapped back to the piece being lifted at that moment. The woman held the piece for a while, staring at it. Nothing happened.

"It must be the gloves," I suggested. "I touched it with my bare hand."

"Jesus," said Jack. "Don't try it, Lori." He stood straight, raising his voice. "Hey, anyone noticed their fingers sinking in? Yeah? Well, quit touching it, will you? How am I supposed to analyze this crap if everyone's been manhandling it?"

"But it's been in the ocean, Dr. Toszak, it's already plenty contaminated with Terran bio— "

"Excuse me? *Terran?*" Jack snorted. "You kids have been watching too much TV."

Lori looked defiant. What if she's right, I thought. What if this is what it looks like: alien space pods. Empty alien space pods. I bit my lip to keep my expression neutral.

Scratching his beard, Jack abruptly turned my way, took my arm and muttered into my ear. "Tell me, Celia, are you and Ron still together, or what?"

Ignoring Jack's question, I looked at Lori and continued as mildly as I could. Actually, I felt at the time as if I was in a sort of trance, or bubble of non-reality. *None of this is real. I'm not real. The universe is a construct of my immortal brain*. "When you bend it, it returns to its original shape."

"Heck, that's nothing new," said Lori. "Tell you the truth, I think this is stupid. I mean, are we thinking about the possibilities here?" Some of the others nodded. "Come on, you know what I mean."

"I have an imagination too, Lori, and I'm interested in any and all ideas," snapped Jack.

I drew him aside. "Just to let you know…no, we're not back together. It was just an experiment."

He looked straight into my eyes, obviously troubled. "An experiment that went awry, right?"

Maybe it was the general excitement making me giddy, or maybe it was the way he said it, but I burst out laughing.

Before he could react, a soldier at water's edge started blaring through a megaphone. "Get out of the water!" The surfers had been noticed. I felt guilty for forgetting about them. What if they were in danger? "Get to shore immediately! There is toxic waste in the water!"

Even though I couldn't see them, I knew exactly what was happening now. The surfers were giving the soldier the finger. Inwardly I smiled. It would take more than some feeble government threat of toxic waste to get a dedicated surfer to shore.

It did take more. A Zodiac was deployed from one of the vehicles, hustled to the water by six soldiers and tossed in. Two of them hopped aboard, fired up the motor and took her out.

What would happen next? Would Ron and I be banished soon, under threat if we blabbed? What could they really do to us?

The surfers were quickly rounded up and brought in. The Zodiac scooted halfway up its rubbery length onto the sand and let them off. They were dripping, puzzled, and surprisingly amiable, considering.

The first one onto the beach was a man, about five foot six, a little muscular guy with gorgeous blond hair in tangled curls. He grinned and gawked around at everyone. His squinty blue eyes were outlined with the indented marks of goggles hanging now on their strap around his neck. He walked forward as the others clambered out, another man and two women.

One of the young soldiers directed the group over to one side of the all-terrain vehicle where they were apparently to be questioned. As the blond turned, I noticed that his goggle strap was blending with the flesh and hair on his neck, as if it was sinking in, or becoming part of him. Or that he was becoming part of it. I blinked and looked again. The black rubber dissipated into his tanned flesh like paint into water.

I took a couple of steps backwards and bumped into Ron, but I couldn't stop staring at the surfer. What the hell was happening to him?

He'd been in the water all this time. The whole group had probably arrived at sunup and been bouncing on the waves ever since. I held my breath, watching. Perhaps I was seeing things, making more of a tense situation than I should.

I looked at the other surfers. One of the women had a strand of kelp stuck to her leg; she leaned over and sort of absently *stroked* it into the rest of her leg, the green of the seaweed becoming part of the black rubber wetsuit, leaving it with a spreading brownish stain.

"Did you see that?" Ron hissed in my ear. He'd taken my upper arms in his hands and was squeezing painfully hard. I found myself being shuffled backward. "Did you *see* that?"

Jack arrived and started to question the foursome, trying to seem laid-back and non-governmental in his plaid shirt, but all of a sudden he stopped in mid word. I heard him emit a loud huff of surprise over the breakers' roar.

One by one everyone on the beach realized that the action had heated up. Instinctively the scientists and several of the officers gathered at a respectful distance. Four of the soldiers trained their weapons on the surfers, and the rest deployed themselves rapidly along the beach, weapons pointed seaward as if battalions of mermaids were going to come flopping out. At last something definite had happened. Everyone had made the connection: *there's something in the water*.

"Should we try to get the hell out of here?" I was very glad right now to have Ron's body pressed against mine, even if it was trembling.

"Christ, I don't know." His voice was very serious, but not, I noted, panicky. Bless him. "Look, we both fooled with that stuff. I went for a swim this morning, damn it."

I tried to match his steady tone. "Yes. And you're all right, aren't you?"

"I sure as hell hope so."

I shook my head, trying to think. Something in the water. An alien disease in our ocean? Where did it come from, how fast would it spread? Could we control it?

Or was this all some crazy hallucination?

Silence from Ron. These must be the same questions occurring to those in charge, if anyone really was. Jack Toszak was hanging in there, sticking close to the surfers. None of them had spoken as far as I knew; they were silent as fish. No one seemed to know what to do, though I suspect many of the military would have liked to start shooting. But the kids still looked a lot like harmless teens, grinning and shuffling their feet in the warm sand, though now they seemed to be wearing body paint instead of wetsuits. There was no real demarcation between skin and rubber, it was all one smooth blended substance. Their hair had started to look like strokes of paint on their scalps.

The helicopter was still patrolling up and down, and the ship had been joined by two larger vessels.

Suddenly the copter rose about a hundred feet higher in the air, as if to avoid something in the water below. Before anyone could react to this, one of the soldiers on shore let out a yelp and started firing off bursts at the water.

Some of the men dropped to the ground fast, the rest of us gawped around stupidly. There were sea lions coming out of the breakers, five or six of them dragging their way energetically toward us, their doggy faces eager, their oily black eyes looking around. Dozens more were out just past the surf—I could see their round wet heads. Fish were leaping in great glistening arcs like fountains. All of a sudden the water was seething with activity, like a choreographed display at Sea World, magnified and weird beyond words.

Several of the soldiers fired point blank into the closest animals, but there was no reaction. Some puckering of their skin, then nothing. No blood, no pain evident.

At least ten otters flipped sleekly through the edge of foam at the front of the sliding waves and pattered quickly toward us.

"Are the fish going to come out too?" Ron sounded breathless.

"And what about the urchins and abalone and anemones?"

"And don't forget the kelp." Ron pointed at the Zodiac, its hind end bouncing gently in the waves, its front half up on the sand. Fronds of seaweed were wrapping themselves around it, sinking into the rubber like water into sand. The Zodiac began to look a lot like the stuff we originally found, vague shimmering patterns blooming on its curved hide. Then it suddenly dissolved into the sand, leaving only its engine and metal fittings behind.

Everyone was well back from the waterline by now, the four surfers herded along at gunpoint. The seals and otters—any sea creature, I realized, with the capability of movement on land—followed us up onto the dryer sand a few feet, and then they all turned back and re-entered the water. A line of them at the edge of the surf watched us with what I hope was nothing more than curiosity. The helicopter maintained a respectful distance from the water.

The sun was high, and the tide was on its way in again.

∞

Ron and I, and the scientists, were hustled into vehicles and removed, abandoning the beach to the soldiers. I heard later that the whole coastline was evacuated that day, a hell of a job. Ron and I were taken to a local airstrip, loaded on a plane and removed to a quarantine facility at the Naden forces base near Victoria. Our luggage from the resort showed up the next day.

We were put in separate rooms, and I didn't see Ron again for a couple of days. We talked on the phone, but his replies to my questions were terse and defensive. He was scared, I knew it. Who wouldn't be?

Being quarantined was like being stuck in a no-frills hotel for the world's most boring symposium, at which there wasn't even the reward of drinks in the evenings. I joked about it at first with Ron, until I noticed that he wasn't answering in the same tone. On the third day he didn't answer me at all.

They let me see him. Behind glass. Oh, Ron. What are you now? Not human anymore—an alien in man's shape. I had to look away from his mildly curious gaze, it was so like the way he'd looked at me when we first met. Except that this time there was no future in it, there was nothing.

Up until that moment, I hadn't really been scared.

He was whisked away from Naden to California's Scripps Institute of Oceanography, where much of the work was being coordinated. Apparently quite a few changed people had been found or captured, and were being studied there.

"You'll be at Naden for at least a month, Dr. Muir," I was told. "We can set you up with a computer, a modem perhaps? Whatever we can do...." *I'd like to get out, please.* Sorry, No. At least I could follow the news, try to come up with ideas.

Endless questions, blood and tissue tests, hard suspicious looks. What did I know? I saw as much as they did of how it started. The TV told me that something awful had happened to the Earth. Everyone knows that our planet is three quarters ocean—well, three quarters of our home was being taken over by an alien. How does it feel?

Coastlines everywhere were in turmoil. Frightened, confused people being evacuated and not knowing why. Many countries had nowhere to put the people; wars broke out every day. It was ghastly, watching, knowing that I'd been there at the beginning. Alien space pods, god damn it.

Finally, four weeks later, I was grudgingly pronounced uncontaminated and allowed to resume my life, or what remained of it.

∞

My neighbour Andrea had kept on feeding Clytemnestra, and I made a note to reimburse her for the cat food she bought, plus something extra for her trouble. Andrea left a forwarding address in Edmonton and moved out the day I came home, roaring away in her Volvo wagon. Clytie was, naturally, aloof and cranky at first, but she warmed up fast and was on my lap while I checked my e-mail.

Something new had popped into being during the short time I'd been in transit from Victoria across the strait to Vancouver.

Jack Toszak had finally decided to clue me in.

I'm in San Diego at Scripps, he wrote. *Phil Mackenzie, a chemical oceanographer with another degree in robotics, is in charge of the north Pacific region. Everyone is scared, hurting for sleep, and generally nuts. There's a lot going on, and we need people who can think laterally. Call me when they spring you, okay?*

This sounded like an oblique job offer. But did I want it? My sister lived in British Columbia's interior; perhaps I should hole up with her, safely away from the ocean.

Clytie let me get up and make coffee, stropping my legs the whole time. I found a tin of tuna in the cupboard, and almost gave it to her as an apology for being away for so long, but couldn't. There might never be any more tins of tuna. She got a large piece of cheese instead.

I dialed Jack's office, coffee in one hand. He picked up on the first ring. "Toszac."

"Uh, Jack? It's me, Celia. I'm out."

"Celia, wow! This is terrific! Listen, you've got to get down here."

"Well, I—"

"We're making headway, but we need more people."

"I can't see that you'd have any trouble—"

"Yeah, well, the trouble is getting the *right* people. Every wacko on the continent has shown up and brought a theory; we need people with level heads. I didn't see you panicking on the beach when this all started."

"Well, I...well, thanks. Actually I'm not really sure—"

"Celia—just listen. If we're going to get anywhere, we need people with imaginations, people who aren't afraid." Pause.

But I *was* afraid. Who on Earth wouldn't be?

Something began to tap in the background. Jack rattling his pen on the desktop, ta-ta-ta *tat*.

"Jack," I asked, "Have you seen Ron at all?"

Another pause. "Ron's doing all right, Celia," he said at last. "I haven't...uh, haven't talked to him. He's being looked after."

"Looked after. Oh, God." I put down the coffee and covered my eyes.

Was my husband truly an alien now, in a tank? The image was there: Ron in the water, hands fanning gently, fully dressed, his eyes like those of the sea lions on Long Beach, watching me with mild interest.

"I'm sorry, Celia."

"Yeah. Okay." After a bit Jack continued talking, his voice artificially hearty, as if lecturing students.

"How can I explain what's happening?" The tapping started up again. "You've been watching the news, I guess. Doesn't say much, does it? Actually, nanotech on a biological instead of mechanical level is the best way to look at it, at least as an instant paradigm for now. The template information is vectored through an RNA analogue, something like a stripped-down virus. It seems to be pretty darn compatible with our sealife." Jack didn't stop for breath; he never has. "Probably designed that way—"

"Designed?"

"Didn't just grow. It's ingested, or enters through cuts, mucous membranes, whatever."

I swallowed. "So the tabloids have it right: we've been invaded."

Silence. Then, "Yeah."

"Okay. So it's in the north Pacific. Any chance of controlling it?"

"Impossible. It replicates itself, searches out biomass and takes over wherever it can, like an extremely opportunistic virus. The ocean currents carry it, and pretty soon it will be everywhere."

"Everywhere."

"Yeah. All the oceans are connected. The amount of biomass in them is stupendous, when you include things like krill and plankton, and all of it we've been able to track—*all of it*—is being converted to the alien template. The damnedest thing is that everything looks pretty much the same as before it changes, except for that spooky effect when things merge. It gives me the creeps."

My coffee had gone cold. "Is that the technical term?"

"Well, yeah, actually."

After short silence, I asked, "What about oxygen production? If the phytoplankton changes, there goes ninety percent of the world's source."

"Now that's something we've been working on pretty hard," he replied. "And it seems we're in luck. Oxygen is being produced—and at a two percent higher rate than before."

"What could that mean?"

"Maybe nothing, except that it's damned fortunate."

"Yeah."

And then, blessedly, he stopped talking. I've had the worst, after all. Poor Ron. I think it was my idea to go to Long Beach.

I chewed my lip. What the hell. It would be only a matter of time before port cities like Vancouver were pretty much abandoned, with frightened soldiers at every intersection. Perhaps my work in calcium carbonate crystal production in shells would come in useful somehow. "Jack, if you can put in the word for me, I'll be there as soon as I can arrange it."

"Terrific. We'll keep you busy, don't worry." I could hear the smile in his voice.

I rinsed my cup in the sink and the familiar, cherished view of Kitsilano Beach was there between the buildings, blue and gold, partially obscured by several rows of shiny new razor-wire fencing. I couldn't see any people or animals.

They needed me, an inorganic chemist. Hell, they needed everybody.

Now all I had to do was find out if there were restrictions on cats coming into the States. In view of what was happening, the idea of quarantining Clytie actually made me laugh.

∞

Less than a week later, Jack and I were leaning over the metal railing around a salt-water pool full of children. The California sun beat down on our heads. The move had gone well. Bureaucracy had caved in to the new threat, and Clytie and I were settled into a motel near Scripps.

The kids in the pool still had bathing suits on, or at least it looked that way, bands of colour across their little bottoms. They splashed just like normal kids, but the noises they made sounded more like the whirring and squealing of machines.

Dissection has been done, of course, on some of the animal forms. We've found out a lot, but learned almost nothing.

Their bodies, Jack told me, were now made of something neither flesh nor plastic. Samples were easy to get, as they didn't seem to feel pain (nor respond to anaesthetic), but a complete dissection had not been attempted on any of the children. Some had parents with them, also in tanks; there were unchanged moms and dads quartered as I was near Scripps. What they might be hoping for I couldn't imagine.

"These kids..." My throat closed right up, watching the children. They swam around and around, not seeming to need to come up for air. "A day at the beach. Mom looks up, and the sea has taken her babies away."

"Yeah." Jack lacked his usual animation. Maybe it was getting to him too, now that the first thrill of strangeness was gone. What the hell were we going to do?

There were hundreds of task-groups in all disciplines around the world, all trying to come up with answers. Nothing short of poisoning our own seas seemed able to stop the spread, and even that desperate act was beyond our technology. Communication was the number one priority, but I felt that if it was possible, it wouldn't be in any ordinary form. We might not recognize it at all.

Jack turned away from the tank and took my hand in his. "You're cold," he said, rubbing it between his warm, stubby-fingered paws. I knew he wanted more than friendship. I'd always thought he was brilliant but never realized how thoroughly nice a guy lurked behind that lumberjack beard. He had offered me crash space at his apartment until I could find my own, but I'd turned him down; a motel was fine for Clytie and me now. I didn't want to let things get away from me. Somehow this planet-wide threat had made love seem trivial; why? Loyalty seemed to be the better emotion: loyalty to Ron in his misfortune? Loyalty to the human life-form itself? I didn't know how to talk about it, so I didn't. I worked instead.

"Come on," he said gruffly, still holding my hand and pulling me away from the tank. "It's got to be coffee time somewhere in this pile of concrete."

∞

In late August I was offered a place on the next team going out to FLIP, the Floating Instrument Platform. It had been towed to a position off the south coast of Hawaii and had done its patented tilt to vertical. Most of its length was nose-down, underwater, and it was crammed with people and instruments, including the imaging technology that generates something called Acoustic Daylight, which lets us see what's down there via computer analysis of the sounds generated by natural bubbles in the ocean. The technician running it was eager to point out what each dim, grainy blur meant.

"That's an eyelash," said Anne, a Scotswoman with a mass of flyaway ginger hair held in a big plastic clip. She pointed to a shimmering truncated curve half off the screen. "That's what we're calling them, anyway. This one's about 50 metres long. And there's a common form—see that hair-like squiggle?"

"Yeah." I traced its loop with my fingernail on the screen. To me it looked like a badly-coiled hose about a mile long. "The stuff is similar to something I've been working with—a polymer consisting of a chain of aspartic acid molecules. When I added a little of it to a solution of calcium carbonate, some really weird spiralling crystals formed. Sort of a combination gel-crystalline substance that we were trying to learn how to control and use."

"Use for what?"

"Industrial materials of various kinds." I shrugged. "Looks like we've been outdone by the alien, though. No patents for us."

Anne didn't laugh. "They must be building something down there," she said. "Something big. Like giant shells perhaps."

I shivered at the image.

The FLIP was stationed at the edge of Hawaii's ancient volcano, where the frozen lava sloped down and down into the immense night of the sea. Surrounded by metal and glass, we were safe in the water, but sealant and lubricants—anything organic in contact with the water—was suspect and constantly monitored.

There were other ships around, Navy vessels. As we watched the screen, a sub cruised dead slow below us, 700 metres under the surface. Its passage added spurious brilliance to the bubble-generated "daylight."

Anne drew my attention to a cluster of bright blips. "Those are—or were—humans. You can tell by the way they bounce the signal." She hit a few keys on her computer and squinted at her screen. "I've seen this group before—they've been busy."

"Busy? Or just moving in response to the currents, or to light, or...."

"Oh, definitely purposeful movement. I don't hold with those who say it's a mindless invasion of spores or viruses or whatnot. That might've been so at the start, but there's intelligence there now, I'm sure of it."

"But which is better—mindless instinct or thoughtful purpose? We'll still suffer." I shuddered again and Anne felt it.

She patted my arm and cocked her head pertly. "Well, we'll have to wait and see, won't we? There's a heirarchy among them. Beings that were once mammals—dolphins, humans and so on—tend to act as shepherds or supervisors of work the more primitive forms carry out."

"Yet when we analyze the tissues, they're all the same."

"I wouldn't know about that. All I do is run this thing," she said, slapping her console cheerily.

Something big, she'd said. Building their new home, at the bottom of our ocean, and there was nothing we could do to stop them.

∞

The water's catalytic change was progressing just as Jack had explained, gradually taking over the planet's oceans. It had not penetrated fresh water, needing a concentration of at least 1 percent sodium chloride and other salts to vector the virus-like plague. Thank God for that. Thank God for a lot of things—not the least of which was plankton's continued photosynthesis. Was that just a lucky break? Or did these facts mean more?

I was back at Scripps again, watching some nice clear video of a motley assortment of life off the coast of Mexico at about 200 feet down. It was eerie to see humans swimming purposefully so far under the surface.

Not humans. Like the children in the salt-water tank, they only *looked* like humans. But then, what were they?

A woman's face flashed on the screen, her legs kicking her past the camera's view. She looked like a tourist, blonde with the remnants of a red bikini like blurry paint on her skin. Then a seagull, its wings flapping slowly in the water, gleamed plastic-white as the spotlights caught it. Whirling shrimp, and the huge grey shoulder of a whale.

Jack had just got back from the south Atlantic where he'd been coordinating collection of species samples from untainted water. He'd checked in with me last night, and arranged to meet today. I was surprised at how much I'd missed him.

I picked up the phone. Jack sounded tired, but glad to hear me. I suggested we meet outside.

"Good idea. See you in five minutes."

Carrying two large coffees, their plastic lids beading with steam, I walked under a sky punctuated with tiny clouds to the tank where Ron and three other adult ex-humans dwelled. The clouds were moving fast, light swelling and vanishing as I leaned on the rail. Thick protective glass was between us, in case of splashes.

Ron immediately swam over and looked up at me, his face blank as usual. I bit my lip and tried to keep looking back without flinching. *Do you blame me? Is there a remnant there of the human you used to be?*

He stared, then moved a little, dipping his head and turning one shoulder as if he were about to dismiss me with a snide comment. My stomach tightened as I came completely alert. He did the same thing again, still watching.

That's a Ron thing to do. Damn it, he's trying to tell me something.

Jack arrived just then, touching my arm gently and making me jump. "Hey, you're tense," he said, taking position beside me to watch the tank. His arm went around my shoulders briefly, then he followed my pointing finger to look down at the water.

"Keep your eyes on Ron," I whispered.

Ron had once boasted thick salt-and-pepper hair waving back from a high, intellectual forehead. Now the top of his head looked more as if a rough brush had painted strokes of grey across his scalp, barely representative of "hair." His shoulders gleamed under the sun. He was still looking directly at me.

"Jack," I whispered, "I think there's some kind of communication attempt going on. Some kind of body language thing."

Jack squinted down at the glinting water, at the bright, mild eyes of the creature looking up.

"Okay," he said carefully. "What makes you think that?"

I replied slowly, uncertainly. What if it was just my imagination? "It used to be a joke. *Speaking Ron.* My sister gave me hell when I tried to decipher his moods and expressions. She said I'd do better learning to speak French—look, did you see that? That thing he's doing, turning away like that—it means he's afraid and trying not to show it."

Ron ducked his head underwater and up again. "I used to think he was being aloof and deliberately incomprehensible when he did that."

"Celia—are you sure?"

I nodded, forcing myself to take a long slow breath.

"It took me a long time to learn Ronnish, but I think I'm getting it. Right now he's daring me to look away. It really means he wants to talk but is too proud to ask; something I picked up about him too late to matter for our marriage." I had to turn away from Ron and the dark-bright salty water he swam in. "He—*it*— wants to talk! Oh, Jack—what's going on?"

Jack said nothing, but he put his arms around me tight, and I felt a brief kiss on the top of my head. "Celia, do you want to leave?"

"No! How could I, now?" I gestured at the tank. "This might be a door opening. It might be the breakthrough we need."

"It might just be a coincidence, a fluke of movement or mimicry. The others aren't doing anything, they're just floating."

I shook my head, my eyes on Ron again. He had let himself sink till his head was underwater, but he was still looking at me. It was true, the other three ex-humans were quiescent, but it seemed to me that they were in an attitude of attention. Watching, but for what? Waiting to see what we would do.

Ron started to back away in the water, using his hands as adeptly as if he'd been born with fins.

I vaguely heard Jack say something about video, *we'd better get video of this*, and then I felt him touch my arm and leave.

Soon there would be a crowd here, and Ron had never liked crowds.

I felt a momentary compulsion to jump into the tank with him, to take him by whatever his shoulders were made of now, and make him talk. Shake him, yell at him. *Talk to me! Tell me what you want! Tell me who you are!*

But we'd never connected when we'd been married—why should we now? He'd always made me work at understanding him, and he'd been so glad, so secretly superior, when I'd failed. Or had he?

I had to blink away tears. "God damn you. You and your head games. You think I'll give up? You think any of us will?" I realized I was shouting, my hands pressed against the glass. I'd never yelled at him when he'd been human. I'd prided myself on my control. "I won't give up. Not this time."

He bobbed in the tank, watching.

My anger faded quickly. If I had ever really loved him, wouldn't I follow him now into the water? Wouldn't I give up my humanity for my mate?

It didn't matter; he was never mine to keep or to give up. He was as distant as the sea, always; incomprehensible as a dream. But like a dream, full of hints, laden with floating threads with which to pull up meaning, as an Inuit will pull up a seal from the dark eternal ocean.

He rolled his shoulder, blinked slowly and looked away at last. He let himself sink, and began circling the tank in a leisurely inhuman glide. He was watching me sideways, and I could feel my instinctive antennae bristle.

"Oh, you're good," I whispered. He couldn't hear me, and it didn't matter. He knew me, I knew him.

There would be communication, I knew that now, no matter how fragile the connection here today. But it would be on the intimate level of the body's signals, mate to mate. Not like talk or sex or fighting or even telepathy—more like the interior hormonal messaging that goes on inside your own body, so instinctive that you don't have to think about it. The way a married couple will learn to interpret each other's moods and wants by the movement of an eyebrow or the turn of a shoulder.

The way I had learned Ron's, too late.

Ron, or whatever he is now, will be the ocean's emissary, and I the land's. We'll talk. In some new way, we'll talk.

Then Jack was beside me again, excited, directing a group of researchers with video cameras and notepads. A crowd gathered fast.

I ignored their bustle and chatter.

My husband and I will never touch each other again. But we'll learn about each other, man and woman, sea and land.

And we'll never, ever, forget that last forever walk on the beach, the mist flying off the water like smoke. ∞

Games of Sea

∞ Sandra Kasturi ∞

Let us play Sea, then,
you and I
while the evening is spread out against
the prow of the world
and strange games can be found
in the hands and minds of children—
every shell, a boat,
every bone, an oar,
every droplet, an ocean

each empty box, a universe

Can't we play Sea, then
you and I
with a world you have been keeping
in one pocket
or another:

a small box
full of shell
and bone
and water
can be thrown into the air
and suddenly

we are
falling into
rowing off
the edge

of the world

(continues…)

asea
asky
adrift

on a vast and crowded ocean
in our pearlescent boat
pulling on oars of bone
waving
to people in ships
more city than ship
to people in cities
more ship than city

flying across the infinite waves
over submerged towers
and sunken forests
past glamorous monsters
and fabulous beasts
every one of us transmogrified
by the light of this changeling Sea

We will hold hands, then,
you and I,
while the evening is still spread out
across the prow of our bobbing
bobbing boat,
children again,
buoyed only by light,
adrift and adream
across the star-streaked oceans and skies
and the floating ephemeral cities
of all the invented worlds of men. ∞

The Edge of the World

∞ Sara Simmons ∞

ANNAVIS KNEW THAT THEY weren't going to sail off the edge of the world. She held to that, as her hammock swayed amid the whispers of night in the farthest south. She had worked through the proofs herself, her second year at the Naval College, but it was hard to believe that the mathematics had any meaning here. Overhead, the sky was cracked where it stretched tight over the rim of the world and although the sun was long set its trapped light flamed along the fractures.

They were sailing closer and closer to the long dotted line on the chart, so similar in appearance to the other lines which showed longitude and latitude and the borders of kingdoms. Soon she would know what kind of boundary this was, that was marked the Edge of the World.

She needed to sleep, not go over the geometry of the proof one more time, looking for the false assumption that would doom them all. Tomorrow *Soltys* would reach the line, and when that moment came Annavis wanted to be rested and ready.

But she had lost the knack of sleep. She sat up, gripping the edges of the hammock. What should have been rough canvas had the live softness of fur. It rubbed against her hand, wanting to be stroked. Annavis smiled. The softness tickled her fingers and palms. Then she froze, catching a scream in her throat. Her hands didn't feel like her own. A long breath later, she remembered. She had taken off her rings at the start of the voyage, the rings that showed her place in the Great Houses, when she found that they kept her from commanding *Soltys* properly.

She gave the hammock a final stroke. There had always been stories about ships coming alive as they sailed south—she had doubted them once. Every day of the voyage *Soltys* had become more awake, reaching out to her crew until they had chosen to join her, to feel the wind in their sails and the touch of water on the planking brushing their own skin. Annavis had kept apart. She had always chosen the unknown, but to her the greatest unknown was to see the edge of the world with her own eyes.

Silently, she swung herself to the deck. As her bare feet touched the planking she felt a guilty pleasure. For a moment she was no longer a captain but a small child, stealing out of bed to creep through the mysteries of the adult world.

Except for the helmsman, the deck was empty. He was steering, his back to her and his concentration fixed on the sails. As Annavis went past him she saw that his eyes were shut—he didn't need vision any more to keep *Soltys* steady on her course. *Soltys* herself was very much aware of the feet on her deck, the empty hammock.

She reached the mast. From the shadow of the weather shrouds a hand reached out to stop her. She froze.

"Captain," Mehen said, in a quiet voice, less harsh than a whisper.

"What is it?" said Annavis, her voice low as well so as not to wake up the night. She wanted to brush past him, but she couldn't. They were the only two people left on board who could speak to each other with human voices.

When she first met Mehen, she had thought of him as the other side of herself, the side without ambition. He could have been her, he could have gone to the Naval College, become captain of *Soltys*. But he hadn't, and that one difference had become all the difference in the world.

He had changed, she thought. At the start of the voyage he would have been content to sail with *Soltys* wherever she went through the islands. He would have taken the chance to become part of her without another thought. But Annavis had shown him that he could direct his course and now the world was full of peril.

Annavis searched for something else to say. "You should be in bed."

"And you," said Mehen absently. He stared aft, where the blind helmsman steered the ship into the south, into the trapped light of the sun. "They are joined so tightly to her, she will bleed if you cut them."

"But not you," said Annavis.

"No, not me. I bleed well enough on my own." He paused. "We should reach the edge tomorrow."

"Yes. If all goes well." The words sounded loud and ominous, so she reached out and tapped the wood of the mast. At the touch she thought *Soltys* shivered a little and turned to look at her.

"And then?" asked Mehen. "What happens then?"

"That depends on what we find there." Annavis knew better than to talk out her fears with him. They were frightened of such different things that it had taken her a long time to see that Mehen was afraid at all.

All the same she asked: "What do you think is there?"

"I don't know. There are no stories this far south." No stories. Perhaps there was nothing to have stories about. Perhaps the edge of the world was a blank wall where the sky came down to the sea. Or, worse, there might only be the grey waves marching on, paying no attention to a line on a chart drawn thousands of miles away and leaving Annavis with only the dreadful blankness where a dream has come true, but there are no new dreams crowding up behind.

But these were her own concerns, and didn't explain why Mehen had stopped her. She waited a minute, then, when he made no movement, asked again, "What is it?"

He didn't answer at once, then finally asked, "How far is far enough?"

"I don't know," said Annavis, her mind tickled into laughter by the question. "Is there such a thing?"

"There must be!" He gripped her arm. "Sooner or later there must be a point for turning back. The world does not go on forever."

She saw that what really frightened him was that he did not think she was afraid. Or if she was, she wasn't afraid of the right things. She didn't know how to reassure him. "If the world doesn't go on, then neither can we. We'll see tomorrow." She shook herself free and hurried past him. He didn't follow.

She reached the bows and leaned forward over the rail. Beneath her tumbled the endless white flutter of the bow wave. *Soltys* swayed on and on into the south, making no fuss, so silent in her going her speed was unremarked until you noticed how fast the water was flung aside and left behind.

Ahead of her the bowsprit stretched out, an airy construction of wood and rope and canvas, leading the cutter into the night. Annavis looked at it and smiled. "Just a little farther."

She swung herself up, holding on to the forestay. There was dew on the smooth surface of the spar, damp and slippery to her bare feet. Moving with cautious balance, she lowered herself until she could curl her toes around the footrope. Beneath her the water slid by, not yet disturbed by *Soltys's* passage.

At the bowsprit end, beneath the high curve of the jib, she settled herself astride the spar. She wrapped her toes around the cold rough chain of the bobstay.

She felt herself precariously balanced, poised in the midst of the air. Ahead the sky blazed, the horizon closer now. She had learned a poem once, a fragment of which she still remembered—*I'll wait out near the rim of the world, where the starry sea dissolves in the sky*. The image had stayed with her, when she had forgotten who was waiting, and why.

"How far is far enough?" she asked *Soltys*. *Soltys* made no reply but held steady on her course. Annavis looked down at the waves rolling beneath her. She tried to imagine turning back, now, and felt herself shake at the thought. She might have found a reason every day of the voyage, but she had fought so long against the idea of "far enough."

Suddenly she was standing, balanced on the bowsprit end, her fingers clutching at the luff of the jib. And at the touch of the wood on her bare feet she remembered.

She had crept from her bed to visit the library, to look at the charts and the great atlas and the books of voyages. Even then she had wanted to sail to the edge of the world. There were lights still burning in the halls and she kept near the walls, on the bare floor beside the carpet. But ahead of her a door stood open, splashing lamplight across her path. She stopped. She knew the voices.

Uncle Umbral ruled House Cabral. Annavis could picture him, his hands heavy with House-rings, alliances and betrayals written there in jewels for those who could read. He frightened her these days. He had brought a new ruthlessness to the games the Great Houses played among themselves as they ordered the ruling of the kingdom. He soon drove out anyone who was not willing to match his ferocity.

Annavis crept closer. Her cousin Iavan stood in front of the desk, and word by word Uncle Umbral destroyed him.

"I'll leave!" cried Iavan at last. "You'll never find me."

"You are mine," said Uncle Umbral. The lamplight twisted his rings. "Mine, like all in this House. You cannot go far enough."

The wind veered a little, its breath shifting on her cheek. The headsails sighed and shivered and the rustle of the bow wave changed its note. Three of the hands came up through the forehatch and padded aft to tend the sheets. Annavis twisted to watch them, almost falling. They did not look up as they soothed the fluttering luffs, but tilted their heads as if listening, all three pulling together without speaking. Then they cleated and coiled the lines, very gently, and went away.

Annavis blinked, hard. She had seen something private, the cutter caring for herself. She sat down again. *She will bleed if you cut them.* There might be a way to join *Soltys*, at least for a little while.

She pulled her rigging knife from the sheath at her belt and held it for a moment, considering her hands in the sky-light. She had taken off her House-rings when she became captain of *Soltys* but even after so long she could see where she had worn them—deep creases at the roots of her fingers, and pale, untanned marks like scars.

She chose the least ring-marked finger and drew the knife-edge across it—a sharp, thin pain. The knife slipped and gashed her palm. She stared for a long moment, horrified. Then a drop of blood fell on the bowsprit and the whole ship shuddered. She pressed the cut to the wood and felt it all—the touch of the wind on her sails, the balancing weight of the keel so far below, all the different forces of air and water that cradled her as she bent them to her desire. She sang to herself, wordlessly. Her own hands moved on her wheel, easing her to meet a wave. A halyard had come adrift from her pinrail and lay in sprawled loops on her deck, but she tucked it back in its place. She stared into the burning sky from the bowsprit end. Her shrouds hummed with the wind in them and she opened her mouth to shout, but then she was back astride the hard spar, shrunk again to a single body.

Annavis breathed deep and looked down. Her hand was no longer bleeding. She still held the knife. She cleaned it carefully and put it away, not tempted to make another cut.

Soltys followed her into the south. She turned, looking back along the whole length of the cutter. The northern sky was darker and there were stars visible. Against them *Soltys* was hugely beautiful, like a mountain, terrifying and reassuring. All at once Annavis felt her lost sleep come back and she climbed in from the bowsprit end.

She looked for Mehen in the shadows as she passed. She thought that she might be able to talk to him now. But he was gone, to bed she hoped, so she went back to her hammock and slept.

∞

Dawn came and with it the world changed, from this to that, from that to this. *Soltys* strode on, sailing through the melting islands as easily as the solid sea.

Annavis woke with the light. The sky was coming closer, stretched tight over the fraying edges of the world. She stared forward but there was nothing to see yet.

She went below to her cabin. Her charts were all here, and the books of voyages which had fed her dream—all useless now. And, as if she needed telling what kind of country she had strayed into, her desk was open and the chess set within it spread out, the pieces playing by themselves. She couldn't tell who was winning. She hoped it didn't matter.

She washed herself and dressed with thorough care, refusing to let herself hurry. She brushed her hair an extra hundred strokes before pulling it back into the intricate braid called the Captain's Knot. She thought her hands were shaking, but in the mirror they were quite still.

When she went back on deck the scene had changed utterly. The sky filled the whole world. The islands and the sea had melted finally together. The water was strangely opaque, and *Soltys's* wake held glimpses of rocks and trees. The world was crumbling. Gaps of nothingness opened in the water, but *Soltys* and the waves flowed smoothly around them. A ship couldn't sail into what wasn't there.

Annavis took her telescope and went forward. Up ahead, on the strangely near horizon, was a line of white foam where the waves were breaking against the sky. Beyond that line, though, the waves went on, their angle bent. Annavis might have thought a mirror hung there, except that there was no *Soltys* reflected.

At Annavis's order *Soltys* hove to within hailing distance of the skywall. The waves were feeling the edge and she bounced uneasily in the chop. Annavis studied the sky through the telescope. She had expected to find great cracks and tears but it was solid here—no way through. This was as far as she could go, but it was not far enough.

She lowered the telescope. She saw Mehen open his mouth to speak and quickly raised it again and swept along the line of the sky. Far to the left—to the east, if there were such a thing as east here—was a dark line on the brilliance, like a black thread rising from the sea. The spray leapt high around it.

Anything was better than turning back. The line was a crack, a crack in the sky. Through it she could at least see what lay beyond.

"Make sail," she said, and *Soltys* turned to the east. She took the wheel herself and edged *Soltys* closer to the barrier, balancing wind and current against each other.

"Captain," said Mehen. "What are you going to do?"

"Sail through, if I can," said Annavis, her mind distracted, so busy with her steering that she was nearly as much a part of *Soltys* as the rest. "Don't you want to see what's there?"

"Oh yes," said Mehen, and hearing her own longing in his voice she could not doubt him. "But how far?"

"Far enough," said Annavis with a laugh.

"How far?" he asked, stubborn.

Annavis became aware of all of *Soltys's* faces turned to hear the answer. She did not think she would be going anywhere unless she gave it.

She fought back her impatience, wishing them all gone, wishing she didn't need them. "For an hour. For two turns of the glass we'll sail beyond the barrier. Then we turn for home.

Mehen nodded, for all of them. He turned over the half-hour glass that measured the ship's time.

Annavis thought suddenly that the answer would have been the same if she had said a day, or a year and a day—the fact of the limit was all that mattered. She felt cheated. Only an hour! But then she had to laugh. She had chosen the limit herself.

She could see stars through the crack. A great wind sprang up behind them. Soltys hesitated for a moment, then leapt forward, heading straight for the sky. Her shrouds creaked with the strain and the end of the boom dipped towards the sea. The crack gaped before her, big enough to take a whole fleet. Annavis shouted aloud, full of the joy of speed and the edge of disaster, and felt the ship shout with her through thirty mouths. A wave broke against the crack. The white water spurted high, striking Annavis in the face so that she gasped.

The next minute Soltys was across and she knew that the boundary was the only thing left that was real. The sun was gone, left far behind, and dark water stretched in every direction.

And she saw the stars, that would never fade with the dawn. They marched in their thousands, with no sky between her and them, and she cried out, another piece of verse she had thought long forgotten:

Oh may it be—
That I am broken as the dawn
With the rushing world beneath me
And only the stars to tell me I am wrong.

And then she was silent, because even the stars didn't care. She was happy to remember her ship and look away.

Soltys had steadied herself after her wild rush. The black water held her gently. The wind that brushed Annavis's face did not touch her and the mainsail hung in vertical creases, limp and useless. Still, she was moving. Moving away from the faint line of light which marked the crack they had passed through. By the compass she was still heading south. Annavis let go of the wheel, but the course didn't waver.

Far ahead, where the stars began to fade, she saw a faint glow, like a great light seen from far out at sea. It reached out to her like a promise, telling her that the edge of the world was not the end of everything. She turned to point it out to Mehen, to convince him, and through him Soltys, that they must go far enough to see what the light held for them.

Mehen was gone. Soltys was crewed by wraiths now—thin

insubstantial creatures in grey rags, which moved as if they would vanish at any moment. Annavis stood very still with her words still in her mouth, choking her.

One of the wraiths came up to her and stared into her eyes from Mehen's face. It tried to put its hand on her arm but it had no substance that could grasp her. It mouthed words at her she could not hear, and when she did not understand it bowed its head and went away.

She was alone. She felt that she had wished them into ghosthood. She could do as she liked now—there was no one left to hold her back.

She had made a promise, though. She looked to see how much of her hour she had left. But the sand was stopped in the hourglasses. When she tried to count her breaths she found there was nothing telling her to breathe. The numbers blurred and twisted into each other, until Annavis had to admit that what she had called an hour was not a thing that had any meaning here. She looked back at the glass and found that while she wasn't watching some sand had fallen through.

And far ahead the light beckoned, a little closer now as *Soltys* glided on. Annavis stood amidst the wraiths and watched it draw nearer. Overhead the mast reached up to the stars and from it stretched the rigging and the limp sails, pale in the starlight.

Out of the corner of her eye she saw a cat-shape and an instant later felt hot breath on her hand and the rub of fur against her leg. *Soltys* echoed with purring thunder. Sleekly muscled, the furred air leapt and balanced on the guns, the rails, stretched to peer at the binnacle. Vines grew where each paw touched. They tangled around the backstays and the useless sheets. The leaves framed black, glittering eyes.

The wraiths were changing too, becoming more solid. They moved about the deck with quick darting motions. Their grey rags glowed with silvery jewels—scales. She saw one arch its back and flick its tail, swimming in the air.

Annavis had scales growing on her own hands. They covered the old marks left by her House-rings, the gash on her palm. They glittered like moonlight on the wave-patterned sea, like the sky at the edge of the world. Her clothes were gone—furred air brushed her bare knees.

She might have been afraid, she knew. She felt the possibility in a corner of her mind. She might have run shrieking over the cutter's side into the black not-water. But she felt only a fierce desire to go on into this new unknown, to see what lay on the far side of the transformation.

She looked up. There were vines curled in the shrouds, reaching to the swaying masthead. She lifted her scaled arms to the stars.

The wraith with Mehen's face returned. It pointed urgently astern. For the first time Annavis looked back and saw how very far they had come. She shook her head and pointed ahead, where the glow was becoming the lights of a great city.

The half-hour glass was empty. The wraith turned it, and the sand poured through like water.

Annavis filled with anger. How dare it? Glittering, her new hands moved to strike. She couldn't let them—this was Mehen, and she had promised to go back. "All right," she said heavily.

The Mehen-wraith turned to the wheel, but it could not grip the spokes. "Let me try," said Annavis, but her scaled hands were clumsy and she could not find a hold. For the first time since crossing the boundary she was afraid. She had never thought that they might not be able to turn back. And at the same time she felt a guilty joy. She had tried—it wasn't her fault. Now she could keep going, find out what she was changing into.

But the Mehen-wraith gestured to the knife at her belt. She knew what it wanted and drew it from the sheath, not surprised that she had no trouble gripping the handle. She drew the edge across the scales and felt it cut, deep. She hadn't expected pain. She screamed and dropped the knife.

"No!" she said. "I can't!"

The Mehen-wraith stared, and all the unseen beasts, and *Soltys* too, between the vine leaves. Annavis took a step back, away from all the eyes. Her shoes had vanished and as her foot touched the planking she was in the corridor of House Cabral again, watching through Uncle Umbral's door.

It was herself standing in front of the desk, her hair pinned up in the Captain's Knot for the first time. The day she had been told she would command *Soltys*.

"She is *Soltys*," said the other Annavis. "She is outside of the House-games. I will take her where I wish."

"Nothing is outside of the House-games," said Uncle Umbral. "Not any more. I make my own rules." He smiled, and twisted at the rings on his hands.

"Then I can too." But she knew he would not rest until he had *Soltys* as well as Annavis in his grasp.

Watching, Annavis felt the old fury again, but it was anger more than fear, and she saw a change in Uncle Umbral, a new wariness. He could crush cousin Iavan, but he couldn't crush her. Unless she let him.

She had sailed away before she had finished that transformation, looking instead for a place on the charts where he couldn't follow. Now she wanted to see what would happen if she returned to confront Uncle Umbral with all the glory of a voyage to the edge of the world behind her. She didn't have to hide here forever, on the far side of the sky.

"This is far enough."

She bent and picked up the knife again and began to scrape at the scales. She knew what to expect this time and set her teeth against the pain. With each cut she saw the lights of the city fading back into a vague glow. The vines withered and the beasts stepped back into the air.

Her eyes were full of tears, but she knew when the last scale was gone. She took the wheel then, feeling *Soltys* alive beneath her touch. Slowly, the cutter responded, turning back to the wall of the sky.

Mehen touched her arm. He looked as desolate as she felt. "It's all right," said Annavis. But right then she didn't believe it. Uncle Umbral seemed very small and far away.

It grew colder. The crew huddled in the stern, staring back at the light until it vanished. Annavis tried counting again, with no more luck than before. At last the sky loomed up before them, smooth and black. Annavis picked out the crack, the only bright point, and steered through. For a long moment they hung poised in a fury of wild water.

Something gave, and *Soltys* fell through into sunlight. "Oh!" said Annavis, and flinched as if she had been struck. Mehen was limping, hunched sideways. Even *Soltys* picked her way among the waves as if she knew she would lose any challenge she made.

Annavis's hands hurt. She looked at them, expecting to see bent and broken claws. They were whole and unmarked—no scars or lines, or any sign that she had ever worn House-rings. Hands to start fresh with. But where they touched the spokes she still felt the raw patches where she had scraped her scales away. She couldn't tell how long it would take her to heal. ∞

The Oceanographers

∞ M. Arnott ∞

The oscilloscope's green face betrays
the same white signature of shock:
whatever strikes at our cable's claw
in the abyss, we recognize
the anger.
    gathered on deck in silence,
we watch as the drum winds grimly back,
winds its miles of wet black cable
up through the cheerful foam.
            What shape
(armour? a mermaid, dead, or a parchment
of blasphemous calligraphy?)
that "it" down there will assume this time,
not noon itself, our scientist, can guess. ∞

Chaff

∞ M. Arnott ∞

Did someone from that rubbled house
stand in this orchard here along the fence
as I do now, listen as birds whisper
catastrophe, and ask his heart
whose name would be recorded with the chosen?

Impossible to know if the eyes
that searched the blue above these apple branches
saw the same blue and the same leaves
as ours, much less to comprehend those cobwebs
of consequence their reason spun
from postulates and axioms quite patent
to them. We never quite caught on.
And now of course it's far too late to ask them.

We didn't know ourselves. The gale
scattered the grain and left the chaff, and only
when we stood, when we saw each other's face
did we understand, with some discomfiture,
that we had been those aliens,
that long-suspected, undesired presence
which used their markets, picked their fruit,
laughed at their jokes, but never quite correctly. ∞

The Dark Hour

∞ A.M. Dellamonica ∞

BROTHER WASN'T THE FIRST CROW Momma brought home, for she had loved anything that flew. If they saw a dragonfly or wasp crushed on the street she would be sharp and angry for days. She brought home sparrows, robins, even pigeons and seagulls. They often had three patients in the house, and once the count reached seven. She taught her son how to dress their injuries, what they ate and how to feed them.

They kept each bird until it healed, until Momma said, "The sky wants this one back." Then the two of them would set it free.

Days after she rescued Brother, a black ball of feathers flailing in wet leaves, Momma was killed by a white riot cop. Her son divorced his species, changing his name to Oriole and taking the crow as his only family. An orphanage run by Momma's church took them in, and he lived there in silence for two years. He didn't say a word to another human, black or white, until Contact, the day that emissaries of seven alien races came to Earth, transmitting messages of friendship from their fragile, exquisite spaceships.

The nuns found him outside that night, face tilted to the stars, mumbling alien words. His voice was hoarse from lack of use—like Brother, he croaked.

"Yah Kurar. Sky's calling," he said, as Sister Beverly carried him to bed.

∞

Oriole woke to a mechanical drumbeat—whoosh-clank, whoosh-clank—and the knowledge that he should have been in agony. Losing shipmesh was like soaking your nerve ends in acid. That was what Union veterans said, and it had been true, though nobody told him the acid would be electrified, boiling, and laced with diamond grit.

But now there was no pain. His body was quiet, almost numb, and beneath the pumping sound he could hear rustling, like feathers rubbing together.

Struggling against torpor, he tried to clench his uncooperative hands into fists. Jackers had boarded his ship, torn him out of mesh, and the effects of the tearout had left him helpless to defend *Corvus*.

He managed to lift his eyelids and saw the dark length of his arm vanishing under a gold quilt, so that for a moment he thought it had been amputated. Beyond the rise of his covered legs, two girls were standing at the foot of the bed. Panic and fury beat in his lungs—were they with the jackers or prisoners like him? Then he adjusted to the dimness and saw they weren't girls at all, but women. Nandi women.

Nandi prisoners, he wondered, who'd dare? It didn't make sense. Too disoriented to think clearly or fast, he flailed with fear and his chaotic impressions—the pumping, the weight of blankets, a sound like children's voices—and his mind stirred up an answer. He'd been rescued.

My ship, he tried to say, but the muscles in his jaw and throat remained dead.

The women wore a traditional white overdress which covered garments of darker, silky fabric. The sleeves of the underdresses were intricately embroidered, symbols of the wearer's profession, family, and rank. One woman's adornments were impressive, intricate gold stitches on the sleeves of a red and yellow dress. Her companion, a younger woman, wore an underdress the deep purple of a bruise. The stitches on her sleeves were black.

The Nandieve vaguely resembled *Homo Sapiens*, though they were smaller, with bodies covered in tawny gold fur. Unoriginal Earther journalists often compared them to lions. They were gangly, with round black eyes, but their legs, arms, and hearts were all in roughly the same place as a human's.

Similarities, yes, and differences, too. Their backs were as supple as young vines, and the hands at the ends of their long arms had only two fingers which nestled against a sinuous, triple-jointed thumb.

Unlike Earthers, they didn't go around jacking spaceships.

Something about their silence made him uneasy. He forced himself to breath slowly, in and out, and was suddenly aware of the tension between the women, so strong it pressurized the room. Their necks were stiff, angry. They were not looking at each other.

"Yah Kurar," he said, his tongue a sandbag. It was the traditional Nandi greeting. It meant "welcome the future."

The older woman turned. "You are safe," she said in Sludge, laying long fingers across his brow. The sensation sizzled across his skin, triggering tearout spasms, and she waited until his head stopped jerking. "You're on Angellan, in my home. My name is Ghala."

"*Corvus*? My ship?" he asked in Nandi.

"My cousin, Saale, allowed the jackers to escape." Sludge still: they kept their tongue for themselves. He remembered slaving to learn the vocab. He'd never used it outside the language class.

"Cousin?"

"She captains the ship that saved you," she explained. "The jackers would have killed you both."

"Both?" he groaned. "My prentice survived?"

She turned his head gently and he saw Mueller in the bed beside him, the tense strand of a breathing tube clamped over his nose and chin. The tube stretched to the bedside, to a fat bellows wheezing inside a metal press.

"I thought they killed him."

"We don't expect him to live," Ghala said. "I'm most sorry."

"He will suffocate during minatte," the other woman said, and the fur on Ghala's cheeks bristled with anger.

Minatte. In Sludge, they called it the dark hour, the daily religious pause when everything on Angellan was shut down. Power, water, ships, dataweb, everything technological, even the spaceport, all of it was dead for the eighty-three minutes that comprised a Nandi hour.

"The respirator's going to shut off?"

"I'm afraid so," Ghala said.

"Is one of you going to help him?" he asked.

"You can pump the breather." The voice drifted over Ghala's shoulder.

"You are too weak," Ghala said, her voice sharp.

"Can't you pump it?"

"I am here on your behalf," Ghala said. "Not his."

"Can't you help him on my behalf?"

"He cannot survive, Oriole. Leave him behind."

"We aren't certain," the younger woman said. "I think—"

"I'll do it," he said.

She pushed the respirator into reach, and Oriole examined Mueller's slack white face. He fumbled the bellows out of its metal frame with twitchy fingers. Just as the lights dimmed and died for minatte, he squeezed, driving air into Mueller's lungs. Ghala stalked out of the room into the darkened hall.

He remembered the first time he meshed with *Corvus* for a race, the Union charity cup. He'd bet the income for three runs, sending the winnings to the Moonmine safety fund when he won.

"Sky wanted her back," he muttered, but it only made him angrier. *Corvus* wasn't freed. She was taken by humans, just like Momma.

He forgot the younger woman until she moved, startling him. Straightening the back of her overdress, she flipped the cloth layers loose like a bird shaking out its wings, perched on the edge of a stool and opened a satchel slumped beside it. Digging inside, back bent like a swan's neck, she littered the floor with empty tubes, small pots, leaves steeping in water, and a gelatinous substance like wax or flesh.

"Is that medicine?" he said.

"No." Light flared beside her, a fat clay tube blazing with white flame. "I'm making these," she said, pointing at the lamp with one black nail.

"Why?"

"It's customary, during minatte."

"My name is Oriole."

"You're welcome here." Her voice was hoarse, as his had been after two years of silence. She kept her head bowed.

"Am I disturbing you?"

"No."

"What's your name?"

Now she looked surprised. "It is Keste," she said. "I am ablun."

"Evoker?" he translated the word. "Lamenter."

"Yes. Advocate for the dead."

"A…police officer?" he asked uncertainly.

"Perhaps, in this case. If Mueller dies I'll investigate the jacking."

"Only if he dies?"

"He's alive now. I cannot act."

"He's not going to die," Oriole said.

"I hope not." She looked up, her fine golden features starkly lit by the brightness of the flame. "He moved, once. Cried out. We've asked Earth for medical advice."

He'd taken Mueller aboard on his last run, had found him sensible and good-tempered. He would have been the fourth Earther in the Union, after Oriole and two others.

"Who can I get to find my ship?"

"Is it not insured?" she asked.

He scowled and considered dropping the bellows. If Mueller died, Keste would hunt the jackers. The Nandi were a powerful race.

She seemed to guess his thought. "By now your ship is stripped. The parts are probably in a black-market hangar out on the Edge."

Her voice was gentle, but as she spoke his wrist muscles began to burn. His fingers trembled and pain followed, tracing a path from the wrist in an agonizing route up his arm, through his shoulders, making a furnace of his chest.

He gritted his teeth, still pumping, and turned away from her. She mixed her chemicals, not seeming to expect a reply.

∞

"Lewis was such a nice name," fretted the Aunt, a distant stranger from England who spoke like a television lady. Her skin was black, but her husband and her heart were white. That was what Momma said.

"You'll have to accept he's Oriole now," said Sister Beverly.

"How'd he get the shiner?" asked Aunt's husband.

Reluctantly, the nun told them. Since Contact, Oriole had devoured information about the abilities of other races. He had studied the prophetic talents of the Purvaran crones, the telepathy of the Unjoulatii. He combed flexjournals for stories on alien physiognomy. He tried to guess his teachers' thoughts.

When alone, he stared at his scant collection of toys, trying to move them with his will.

"He was trying to push a toy train," Sister Beverly said.

Oriole, his nose pressed to the window, ignored them, scanning the sky. He'd thought he had succeeded. The little blue engine had trembled, on the edge of motion. But he had been holding his breath while he strained to make it go. The motion he saw was a betrayal by his eyes as he passed out from lack of air.

"He fell," she finished. "And struck his head on a table."

"Kid knocked himself out trying to be a Deev?" The husband coughed, hiding laughter.

Sister Beverly said, "I hope you'll review the report from the psychologist."

The Aunt flushed. "We brought a cage for the raven."

"Crow," Sister Beverly said. Oriole felt her eyes on him. He'd told her they'd bring a cage. "He set Brother free this morning."

"Oh," said the Aunt, relieved. "Good boy, Lew—good boy. Come with Auntie now." She held out a hand for him.

He squeezed his fists into his pockets, out of reach.

∞

"You are kind, but you need not concern yourself with my niece," Ghala said.

"I like her." He'd already tried to get out of bed, but his knees collapsed as soon as he put weight on them, and he almost pitched over onto Mueller. As he fell, snatching the young man's quilt in an attempt to save himself, he thought his prentice's eyebrow twitched into a frown.

Ghala traced the Union gold woven into the sleeves of the night-robe they'd given him. Clearly, Oriole outranked Keste. "Ablun tend to the dead. Looking back to her holds away your future."

"I have nowhere to look but back," he said, struggling with a lump in the pillows.

The Nandi prided themselves on looking forward. Angellan was a garden: not a hive was moulded whose impact on the ecosystem hadn't been projected for centuries, no tree was planted whose harvest was not calculated. As a teenager Oriole had revered them, but when he went to work Moonmine and saw the mountains of waste piling up on the landscape, he'd seen how little the future of Earther's dirt mattered to them.

Ghala straightened the pillow. "Your insurance will buy another ship."

"They can buy a new ship," he said, "They can't replace *Corvus*."

"You had personal possessions on board?"

"That's not it," he said. His leg spasmed, exposing his black and vulnerable toes.

She tucked the sheet back over them. "You should rest. Stress can increase the neural damage."

"When is the next minatte?"

"This evening," she said.

"Same time of day?"

"Later," she said. "A full day passes before it begins again."

"And will Keste come?"

"The vigil is permitted but not required," she said, radiating disapproval. "You should discourage her."

"I'll need to be awake next minatte. For Mueller."

"Of course." She dropped a band into his hands, a strip for his undersleeve, more gold embroidery and a few streaks of red. "This says you are my guest. I'll get a tapestry for your door."

"I appreciate it, Ghala. But about Keste…"

She pinned the fabric to his shoulder with two efficient jabs. "She is no more than one of the dead herself," she said, and ended the discussion by leaving.

∞

At fourteen Oriole was hoarding credits, working two jobs and asking for money for his birthday and the holidays. At sixteen he got a waiver from his social advocate and a job at Moonmine, wrestling the elements and daring the overtime regs. Three years later he was on Thistledown space station, the Union's pioneer Earther prentice.

Blissfully, precociously, licensed at twenty-one, he worked a ship he'd leased from the Union, flying danger runs.

Oriole was twenty-four when he bought his wings.

Corvus unlocked when he blinked his eye, powered up and down as he clenched and unclenched his jaw. She was sleek, insectile, a bright haven of metal and biomesh flashing between his brothers, the calm and hateless stars. In her flypit, Oriole stretched out his hands to extend towing fields, clawing salvage from the cool womb of space. He piloted with sure turns of his head, blinked to bring the stars closer and closer with each minor adjustment of the sensors.

No risk runs for this ship. Oriole took salvage jobs and passengers. He spent his income on maintenance, upgrades, insurance, and jackproofing. *Corvus* was as jack-proof as technology could make her.

It wasn't enough.

∞

"Have you read your flims?" Ghala asked. He was steady enough to walk and she was leading him through the gardens.

"Mostly get-well messages." Oriole said.

"Big family?"

"Friends," he said. Sister Beverly sent a short note, the first he'd received in years, urging him to visit. "The Union filed my jacking claim. They'll deliver the new ship here, if that's all right."

"Certainly. You'll be recovered by the time it arrives." When he didn't answer, she studied him with her shiny black eyes. "You are still depressed."

He looked back at the hive, a round bulb of grey stone. A sharp golden needle emanated from its roof: the catch which absorbed bursts of airborne energy from the power plants. Everything on Angellan seemed to be in flight: floats drifted over the hives in a glimmering layer, making a shifting mosaic of the sky. "I worked ten years for that ship."

Comprehension rippled through her features. "The ship was your minatten?"

"Minatten?" Sludge translated the word to 'night hobby.'

She pointed at a powerburst, the floats. "What we make in the light of day, we call that betatten," she said. "It is taxed: some for the present, more for the future." Her words had the cadence of a recitation.

"What about the past?"

"The past is dead. It is like gravity, holding you back from the future. But what you make during the minatte is your own."

"Minatten," he mused. "Like Keste's lamps?"

"Yes," she sighed. "Like that."

"*Corvus* wasn't homemade."

"When we meet offworlders who have built something for themselves—for their souls, we say—we call it minatten too."

Just then Keste appeared, walking down from the flower-laden slopes of the upper garden, a dark purple bloom between her fingers. When she saw Ghala and Oriole she changed direction, flowing into another path with the habitual discretion of the outcast. A moment later she reappeared and started up the hill again. Voices—children—taunted her from the path. A clod of dirt arced out of the trees, spattering into bits at her feet, little dots of black pelting her purple underdress.

Ghala wrapped her fingers around his wrist. "I grieve for your minatten," she said. "But you cannot replace *Corvus* by creating life where there is none. Let Mueller go."

"He screamed yesterday when I was pumping his lungs."

"Reflex. Your friend's dead. Leave him to Keste."

"He was my prentice," Oriole said. "My responsibility."

"Will you leave if he is still clinging to life? Will you stay in our home and sacrifice yourself to him? If you let him die Keste may find the jackers, and if she does..."

"Don't pretend she can still catch *Corvus*," he said. "You'd do anything to make me believe Mueller's dead. But you can't bribe me, Ghala. My ship's gone."

She pulled back, startled by his rage, and Oriole wobbled without her supporting arm.

"Yes, of course it is," she said. "Forgive me."

He thought he'd stopped hoping, but his chest burned anyway.

Later at minatte he was glad to see Keste, piling handfuls of pulp onto a handmade strainer. She looked less guarded, more cheerful.

"Ghala says you don't have to be here."

"I rarely have duties in this part of the hive," she said. "Am I disturbing you?"

"Absolutely not," he said. "Those are your minatten. Do you sell them?"

"Yes," she said. "My brother makes stands for them."

"So there is someone here who speaks to you."

She rocked slightly on the stool. "No, he was sent to Earth. I give some lamps away without stands. I'm saving the rest for his return."

He took the bellows out of the press and leaned against the sickbed, facing her as he pumped Mueller's lungs. "When my mother died I was sent to live with strangers. They made sure I knew I wasn't wanted."

"You are good to be concerned, but our situations are different."

"How?"

"Everyone here has a place."

"Your family values your place?" He barked sarcastic laughter.

She looked troubled and unwilling to answer. "My place is very important," she said. "You cannot understand."

"Keste, listen," he said. "Every year my aunt filed a request with the social advocate to have me put back in institutional care. She'd say, 'you're unhappy, aren't you darling? Write a nice note to your advocate, now, and ask her to send you to school.'"

"Did you write it?"

"They couldn't fund a kid with solvent kin."

She set the mesh screen on an empty drum and began pounding the pulp. The rhythm of her hands and the patter of it dribbling into the drum throbbed between the wheezes of the bellows.

He spoke over the noise. "Doesn't it make you angry?"

"Ablun make no wealth," she said. "Our maintenance is stolen from the future. We look back. We're…"

"Necessary," he said.

"Deviant. Flawed. Corrupt." With each word she pounded the pulp harder, but her face remained serene.

"You're none of those things."

"Even as a child I could not walk away from the past," she said. "Do not feel sorry for me, Oriole. I chose this."

"Why?" he asked, voice hoarse, like a heartbroken child.

"I'll show you," she said.

∞

Gul, his flight mentor, was a cranky old pilot from a water-dwelling race. Eccentric, testy, and paranoid, he was never as happy as when preparing for disaster.

"Ships crash, Earthchild," Gul said the day they met.

"Don't call me that," he said.

"Pilots crash, uh huh, they get jacked. Have to survive. You're ready for that?"

"I doubt it," he'd grumbled. Crash survival rates were low.

A rush of bubbles—at that point Oriole couldn't tell the alien from the water it swam in—swirled through the pinkish liquid in Gul's tank. "You're not deathseeking?" The words came through the translator in uninflected Sludge, and Oriole knew he was close to losing a mentor.

"No. 'Course not."

"Can you make rope from weeds, Starchilde?"

"No."

"Rope's vital for a landwalker," Gul observed. "Catch prey, bind bones, uh huh."

For months after that, in the pauses between their runs, Gul had him fishing reeds and thistles out of swamps, slicing out their minuscule tendons and plaiting them into threads. Eventually the process of making rope wove itself into his dreams.

∞

Keste took him to a funeral.

The dead child was braced in a standing position, eyes open, hand outstretched. Her overdress fluttered in the wind, and the stitching on her undersleeves climbed to her shoulders, greens and yellows giving way to black and deep purple.

Keste wore an underdress like none he'd ever seen, a rainbow of daubed colours, sleeves stitched and overstitched until they were bulky with the weight of thread.

"What do you do when there's an accident?" he whispered. "When the body's torn up?"

"Hologram."

Mourners streamed past the body, laying flowers and gifts on the ground at the girl's feet. As they rose they seized the limp hand, pressed it once to their forehead, and then walked on without looking back, toward the girl's family hive.

"The turnout's huge," he said.

"Everyone goes to funerals when they can."

"You mean they don't know her?"

"Only a few."

They followed the procession into the hive's great hall and he watched Keste move among the mourners. Everyone responded to her presence. The girl's family spoke to her, telling her the child's business, leaving last messages. In one or two cases they wept, and she held them.

As time passed he saw more and more of the Nandieve, steeped in grief and liquor, addressing Keste by other peoples' names.

She was the centre of attention: hostess and priestess all at once—working the crowd, the Aunt had called it. Sought by everyone, Keste consoled them, advised them, cajoled them gently into laughter. She shone with happiness: her black eyes radiant with life and cheer, she talked to them all, high and low, picking up conversations begun at other funerals, speaking of their lost relatives with compassion and ease.

Away from Keste, Oriole couldn't help seeing they were separated like layers of oil. Those wearing gold spoke to each other, to the ones with yellows and oranges, to him with his Union ranking. They seemed not to see anyone else. The reds clustered in a corner, chatting. They bowed slightly when Oriole passed. The rest dropped their eyes when he was near.

"How are you feeling?" Keste had crept up on him, fur flat against her face, a mischievous expression. She handed him a glass of red wine.

"It's from Earth," she said. "It's not very strong—it won't affect your recovery."

He looked into the glass. "I generally drink üshen."

"How I envy you. You're so well travelled," she said, pinching a loop of loose thread from the embroidery on her arm, tugging it out of the welter of stitches. "What is your homeworld like?"

"Nothing like this," he said, sweeping an arm at a window to indicate the busy Nandi sky, filled with floaters and powerbursts. "If you really want to mix cultures you should go to Thistledown."

"My brother told Ghala he'd never seen anything like it," she said, voice wistful.

"If Mueller dies you'll have to go," he said, suddenly inspired. "To track down the jackers."

Her head jerked up and the thread popped loose. "I hadn't thought of it," she said.

"Any investigation would start there," he said.

"Thistledown," she said. "Is that your home now?"

"I lived on *Corvus*." He rolled wine on his tongue.

Keste's face grew serious and she tucked the strand of thread in her pocket. "Your minatten and your home, too," she said. "And your prentice all at once. How terrible."

"Why don't I tell you about Thistledown," he said. His voice was suddenly thin and hoarse.

"Is that where you first saw *Corvus?*"

"It doesn't matter," he said.

"Now is the mourning time, Oriole," she said. "Talk about your loss. Leave it in the past."

"I don't need comforting," he said.

"Your ship is gone," she said. "You must move forward."

His arm shook as he set the wine down, sloshing it over his fingers. "The only thing I want to leave behind is this party."

"I'm sorry," Keste said.

"Can you take me back to the hive?"

She shook her head. "You'll have to go with Ghala when she leaves."

"What about you?"

"The girl did not die until the mourners left her. This is her first night as a spirit."

"You stay with her?"

"We believe that in the future the dead are waiting for us, that we will be reunited. If the girl's spirit is troubled she may tell me how to ease her voyage. She leaves us behind too."

"Justice agent, grief counsellor, and now mystic?" he said. "I suppose you'll bury her as well."

"Who else?"

∞

His first formal dinner at the hive was a few nights later. The table curved through a dining hall as large as a hangar, a continuous serpentine surface of shining golden wood. He was seated miles away from Keste, who ranked lower than most of the children. Hundreds of Nandi sat between them.

Ghala had him next to an energetic young man who was courting one of her daughters. "He is a highly placed garden designer," she told him in a low voice, when the young man's attention was distracted. "He's very interesting."

The table was alive with conversations, most in Nandi, a few—politics and news—in Sludge for Oriole's benefit. The sound rolled up and down the tables as people discussed a topic with their peers, and then listened as their neighbours on either side picked up the conversation. In this way they managed to address and answer each other without breaching the protocol.

"I didn't know you kept things this formal at home."

"This is a celebration. We have heard my nephew is coming home."

"Keste's brother?"

"My sister's child, Juie. He has been on Earth for six of your years."

"Does she know?"

"I'm sure she's heard," she sighed. "You don't think of your ship so much now, do you?"

"I can think about two things at once," he said dryly.

"You should pick two different subjects," she said. "Your new ship. Your recovery."

"I'm healing all right," he said, allowing his hand to wobble in midair as a joke.

"When was the last time you went home to Earth?"

"I probably couldn't find it," he said.

"You're a hero there, I understand."

He shrugged. "Ghala, minatten are completely handmade, right?"

"Yes."

"Where do you get the raw materials?"

She beamed. "You are taking up a night hobby?"

"Nothing during the dark hour. I'm not giving up on Mueller."

"And minatte is when you see Keste. She sits waiting for him to die and you prevent it."

"I'm not obsessed with her," he said sharply, and heads turned.

Ghala smoothed down the spikes of fur on her cheeks and offered him a helping of moist, bluish vegetables. "We keep wildlands for minatten supplies," she said. "The boys can show you."

He could follow the phrase as it slipped into conversations trickling down the table. "The offworlder wants to go to the wildlands tomorrow. Perhaps Yuken and Jeft will take him."

∞

He saw his first ship on the trip to Moonmine. It was a Tuesday, two days after he turned sixteen. He had faced down his advocate for the waiver Monday morning. The mine had already hired him as a sampler: he'd studied the necessary chemistry and geology, and learned Sludge, Purvaran, and Nandi for good measure.

Hangars landed and took off all the time at the port outside Baton Rouge, but hangars had never interested him. They were little more than glorified elevators. Massive, powerful carriers, they took real spacecraft in and out of gravity fields.

Uncle paced behind him as he watched the ships being towed in and out of the hangar for feeding and loading, their silver forms glistening inside the jelly and nerve tissue of the flightmesh that encased them.

"You think that thing'll leave on time?" Uncle asked.

"You don't have to stay," Oriole said, not taking his eyes off the ships. He had accessed thousands of pictures on the flexjournals, but he was still breathless at the sight of them. They looked like wasps suspended in their eggs: the three bulbs of the cabin, hold and engines wedded together like a head, thorax and abdomen, the spindles extending into the jelly like legs and antenna and wings.

"You'll be halfway home before I make it out of the boonies," Uncle muttered.

"I'm not coming back." He was already trying to excise the New Orleans accent from his English, to speak with the flat tones of an offworlder.

“They’re not going to put up with sulking. They’ll expect you to act like a human being and fit in.”

“I’ll fit in,” he said.

“Advocate says we have to take you back if you get fired before you’re eighteen.”

“You won’t be seeing any more of her, either,” he said. He leaned on the glass, leaving a circle of condensed breath around his chin, and Uncle shrugged and walked away.

∞

Gul would be happy to know his survival training got some use, Oriole thought, as he secured the frame of his sieve. He poked homemade strands of thread through the holes he had bored through the wood, tying, tightening. He crossed the lines, knotted, bounced the flat of his hand against the mesh surface until he was satisfied it would hold.

Then he took the stone rolling pin—he’d traded Jeft for six feet of rope—and fitted it into the grooves. Tightening the pegs, he rolled it back and forth across the frame. Like that he had a home-made pulp strainer.

He stayed up through the night, carving, putting finishing touches on the frame. As the sun rose over the gardens he was more rested than he’d been since the jacking. It had been that way in *Corvus*, too; a few useful hours in shipmesh were always more energizing than whole shifts of sleep.

Corvus. The thought of her made his chest ache.

Fleeing memories, he groped his way down the hive, following the colours of the carpet, looking at the tapestries which hung on the hundreds of portals. At last he spotted the sombre bruise-purple silk, the black stitches. She’d been relegated to the basement.

Oriole pushed the tapestry aside.

Keste’s chamber was more theatre than bedroom. A round space with a high ceiling, it was like a vault: the walls were made of blackened wood, the floor from black stone. Light came through slits in the wall, radiating a baleful yellow onto the dull floor.

Hundreds of tapestries hung from the ceiling, banners of colour and stitching, some dangling so low they brushed the top of Oriole’s head.

He raised his hand, brushed their bottom edges, watched the different colours slide over his fingertips. Across from the door was a tapestry he recognized. Its stitching and clan colours were those worn by the young girl whose funeral he had attended. Keste must have buried all of these Nandi.

Everything in the room was hand-made: the rough-hewn bed, a stool lashed together with vines, a chunky desk. The knobs on the bedposts were carved into busts, the heads of a boy and a girl. Keste and her brother?

Beside the bed, waiting for minatte, hand-made stands held a trio of Keste's lamps in the centre of the room. There was nothing else in the room, not even a flexjournal reader.

Picking his way to the bed, Oriole peered underneath. Baskets of clothing crowded each other for the meagre space, like baby birds in a nest. The lampmaking satchel was beside them. Oriole fished inside for Keste's pulp strainer.

The frame he'd made to replace it was unabashedly wedded to his past, carefully etched with images of Brother, of jasmine leaves, a dragonfly, bamboo, clouds, even tools they'd used on Moonmine. He'd never been good enough to etch faces, so he'd carved things that reminded him of his friends on the Mine and in the Union. *Corvus* graced the long wooden sweep of a handle he'd dotted with stars.

He switched the frames and climbed to his feet. A rush of vertigo chased him: he'd got up too quickly.

Suddenly, he felt the years-lost scratch of talons on his forearm.

"Brother?"

His vision cleared, taking the sensory hallucination with it, leaving him listening for the sound of beating wings.

Goddamn jackers. His nervous system would never be optimal again. Three tearouts was the most anyone had survived. He sat down heavily on the bed, trying to catch his breath.

The tapestries fluttered and Keste slipped inside.

At first she didn't see him. She closed the door and leaned against the black wall, her eyes roaming the room, dirt on her hands and overdress. She looked contented and cheerful. She muttered a snatch of an old poem he'd taught her. The words seemed to slide into the tapestries and then echo back, making it sound like there were dozens of people there, all speaking with lowered voices.

Suddenly she twitched, startled, and looked down at him.

"Should I go?" he asked.

"No, I'm just surprised," she said. "Nobody comes here."

"I wanted to leave you something."

Stunned, she brushed soil from her hands. "A gift?"

He nodded.

She held herself there at the entrance, just for a moment, before rushing down the steps. His face grew warm as she held out her hands for the frame.

Hopping up onto her stool, she waved him back at the bed as he was about to rise. The headboard clicked faintly as he settled, as if something had landed there beside him. He did not turn his head.

"It's lovely," she said. "It has minatten spirit, even if you didn't do it during minatte."

"I have a lot of dark hours," Oriole said.

Her hands traced the stars on the frame, pushed the roller back and forth, and settled on *Corvus*. The Nandi didn't cry, but emotion stiffened her spine, making her seem as though she'd gotten taller, grown.

"You are profoundly stubborn," she said.

"Keste, you must be the only one who hasn't been off-world."

She set the frame down. "Is that how you solve everyone's problems? By jacking them from home?"

"If Mueller dies…"

She closed her eyes. "Don't say any more."

He felt himself growing cold. Maybe they'd caught the jackers, and she wouldn't be able to leave after all. "What's happened?" he asked.

She handed him a flims. It was from Earth Medical, English translated into Nandi. His feelings knotted in a stringy mass. They'd included Mueller's living will.

"It says…"

"I can read Nandi."

"Sorry."

"It says there's a chance."

"His instructions specifically address biomesh tearout."

"Have you…released him?"

"I wanted to tell you first."

He looked away, took a deep breath. "So you'll have to track down the jackers."

She nodded. "I will need to go to Thistledown."

"Can I take you?" he asked.

"As Mueller's flight mentor you're entitled."

"I'll look up the protocol so I don't offend anyone when I ask."

She laughed, a chuckle that nearly brought tears to his eyes. "You're very insightful. Sometimes."

∞

Sister Beverly kept trying to get him back to Earth.

She wrote when he got his license, again to congratulate him when he got his ship. The flexjournals ran filler stories about his progress in the

Union, and she'd write to say she'd seen an article, why didn't he come and see how proud they all were?

She wrote him when the Aunt died.

"I hope you'll come home," she wrote. "Your uncle is taking the loss hard and would be comforted by seeing you."

In the end he didn't even send flowers.

After that her communications got rare. Before the get-well flims she sent him after the jacking, Oriole hadn't heard from her in two years.

∞

"I can't do it, but we can wait for minatte," Keste said. "It's almost time."

"No," Oriole said. "Thanks."

"I'd hoped he might recover."

"Me, too," he said.

"It was terribly bad luck," she said.

"He was just too new to shipmesh," Oriole said. He unclenched his fists, rubbed his hands together. He put icy fingers on the respirator, pulled it from his prentice's face, drawing the hose clear of his mouth. The mask had left a mark around his jaw, a red fissure. "If you're gonna stage a miracle recovery, kid, now's the time," he whispered in his rusty English.

Mueller didn't manage even one breath on his own.

They stood together, contemplating the body on the bed, a husk that once contained an sensible young pilot. Oriole had a vivid memory: Momma crying over the flattened remains of a robin.

"You won't carry him around too?" Keste asked.

"I barely knew him," he said bitterly.

Keste climbed onto the bed, crouching on her knees beside Mueller, and stroked his face with the backs of her hands. "I would imagine he admired you very much."

Oriole fled, stumbling outside on numb legs.

The yard was empty.

Groomed to immaculate perfection, every leaf seemed to shine, every tree reached gently for the next. Every curve of the hive gleamed like bone in the orange glow of the Nandi sun. Music played softly from points he couldn't locate, bathing the grounds in soft melody.

Loitering near the float park, Ghala and her husband were the only members of the family in sight. The sunlight on them was brightening, making the gold stitches on their sleeves shine. Oriole glanced up. Floats were parking for the approaching minatte, and the mosaic of traffic was crumbling as the sky cleared.

Ghala waved him over. "Mueller?"

"In the past," he said.

She missed his sarcasm, looking pleased and relieved, like someone whose prentice has finally mastered a critical lesson. "You will leave us soon?"

"My ship's being delivered tomorrow."

"And are you looking forward to your new ship?"

"I'm looking forward to being in space again."

"Have you named it?"

"I was thinking about *Vespa.*" He was about to say something more, about Keste, when a green float raced over the hills towards the hive. Ghala clapped. There was a hiss, and a gush of perfume washed through the float park.

"Is something going on?" he asked.

"It's my nephew."

"Keste didn't say..." Ghala's husband drove the words back into his throat with a long, cold glance.

The float latched into a berth and a young man, lithe and excited, bounded out before it had settled on the ground. He leaped into Ghala's embrace. "Almost forgot minatte," he laughed. "Had to speed."

Oriole tried to fade back so they could have their reunion, but Ghala seized his hand.

"Oriole, guest, this is my nephew, Juie."

"You make stands for lamps, I hear," Oriole said in Nandi.

The young man regarded him with warmth. "Oh, there's never time on Earth," he said. His English had a Southern lilt to it.

"You were in New Orleans," Oriole guessed.

Juie nodded. "Lampstands are tricky," he said. "Tougher than they look, and I'm out of practice. I might just take up minatten poetry."

"Keste's been saving lamps..."

"Let's go inside," Ghala interrupted, encircling them both with her arms, nudging them toward the open portal of the hive.

Keste was there.

She was coming out of the house in pursuit of Oriole. Seeing Juie, her face bloomed with surprise. The fur on her cheeks rippled with pleasure, and she extended her hand. The sunlight caught the purple of her underdress strangely, and it seemed to shimmer into a shade of silver, like mercury, like the scales of a fish or the skin of a spaceship.

Juie reached halfway across the distance and then they both froze, let their hands fall. His uncle jostled him sharply. "Have you learned nothing?" he demanded in Nandi.

"They haven't seen each other in six years," Oriole said, but Juie was already turning his face to Ghala.

"Is this a funeral?" Ghala's husband hissed, seeming to address Juie instead of Keste. "Has someone died?"

Keste's head dipped and she drifted silently away.

"Come, Oriole," Ghala said.

He tore free and went after Keste. She was hunched over Juie's float, running her fingers over its surface as if she was petting the flank of a beast.

"Hit it," he suggested. "You're angry. You'll feel better."

Her fingers curled up and she raised her arms above the float, her spine stiff with stitched up emotion. Then she let her arms drop. "I'm not angry."

Oriole punched the float for her, setting it a-quiver and jolting pain down his arm. "My ship will be here tomorrow. We can leave on the first hangar out."

"Yes," Keste said. "He looked well, didn't he?" She continued into the garden without waiting for an answer.

"One more day," he whispered.

Once he got her into space, he knew she wouldn't return. She'd been willing to give up the comforts of a normal life for the funerals, where she could move among people and speak to anyone. At Thistledown, she could do the same with no sacrifice at all.

He could set her free.

∞

Momma had never tamed the birds she kept at home, curing them fast and sending them back to the wild. If she'd lived, Brother would have gone a month after she rescued him. After so many years, he wasn't sure the crow remembered what freedom was.

He'd remember pretty quick if someone tried to cage him.

They rose before dawn on the day the Aunt was coming and crept out of school. Brother greeted the cold morning like a friend, shaking his feathers, hopping and croaking.

Oriole took him to a long, twisted alley walled by huge buildings on either side, so tall they blotted out a sky which was overcast: starless, moonless. He sat on an old crate and fed the bird roasted sunflower seeds, tempting him into reach and then throwing the seeds over him. It was an old game, a favourite with them both.

"Maybe we could both run away," he said. Brother paused in mid-peck. Boys can't live like birds, his gaze seemed to say. Oriole was already shivering in the cold air, a chill the crow didn't feel.

"If I could fly we could go away together," he said. He bounced a seed across the pavement and Brother devoured it.

He'd hated this part, had cried and fought Momma the first time they'd set a bird free. After she died he'd forgotten he was ever mad at her, but now he remembered that day. She'd carried him all the way home, punching and kicking.

He rubbed his eyes with the palms of his hands, stinging them with salt from the seeds.

Later on, he'd behaved better, though sometimes Momma would have to say, "Don't make me drag you home," before he turned his back on the tiny guest they were forcing out into the harsh and violent world.

He got to his feet. "Bye, Brother," he said, his voice trembling.

Brother hopped closer and he retreated, tossing a seed. Brother jumped on it; Oriole widened the distance between them.

The crow croaked, tilted his head.

"You have to go now," he said. He pitched another seed, but the bird fluttered over it, landed on a brick windowsill just inches from his head. He lashed his arm at the sill, driving the crow into flight and scraping his wrist on the bricks. He shrieked in frustration and pain, grabbing the wrist, and the tears began to flow.

Brother landed on the ground in front of him, scolding him now, ignoring Oriole when he stamped his feet to scare him off.

"Go!" Weeping hysterically, he kicked him.

It was barely a push, just enough to scare Brother into the air, but as soon as he did it he was sick, sure he'd struck too hard, that he'd broken bones and killed him.

"Get lost, you dumb bird," he screamed. "Sky's calling you." He threw the last of the seeds.

Brother circled once, still scolding, and then soared away into the brightening sky, vanishing over the tops of the buildings. Oriole pelted away down the alley, sobbing, so blinded by tears that he nearly didn't find his way back to school.

Back in his room, he watched at the window, rocking and holding his scratched wrist with his other hand, squeezing it tighter and tighter as the sun continued to rise.

Brother never came.

∞

Ghala had made him a bag for his clothes and the family had filled it with tunics and trinkets. He had a minatten bracelet from one of the boys, a hologram of the busy Angellan sky, a slender wallet for flims, his door tapestry, a datachip loaded with starcharts, a journal, even a simple game from the children. The fabric of the bag stretched like a filled belly. He'd never received so many gifts in his life. *Vespa* wouldn't be *Corvus*, but Oriole could glimpse a future worth welcoming: unpacking the gifts, getting Keste installed in the passenger cabin, showing her the stars.

She was the hangar, looking cheerful and nervous all at once. Her satchel was half empty, just a tapestry and a bag of pots for making lamps.

"Excited?" Oriole asked, as they stepped into the hangaryard, putting some distance between them and the float park, where Ghala and Juie were watching. Nobody had spoken on the trip to the spaceport.

"I could hardly help it," she said.

A young Nandi man with blue undersleeves was playing a sprightly tune on a green instrument, and she wove her head slightly in time to its beat. Oriole copied her movements roughly, and suddenly they were dancing, side by side, bodies swaying in the current of fast, high notes.

The musician spotted them. His gaze riveted on Keste, and he stopped playing.

Oriole kept dancing. "Don't stop," he said. "I'll sing you a mining tune."

"We'd better," Keste said, laughing. "Ghala's nerves won't take the strain."

"I guess we can afford to be merciful," he grinned.

"If we kill her I'll have to stay and bury her," she said, and clapped her hands over her mouth.

"Wickedness," Oriole teased, and then he spotted a glass spindle filled with pink liquid rolling towards them.

"Gul?"

The tank's scanners were pointed at Oriole, robotic arms laden with datachips and recorders. A long tassel of fabric with the gold stitching of the Union rank trailed from one slender metallic arm, rippling in the breeze like a flag.

"Is that a machine?" Keste reached out to touch it, her eyes sparkling with excitement.

"This is my flight mentor," he said. Keste yanked her hand back, startled.

"Here, Starchilde," Gul's voice resonated from the speaker at the base of the tube. "Told you jackers, huh didn't I?"

"You told me," Oriole said.

"Recovered?" One of the robot arms poked his hand.

"Well enough." He took the arm and pulled until the mechanism whined, showing Gul the steadiness of his grip.

"Don't hazard you made much rope."

"I made thread," he said. "Gul, this is Keste. She's leaving with us."

Keste ducked her head shyly at the tank.

"Leaving, uh huh, with you."

The sides of the hangar peeled away and two silver ships appeared: Oriole's new wings, and Gul's beloved, battered *Darter*. A crew hooked up to *Darter* and towed her off the hangar.

"You're doing business?"

The tank gurgled. "Important delivery contract."

"But…you're still in bioloads?"

"Starchilde," he teased. "Would I change, huh, and not say?" Keste was staring at his tank with unabashed curiosity; Gul condensed into thick pink mush so she could see him.

"Come on, Gul. Nandi don't import species."

"True, huh, but Nandi import criminals."

Keste gasped softly.

"Criminals?"

"Exotic, huh, but still bioload."

"What criminals?"

"He means the jackers, Oriole," Keste said.

"I have them on my ship," Gul said smugly.

"What?" Spots danced in front of his eyes.

"Delivery now, huh, to authorities," Gul said.

"How did…" His throat closed over the words. "The Union get lucky?"

"No, uh-uh. Earth offered reward day you lost *Corvus*."

"You mean Moonmine."

"Moonmine suggestion, maybe. Earth paid. You're pride to them. First pilot, famous. Want to see the jackers?"

"No."

"You are a strange peopleboy, Starchilde," said Gul. "Where are the authorities?"

"I'll take charge of them," Keste said. Her voice was hoarse.

He caught her by the arm, vaguely aware of the shocked face of the musician. "Come anyway," he said. "Come because you want to."

She was looking at his new ship, shaking so hard you'd think she'd been torn out of shipmesh. Her spine was rigid with distress.

"Keste," he said.

She shook her head slightly. "I don't have duties offworld anymore. I have to stay to prosecute the jackers."

"Someone else will do it," he said.

"Oriole, I couldn't come back."

"What would you have to come back to?" he said.

"You can still go back to Earth," she said, speaking Nandi at last. "You're not banned. They love you."

"I've never gone back," he said.

"Perhaps you should."

"It's not my home. They're not my people," he shouted.

"Neither am I." She pointed at Ghala and Juie. "They're my people, Oriole, and I don't need to be rescued from them."

She turned, took a breath, and spoke to Gul. "I'll call prisoner transport."

"Hurry," Gul said. "Prisoners escape, they cause trouble."

"They'll be here soon," she promised.

"Keste!" Oriole hissed.

She reached into her satchel and took out a finished lamp, held it out.

"Come with me," he said again.

"Please take it."

He pulled his hands away, knotting fists behind his back.

She shook her head, set the lamp at his feet. As she straightened his hand brushed her forehead. She turned and walked away. She didn't look back.

The musician began to play again, his notes hot and angry, chasing her slow steps like small birds driving crows from their nesting grounds.

Gul rolled closer. "Pretty ship, uh?"

"Uh huh," Oriole said. He stared across the field at Keste, willing her to return, to turn back and look at him. He imagined he had her, that her steps were slowing.

"Name her soon? Union log wants confirmation, uh huh identity coding?"

Keste paused at the float steps, just for a moment. Then she pulled herself into her family's waiting float, against the traction of his will.

"Starchilde," Gul said. "Bad luck, huh, ships without names."

The float dipped over the hill.

"Call her…"

It glided out of sight.

"Call her…*Nevermore*," he said. ∞

Why Starships Should Be Named For Moths

∞ Peter Bloch-Hansen ∞

The stars kill those who love them.
They aren't bright twinkles
scattered over a velvet night,
but blinding light,
flame,
rage.

Still, we love them,
tracing among them
shapes that match the spaces
in our hearts,
weaving through them
stories,
tales—
love,
courage,
treachery, sacrifice.

We build great ships,
plan great, precise, arcing journeys,
yearning,
yearning to change,
fly out of our green, nibbling little lives,
to touch,
enter,
be
that brightness. ∞

Home Again, Home Again

∞ Cory Doctorow ∞

THE KIDS IN MY LOCAL bat-house breathe heavy metals, and their gelatinous bodies quiver nauseously during our counseling sessions, and for all that, they reacted just like I had when I told them I was going away for a while—with hurt and betrayal, and they aroused palpable guilt in me.

It goes in circles. When I was sixteen, and The Amazing Robotron told me he needed to go away for a while, but he'd be back, I did everything I could to make him guilty. Now it's me, on a world far from home, and a pack of snot-nosed jellyfish kids have so twisted my psyche that they're all I can think of when I debark the shuttle at Aristide Interplanetary, just outside my dirty ole Toronto.

The customs officer isn't even human, so it feels like just another R&R, another halting conversation carried on in ugly trade-speak, another bewilderment of queues and luggage carousels. Outside: another spaceport, surrounded by the variegated hostels for the variegated tourists, and bipeds are in bare majority.

I can think of it like that.

I can think of it as another spaceport.

I can think of it like another trip.

The thing he can't think of it is, is a homecoming. That's too hard for this weak vessel.

He's very weak.

∞

Look at him. He's eleven, and it's the tencennial of the Ascension of his homeworld—dirty blue ball, so unworthy, yet—inducted into the Galactic fraternity and the infinite compassion of the bugouts.

The foam, which had been confined to just the newer, Process-enclaves before the Ascension, has spread, as has the cult of the Process For Lasting Happiness. Process is, after all, why the dirty blue ball was judged and found barely adequate for membership. Toronto, which had seen half its inhabitants emigrate on open-ended tours of the wondrous worlds of the bugout domain, is full again. Bursting. The whole damn planet is accreting a layer of off-world tourists.

It's a time of plenty. Plenty of cheap food and plenty of cheap foam structures, built as needed, then dissolved and washed away when the need disappears. Plenty of healthcare and education. Plenty of toys and distractions and beautiful, haunting bugout art. Plenty, in fact, of everything, except space.

He lived in a building that is so tall, its top floors are perpetually damp with clouds. There's a nice name for this building, inscribed on a much-abused foam sculpture in the central courtyard. No one uses the nice name. They call it by the name that the tabloids use, that the inhabitants use, that everyone but the off-world counselors use. They call it the bat-house.

Bats in the belfry. Batty. Batshit.

I hated it when they moved us into the bat-house. My parents gamely tried to explain why we were going, but they never understood, no more than any human could. The bugouts had a test, a scifi helmet you wore, and it told you whether you were normal, or batty. Some of our neighbors were clearly batshit: the woman who screamed all the time, about the bugs and the little niggers crawling over her flesh; the couple who ate dogturds off the foam sidewalk with lip-smacking relish; the guy who thought he was Nicola Tesla.

I don't want to talk about him right now.

His parents' flaw—whatever it was—was too subtle to detect without the scifi helmet. They never knew for sure what it was. Many of the bats were in the same belfry: part of the bugouts' arrogant compassion held that a couple never knew which one of them was defective, so his family never knew if it was his nervous, shy mother, or his loud, opinionated father who had doomed them to the quarantine.

His father told him, in an impromptu ceremony before he slid his keycard into the lock on their new apt in the belfry: "Chet, whatever they say, there's nothing wrong with us. They have no right to put us here." He knelt to look the skinny ten-year-old right in the eye. "Don't worry, kiddo. It's not for long—we'll get this thing sorted out yet." Then, in a rare moment of tenderness, one that stood out in Chet's memory as the last of such, his father gathered him in his arms, lifted him off his feet in a fierce hug. After a moment, his mother joined the hug, and Chet's face was buried in the spot where both of their shoulders met, smelling their smells. They still smelled like his parents then, like his old house on the Beaches, and for a moment, he knew his father was right, that this couldn't possibly last.

A tear rolled down his mother's cheek and dripped in his ear. He shook his shaggy hair like a dog and his parents laughed, and his father wiped away his mother's tear and they went into the apt, grinning and holding hands.

Of course, they never left the belfry after that.

∞

I can't remember what the last thing my mother said to me was. Do I remember her tucking me in and saying, "Good night, sleep tight, don't let the bedbugs bite," or was that something I saw on a vid? Was it a nervous command to wipe my shoes on the way in the door? Was her voice soft and sad, as it sometimes is in my memories, or was it brittle and angry, the way she often seemed after she stopped talking, as she banged around the tiny, two-room apt?

I can't remember.

My mother fell away from speech like a half-converted parishioner falling away from the faith: she stopped visiting the temple of verbiage in dribs and drabs, first missing the regular sermons—the daily niceties of Good morning and Good night and Be careful, Chet—then neglecting the major holidays, the Watch out!s and the Ouch!s and the answers to direct questions.

My father and I never spoke of it, and I didn't mention it to the other wild kids in the vertical city with whom I spent my days getting in what passed for trouble around the bat-house.

I did mention it to my counselor, The Amazing Robotron, so-called for the metal exoskeleton he wore to support his fragile body in Earth's hard gravity. But he didn't count, then.

∞

The reason that Chet can't pinpoint the moment his mother sealed her lips is because he was a self-absorbed little rodent in those days.

Not a cute freckled hellion. A miserable little shit who played hide-and-seek with the other miserable little shits in the bat-house, but played it violently, hide-and-seek-and-break-and-enter, hide-and-seek-and-smash-and-grab. The lot of them are amorphous, indistinguishable from each other in his memory, all that remains of all those clever little brats is the lingering impression of loud, boasting voices and sharp little teeth.

The Amazing Robotron was a fool in little Chet's eyes, an easy-to-bullshit, ineffectual lump whose company Chet had to endure for a mandatory hour every other day.

"Chet, you seem distr-acted to-day," The Amazing Robotron said in his artificial voice.

"Yah. You know. Worried about, uh, the future." Distracted by Debbie Carr's purse, filched while she sat in the sixty-eighth floor courtyard, talking with her stupid girlie friends. Debbie was the first girl from the gang to get tits, and now she didn't want to hang out with them anymore, and her purse was stashed underneath the base of a hollow planter outside The Amazing Robotron's apt, and maybe he could sneak it out under his shirt and find a place to dump it and sort through its contents after the session.

"What is it about the fu-ture that wo-rries you?" The Amazing Robotron was as unreadable as a pinball machine, something he resembled. Underneath, he was a collection of whip-like tentacles with a knot of sensory organs in the middle.

"You know, like, the whole fricken thing. Like if I leave here when I'm eighteen, will my folks be okay without me, and like that."

"Your pa-rents are able to take care of them-selves, Chet. You must con-cern your-self with you, Chet. You should do something con-struct-tive with your wo-rry, such as de-ciding on a ca-reer that will ful-fill you when you leave the Cen-ter." The Center was the short form for the long, nice name that no one ever used to describe the bat-house.

"I thought, like, maybe I could be, you know, a spaceship pilot or something."

"Then you must stu-dy math-e-mat-ics and phy-sics. If you like, Chet, I can re-quest ad-vanced in-struct-tion-al mat-e-rials for you."

"Sure, that'd be great. Thanks, Robotron."

"You are wel-come, Chet. I am glad to help. My own par-ent was in a Cen-ter on my world, you know. I un-der-stand how you feel. There is still time re-main-ing in your ses-sion. What else would you like to discuss?"

"My mother doesn't talk anymore. Nothing. Why is that?"

"Your mo-ther is..." The Amazing Robotron fumbled for a word, buried somewhere deep in the hypnotic English lexicon baked into its brain. "Your mo-ther has a prob-lem, and she needs your aff-ec-tion now more than e-ver. What-ev-er rea-son she has for her si-lence, it is not you. Your mo-ther and fa-ther love you, and dream of the day when you leave here and make your own way through the gal-ax-y."

Of course his parents loved him, he supposed, in an abstract kind of way. His mother, who hadn't worn anything but a bathrobe in months, whose face he couldn't picture behind his eyes but whose bathrobe he could visualize in its every rip and stain and fray. His father, who seemed to have forgotten how to groom himself, who spent his loud days in one of the bat-house's workshops, drinking beer with his buddies while they played with the arc welders. His parents loved him, he knew that.

"OK, right, thanks. I've gotta blow, 'K?"

"All-right. I will see you on Thurs-day, then?"

But Chet was already out the door, digging Debbie Carr's purse from under the planter, then running, doubled over the bulge it made in his shirt, hunting for a private space in the anthill.

∞

The entire north face of the bat-house was eyeless, a blind, windowless expanse of foam that seemed to curve as it approached infinity.

Some said it was an architectural error, others said it was part of the bat-house's heating scheme. Up in nosebleed country, on the 120th level, it was almost empty: sparsely populated by the very battiest bats, though as more and more humans were found batty, they pushed inexorably upwards.

Chet rode the lift to the 125th floor and walked casually to the end of the hallway. At this height, the hallways were bare foam, without the long-wear carpet and fake plants that adorned the low-altitude territories. He walked as calmly as he could to the very end of the northern hall, then hunkered down in the corner and spilled the purse.

Shit, but Debbie Carr was going girlie. The pile was all tampons and makeup and, ugh, a spare bra. A spare bra! I chuckled, and kept sorting. There were three pennies, enough to buy six chocolate bars in the black-market tuck-shop on the 75th floor. A clever little pair of folding scissors, their blades razor-sharp. I was using them to slit the lining of the purse when the door to 12525 opened, and the guy who thought he was Nicola Tesla emerged.

My palms slicked with guilty sweat, and the pile of Debbie's crap, set against the featureless foam corridor, seemed to scream its presence. I spun around, working my body into the corner, and held the little scissors like a dagger in my fist.

The guy who thought he was Nicola Tesla was clearly batty. He was wearing boxer-shorts and a tailcoat and had a halo of wild, greasy hair and a long, tangled beard, but even if he'd been wearing a suit and tie and had a trip to the barber's, I'd have known he was batty the minute I laid eyes on him. He didn't walk, he shambled, like he'd spent a long, long time on meds. His eyes, set in deep black pits of sleeplessness, were ferociously crazy.

He turned to stare at me.

"Hello, sonny. Do you like to swim?"

I stood in my corner, mute, trapped.

"I have an ocean in my apt. Maybe you'd like to try it? I used to love to swim in the ocean when I was a boy."

My feet moved without my willing them. An ocean in his apt? My feet wanted to know about this.

I entered his apt, and even my feet were too surprised to go on.

He had the biggest apt I'd ever seen. It spanned three quarters of the length of the bat-house, and was five storeys high. The spots where he'd dissolved the foam walls away with solvent were rough and uneven, and rings of foam encircled each of the missing storeys above. I couldn't imagine getting that much solvent: it was more tightly controlled than plutonium, the subject of countless action-adventure vids.

At one end of the apt stood a collection of tall, spiny apparatus, humming with electricity and sparking. They were remarkable, but their impact was lost in what lay at the other end.

The guy who thought he was Nicola Tesla had an ocean in his apt. It was a clear aquarium tank, fifteen meters long and nearly seventeen high, and eight meters deep. It was dominated by a massive, baroque coral reef, like a melting castle with misshapen brains growing out of it.

Schools of fish—bright as jellybeans—darted through the ocean's depths, swimming in and out of the softly waving plants. A thousand neon tetra, a flock of living quicksilver sewing needles, turned 90° in perfect unison, then did it again, and again, and again, describing a neat, angular box in the water.

"Isn't it beautiful? I'm using it in one of my experiments, but I also find it very *calming*."

∞

I hail a pedicab and the kids back on my adopted homeworld, with their accusing, angry words and stares vanish from my mind. The cabbie is about nineteen and muscular as hell, legs like treetrunks, clipped into the pedals. A flywheel spins between him and me, and his brakes store his momentum up in it every time he slows. On the two-hour ride into downtown Toronto, he never once comes to a full stop.

I've booked a room at the Royal York. I can afford it—the stipend I receive for the counseling work has been slowly accumulating in my bank account.

Downtown is all foam now, and "historical" shops selling authentic Earth crapola: reproductions of old newspapers, reproductions of old electronics, reproductions of old clothes and old food and other discarded cultural detritus. I see tall, clacking insect-creatures with walkman headphones across their stomachs. I see squat, rocky creatures smearing pizza slices onto their digestive membranes. I see soft, slithering creatures with Toronto Blue Jays baseball hats suspended in their jelly.

The humans I see are dressed in unisex coveralls, with discreet comms on their wrists or collars, and they don't seem to notice that their city is become a bestiary.

The cabby isn't even out of breath when we pull up at the Royal York, which, thankfully, is still clothed in its ancient dressed stone. We point our comms at each other and I squirt some money at him, adding a generous tip. His face, which had been wildly animated while he dodged the traffic on the long ride is a stony mask now, as though when at rest he entered a semiconscious sleep mode.

The doorman is dressed in what may or may not be historically accurate costume, though what period it is meant to represent is anyone's guess. He carries my bag to the check-in and I squirt more money at him. He wishes that I have a nice stay in Toronto, and I wish it, too.

At the check-in, I squirt my ID and still more money at the efficient young woman in a smart blazer, and another babu in period costume—those shoes look painful—carries my bag to the lift and presses the button.

We wait in strained silence and the lift makes its achingly slow progress towards us. There are no elevators on the planet I live on now—the wild gravity and wilder windstorms don't permit buildings of more than one story—but even if there were, they wouldn't be like this lift, like a human lift, like one of the fifty that ran the vertical length of the bat-house.

I nearly choke as we enter that lift. It has the smell of a million transient guests, aftershaves and perfumes and pheromones, and the stale recirc air I remember so well. I stifle the choke into my fist, fake a cough, and feel a self-consciousness I didn't know I had.

I'm worried that the babu knows that I grew up in the bat-house.

Now I can't make eye-contact with him. Now I can't seem to stand naturally, can't figure out where a not-crazy puts his hands and where a not-crazy puts his eyes. Little Chet and his mates liked to terrorize people in the lifts, play "who farted" and "I'm gonna puke" and "I have to pee" in loud sing-songs, just to watch the other bats squirm.

The guy who thought he was Nicola Tesla thought that these games were unfunny, unsophisticated and unappetizing and little Chet stopped playing them.

I squirt extra money at the babu, after he opens my windows and shows me the shitter and the vid's remote.

I unpack mechanically, my meager bag yielding more-meager clothes. I'd thought I'd buy more after earthfall, since the spaceports' version of human apparel wasn't, very. I realize that I'm wearing the same clothes I left Earth in, lo those years before. They're hardly the worse for wear—when I'm in my exoskeleton on my new planet, I don't bother with clothes.

∞

The ocean seemed too fragile to be real. All that caged water, held behind a flimsy-seeming sheet of clear foam, the corners joined with strips of thick gasket-rubber. Standing there at its base, Chet was terrified that it would burst and drown him—he actually felt the push of water, the horrid, dying wriggles of the fish as they were washed over his body.

"Say there, son. Hello?"

Chet looked up. Nicola Tesla's hair was standing on end, comically. He realized that his own long, shaggy hair was doing the same. The whole room felt electric.

"Are you all right?" He had a trace of an accent, like the hint of garlic in a salad dressing, an odd way of stepping on his vowels.

"Yeh, yeh, fine. I'm fine," Chet said.

"I am pleased to hear that. What is your name, son?"

"Chet. Affeltranger."

"I'm pleased to meet you. My name is Gaylord Ballozos, though that's not who I am. You see, I'm the channel for Nicola Tesla. Would you like to see a magic trick?"

Chet nodded. He wondered who Nicola Tesla was, and filed away the name Gaylord for making fun of, later. In doing so, he began to normalize the experience, to structure it as a story he could tell the other kids, after. The guy, the ocean, the hair. Gaylord.

A ball of lightning leapt from Tesla/Ballozos's fingertips and danced over their heads. It bounced around the room furiously, then stopped to hover in front of Chet. His clothes stood away from his body, snapping as though caught in a windstorm. Seen up close, the ball was an infinite pool of shifting electricity, like an ocean of energy. Tentatively, he reached out to touch it, and Tesla shouted "Don't!" and the ball whipped up and away, spearing itself on the point of one of the towers on the opposite side of the room.

It vanished, leaving a tangy, sharp smell behind.

The story Chet had been telling in his mind disappeared with it. He stood, shocked speechless.

The guy who thought he was Nicola Tesla chuckled a little, then started to laugh, actually doubling over and slapping his thighs.

"You can't *imagine* how long I've waited to show that trick to someone! Thank you, young Mr. Affeltranger! A million thanks to you, for your obvious appreciation."

Chet felt a giggle welling up in him, and he did laugh, and when his lips came together, a spark of static electricity leapt from their seam to his nose and made him jump, and laugh all the harder.

The guy came forward and pumped his arm in a dry handshake. "I can see that you and I are kindred spirits. You will have to come and visit again, very soon, and I will let you see more of my ocean, and maybe let you see 'Old Sparky,' too. Thank you, thank you, thank you, for dropping in."

And he ushered Chet out of his apt and closed the door, leaving him in the featureless hallway of the 125th storey.

∞

I had never been as nervous as I was the following Thursday, when my regular appointment with The Amazing Robotron rolled around again. I hadn't spoken of the guy who thought he was Nicola Tesla to any of my gang, and of course not to my parents, but somehow, I felt like I might end up spilling to The Amazing Robotron.

I don't know why I was worried. The guy hadn't asked me to keep it a secret, after all, and I had never had any problem holding my tongue around The Amazing Robotron before.

"Hel-lo, Chet. How have you been?"

"I've been OK."

"Have you been stud-y-ing math-e-mat-ics and phys-ics? I had the supp-le-ment-al mat-e-rials de-liv-er-ed to your apt yes-ter-day."

"No, I haven't. I don't think I wanna be a pilot no more. One of my buds tole me that you end up all fugged up with time an' that, that you come home an' it's the next century an' everyone you know is dead."

"That is one thing that hap-pens to some ex-plor-a-tor-y pilots, Chet. Have you thought a-bout any o-ther poss-i-bil-i-ties?"

"Kinda. I guess." I tried not to think about the 125th story and the ocean. I was thinking so hard, I stopped thinking about what I was saying to The Amazing Robotron. "Maybe I could be a counselor, like, and help kids."

The Amazing Robotron turned into a pinball machine again, an unreadable and motionless block. Silent for so long I thought he was gone, dead as a sardine inside his tin can. Then, he twitched both of his arms, like he was shivering. Then his robot-voice came out of the grille on his face. "I think that you would be a ve-ry good coun-sel-or, Chet."

"Yeh?" I said. It was the first time that The Amazing Robotron had told me he thought I'd be good at anything. Hell, it was the first time he'd expressed *any* opinion about anything I'd said.

"Yes, Chet. Be-ing a coun-sel-or is a ve-ry good way to help your-self un-der-stand what we have done to you by put-ting you in the Cen-ter."

I couldn't speak. My Mom, before she fell silent, had often spoken about how unfair it was for me to be stuck here, because of something that she or my father had done. But my father never seemed to notice me, and the teachers on the vid made a point of not mentioning the bat-house—like someone trying hard not to notice a stutter or a wart, and you *knew* that the best you could hope for from them was pity.

"Be-ing a coun-sel-or is ve-ry hard, Chet. But coun-sel-ors sometimes get a spec-ial re-ward. Some-times, we get to help. Do you re-ally want to do this?"

"Yeh. Yes. I mean, it sounds good. You get to travel, right?"

The Amazing Robotron's idiot-lights rippled, something I came to recognize as a chuckle, later. "Yes. Tra-vel is part of the job. I sug-gest that you start by ex-am-in-ing your friends. See if you can fi-gure out why they do what they do."

I've used this trick on my kids. What do I know about their psychology? But you get one, you convince it to explain the rest to you. It helps. Counselors are always from another world—by the time the first generation raised in a bat-house has grown old enough, there aren't any bats' children left to counsel on their homeworld.

∞

I take room-service; pizza and beer in an ice-bucket: pretentious, but better than sharing a dining-room with the menagerie. Am I becoming a racist?

No, no. I just need to focus on things human, during this vacation.

The food is disappointing. It's been years since I lay awake at night, craving a slice and a brew and a normal gravity and a life away from the bats. Nevertheless, the craving remained, buried, and resurfaced when I went over the room-service menu. By the time the dumbwaiter in my room chimed, I was practically drooling.

But by the time I take my second bite, it's just pizza and a brew.

I wonder if I will ever get to sleep, but when the time comes, my eyes close and if I dream, I don't remember it.

I get up and dress and send up for eggs and real Atlantic salmon and brown toast and a pitcher of coffee, then find myself unable to eat any of it. I make a sandwich out of it and wrap it in napkins and stuff it into my day-pack along with a water-bottle and some sun-block.

It's a long walk up to the bat-house, but I should make it by nightfall.

∞

Chet was up at 6h the next morning. His mom was already up, but she never slept that he could tell. She was clattering around the kitchen in her housecoat, emptying the cupboards and then re-stacking their contents for the thousandth time. She shot him a look of something between fear and affection as he pulled on his shorts and a T-shirt, and he found himself hugging her waist. For a second, it felt like she softened into his embrace, like she was going to say something, like it was normal, and then she picked up a plate and rubbed it with a towel and put it back into the cupboard.

Chet left without saying a word.

The bat-house breathed around him, a million farts and snores and whispered words. A lift was available almost before he took his finger off the summon button. "125," he said.

Chet walked to the door of the guy who thought he was Nicola Tesla and started to knock, then put his hands down and sank down into a squat, with his back against it.

He must have dozed, because the next thing he knew, he was tipping over backwards into the apt, and the guy who thought he was Nicola Tesla was standing over him, concerned.

"Are you all right, son?"

Chet stood, dusted himself off and looked at the floor. "Sorry, I didn't want to disturb you…"

"But you wanted to come back and see more. Marvelous! I applaud your curiosity, young sir. I have just taken the waters—perhaps you would like to try?" He gestured at the ocean.

"You mean, swim in it?"

"If you like. Myself, I find a snorkel and mask far superior. My set is up on the rim, you're welcome to them, but I would ask you to chew a stick of this before you get in." He tossed Chet a pack of gum. "It's an invention of my own—chew a stick of that, and you can*not* transmit any nasty bugs in your saliva for forty-eight hours. I hold a patent for it, of course, but my agents report that it has been met with crashing indifference in the Great Beyond."

Chet had been swimming before, in the urinary communal pools on the tenth and fifteenth levels, horsing around naked with his mates. Nudity was not a big deal for the kids of the bat-house—the kind of adult who you wouldn't trust in such circumstances didn't end up in bat-houses—the bugouts had a different place for them.

"Go on, lad, give it a try. It's simply marvelous, I tell you!"

Unsteadily, Chet climbed the spiral stairs leading up to the tank, clutching the handrail, chewing the gum, which fizzed and sparked in his mouth. At the top, there was a small platform. Self-consciously, he stripped, then pulled on the mask and snorkel that hung from a peg.

"Tighten the straps, boy!" the guy who thought he was Nicola Tesla shouted, from far, far below. "If water gets into the mask, just push at the top and blow out through your nose!"

Chet awkwardly lowered himself into the water. It was warm—blood temperature—and salty, and it fizzled a little on his skin, as though it, too, were electric.

He kept one hand on the snorkel, afraid that it would tip and fill with water, and then, slowly, slowly, relaxed on his belly, mask in the water, arms by his side.

My god! It was like I was flying! It was like all the dreams I'd ever had, of flying, of hovering over an alien world, of my consciousness taking flight from my body and sailing through the galaxy.

My hands were by my sides, out of view of the mask, and my legs were behind me. I couldn't see any of my body. My view stretched 8m down, an impossible, dizzying height. A narrow, elegant angelfish swam directly beneath me, and tickled my belly with one of its fins as it passed under.

I smiled, a huge grin, and it broke the seal on my mask, filling it with water. Calmly, as though I'd been doing it all my life, I pressed the top of my mask to my forehead and blew out through my nose. My mask cleared of water.

I floated.

The only sound was my breathing, and distant, metallic *pink!s* from the ocean's depths. A school of iridescent purple fish swam past me, and I lazily kicked out after them, following them to the edge of the coral reef that climbed the far wall of the ocean. When I reached it, I was overwhelmed by its complexity, millions upon millions of tiny little suckers depending from weird branches and misshapen brains and stone roses.

I held my breath.

And I heard nothing. Not a sound, for the first time in all the time I had been in the bat-house—no distant shouts and mutters. I was alone, in a vast, personal silence, in a private ocean. My pulse beat under my skin. Tiny fish wriggled in the coral, tearing at the green fuzz that grew over it.

Slowly, I turned around and around. The ocean-wall that faced into the apt was silvered on this side, reflecting back my little pale body to me. My head pounded, and I finally inhaled, and the sound of my breathing, harsh through the snorkel, rang in my ears.

I spent an age in the water, holding my breath, chasing the fish, disembodied, a consciousness on tour on an alien world.

The guy who thought he was Nicola Tesla brought me back. He waited on the rim of the tank until I swam near enough for him to touch, then he tapped me on the shoulder. I stuck my head up, and he said, "Time to get out, boy, I need to use the ocean."

Reluctantly, I climbed out. He handed me a towel.

I felt like I was still flying, atop the staircase on the ocean's edge. I felt like I could trip slowly down the stairs, never quite touching them. I pulled on my clothes, and they felt odd to me.

Carefully, forcing myself to grip the railing, I descended. The guy who thought he was Nicola Tesla stood at my side, not speaking, allowing me my reverie.

My hair was drying out, and starting to raise skywards, and the guy who thought he was Nicola Tesla went over to his apparatus and flipped a giant knife switch. The ocean stirred, a puff of sand rose from its bottom, and then, the coral on the ocean's edge *moved.*

It squirmed and danced and writhed, startling the fish away from it, shedding layers of algae in a green cloud.

"It's my latest idea. I've found the electromagnetic frequencies that the various coral resonate on, and by using those as a carrier wave, I can stimulate them into tremendously accelerated growth. Moreover, I can alter their electromagnetic valences, so that, instead of calcium salts, they use other minerals as their building-blocks."

He grinned hugely, and seemed to want Chet to say something. Chet didn't understand any of it.

"Well, don't you see?"

"Nuh."

"I can use coral to concentrate trace gold and platinum and any other heavy-metal you care to name out of the seas. I can prospect in the very water itself!" He killed the switch. The coral stopped their dance abruptly, and the new appendages they'd grown dropped away, tumbling gracefully to the ocean's floor. "You see? Gold, platinum, lead. I dissolved a kilo of each into the water last night, microscopic flakes. In five minutes, my coral has concentrated it all."

The stumps where the minerals had dropped away were jagged and sharp, and painful looking.

"It doesn't even harm the fish!"

∞

Chet's playmates seemed as strange as fish to him. They met up on the 87th level, where there was an abandoned apt with a faulty lock. Some of them seemed batty themselves, standing in corners, staring at the walls, tracing patterns that they alone could see. Others seemed too confident ever to be bats—they shouted and boasted to each other, got into shoving matches that escalated into knock-out brawls and then dissolved into giggles. Chet found himself on the sidelines, an observer.

One boy, whose father hung around the workshops with Chet's father, was industriously pulling apart the warp of the carpet, rolling it into a ball. When the ball reached a certain size, he snapped the loose end, tucked it in and started another.

A girl whose family had been taken to the bat-house all the way from a reservation near Sioux Lookout was telling loud lies about home, about tremendous gun-battles fought out with the Ontario Provincial Police and huge, glamorous casinos where her mother had dealt blackjack to millionaire high-rollers, who tucked thousand dollar tips into her palm. About her bow and arrow and her rifle and her horses. Nobody believed her stories, and they made fun of her behind her back, but they listened when she told them, spellbound.

What was her name, anyway?

There were two boys, one followed the other everywhere. The followee was tormenting the follower, as usual, smacking him in the back of the head, then calling him a baby, goading him into hitting back, dodging easily, and retaliating viciously.

Chet thought that he understood some of what was going on. Maybe he'd be able to explain it to The Amazing Robotron.

∞

I never thought I'd say this, but I miss my exoskeleton. My feet ache, my legs ache, my ass aches, and I'm hot and thirsty and my waterbottle is empty. I'm not even past Bloor Street, not even a tenth of the way to the bat-house.

∞

The Amazing Robotron seemed thoughtful as I ratted out my chums. "So, I think they need each other. The big one needs the little one, to feel important. The little one needs the big one, so that he can feel useful. Is that right?"

"It is ve-ry per-cep-tive, Chet. When I was young, I had a sim-i-lar friend-ship with an-other. It—no, *she*—was the lit-tle one, and I was the big one. Her pa-rent died be-fore we came of age, and she left the Cen-ter, and when she came back to visit, a long time la-ter, we were re-ver-sed—I felt smal-ler but good, and spec-ial be-cause she told me all a-bout the out-side."

Something clicked inside me then. I saw myself inside The Amazing Robotron's exoskeleton, and he in my skin, our roles reversed. It lasted no longer than a lightning flash, but in that flash, I suddenly knew that I could talk to The Amazing Robotron, and that he would understand.

I felt so smart all of a sudden. I felt like The Amazing Robotron and I were standing outside the bat-house, *in* it but not *of* it, and we shared a secret insight into the poor, crazy bastards we were cooped up with.

"I don't really like anyone here. I don't like my Dad—he's always shout-ing, and I think he's the reason we ended up here. He's batshit—he gets angry too easy. And my Mom is batshit now, even if she wasn't batshit before, because of him. I don't feel like their son. I feel like I just share an apt with these two crazy people I don't like very much. And none of my mates are any good, either. They're all either like my Dad—loud and crazy, or like my Mom, quiet and crazy. Everyone's crazy."

"That may be true, Chet. But you can still like cra-zy peo-ple."

"Do *you* like 'em?"

The Amazing Robotron's idiot lights rippled. *Gotcha*, I thought.

"I do not like them, Chet. They are loud and cra-zy and they on-ly think of them-selves."

I laughed. It was so refreshing not to be lied to. My skin was all tight from the dried saltwater, and that felt good, too.

"My Dad, the other day? He came home and was all, 'This is a con-spiracy to drive us out of our house. It's because we bought a house with damn high ceilings. Some big damn alien wanted to live there, so they put us here. It's because I did such a good job on the ceilings!' Which is so stupid, 'cause the ceilings in our old house weren't no higher than the ceilings here, and besides, Dad screwed up all the plaster when he was trying to fix it up, and it was always cracking.

"And then he starts talking about what's really bugging him, which is that some guy at the workshop took his favorite drill and he couldn't finish his big project without it. So he got into a fight with the guy, and got the drill and then he finished his big, big project, and brought it home, and you know what it was? A *pencil-holder!* We don't even *have* any pencils! He is so screwed up."

And The Amazing Robotron's lights rippled again, and a huge weight lifted from my shoulders. I didn't feel ashamed of the maniacs that gave me life—I saw them as pitiful subjects for my observations. I laughed again, and that must have been the most I'd laughed since they put us in the bat-house.

∞

I'm getting my sea-legs. I hope. My mouth is pasty, and salty, and sweat keeps running down into my eyes. I never even began to realize how much support the exoskeleton's jelly-suspension lent me.

But I've made it to Eglinton, and that's nearly a third of the way, and to celebrate, I stop in at a coffee-shop and drink a whole pitcher of lemonade while sitting by the air-conditioner.

I got the word that they were tearing down the bat-house only two weeks ago. The message came by priority email from The Amazing Robotron: all the bats were dead, or enough of them anyway that the rest could be relocated to less expensive quarters. It was barely enough notice to get my emergency leave application in, to book a ticket back to Earth, and to finally become a murderer all the way.

Damn, I hope I know what I'm doing.

∞

The guy who thought he was Nicola Tesla told me all kinds of stories, and I was sure he was lying to me, but when I checked out the parts of his story that I could, they all turned out to be true.

"I don't actually *need* to be here. I've come here to get away from all the treachery, the deceit, the filthy pursuit of the dollar. As though I need more money! I invented foam! Oh, sure, the Process likes to take credit for it, but if you look up the patent, guess who owns it?

"Master Affeltranger, you may not realize it to look at me, but I have some *very* important friends, out there in the Great Beyond. With important friends, you can make a whole block of apts simply disappear from the record-books. You can make tremendous energy consumption vanish, likewise."

He spoke as he tinkered with his apparatus, which hummed alarmingly and occasionally sent a tortured arc of electricity into the guy who thought he was Nicola Tesla's chest.

It happened three times in a row, and he stamped his foot in frustration, and said, "Oh, *do* cut it out," apparently to one of his machines.

I'd been jumping every time he got zapped, but this time, I had to giggle. He whirled on me. "I am not trying to be *amusing*. One thing you people never realize is that the current has a *will*, it has a *mind*, and you have to keep it in check with a firm hand."

I shook my head a little, not understanding. He waved a hand at me, frustrated, and said, "Oh, go have a swim. I don't have time to argue with a child."

I climbed into the ocean, and the silence embraced me, and the water tingled with electricity, and my consciousness floated away from my body and soared over an alien world. Like a broken circuit, I disconnected from the world around me.

∞

Chet's father came home with a can of beer in his hand and the rest of the six-pack in his gut. He walked over to the vid, where Chet was researching the life of Nicola Tesla, which took forever, since he had to keep linking back to simple tutorials on physics, history, and electrical engineering.

Chet's father stooped and took the remote out of Chet's hands and opened up a bookmarked docu-drama about the coming of the bugouts. Chet opened his mouth to protest, and his father shouted him down before he could speak. "Not one word, you hear me? Not! One! Word! I've had a shithole day and I wanna relax."

Chet's mother dropped a plastic tumbler, which bounced twice, and rolled to Chet's toe. He stepped over it, walked out the door, and took the elevator to the 125th floor.

Chet burst into the guy who thought he was Nicola Tesla's apt and screamed. Nicola Tesla was strapped into a heavy wooden chair, with a metal hood over his head. Arcs of electricity danced over his body, and he jerked and thrashed against the leather straps that bound his limbs. Unthinking, Chet ran forward and grabbed the buckle that bound his wrist, and a giant's fist smashed into him, hurling him across the room.

When he came to, the electric arcs were gone, but the guy who thought he was Nicola Tesla was motionless in his straps, under his hood.

Carefully, Chet came to his feet, and saw that the toe of his right sneaker had been blown out, leaving behind charred canvas. His foot hurt—burned.

He hobbled to the chair and gingerly prodded it, then jerked his hand back, though he hadn't been shocked. He bit his lip and stared. The wood was quite weathered and elderly, though it had been oiled and had a rich, well-cared-for finish. The leather straps were nightmarishly thick, gripping the guy who thought he was Nicola Tesla at the bicep and wrist, at the thigh and calf and ankle. Livid bruises were already spreading at their edges.

Chet was struck by a sudden urge to climb into the ocean and *stay* there. Just *stay* there.

Under the hood, the guy who thought he was Nicola Tesla groaned. Chet gave an involuntary squeak and jumped a little. The guy who thought he was Nicola Tesla's body snapped tense. "Who's there?" he said, his voice muffled by the hood.

"It's me, Chet."

"Chet? Damn. Damn, damn, damn." His right hand bent nearly double at the wrist and teased the buckle of the strap free. With one hand free, the guy who thought he was Nicola Tesla quickly undid the straps on his upper body, then lifted away the hood. He pointedly did not look at Chet as he doubled over and undid the straps on his legs and ankles.

Gingerly, he stood and stretched, then sighed tremendously.

"Chet, Chet, Chet. I hope I didn't frighten you too badly. This is Old Sparky, an exact replica of the electric chair at Sing-Sing Prison in New York. Edison, thief and charlatan that he was, insisted that his DC current was safer than my AC, and they built a chair that used my beautiful current to execute criminals, by the hundreds.

"Nicola Tesla and I became one when I was eight years old, and I received a tremendous shock from an electrified fence. I was stuck to it, glued by the current, and after a few moments, I just relaxed into the current—befriended it, if you will. That's when the spirit of Nicola Tesla, a-wandering through the wires for all the years since his death, infused my body.

"So now I use Old Sparky here to recharge—please forgive the expression—my connection with the current. I once spent eight years in the chair, when I needed to disappear for a while. When I woke, I hadn't aged at all—I didn't even need to shave! What do you think of that?"

Chet was staring in horror at him. "You electrocute yourself? On purpose?"

"Why, yes! Think of it as a trick I do, if it makes you feel better. I could show you how to do it..." he trailed off, but a look of hunger had passed over his face.

∞

I get all kinds of access to bat-house records from the vid in my apt on my new world. No one named Gaylord Ballozos ever lived in any bat-house. Apt 12525, and the five above it, were never occupied. The records say that the locks have never been used, the doors never opened. It won't be searched when they evacuate the bat-house.

That's what the records say, anyway.

Electricity gives me the willies. The zaps of static from the dry air of the FTL I took home to Earth made me scream, little-boy squeaks that made the other passengers jump.

I don't remember that it was ever this hot in Toronto, even in the summer. The sky is all overcast, so maybe it's a temperature inversion. Up here at Steeles Avenue, I'm so dehydrated that I spend a whole dime on a magnum of still water and power-chug it, though you're not supposed to drink that way. Almost there.

∞

The other kids in the abandoned apt on the 87th floor ignored me. They'd been paying less and less attention to me, ever since I started spending my afternoons up on 125, and I was getting a reputation as a keener for all the time I spent with The Amazing Robotron.

That suited me fine; the corner of the gutted kitchen was as private a space as I was going to find in the bat-house. I had the apparatus that Nicola Tesla had given me plugged into the AC outlet under the sink. I closed my eyes and breathed deeply, concentrating on the moments after my breath left my chest, that calm like the ocean's silence. Smoothly, I reached out and grasped the handle of the apparatus and squeezed.

The first time I tried this, under Nicola Tesla's supervision, I'd jerked my hand away and squeezed it between my legs as soon as the current shot through me. Now, though, I could keep squeezing, slowly increasing the voltage and amperage, relaxing into the involuntary tension in my muscles.

I'd gotten so good at it that I'd started using the timer—I could lean into the current forever without it. I had it set for three hours, but when the current died, it felt like no time at all had passed. I probed around my consciousness for any revelation, but no spirit had come into my body during the exercise. The guy who thought he was Nicola Tesla didn't know if there were any other spirits in the wire, but it stood to reason that if there was one, there had to be more.

I stood, and felt incredibly calm and balanced and centered and I floated past the other kids. It was time for my session with The Amazing Robotron.

"Chet, how are you fee-ling?"

"I'm well, thank you." Nicola Tesla spoke well and carefully, and I'd started to ape him.

"And what would you like to dis-cuss to-day?"

"I don't really have anything to talk about, honestly. Everything is fine."

"That is good. Do you have any new ob-ser-va-tions about your friends?"

"I'm sorry, no. I haven't been paying much attention lately."

"Why hav-en't you?"

"It just doesn't interest me, sorry."

"Why does-n't it in-ter-est you?"

"I just don't care about them, to be frank."

The Amazing Robotron was absolutely still for a moment. "Are things well with your par-ents, too?"

"The same as always. I think they've found their niches." *Find your niche* was an expression I'd pirated from the guy who thought he was Nicola Tesla. I was very proud of it.

"In that case, why don't we end this mee-ting?"

I was surprised. The Amazing Robotron always demanded his full hour. "I'll see you on Wednesday, then?"

"I'm af-raid not, Chet. I will be gone for a few months—I have to return home. There will be a sub-sti-tute coun-sel-or arri-ving next Monday."

My calm center shattered. Sweat sprang out on my palms. "What? You're leaving? How can you be leaving?"

"I'm so-rry, Chet. There is an em-er-gen-cy at home. I'll be back as soon as I can."

"Frick that! How can you go? What'll I do if you don't come back? You're the only one I can talk to!"

"I'm so-rry, Chet. I have to go."

"If you gave a shit, you'd stay. You can't just leave me here!" I knew as I said it that it didn't make any sense, but a picture sprang into my mind, one that I'd been carrying without knowing it for a long time: The Amazing Robotron and me as an adult, walking away from the bat-house, with suitcases, leaving together, forever. I felt a sob hiccough in my throat.

"I will re-turn, Chet. I did-n't wish to up-set you."

"Frick that! I don't give a shit if you come back, asshole."

∞

Chet went straight to 87 and plugged in to the apparatus. He didn't set the timer, and he stayed plugged in for nearly two days, when two fighting boys tumbled into him and knocked his hand away. He was centered and numb again, and didn't have any sense of the intervening time. He didn't even have to pee. He wondered if he was trying to commit suicide.

He checked his comm and got the date, noticed with distant surprise that it was two days later, and wandered up to 125.

The guy who thought he was Nicola Tesla shouted a distant "Come in" when Chet tapped on the door. He was playing with his ocean again. Chet felt his hair float up off his shoulders. He stopped and watched the coral squirm and dance.

"I spent nearly two days on the apparatus," Chet said.

"Eh? Very good, very good. You're progressing nicely."

"My counselor has left. He had to go home."

"Yes? Well, there you are."

"What were your parents like?"

"Nicola Tesla's father was a bishop, and his mother was an illiterate, though she was a gifted memnist and taught me much about visualization."

"No, I mean *your* parents. Mister and Missus Ballozos. What were *they* like?"

The guy who thought he was Nicola Tesla shut down the ocean and watched the lumps of ore tumble to the sand. "Why do you want to know about *them?* Are you having some sort of trouble at home?" he asked impatiently, not looking away from the ocean.

"No reason," Chet said. "I have to go home now."

"Yes, fine."

∞

"The hell have you been, boy?" Chet's father said, when he came through door. His father was in front of the vid, wearing shorts and a filthy T-shirt, holding the remote in one hand. Chet's mother was sitting at the window, staring out into the clouds.

"Out. Around. I'm okay, okay?"

"It's not okay. You can't just run around like some kind of animal. Sit the hell down and tell me where you've been. Your counselor was here looking for you."

"Robotron? He was here?"

"Yes he was here! And I had to tell him I didn't know where my damn kid was! How do you think that makes me look? You know how worried your mother was?"

Chet's mother didn't stir from her post by the window, but she flinched when Chet's father spoke. Chet swallowed hard.

"What did he want?"

"Never mind that! Sit the hell down and tell me where you've been and what the hell you thought you were doing!"

Chet sat beside his father and stared at his hands. He knew he could outwait his father. After half an hour, Chet's father turned the vid on. Four long hours later, he switched it off, and went to bed.

Chet's mother finally turned away from the now-dark window. She reached into the pocket of her grimy bathrobe and withdrew an envelope and handed it to Chet, then turned and went to the apt's other room to sleep.

My name was on the outside of the envelope, in rough script, written with awkward exoskeleton manipulators. I broke its seal, and it folded out into a single flat sheet of paper.

DEAR CHET, it began. At the bottom of it was a complex scrawl that I recognized from the front of The Amazing Robotron's exoskeleton. It must be some kind of signature.

> DEAR CHET,
>
> I AM SORRY TO HAVE TO LEAVE YOU SO SUDDENLY, AND WITHOUT ANYONE ELSE TO TALK TO. THERE IS AN EMERGENCY AT MY HOME, BUT I WOULDN'T GO IF I DIDN'T BELIEVE THAT YOU WERE ABLE TO HANDLE MY ABSENCE. YOU ARE A VERY PERCEPTIVE AND STRONG YOUNG MAN, AND YOU WILL BE ABLE TO MANAGE IN MY ABSENCE. I WILL BE BACK, YOU KNOW.
>
> YOU WILL BE ALL RIGHT. I PROMISE.
>
> THIS ISN'T EASY FOR ME TO DO, EITHER. IT MAY BE THAT I AM THE ONLY ONE YOU CAN TALK TO HERE AT THE CENTER. IT IS LIKEWISE TRUE THAT YOU ARE THE ONLY ONE I CAN TALK TO.
>
> I WILL MISS YOU, MY FRIEND CHET.

The writing was childish, with many line-outs and corrections. Reading it, I heard it not in The Amazing Robotron's halting mechanical speech, but in my own voice.

I didn't cry. I held the letter tight in my hand, as tight as I ever held the apparatus, and leaned into it, like it was a source of strength.

∞

They haven't even started work on the bat-house. There are bugout saucers hovering all around it, with giant foam-solvent tanks mounted under their bellies. A small crowd has gathered.

I take off my jacket and lay it on the strip of grass by the sidewalk across the street from the bat-house. I pull off my soaked T-shirt and feel a rare breeze across my chest, as soothing as a kiss on a fevered forehead. I ball up the shirt, then lay down on my jacket, using the shirt as a pillow.

The bat-house is empty, its eyes staring blind, vertical to infinity. The grotty sculpture out front is gone already, and with it, the sign with the polite, never-used name. It is now just the bat-house.

I check my comm. The dissolving of the bat-house is scheduled for less than an hour from now.

∞

The new counselor was no damn good. It wore a different exoskeleton, a motorized gurney on wheels with three buzzing antigrav manipulators that floated constantly around the apt, tasting the air. It called itself "Tom." I didn't call it anything, and I limited my answers to it to monosyllables.

The next time I came on the guy who was Nicola Tesla in his chair, the letter was in my pocket. I took a long swim in the ocean, and then I stripped off my mask and spit out the snorkel, took a deep breath and dove until my ears felt like they were going to burst. I stared at my reflection in the silvered wall of the tank. Through the distortion of the water and the sting of the salt, my body was indistinct and clothed in quicksilver, surrounded by schools of alien, darting fish. I didn't recognize myself, but I didn't take my eyes away until my lungs were ready to burst and I resurfaced.

The guy who thought he was Nicola Tesla was still thrashing away at his straps when I climbed down from the ocean's top. At one side of Old Sparky, there was a timer, like the one on my apparatus, and a knife-switch for timed and untimed sessions.

I stared at him. My life unrolled before me, a life distanced and remote from the world around me, a life trapped in my own deepening battiness. Before I could think about what I was doing, I flipped the switch from "timed" to "untimed." I took one last look at the ocean, looked again at Nicola Tesla, my friend and seducer, stuck to his chair until someone switched it off again, and left the 125th floor.

∞

I took the apparatus apart in the kiddy workshop, stripped it to a collection of screws and wires and circuit boards, then carefully smashed each component with a hammer until it was in thousands of tiny pieces.

It took me two days to do it right, and not a moment passed when I didn't nearly run upstairs and switch off Tesla's chair.

And not a moment passed when I didn't visualize Tesla's wrath, his betrayal, his anger, when I unbuckled him.

And not a moment passed when I didn't wish I could plug in the apparatus, swim in the ocean, take myself away from the world and the world away from me.

The Amazing Robotron returned at the end of the second day.

"Chet, I am glad to see you a-gain."

I bit my lip and choked on tears of relief. "I need to leave here, Robotron. I can't stay another minute. Please, get me out of here. I'll do anything. I'll run away. Get me out, get me out, get me out!" I was babbling, sniveling and crying, and I begged all the harder.

"Why do you want to leave right now?"

"I—I can't take it anymore. I can't *stand* being here. I'd rather be in prison than in here anymore."

"When I was young, I left the Cen-ter I was rais-ed in to attend counsel-ing school. You are near-ly old e-nough to go now. May-be your parents would let you go?"

I knew he had found the only way out.

I started work on my father. I wheedled and begged and demanded, and he just laughed. For three whole days, I used begging as a way to avoid thinking of Tesla. For three days, my father shook his head.

I cried myself to sleep and wallowed in my guilt every night, and when I woke, I cried more. I stopped leaving the apt. I stopped eating. My mother and I sat all day, staring out the window. I stopped talking.

One morning, after my father had left, I dragged a stool to the window and pressed my face against it. My mother clattered around behind me.

"Go," my mother said.

I gave a squeak and turned around. My mother had folded my clothes in a neat pile and had laid a canvas bag beside it. She had the vid remote in her hand, and on the screen was a waiver for me to go to school. We locked eyes for a moment, and I moved to go to her, but she turned and stormed into the kitchen and started to clean the cupboards, silent again.

I left that day.

∞

The saucers lift off to-the-second on-time. The crowd, which has grown, sighs collectively as the saucers disappear over the haze, then a fine mist of solvent rains down on our heads. It's as salty as sea-water, and the bathhouse trembles as it begins to melt. Streams of salty water course down its sides.

The top of the building comes into view, the saucers chasing it down as it dissolves, spraying a steady blast of solvent.

I tense as the building's top reaches what I estimate to be 150. My calves bunch and my breath catches in my chest. I feel like I'm drowning, and the building's top crawls downwards, and my feet are sloshing to the ankles in dissolved foam, that runs off into the sewers.

I stay tense until the building's top is far beneath what *must* be 125, then I exhale in a whoof of air. My head spins, and I brace my hands against my thighs. I'm not looking up when it happens, as a result.

The first sign is when the great tide of green, scummy, plant-stinking water courses down over us, soaking us to the skin, blinding me and sending me reeling in reverie. Did I see hunks of dead, petrified coral crashing around me, or did I imagine it?

A brief second later the building's top emits a bolt of lightning that broke even Tesla's record for man-made lightning, recorded at nearly a kilometer in length. A clap of thunder accompanies it, louder than any sound I have ever heard, and it its wake I am perfectly deaf, submerged in silence.

The finger of lightning crawls through space like a broken-back rattler, and my hair rises from my shoulders. In the presence of so much current, I should be petrified, but it is magnificent. The finger seeks and seeks, then contacts one of the saucers and literally blasts it out of the sky. It plummets in slow-motion, and as it does, the building's top descends even further, and I *swear* I see the chair falling from the building's edge, and the man strapped inside it had not aged a day in all the lifetimes gone by.

∞

Chet's comm died somewhere in the lightning strike, but the emergency crews that took him away and looked in his ears and poked him in the chest and gave him pills take him back to the Royal York in a saucer, bridging the distance in a few minutes, touching down on Front Street. The Royal York's doorman doesn't bat an eye as he gets the door for him.

The elevator ride is fine. He is still wrapped in the silence of his deafness, but it's a comforting, *centering* silence.

Once Chet is back in his room, he fires up the vid and starts writing a letter to The Amazing Robotron. ∞

Nightfall

∞ Susan A. Manchester ∞

"Even if children fall and stars
and elephants and dark spaces
from the sky, it does not matter.
Eventually, there will be
a soft landing. Eventually,
they ride the wave of some note
from a golden trumpet sustained
loud and long. Even the black
holes forming craters on the earth
cannot matter, if the sound of violins
cushions the fall. Each landing,
no more than a ripple on the pond,
finally touches every shore
at the same time. It is and
always will be all right
for anything to fall from the sky.
Trust me," the Night said. ∞

Rice Lake

∞ Ursula Pflug ∞

ALEXIA CALLED HER FRIEND JILL. "Jill," she said, "I want to come visit for the week-end. Can you come pick me up?"

"Sure," Jill said. "There's a party at Elizabethville. Six o'clock."

"Bye."

Elizabethville, a tiny village near Port Hope. Their friend Raven didn't live there any more. Moved to the city, gone down to T.O., the Big Smoke, to pursue his career as a freelance programmer. An opposite move to her own; she and Frank were from Toronto, just as Port Hope was Raven's home town.

Winter parties at Elizabethville; Alexia and Frank used to go there when Gerrard was four, the baby Sarah a year or two old, still nursing. They'd stay over, in one of the many upstairs bedrooms, the doors each painted a different primary colour. Alexia, seeing them, had thought she wanted to paint her doors like that. Now Raven was gone, and Rita and Andrea lived there. Still had parties in that house that was always, in Alexia's memories, even the summer ones, surrounded by faded brown earth, patched snow, winter trees.

Raven gone. Everything goes. It had been a year of breaking circles; not just her friend leaving for the city but couples Alexia loved splitting up and moving far away from each other, far from her.

One winter her daughter Sarah, then two, had surprised her, picked up an old birthday invitation off the floor, pretended to read, saying: "It says we're invited to a party at Elizabethville on Saturday." And an hour later Raven had called, inviting them.

Alexia had looked at her daughter, astonished. Another Voyager then. Not much she could do about it, either way, although she hadn't been Played herself in years. The Game. Only Jill, of all their old Voyager circle, still had huge circles she'd drawn on the earth in front of her cabin, barely visible under the new grown, unmowed grass, in different pastel colours of children's sidewalk chalk. Circles. They'd never faded, even after years of rain. When the grass, unwatered, went bald and dry in mid-July you could still trace their thick outlines. What had

Jill used to draw those circles, that they'd last like that? Not sidewalk chalk after all, but memory. Her memories of The Game.

Alexia remembered a time she'd been Played with her father. That had been about circles too. Perhaps eleven, she'd gone with him to the snowy school yard across the street from the Toronto house where they lived. Circles they'd drawn in the snow, or perhaps uncovered. The circles had caught fire. She'd never remembered it before that moment, the way she always forgot when she'd been played by The Game. That time, Alexia suddenly understood, had been about gathering strength to survive her mother's coming death, that neither of them knew about. And yet The Game had known; The Game always knew. Why else would it have chosen that moment to Play them, making fire circles in snow?

But there was Jill's VW bus door slamming in the driveway; Alexia grabbed earrings and her green jean jacket, shouted good-bye to Frank and the kids.

∞

The two women poked through Jill's junk. Jill had acres and acres of junk: fridges, toasters, stoves, nails, screws, ironing boards, doors, windows, shoes, toy tractors, motors, screen doors, window frames, chairs, tables, beds, skis.

Jill's father collected it all, slowly, over many years, from the dump and out of people's roadside garbage. Now at the height of summer it was almost entirely covered by the carroty foliage of Queen Anne's lace, her white umbelled heads.

Alexia asked Jill why and her friend said: "My father walked barefoot through Russia in the snow. He doesn't want us ever to go without."

Alexia loved the way Jill looked, as if she was a larger version of herself. Tall, slender but broad-shouldered and strong, with large brown doe's eyes, a thick wash of adventuresome brown hair. Alexia was tall, but not so tall as Jill, large-eyed, but not as deer-like as Jill, had brown hair she'd taken to cutting short again. Sometimes, hugging Jill, her head reaching Jill's neck, she felt for a moment as though she was hugging her missing mother. Her mother who stayed young in Alexia's memory, the same age as Jill was now when she died.

Jill built a small house out of her father's junk piles, furnished it. Most of the junk was rotting now. Alexia left her friend at the house to walk the beautifully mown paths between the junk piles, where Jill had been sorting. A coffee can for screws, one for nails, a plastic tray of hammers. Alexia could see where Jill had been, as though by trails of glistening snail slime. Each time Jill found another tool she added it to the hammer tray,

Alexia surmised, although she hadn't brought it back to the house yet. The screws and nails she had, though; they held her house together.

"We always talk a lot about memory, forgetting," Jill said when Alexia got back, and it suddenly seemed appropriate that her house was built out of other people's forgotten memories.

"What will you do with your life now?" Alexia asked her, just as she did once a year.

Her answer was always the same: "There's enough work here for a lifetime. I'm sorting my father's junk."

Alexia had the sense not to laugh.

In Jill's garden, among piled straw for mulch, rows of scarlet runner beans, beets and cucumbers, the wild mullein was left unpulled, and, manured, it grew taller than the garden fence; huge candlesticks, opening yellow flowered after rain. Alexia's son Gerrard one summer dipped them in melted paraffin, sprinkled them with the same crystals used in fire-logs: torches, they burned green and red and blue. Then, later, Alexia read the settlers did that too, although of course they used beeswax, and didn't have the chemical colours.

Jill had a heavy-duty extension cord that ran up to the main house, supplied her power. Jill and Alexia followed the orange snake through hedgerows, a pile of rusting toy tractors, and an abandoned outdoor seating arrangement made of small cable spools. They were looking for a bottle opener; on the drive down they'd accidentally bought non-twist-off beer.

"My mother won't come up from the city any more," Jill said. "She hated that there were seven spatulas in the drawer for turning bacon; she could never find the wooden spoon."

"Or the day she wanted one of the seven spatulas there were three corkscrews, twelve salad forks and sixteen paring knives obscuring her view of it," Alexia replied.

"Such perfidy," Jill said. "My father's so rich."

"Makes you wonder why anybody ever buys anything," Alexia said.

"Makes you wonder," Jill replied. "Although some of them are a bit rusty, or bent."

"Or melted," Alexia said, holding up a blackened, spongy green plastic spatula. "So what are you building this year?" she asked, the bottle-opener found, because Jill was always building something.

"A fieldstone deck," Jill said, as they made the return journey, past a circle of foxgloves, several screen doors and an oil painting of a child, perched, somewhat precariously, on top of a winding split rail snake fence.

"With ramps for Michael."

Michael with an angel's name. Alexia didn't think of that with every Michael she knew, but she always did with Jill's son, who rolled through life in a wheelchair. There were ramps she'd built out of dismantled wooden factory pallets, going up and down the sloping hills, through the neglected orchard, to the outhouses full of neatly stacked *National Geographics*, and, pinned to the wall, the old Peterborough Petroglyphs poster, that they used to hand out free, before the funding cuts. Everyone had that poster pinned to the rotting cedar walls of their outhouses; in fact, Alexia thought, it was the only place you could find them any more, only the outhouse walls that hadn't forgotten.

So many things gone.

Sometimes Jill walked at night, from town to town, with a flashlight, her son rolling along in his wheelchair beside her, his knuckles blackened and callused from bumping into things. Jill drew then, in a black hard covered notebook like the kind both women used to draw and write in when they were in high school, before their dreams went to sleep, a lake drowning. They didn't know then that those dreams would come easily for such a few short years; that they would have to work hard, the rest of their lives, to keep one scant light of them awake. Jill borrowed her son's oil pastels, drew bright red cornstalks, purple skies. Who am I, Alexia thought, to say you have never seen such a thing, it's never been? I don't walk those roads at night, through to the twilit hours close to dawn, just in time to eat bacon and eggs at the highway truck stop when it opens at six.

"What did we do, after high school?" Jill asked, opening both women beer, back at the little wraparound porch of her cabin, built, of course, out of junk wood. Basil and pumpkins grew out of old creamers. One of the pumpkin vines had climbed in the front window of the house. "I want to grow indoor pumpkins," Jill added, catching Alexia's bemused stare.

"We went west, separately," Alexia answered.

Went west, lived among trees, learned their mystery. Were still learning, come to think of it. A lifelong task; one of the unsung ones that pays only in deepening joy, greater understanding. Why was it so important? Because of The Game.

In The Game there was A Fountain, a Tree. Your job in the game, should you wake one morning into its mystery, aside from allowing yourself to be Played like a tiny animated person in a game board big as life, was to care for The Fountain, The Tree. Any tree could be The Tree, any fountain The Fountain, for a few short glimmering moments. Just as any person could likewise be a Player, be Played for seconds, minutes, hours. Few were chosen and of those, fewer still woke to the intensity. And if, for a few moments, they did realise they were being Played, they forgot almost immediately.

It was hard to remember mysteries so much larger than oneself, retain even one note of the song one heard, the song one was. And yet Alexia knew it was only because she and Jill were Voyagers that they still retained any poetry in their lives at all, any shimmering dreams.

Bottles in hand, they went to look at Jill's second garden, in the old cornfield. "I still don't know why you grow more pumpkins than anyone else," Alexia said, and left for the outhouse. She always did her best thinking in bathrooms.

In the outhouse she wondered why there were drawings of snails hidden on rocks beneath the moss, that one could pull away like a carpet to look at: snails drawn by time. Once, very young, up north, Alexia had thought how the entire landscape was a clever stage set, a prop built by some master theatre designer, her motives unknown, other than her evident, passionate love of beauty. As though one could peel it away like moss too, see the true meaning of things, the writing on the wall, or on the rocks, as it were. A Game thought, she figured, yet that's how the natives preserved their rock carvings before the government built that shiny new white house for them. In the old days the moss covered the images over; people peeled it back only when they went to look at the petroglyphs, savouring them a few times each year. Like the chalk circles under Jill's wildflower meadow of a lawn. "And we think we know something about preservation," Alexia said quietly, staring at the curled and mildewed poster, reaching for toilet paper. Even when she first moved to the country, approached the petroglyphs on then unkempt wilderness trails, peered through a wire fence, she could still feel them. Now she felt the building. "And that's the whole point of The Game, isn't it," Alexia whispered, "is feeling things. Feeling picture stories. "

Alexia picked up the top copy in the ubiquitous stack of bright black and yellow. She was sure *National Geographics* bred in the closets at her own farm too. Something in cardboard boxes, in dust and darkness, that they required to propagate. She leafed through them, looking for Game clues. What if they could begin to be Played again, as they hadn't in years?

No pictures of fountains, nor of circles, whether drawn by chalk or fire. Nothing that gave her that strong rinsed feeling. Lots of pictures of trees, but none of The Tree. She longed to be Played, to be in a story so real and true it took on its own life, shaped the storyteller, a reverse creation.

It's not really me who ever made the stories, she thought, but the stories that made me. And who didn't long to be made anew, as often as possible? She called for The Game, a kind of prayer. Why did they stop being Played? Because so few did. Because they grew up. Because it was hard when no one understood or cared. Much easier to forget, give up, let the flames die. Alexia heard a car pull up, sighed, set aside her reading, her thinking, her searching.

The men had arrived: Jill's new beau Ben and his buddy Milo. They'd only take the one vehicle: Ben's trusty, rusty Chevy Nova, of indeterminate, elderly vintage. The trunk had a cooler full of beer. At the party Jill took Alexia aside, asked what she thought of Ben. "He seems nice," Alexia said, and not: He will go. He's one who goes, not one who stays.

Jill went outside alone to look at the stars, the northern lights, shimmering in green curtains, didn't call them out, so absorbed she forgot to tell them till later. Jill's always seeing things the rest of us don't see, Alexia thought. Drank beer, talked to Andrea and Rita about families, to Ben and Milo about fishing, missed Raven, the way things were before, this house, then.

Raven, her one infidelity. They walked in the woods together at a party, years before, under a moon, the children long asleep, Frank too gone up to bed. Raven's long black hair sweeping over his shoulders, his beaten brown leather jacket. A cabin a mile's hike away, belonging to a friend. She thought she'd feel cheap, sleazy, as though she was breaking things. But she hadn't. Felt only love reborn, love she'd given up hope for, settled for the other thing. It's easy to fall out of love with your husband when you're always tired, up in the night, changing diapers, losing patience, sleep, self respect. Love runs away to hide under a fossil rock and then you're just going through life together, a day at a time.

And Raven too had made her sad as he talked with smoky eyes of life gone wrong and she'd thought, I can't save him. Why does one always want to? He can only save me; for this one short moment, a moment to take back into life with me. They'd made a fire outside, drunk scotch, talked until five. Still dark then, in winter. He'd walked her back to the house, gone alone to sleep in the cabin, not wanting to be there when Frank woke. Yet he'd been Frank's friend first. And she'd told her husband eventually, how when love's cup is empty you have to find someone to fill it again. Frank had understood, at least enough not to ditch her. She figured she'd do the same for him. Hoped he wouldn't. Who could stand the anger, the pain?

But something else had happened too, that winter night years before.

Alexia felt it tugging at her. What? A Game thing. Gone like the electric green curtains flickering in the sky, so impressive just two hours before.

∞

Two in the morning, on the way back to Jill's, they stopped to swim in a pond under an old mill. Scrambled down a bank in utter darkness, obscured from moonlight which fell in yellow wavelets on the pond itself by the mill's shadow; scrabbled in the dark, beer bottles in hand. Tomorrow, Alexia guessed, she'd have the poison ivy to prove it. Alexia didn't swim, watched the others; Jill swam in T-shirt and underwear. She must feel shy with these people, Alexia thought: the Jill she knew skinny-dipped whenever she could.

The only unwet one, she sat in the front next to Ben's sidekick. Milo was from Liverpool, in England, and she was enchanted by his cockney accent, so infrequently heard in southern Ontario. Anything new she craved, bloodthirsty for it. Another side effect of motherhood: starvation for stimulation.

Milo was the designated driver, since he spent the party sleeping on Rita and Andrea's couch, had no opportunity to suck beers like the rest of them. She liked Jill's friends, but they weren't Voyagers, didn't shift out of focus just a little as she looked at them, as though part of them inhabited another space, another plane. But that was okay. Not everyone was. The Game hadn't Played them, all night long. Alexia felt more than a little hollow. But why should it, after all, come back for them when they'd abandoned it so long ago? Along with their hopes, their dreams.

"The Game was our hopes and dreams," she said fiercely. Ben and Milo turned to look at her, curious. Milo was sardonic, but Ben smiled kindly as though he almost understood. It was only Jill who laughed in heartfelt agreement.

∞

Alexia lay in Jill's bedroom, an attic loft full of windows, thinking about families, how she wanted to leave her children unburdened, how it was an impossible task, how, sometimes, burns became later gifts. Picked up a National Geographic from the pile beside the bed, a mattress on the salvaged barn board floor, covered by beautiful ragged old quilts that smelled of Jill. Jill's smell, the enormous light of Jill's rooms. Thin[illegible] to be done without.

Jill stood on the stairs to pass her food, to set on the fl[illegible] bed: boiled corn, old and leathery, new potatoes, boiled a[illegible] olive oil, salt and pepper, a little opal basil vinegar. Jill's duvet [illegible] in a homemade case, blue and white striped ticking. Downstairs on the ancient record player, salvaged from a junk pile, Jill and Ben played James Taylor, then Marianne Faithful. "It's like listening to all the years of our lives," Alexia said when she at last came downstairs, feeling social enough to join in coffee, conversation, although Ben was having a breakfast beer. Possibly a good idea, Alexia thought, considering her corrugated cardboard brains.

Jill and Ben drove Alexia home along the south shore of Rice Lake. Alexia thought she saw stories floating there, stories which had only recently been released by the weeds which choked the bottom. Even if she wasn't Played herself, she knew that even this, passing this Game locus, would open out her life in exactly those areas where it felt closed, constricted.

New stories: it made Alexia glad to see them; they seemed glad to be there, morning glories opened after rain. These were stories that had never been heard before. Alexia wanted to stay, rent a houseboat with a slip at Gore's Landing, live on the lake for a month and sit on the deck each morning, pen in hand, transcribing them. She'd have a green Coleman propane pump stove, a yellow enamel teapot, make black tea like her mother for friends who swam out. Like her mother, gone now: the first to go, the loss all other losses were measured against, The Loss that taught her to treasure her family and friends, while she yet had them. Because they too might go. Like Ben would go.

The Game Played. Alexia saw:

In Rice Lake a drowned woman floated, Ophelia-like. She was drowned but not dead. Bigger than Jill and Alexia, much bigger. Almost as big as the lake. Houseboats went out to look at her, and sometimes their propellers became entangled in the long grey green folds of her dress. Not my mother, Alexia thought, a writer not a painter, drowned like Woolf, yet not Virginia, not suicided like both she and my mother, but waiting, dormant. A temporary drowning. What did she write? The landscape.

Jill, Alexia knew, took creative writing lessons from her. Like Alexia herself, trying always to carve a life out of beauty, a poem.

But they'd already taken the north turn up twenty-eight. Alexia enjoyed Ben's swatches of ironic conversation, was briefly sad, feeling again he would go before she ever got to know him properly. If only he'd surrender, let himself be Played. Then he'd stay, Alexia thought, know the beauty and passion he craved were always there, waiting in The Game. [illegible]t go running off to look for it somewhere else, in another woman. [illegible] story so intense it shaped the teller.

∞

Mid-July, so hot they decided to stop at the beach at Serpent Mounds on Rice Lake's north shore. Here there were huge submersible mowers which kept the weeds down, in the roped off swimming area. Alexia ducked under the roped rubber buoys which marked the edge, thinking to swim out, touch only the hem of Her dress. But she returned, having encountered a faceful of weeds, and not Her sodden garment hem at all. A drowned woman, Alexia thought, She still dreams stories so beautiful they might yet change the lives of those living on Her shores.

Afterwards she walked the trails, out of the sun, sheltered by trees beside the bog, felt a little history then; feet which walked there hundreds of years before she came. Feet from Before. Wanted to feel what they felt, why they walked there, built their Mounds there. Why? Because it was beautiful.

They made the last leg of the journey to Asphodel Township, where she lived. Stopped at the mill pond near Alexia's house; a stranger in a new four by four truck asked her the name of the river that pooled there, above the dam where the kids caught crayfish, where Alexia first identified swamp milkweed, a milkweed more delicate, more feminine than its fieldborn cousin, with bright lavender pink flowers and fuzzy, slenderly lanceolate leaves.

"It's the Ouse," Alexia said, thought again of Virginia, her hair spreading behind her like weeds. But those were old stories brought from Europe; the settlers paved the landscape over with old European names. Did Virginia drown herself in England's ooze before or after this river was likewise named? Why were the pioneers unable to think of new names, particular to this continent? Labelling it instead with misspelled, often misplaced native names, or imported names. Unable to read the names which grew here organically, more legible at some times than at others, mushrooms sprouted after rain. Nature's writing, out of rot, compost. Like John Keats: it all comes out of the rag and bone bag, for all writers, nature too.

Alexia's mill pond: was it Lethe or Mnemosyne? Did she come from the city to the country to remember how to be Played, or to forget the pain of her mother's suicide? As if she could, ever, really. Did the ghosts here talk endlessly of the past, or make helpful suggestions about how to live gracefully in the present? Greek legend had it that in the fields of Asphodel, near the gates to Hades a pink lily grew, of the Allium or garlic family, beside Lethe, pool of forgetting, or was it Mnemosyne, pool of memory? What were the ghosts saying? In spring Alexia and her family would go out to the woods to gather wild leeks, a traditional native spring tonic. They boiled them as greens, cut them into salads, ate them whole, raw, while they unshovelled them, not waiting till they got home. Between Hepatica and Spring Beauty they grew: green, outrageous, smelling like a cancer cure. Not called Asphodels, though, but perhaps Cousins of Asphodels.

Alexia prolonged her swim at the dam, she knew, not only because it was so hot, or to swim off the night's beer, but to postpone going home, to pick up again the reins of everyday life, of meals and laundry and sweeping, of mending children's tears.

∞

When she got home Frank was fixing the truck, asked if she'd help. But she said, "I've already run and emptied the dishwasher twice, done and put away two loads of laundry, put on a soup, swept the floor. Besides," she looked at the greasy black engine with some misgivings, "If women had invented transportation, we wouldn't have cars."

"What would we be doing?" Frank asked, raising a wry eyebrow.

"Teleporting," she said, knowing this wasn't a totally pragmatic answer from Frank's point of view, but it got her out of the repair work, this time; other times she did help. She went inside to get a glass of water, load the dishwasher, put on the wash, do all the things she said she'd already done. If they were as reliable as death and taxes, what was the difference if she put them in the past or future tense? She unwound the plastic vines of flowers from the washer so she could open the lid; the machine was a shrine: the closest she came, in this house, to having The Fountain, caring for it. But why was it so important to have a fountain? She barely remembered. Something to do with needing water for those moments when the fire circles burned too hot, burned away The Tree's new growth and not just the dead branches, legacy of winter storms.

∞

Sitting at her winter window, six months later, Alexia hoped the Rice Lake stories were still there, not destroyed by the storm, their text mixed into a hopeless jumble. Perhaps the stories had been tossed by winter waves onto the shore, whole: maybe they were even now spreading northwards, towards Alexia's town, cloaking the hills and valleys with new words, more sincerely heartfelt ways of living. And all, Alexia thought, because Jill walked beside me for so long. Sometimes Alexia thought it was she and not Jill who'd endured the deeper burn, although to outsiders she knew it looked otherwise. People wondered how she could choose Jill for a friend, Jill who was so burdened, and not only burden but gift: Michael with an angel's name, the son who never grew up, or at least, not the way her own children did. Grew larger, sweeter, somewhat smarter; at twenty loved to listen to The Wolf, his classic rock station, chat with his friends on the phone; no longer glued, slowly, carefully, his face a mask of concentration, tools and stereos cut out of Home Hardware catalogues onto bristol board. Alexia had one of his collages, somewhere, kept it safe with Gerry and Sarah's work. But Alexia thought: I always choose the burned as my closest friends; it is they who know how to heal.

She called her friend, got Michael first.

"Hi Michael, it's Alexia. What are you doing?"

"Stereo," Michael answered and squealed by way of punctuation. "Your mum there?" Alexia asked and Michael called out: "Jill! Jill! It's Alexia."

When Jill got on she said that Ben had gone.

"I knew he'd go."

"How did you know?"

"Must be a Game thing."

"The Game is almost lost, from being Played too little."

Had they ever talked about it before? "What was it called?" Alexia asked. "Going West maybe?" Perhaps if they talked about The Game, acknowledged its existence, the giantess wouldn't die.

"Or Broken?," Jill answered, the phone line crackling with winter weather. "There were archetypes, almost like icons that you worked with; the mirror: the fountain, the tree, the circle. There was a whole dictionary of symbolic images; you'd reweave them into endless new patterns, new meanings. Stories."

Excited, Alexia interrupted her friend, rushing on: "The Game was always being played somewhere, an endless Game; you could join in it any place, any time. And you could always tell another Voyager; they shimmered a little. You'd recognize them, walking into a room, although no one else would notice. Or did we call ourselves Explorers? Funny how you forget."

But Jill said, "Funny how much we remember. Maybe it's time."

∞

It was early March. Alexia went to a party in Peterborough, ran, unexpectedly, into an old lover from years before. Raven up from the city. Together they went outside into the night. There was a cracked fountain in the centre of the back yard. Raven leaned on it, looking in; a crack so deep it couldn't hold water, even now, after rain. "It's The Fountain," she realised with a shock that ran through her like electricity: shockingly. Said, "I'm Being Played again. The Game is still here; I thought it was gone."

She watched Raven to see what he would do.

To be a Voyager one must have a fountain to drink at. The water is full of images, of stories one may live out or only read. The water is clear like any water: only to the drinker do the stories becomes legible. Like those Japanese paper flowers that bloom when sunk into a glass of water; myths bloom only when imbibed by a Voyager.

Remembered too: she and Raven, the night of their affair, years before in Elizabethville. A Fountain that night too, a stone outcropping shaped like a shallow bowl, full of rain. She'd seen a story there, read it aloud, told him it was his turn. How does one describe that feeling of being Played, a story told in partnership with The Game? She'd waited, hoping, yet every tale he'd tried to tell had been pulled back into the water before it was done. Told with smoky eyes of life gone wrong, his hands glistening and wet with words but no completion.

He'd said even then he was leaving, moving to the city. Unable to be whole, to make a true story, Raven went instead into the world to tell the bright half he knew. Alexia and Jill stayed home on their country farms, telling stories and painting pictures respectively: intricate and self-reflexive, woven, like intertwining vines or the Celtic patterns in the *Book Of Kells*; their beauty so all encompassing, so complete, so comforting they offered sanctuary. What Voyager who could do that, who could world build beauty so convincingly, would venture far from home, into the world, among the cold starved others who'd never learned the ancient craft? But Raven who'd been Played and lost had gone.

And tonight, again, there was nothing for Raven to drink. His face was illumined, but only half of it, by the moon. The illumined face was happy, but she knew the other, unseen one was not. She watched, knew that soon he would tire of waiting, that with no stories to drink, he would have to leave The Game, just like before. That as he walked away, his snowy footsteps would catch fire. Knew also she would follow, as last time, she had not. Because last time, with the vanity of an Explorer, she guarded her wealth jealously. Because last time her fountain was full and his wasn't.

But this time it was different. This time the Game had nothing to with love, with passion between men and women, if indeed it ever had. Because this time, years later, she knew at last, having half a face was better than none at all. It was the half-faced who made the bridges between the fountain and the world, the pool of remembering and the pool of forgetting. Who stopped the burning. Who cared for the trees, The Tree. ∞

Smokestack in the Desert

∞ J. Michael Yates ∞

WHEN I CROSSED THE DESERT OUTSIDE—as you just did—the smokestack seemed rooted somewhere below the horizon and rose up to pierce the ceiling of cloud. I was certain that beyond the cloud it continued to rise.

That the stack seems to grow even as one approaches is only partially visual illusion. The column itself does, in fact, grow according to work below here at the furnace, weather, and other more subtle conditions.

You're surprised that it requires no more than our number here to keep the furnace incandescent day and night.

Almost none attempt the crossing.

Due to the concentration of the furnace-fuel, we few attendants suffice.

How the stack and furnace— "the plant," if you wish—were established, no one here knows. It won't confront you as mystery for long. You might say there aren't any mysteries here.

We don't know the diameter of the desert—although it seems safe to assume it is always increasing. Keeping the furnace ablaze is, to all of us, much more important than preoccupations with measurements outside.

Of course we're aware that the height of the stack increases—that was clear to each as he approached. That the stack vanishes into clouds of its own creation, is also clear. Clouds of fume and particle level into the rose-grey overcast which reaches as far as vision in every direction.

We don't doubt that the fumes are toxic to all vegetation. And surely you felt the absence of animals, even of vultures, as you approached. The plant is creator, preserver, expander of the desert. Presumably, the more the height of the stack rises, the greater the diffusion of fume-cloud. If increase of the desert area is geometric, or arithmetic, is of no pertinence. Our duties here at the furnace are constant. We depend on our duties, they on us; nothing distracts us.

I pause to offer this slight explanation in order to reassure you that, although we are very intensely employed here, we are not unconscious men, not automatons, not slaves. We have our industry and we have our musings. Like all of us, I think you will, in the long perspective, come to value work above everything. There is, really, after all, only work.

I suppose I needn't remind one who has just traversed that expanse that during your journey and your stay here, the desert has expanded beyond any possibility of your return the direction you came—whichever it was.

And I won't, of course, command you to begin work or suggest duties. There are no commands here. No authority. Each finds his own mode of contribution to the fire and fume. ∞

Within the Mechanism

∞ Yves Meynard ∞

Rending

LONG AFTER THE ANUBINE HAD LEFT, a pall of smoke still hung in the air above the surface of the Mechanism. Slowly it settled onto the metal skin and the small plot of earth and its vegetables; ashes rained down onto the tree that grew beneath the grating, and fouled the pool at the bottom of the hollow drum from which Berrin and Maddus drew their water.

Berrin had been gone three days: a hunting expedition, far away east along the metal aisles of the Mechanism, beyond the thicket of criss-crossing corroded beams they called the Hedge Forest and into the wild area beyond, where much soil had drifted into depressions of the surface. There grass and trees grew, and birds and small animals were abundant.

The hunting had been good; Berrin was skilled with her crossbow. Her bags now bulged with meat. She was quietly happy. She longed to be with Maddus again, in great and sudden bursts of feeling that left her with a dry mouth and a pounding heart.

Her mind adrift in fantasies, she paid only cursory attention to her surroundings. Thus it was only when she was already very near her home that she finally grew aware of the devastation the Anubine had wrought. In sudden terror, she ran the rest of the way, not even thinking to draw the blade she wore strapped to her forearm.

She had known, perhaps, from the moment she perceived the remains of the cloud roiling in the air. In fact, it seemed to her now that she had known before that moment; as the pain of a wound is later remembered to have begun before ever the flesh was cut. She had known that she was too late, that the Anubine had caught Maddus and overcome her. As if it could not have been otherwise.

She found Maddus on the sloping plate behind the house. The Anubine had dismembered her and scattered her limbs about, a discarded puzzle of flesh. Dried blood stained the whole of the metal surface. The head had rolled to the bottom of the incline, and rested face up in the angle of the plate with the main floor. Its features were twisted; in surprise, in terror, in pain? Perhaps, thought Berrin, Maddus had been caught unaware and had not had enough time to be afraid. She doubted it.

The trunk had been hewn in three pieces, and the poured-out innards had been slashed into ribbons. With Maddus' blood the Anubine had drawn a complex symbol on the rear wall of the house. Doubtless it meant something to them, but to a Mere human it was unintelligible. Berrin ignored it as she began to gather the pieces of Maddus' corpse, methodically, the way she used to tidy up their house; and then her numbed mind began to thaw and she was able to scream at last.

∞

Rebuilding

In the end, it surprised her how ordinary the whole thing seemed. For many long minutes, but far less than an hour by the horizon clock, she had raved and gibbered. Then her emotions drained away and her sanity returned. Always she had been like this, feelings coming after a brief delay in a explosive rush, and then utterly spending themselves, leaving behind a composure cold and hard, like the metal of the Mechanism in the night. Only happiness had been otherwise, a slow quiet building-up that did not pause or crest.

Her lover was dead now; her happiness should be ended, but there was one way that she might yet attempt to recapture it. It was forbidden; all her youth in Town Dulade she had heard the prohibition against invoking that gift of the Mechanism. But she had left Town Dulade years ago, to be alone with Maddus, to live as they saw fit, far away into the metal wilderness; she had discarded the prohibitions of her former home.

She finished gathering the fragments of the corpse. She laid them one against the other, roughly recreating the pattern of Maddus' body. Parts were missing, or damaged beyond hope. Half the left hand was crushed to a pulp; the tendons of the right leg were shredded; part of the face had been torn off and flung away, and Berrin could not find it.

Yet in the end what she had assembled of Maddus was enough. She went into the house—what the Anubine had left of it. They had burst a wall, smashed the glass windows, demolished the furnishings; but they had in fact taken nothing, for stealing was not their way. Berrin found the heavy casket she was looking for; it was gashed and battered but unopened. She fit her key inside the lock and opened the lid. Inside the casket were all the fragments she had gathered over the years. A vast selection, full of possibilities.

So she set to work. Inside the casket were crimped needles with a point at either end, shards of gears, small toothed wheels, screws of bronze and nails of brass, clamps that looked like the heads of children with grotesque jaws, coils of barbed wire fine as hairstrands, icicles of melted glass, thin slabs of steel pierced with a myriad holes almost too fine to discern, and much else. Patiently and with precision, Berrin reassembled Maddus. She stapled and sewed shut the tears in the internal organs; fitted metal caps onto the shattered ends of the spine and socketed them together; pinned the arms to the shoulders; to replace the missing fingers she screwed lengths of coppery cylinders onto the carpal bones and set steel cable inside the leg in lieu of a tendon.

She worked until the sun had declined to the edge of the world and drowned her work in shadow. Then she stopped, spent. She might have made some light, but there was no need. She was finished. No matter the outcome, she had done her utmost.

She kneeled, facing the half-disk of the sun, and prayed to the Mechanism, that it might grant her her heart's desire. Under her legs she could feel the thrum of it, the slow energies still coursing through the vast expanse of dying metal, and she begged that they might come to her aid. As if to answer her, the horizon clock clanged out its evening call, and Berrin started. At that moment, Maddus drew a shuddering breath. Berrin went to her, took her into her arms, supporting her head.

Maddus' eyelids fluttered, drew open. The eyes rolled randomly, then fixed on Berrin's face. There was no recognition in them. Maddus coughed long and hard, retched, and finally spat out a clot of blood; in the heart of it gleamed a steel needle.

∞

Remembering

She was like a child in some ways, an infant. She could not control her body, and her limbs would suddenly flail about convulsively, then settle back into immobility. From time to time, groans and whines forced themselves through her throat, random exhalations unrelated to anything else. The metal pins Berrin had set in her flesh were moving about slowly, like thorns in stirred clay. Twice already a sharp projecting edge had scored Berrin's flesh while she tried to restrain Maddus' thrashing limbs.

Toward dawn Maddus began to quiet; her movements had lost some of their spastic quality, and she no longer gave voice. Berrin took some food from her pack and ate, then drank water from her gourd. After a moment's hesitation, she offered some to Maddus, who proved able to swallow the liquid, but closed her lips tightly after a few mouthfuls.

The sky lightened in the east, in the direction of the Hedge Forest. A tremor passed through the skin of the Mechanism: some huge weight shifting far below them, the beat of an escapement so vast its period was measured in years, the collapse of an entire substructure tens of kilometers away… There was no way to tell. Maddus began to mutter indistinctly. Berrin smoothed the other woman's hair away from her forehead; she scratched her palm on the tip of a pin that protruded from the temple.

The distant clock, half-hidden by the northern horizon, its eastern rim gleaming orange, clanged once. The sun had risen in the sky, though they were still in the shadow of the Hedge Forest. Maddus opened her eyes, looked at Berrin. Her lips twisted and quivered; she said, in a voice that seemed to belong to an old man, "Dark it was, and so deep I thought all the lights would leave forever. Was it the Hand that sent for me?"

Berrin shut her eyes and felt tears gather at their corners.

Maddus spoke on, but her voice now was a young girl's. "It came through the garden. The steel leaves, the thorns of gold—they didn't stop it. It took me and…oh!" She convulsed suddenly in Berrin's arms. Her limbs drummed on the ground; the metal fingers of her left hand jetted sparks as they screeched against the old steel. Maddus let out a howl of agony. Berrin tried to restrain her, but Maddus suddenly wrestled herself free and jumped to her feet. Her eyes were open wide, fixed on something that was not there. She pointed at it, spoke a name, whirled and began to run. Berrin rose to pursue, but after a dozen strides Maddus threw herself to the ground, clapped her hands over her head, and was still.

Berrin knelt by her side and waited, stroking her back gently. After a time she drew Maddus up to her feet and led her to what remained of their house. Maddus was now pliant, her face slack and her eyes glazed. Berrin made her sit on a gored cushion, gave her more water and a small amount of food.

An hour or two passed. Maddus regained a measure of awareness. When Berrin offered the gourd she took it in both hands and drank.

Berrin said, "Maddus?" The other woman looked at her blankly. "What is your name?" said Berrin, smiling, though she knew the answer would break her heart.

"Ah-wh… I down't…" said Maddus, words coming blurred and slow. She screwed up her face in concentration and said "I am…Kaph."

∞

Redefining

Berrin had known she could expect no more, yet she had hoped that the mind of Maddus would survive, more or less intact. But mind is an outgrowth of the body; from a torn and patched-up body nothing could emerge but a torn and patched-up mind. Maddus was gone; this woman who called herself Kaph had taken her place. Her memories were incoherent fragments, shards of dreams. They would have to be sorted, assembled, integrated. The work of weeks, months, a lifetime.

To give Kaph a focus, a core of action to cling to while she rebuilt her identity, Berrin enrolled her in the repairing of their home. For two days they busied themselves at it. The destroyed wall could be reassembled, but a gaping tear remained. Some of the furniture was salvageable; other pieces could, with patience, be partially repaired. The vegetables in the plot had been uprooted, but not all the plants were dead.

As a final gesture, the Anubine had set off a low-yield sunweapon at ground level and a crater had been blasted not fifty meters from the house. Through the ruptured skin of the Mechanism could be seen a maze of intersecting pipes, around which glittering cables twisted in double helices. From the depths of the hole a ratcheting sound could be heard, whirring up and down in frequency, sounding in its upper register like a man's hoarse whine.

Some fragments had jarred loose in the explosion and those Berrin decided to scavenge; while Kaph held onto the end of a rope Berrin lowered herself into the hole and gathered up what she could reach. Some of the pipes were burning hot to the touch; some were so cold Berrin lost a patch of skin to them.

In the evening Berrin set out her gleanings on the floor of the house. Kaph sat across from her, squeezing her metal fingers within her flesh ones. As long as she worked, she was calm, absorbed in the task at hand. When she became idle, she grew distressed. Berrin could see emotions flickering across her face and imagined the flow of disconnected images and thoughts passing through the other woman's mind.

She pointed to an odd piece of metal, shaped like a crescent. "What do you think this is, Kaph?" she asked, to distract her.

Kaph's eyes flicked to her face. Her mouth twisted, corners down. "I'd like to know who you are, please," she said.

Berrin looked at the floor. She had not guessed it would be so bitter. "My name is Berrin. You and I were lovers. We came from Town Dulade, a week's march west of here. We knew each other in childhood, we were parted, and met again when I was twenty and you twenty-one. We fell in love and chose to make our life here, because we liked the wilderness and the solitude. And because we thought we had no need to fear the Anubine."

"I don't remember this. I don't remember you. I don't have clear memories of anything. I lived in a garden when I was young, and when I was an old man I ruled in a city high on a great turbine, and I had several children... But I can't have done all this. I'm not a man, I'm not old. I don't know why you would lie to me, but I don't remember any of what you talked about."

"You were killed, Kaph. The Anubine came upon you and killed you, and dismembered your corpse. I rebuilt you, but when you came back to life you were not the same. This is why it's forbidden to reassemble the dead. I thought it wouldn't happen that way, that the tales they told in Town Dulade were lies or legends. Now I know they weren't. I am sorry to have brought you pain, but I loved you, and I wanted you alive again." Berrin was playing with two small gears, knocking them one against the other, again and again, looking at nothing else.

Kaph was silent a long time. She ran her metal fingers through her black hair. Then in a small voice she said, "I remember...the Anubine. I remember...I was surprised, so surprised. Faces, laughs—they held me, something shiny with teeth bit into my skin, and then..." Kaph shuddered. She whispered, "Then they cut off my head. I saw my body fall down. Blood spouting from the neck. Then nothing."

She seized Berrin's arm. "Is that who I was? Is that who she was—?"

"Maddus. Yes. I think those may be her memories."

Kaph bit at her lip. "They've stolen her from me. I won't let them. I want her back!"

"It's no good, Kaph. Let it go. You are who you are now. Best to—"

"No! The Anubine stole my self. I will go after them and get it back."

"...I don't think they have it in their possession, Kaph."

"Do you *know* so? Do you know the Anubine well?"

"No one knows or understands the Anubine. But I don't think they could give you back your old self if they wanted to."

"I'm willing to try. I'll leave next morning." Then Kaph paused, blushed. "Berrin, you have been very kind to me. I haven't said thank you. I'm sorry. I'm sorry to leave, because I think you want me to stay. But I'd like to be the one you loved. That's the only way I know to thank you."

There was much of Maddus in that speech, in the intentions behind it, and yet much that was utterly unlike her. Berrin took Kaph's hand in hers.

"Do what you will. But if you go after the Anubine, I will go with you." Berrin thought that without a purpose, Kaph might collapse, that she would cling to that decision beyond reason and hope because she had no other way to live.

Kaph smiled; the corner of her mouth stretched to touch the metal plate of her right cheek, and the barbed wire that stitched her lips to her chin glittered in the light.

∞

Readjusting

They set off the next day, in pursuit of the Anubine. Berrin's travel equipment was intact, and half of Maddus'—now Kaph's—was usable. Berrin had laboriously cleaned out the hollow drum and the rainwater that gathered there was once more fit to drink, though it still tasted of bitter ashes. They filled their gourds with it.

The trail of the Anubine was easy to follow at first; their booted feet had left deep prints in the soil that drifted over the hollows in the skin of the Mechanism. They had traveled northeast, away from the civilized areas to the southwest. Whether because townsfolk maintained some organized defenses or for some stranger reason, the Anubine never attacked towns. Town-dwellers heard of them from travellers. Living in civilized regions all their life, Berrin and Maddus had been able to believe the Anubine were no threat in this area of the Mechanism. Berrin hated herself every time she recalled her former mindset; she knew she had succumbed to a typical Mere flaw, that of believing reality conformed to her wishes.

Days passed, and the trail led ever-deeper into a country strange to Berrin. Her usual hunting grounds were east and south. Kaph, of course, had no relevant geographical memories.

At night Berrin wondered why she had followed Kaph on this journey. It could not be loyalty to Maddus, for Maddus was dead and gone. Nor could it be the emprise of the flesh she had once lusted for; Maddus' body was now ravaged and scarred, and Berrin must concede to herself that it elicited in her nothing other than pity and revulsion. Was she then loyal to this new person, Kaph? Was it because she had, in a sense, given birth to Kaph, that she followed her now?

She could not understand herself. Perhaps it was better to simply live and ask no questions. Within the Mechanism, answers were too often unwelcome in the end.

They traveled fast. This region of the Mechanism was mostly free of obstacles, a great plain divided into a semi-regular tiling by trenches no more than half a meter wide. In the middle of some of these tiles rose angular tiered mounds five meters high, without openings, shuddering and thudding to an internal movement. Clouds of rust-colored steam leaked from their base.

Tracking the Anubine through this region might have been hopeless, for there was no accumulated soil to keep a record of their passage; but they had continued their labor of destruction, tearing open some of the mounds. From the rents a thick fluid had poured in ropes and drapes and pillows, and swiftly solidified into bright green stone. From one destroyed mound to the next, it was a nearly straight line, still going northeast.

On the fourth day of their pursuit, Berrin and Kaph entered a fertile domain. Soil had drifted deep in this place of considerable relief and plants of all sorts had taken root. Breadtrees grew wild and though their fruit was small and somewhat dry, it filled the stomach. The two women refilled their packs. Berrin brought down a large white bird with a cross-bow bolt.

That night they made camp in a sheltered, quiet nook between two tall bluish cubes; they built a fire of dried branches in a small depression and cooked the bird. After their meal, lying side by side in the tent, they talked of small things. Berrin told a joke which brought crows of laugher from Kaph.

After a time Kaph touched Berrin's shoulder gently.

"Berrin… Did you make love with Maddus often?"

Berrin sighed. "I guess so."

"Do you… Do you want me? You've been kind and…"

"Please, Kaph, it's not meant to be that way."

"I just want to be nice to you."

"Do you want me? Truly?"

"I… No. I'm… Well, Maddus wanted you, I'm sure, but I'm still Kaph. And I think… I think I'd like you to hold me, yes. But not, not really that."

"It's all right, Kaph. It's all right." In fact Berrin was relieved, and ashamed of it. She held Kaph in her arms, and it was a small measure of comfort, but next to the woman's warm living flesh her own skin touched chill metal. A socket she had used in reassembling the shoulder had traveled through the flesh and now she could feel its hard square edges just beneath the skin of Kaph's arm.

∞

Reckoning

It was two days later, close to sundown, that they came upon the martyred Anubine.

This region of the Mechanism was dotted with branching antennas of flexible chromed metal. The Anubine had been lashed to one of these pseudotrees, his feet a full meter above the ground. The black leather bonds had dug deep into his flesh at throat, ankles and wrists. His black-brown dog's head was tilted upwards, his eyes wide open as if gazing into the empty sky. The flesh of his body was nearly white, and hairless.

Berrin felt her heart pounding, not only with excitement but also with fear. Tied and dying the Anubine might be, but she did not trust him to be harmless. Kaph wanted to rush up to him, but Berrin held her back. "Stay at a good distance," she warned.

The Anubine had heard them. Slowly he tilted his head forward. His yellow eyes blinked. His dog's mouth formed words, the lips stretching over the fangs.

"Two Mere females come to look upon my dying. A small audience, but better than nothing. Won't you come closer?"

"Why are you here?" asked Kaph. "Who bound you?"

"My own brothers. It is our way. We bring death to the folk who live on the Mechanism, nor do we fail to include ourselves among them. Ever and anon, we sacrifice one of our own."

"Why do you do it?" asked Berrin, certain in the asking that the question would not be answered meaningfully. But she was surprised.

"The world is at its end, little sisters. The long dream of humanity is nearly over. It is just and fitting that the end of all things be celebrated; we of the Anubine have taken it as our duty. We travel hither and thither and hasten the ruin and downfall of the Mechanism. We kill, and break, and destroy. We are the harbingers of the changes to come. We know we are misunderstood, and we accept this. Yet sometimes it pains us. Would you not comfort me in my dying? I have hardly the breath to talk loud enough to reach your ears at this distance."

"Do you remember me?" said Kaph. "A week ago you killed me and destroyed my home."

The Anubine tilted his head to the side, frowned. "Perhaps I do. If I make abstraction of all the metal…yes, what remains of your flesh is indeed familiar. Of course, now I recall it: you are our most recent kill! But calm yourself; it was not I that took off your head. In any case, you live again; what is your complaint?"

"I'm not who I was! You stole her, you stole Maddus, and I want her back!"

At this the Anubine laughed, a thin strangled laugh, for the bonds cut into his throat. "We do not steal," he said. "When you were killed, the complex of electrical patterns you call your self was dispersed. So it is with everyone who dies. Within the Mechanism, some of these patterns may be picked up by whatever suitable receptors still function; they then enter a conductive net and may be rebroadcast at random moments. At the moment of your reassembly, your nervous system received and was imbued with hundreds of these fragmentary patterns, and these combined with the decayed chemical remnants of the personality that still existed within your brain. Whoever you were is not 'gone'; she is *rent*, into a thousand pieces, each a distorted shred of the whole. You cannot have her back; or else you must ask the Mechanism, most humbly, to regather what lies scattered across its whole expanse."

"Damn you, you fucking piece of abhuman filth!" cried Kaph, trembling.

The Anubine's body twisted within his bonds; his hands clenched and his penis engorged. "Such language, little sister. Education and refinement are sadly lacking in these latter days..." He panted, his red tongue flickering between his teeth.

"How would you like to be killed? We've got a crossbow. We can put a bolt into your eye anytime! What would it feel like to be killed by two Mere women?" Kaph's face was scarlet, and she shook with her anger.

"No...matter." The Anubine's breath now came in ragged gasps, as if he strove in vain to fill his lungs to capacity through the constriction at his throat. "Two Mere women, you say... But even what we call Mere humanity is...not the human norm that was. We have changed so much...beyond the original...model. For thousands of...years now, no one alive on this world...would have been called human...by our forebears. We...are all...distorted...reflections."

His eyes fixed on the two women then, and his pupils dilated until only a thin circlet of gold was left at the rim. Berrin had only a second to react, shoving Kaph sideways with a burst of terrible strength. With a convulsive jerk that nearly tore his bonds loose, the Anubine vomited a stream of blood at them. But the jet missed its target and splashed onto the skin of the Mechanism. Berrin, who had fallen on top of Kaph, rolled to the side and bounded back on her feet.

She took the time to check that none of the liquid had touched them. Then she unhooked the crossbow from her belt and released the safety catch. Legs braced, fists joined at the trigger, she aimed at the Anubine, now gasping and limp within his bonds. Berrin fired. The quarrel whistled through the air and buried itself in the canine head. The Anubine screamed and blood ran from his mouth again, a thin flow without any force. He thrashed and collapsed, dead.

Berrin turned to Kaph. "Are you all right?" she asked.

Kaph stood up, holding her right elbow in her left hand. "Yes...I guess. Why did he do that?" Some blood oozed between her fingers; but it was her own, a dark red, not the Anubine's pale crimson.

"I don't know. I think his blood might be infectious. My mother told me tales of the Paä; it's said if only one drop of their blood enters your body, it changes you, so that you eventually become one of them. Maybe it's that way with the Anubine."

"I knew one of the Paä once," said Kaph. "She was a tall woman with the most extraordinary hair, and she lived in a tower over the Third Flow—" She stopped, mouth still open; passed a hand across her face and continued, "No. I didn't know her. I dreamed her. I heard tales and I made it up."

Berrin went to her, held her gently. Kaph's arm was loose at the elbow and her fingers quivered in palsy. "I'm rent. That was what he said. I can't get her back, can I?"

"I don't know. Why should he tell the truth? I didn't understand half of the words he used, anyway. He was telling us lies, to scare us."

"No. He spoke like someone who knows. I'm sure he wasn't lying. Maddus is gone. You said so yourself in the beginning. It's hopeless, isn't it?"

Berrin sighed. "I'm sorry, Kaph. If the Anubine spoke the truth, you can't become Maddus. And even if he lied, I have no idea how you could do it. I don't think his brothers could or would help you. I feel it would be useless to pursue them any longer."

"I doesn't matter. I'm just so tired. Let's make camp somewhere away from that."

They moved some good distance away, and sheltered at the foot of a large antenna. The Anubine's corpse was visible as a small shape and with dusk it vanished. The riven moon rose, trailed by a cloud of glittering fragments. The chrome trees glowed in the moonlight, like frozen inverted bolts of lightning.

∞

Returning

They set out at daybreak, back toward their home. But it was as Berrin had feared: deprived of a purpose, Kaph's mind began to weaken. Since now she herself believed her identity to be an illusion, a patchwork-construct, the dissolution was accelerated. They traveled for a day, Kaph growing less and less focused by the hour. The next morning found her feverish and delirious. Berrin stayed by her side and gave her water frequently. She tried to soothe her, but nothing she did proved effective.

Like the metal parts adrift within her flesh, assemblages of memories traveled through Kaph's mind and sometimes emerged briefly, crushing her in the grip of hallucinations. She remembered being a little girl, holding a furred pet in her arms in the sunlight, the ghost of a moon still whole riding in the summer sky; next she writhed and wailed like an infant, then screamed of the steel limbs that had rocked her to death; and then in the voice of the old man she had been the first night, she said "The Hand deserted me. I know it. They let me be winched down into the well, and erased me from their remembrance, that they might sleep easily. Who are you who pulled me out? Who are you?"

"Kaph! Kaph!" Berrin called, and shook the other woman. "Remember yourself! Kaph! *Maddus!*" Kaph's flesh stirred under Berrin's hands, muscles rippled and metal joints flexed. Kaph spoke again, but her voice seemed to have become a chorus, and discordant words mingled in her mouth until only a burst of glutinous consonants emerged. In despair and grief, Berrin began to hit her, pounding her fists into the malleable flesh.

Kaph's confusion only increased. Berrin struck her again and again, punching and kicking; finally she grasped Kaph's head, her fingernails gouging the cheeks, and kissed Kaph on the mouth until her own lips had been torn open by the barbed wire. And then she drew her blade and stabbed Kaph in the heart.

It wasn't enough to kill her. The Mechanism had imbued her with abnormal vitality. Her body still stirred; Berrin could imagine the metal parts migrating from now-reknitted flesh into the damaged heart tissue. A child-headed clamp would replace a torn valve; helical springs would stretch themselves along a damaged ventricle...

So she did what the Anubine had done; tore Kaph's body apart and scattered the pieces over the skin of the Mechanism. When she was finished, she felt a surge of relief, overriding everything else she felt. She left the dismembered corpse behind and took the direction of her house.

Of the rest of her trip home she had only fragmentary recollections. She knew she was many days' walk away, but it seemed to take only a few hours before she found herself in sight of her dwelling. Had the Mechanism drunk these memories? Would someone, one day, find herself reassembled, granted a life she did not deserve, owning these shattered recollections, among a thousand incoherent others?

She found herself remembering the Anubine's words: *We have changed so much beyond the original model. We are all distorted reflections*. She felt a distorted reflection herself, of the woman she had been.

Her house was unchanged. Though she and Kaph had scrubbed the wall clean, she could still see the ghost of the symbol the Anubine had drawn with Maddus' blood. She fancied she could grasp some of its meaning now.

She set down her pack, sat on a chair that had been destroyed and then rebuilt. She would grieve in a moment. Grieve for Maddus and for Kaph, and for herself too. And when the grief was past, she would be once more cold and hard, if cracked at the core. She would leave again. Return to Town Dulade for a time, probably, but then go on. Travel in other directions. Hunt for a city built high on a great turbine; for gardens wherein one could find leaves of steel and thorns of gold; or for some place even stranger, some place within the Mechanism where she might, perhaps, be at peace. ∞

The Dragon of Pripyat

∞ Karl Schroeder ∞

"THERE'S THE TURNOFF," said Gennady's driver. He pointed to a faded wooden skull and cross-bones that leaned at the entrance to a side road. From the pattern of the trees and bushes, Gennady could see that the corner had once been a full highway interchange, but the turning lanes had overgrown long ago. Only the main blacktop was still exposed, and grass had made inroads to this everywhere.

The truck stopped right at the entrance. "This is as far as I go," said the driver. He stepped out of the idling vehicle and walked around the back to unload. Gennady paused for a moment to stare down the green tunnel before following.

They rolled out some steel drums containing supplies and equipment, then brought Gennady's motorcycle and sidecar.

The driver pointed to the Geiger counter that lay on top of the heaped supplies in the sidecar. "Think that'll protect you?"

"No." Gennady grinned at him. "Before I came I did a little risk calculation. I compared the risk of cancer from radiation to that of smoking. See? Here the Geiger clicks at about a pack-a-week. Closer in, that's going to be a pack-a-day. Well, I'll just avoid the pack-a-minute spots, is all. Very simple."

The driver, who smoked, did not like this analogy. "Well, it was nice knowing you. Need anything else?"

"Uh...help me roll these behind the bushes there." They moved the drums out of sight. "All set."

The driver nodded once, and Gennady started down the abandoned road to Pripyat.

The tension in his shoulders began to ease as he drove. The driver had been friendly enough, but Gennady's shyness had made the trip here an uncomfortable one. He could pretend to be at ease with strangers; few people knew he was shy. It still cost him to do it.

The trees were tall and green, the undergrowth lush. It smelled wonderful here, better than the industrial area around Gennady's apartment. Pure and clean, no factory smell.

A lie, of course. Before he'd gone a hundred meters, Gennady slowed, then stopped. It all looked serene and bursting with health—a seductive and dangerous innocence. He brought out a filtered face mask he had last worn in heavy traffic in St. Petersburg. For good measure he wrapped his boots in plastic, snapping rubber bands over his pant cuffs to hold it on. Then he continued.

The view ahead was not of a straight black ribbon with sky above, but a broad green tunnel, criss-crossed at all levels with twigs and branches. He'd expected the road would be cracked and buckled from frost heaving, but it wasn't. On the other hand underbrush had overgrown the shoulder and invaded the concrete, where patches of grass sprouted at odd places. For no good reason, he drove around these.

Over the next half hour he encountered more and more clearings. Tall grass lapped like waves around the doors of rusting metal pole-sheds once used for storing farm equipment. Any houses made of lath and plaster had caved in or been burned, leaving only single walls with windows looking from open field to open field. When he spotted the giant lattice-work towers of the power line looming above the trees he knew he was getting close. As if he needed visual confirmation—the regular ticking from the counter in his sidecar had slowly become an intermittent rattle, like rain.

Then without warning the road opened out into a vista of overgrown concrete lots, rusted fences and new forest. Wildflowers and barley rioted in the boulevard of the now-divided highway, and further ahead, above patchy stands of trees, hollow-eyed Soviet-style apartment blocks stared back at their first visitor in…years, possibly.

He shut off the bike and brought out his Pripyat roadmap. It was thirty years out of date, but since it was printed a year before the disaster, the roads would not have changed—other than the occasional oak tree or fallen building blocking his path. For a few minutes he puzzled over where he was, and when he was certain he pulled out his phone.

"Lisa, it's me. I'm here."

"You okay?" She had answered promptly. Must have been waiting. His shoulders relaxed a bit.

"I'm fine. Place looks like a park. Or something. Very difficult to describe." There were actual trees growing on the roofs of some of the apartment blocks. "A lot of the buildings are still standing. I'm just on the outskirts."

"What about the radioactivity?"

He checked the Geiger counter. "It's not too hot yet. I'm thinking of living in a meat locker. Somewhere with good walls that got no air circulation after the Release."

"You're not near the reactor, are you?"

"No. It's by the river, I'm coming from the north-west. The trees hide a lot."

"Any sign of anybody else?"

"Not yet. I'm going to drive downtown. I'll call you when I have the satellite link running."

"Well, at least one of us is having an exciting day."

"I wouldn't exactly call it exciting. Frightening, maybe."

"Well." She said well in that tone when she was happy to be proved right about something. He could practically see her. "I'm glad you're worried," she said at last. "When you told me about this part of the job you pretended like it was no big deal."

"I did not." Well, maybe he had a little. Gennady scratched his chin uncomfortably.

"Call me soon," she said. "And hey—be careful."

"Is my nature."

∞

Downtown was too hot. Pripyat was a Soviet modern town anyway, and had no real centre aside from some monolithic municipal buildings and farmers' markets. The populace had been professional and mobile; it was built with wide thoroughfares connecting large, partially self-contained apartment complexes. Gennady read the cultural still-birth of the place in the utter anonymity of the buildings. Everything was faded, most signs gone, the art overwritten by vines and rust. So he could only identify apartment buildings by their many small balconies, municipal offices by their lack of same. That was the beginning and end of Pripyat's character.

Gennady paused often to look and listen, alert for any signs of human habitation. There were no tire tracks, no columns of smoke. No buses passed, no radios blared from the high-rises.

He found himself on the outskirts again as evening reddened the light. Twelve-storey apartment blocks formed a hexagon here, the remains of a parkette in its center. The Geiger counter clicked less insistently in this neighbourhood. He parked the motorcycle in the front foyer of the eastern-most tower. This building still had a lot of unbroken windows. If he was right, some of the interior rooms would have low isotope concentrations. He could rest there, as long as he left his shoes outside, and ate and drank only the supplies he had brought with him.

The echoes of his boot crashing against an apartment door seemed to echo endlessly, but no one came to investigate. Gennady got the door open on the third try, and walked into the sad evidence of an abandoned life. Three days after Reactor 4 caught fire, the tenants had evacuated with everything they could carry—but they'd had to leave a black upright piano that once they might have played for guests who sipped wine here, or on the balcony. Maybe they had stood watching the fire that first night, nervously drinking and speculating on whether it might mean more work for renovators and fire inspectors.

Many faded and curled photos were pinned to the beige kitchen cupboards; he tried not to look at them. The bedroom still held a cot and chest of drawers with icons over it. The wallpaper here had uncurled in huge rolls, leaving a mottled yellow-white surface behind.

The air was incredibly musty in the flat—a good sign. The Geiger counter's rattle dropped off immediately, and stabilized at a near-normal level. None of the windows were so much as cracked, though the balcony door had warped itself to the frame. Gennady had to remove its hinges, pull the knob off and pry it open to get outside. Even then he ventured only far enough to position his satellite dish, then retreated indoors again and sealed the split frame with duct tape he'd brought for this sort of purpose. The balcony had swayed under him as he stepped onto it.

The sarcophagus was visible from here on the sixth floor. Twenty years ago this room must have looked much the same, but the Chernobyl reactor had still sported the caged red-and-white smokestack that appeared in all early photos of the place. The stack had fallen in the second accident, when Reactor Two went bad. The press referred to the first incident as The Disaster; the second they called The Release.

The new sarcophagus was designed to last ten thousand years. Its low sloping sides glowed redly in the sunset.

Gennady whistled tunelessly as he set up the portable generator and attached his computer, EM detection gear and the charger for his Walkman. He laid out a bedroll while the system booted and the dish outside tracked. As he was unrolling canned goods from their plastic sheaths, the system beeped once and said, "Full net connection established. Hi Gennady."

"Hi. Call Mr. Merrick at the Chernobyl Trust, would you?"

"Trying…"

Beep. "Gennady." Merrick's voice sounded tinny coming from the computer's speaker. "You're late. Any problems?"

"No. Just took a while to find a secure place. The radiation, you know."

"Safe?"

"Yes."

"What about the town? Signs of life?"

"No."

"The sarcophagus?"

"I can see it from here, actually." He enabled the computer's camera and pointed it out the window. "Well, okay, it's too dark out there now. But there's nothing obvious, anyway. No bombs sitting out in the open, you know?"

"We'd have spotted them on the recon photos."

"Maybe there is nothing to see because there is nothing there. I still think they could be bluffing."

Merrick grunted. "There was a release. One thousand curies straight into the Pripyat river. We monitored the plume. It came from the sarcophagus. They said they would do it, and they did. And unless we keep paying them, they'll do more."

"We'll find them. I'm here now."

"You stayed out of sight, I trust."

"Of course. Though you know, anything that moves here stands out like a whore in church. I'm just going to sit on the balcony and watch the streets, I think. Maybe move around at night."

"Just call in every four hours during the day. Otherwise we'll assume the worst."

Gennady sighed heavily. "It's a big town. You should have a whole team on this."

"Not a chance. The more people we involve, the more chance it'll get out that somebody's extorting the Chernobyl Trust. We just barely hold onto our funding as it is, Gennady."

"All right, all right. I know I come cheap. You don't have to rub it in."

"We're paying you a hell of a lot for this. Don't complain."

"Easy for you to say. You're not here. Good night, Merrick."

He stretched out for a while, feeling a bit put out. After all, it was his neck on the line. Merrick was an asshole, and Lisa had told him not to come. Well, he was here now. In his own defence, he would do a good job.

It got dark quickly, and he didn't dare show much light, so reading was out. The silence grew oppressive, so he finally grunted and sat up to make another call.

This time he jacked in to the net. He preferred full-sense interfaces, the vibrant colours and sounds of net culture. In moments he was caught up in a whirlwind of flickering icons and sound bites, all the news of the day and opinions from around the world pouring down the satellite link to his terminal. Gennady read and answered his mail, caught up on the news, and checked the local forecast. Good weather for the next week, apparently. Although rain would have helped keep the isotopes out of the air, he was happy that he would be able to get some sun and explore without inconvenience.

Chores done, he fought upstream through the torrent of movie trailers, whispers of starlet gossip, artspam messages and hygiene ads masquerading as real people on his chat-lines, until he reached a private chat room. Gennady conjured a body for himself, some chairs and, for variety, a pool with some sunbathers, and then called Lisa.

She answered in window mode, as she often did. He could see she was in her London apartment, dressed in a sweatshirt. "Hi," he said. "How was the day?"

"It was okay."

"Any leads on our mythical terrorists?" Lisa was a freelance Net hacker. She was well-respected, and frequently worked for Interpol. She and Gennady talked almost every day, a result of their informal working relationship. Or, he sometimes suspected, maybe he had that backwards.

She looked uncomfortable. "I haven't found anything. Where have you been? I thought you were going to call as soon as you arrived."

"I told you I'd call. I called."

"Yeah, but you're not exactly reliable that way."

"It's my life." But this was Lisaveta, not just some anonymous chat on the Net. He ground his teeth and said, "I am sorry. You're right, I make myself hard to find."

"I just like to know what's going on."

"And I appreciate it. It took me a while to find a safe place."

Her expression softened. "I guess it would. Is it all hot there?"

"Most of it. It's unpredictable. But beautiful."

"Beautiful? You're daft."

"No really. Very green, lush. Not like I expected."

She shook her head. "Why on earth did you even take this job? That one in Minsk would have paid more."

"I don't like Minsk."

She stared at him. "Chernobyl's better?"

"Listen, forget it. I'm here now. You say you haven't found our terrorists?"

She didn't look like she wanted to change the subject, but then she shrugged and said, "Not a whisper on the Net. Unless they're technoluddites, I don't see how they're operating. Maybe it's local, or an inside job."

Gennady nodded. "Hadn't ruled that out. I don't trust this Merrick fellow. Can we check into the real financial position of the Trust?"

"Sure. I'll do that. Meanwhile…how long are you going to be there?"

He shrugged. "Don't know. Not long."

"Promise me you'll leave before your dosimeter maxes out, even if you don't find anything. Okay?"

"Hmm."

"Promise!"

He laughed. "All right, Lisaveta. I promise."

Later, as he lay on his bedroll, he played through arguments with Lisa where he tried to explain the strange beauty of the place. He came up with many phrases and examples, but in the end he always imagined her shaking her head in incomprehension. It took him a long time to fall asleep.

∞

There was no sign that a large group of people had entered Pripyat at any time in the recent past. When Trust inspectors came they usually arrived by helicopter, and stayed only long enough to replace the batteries at the weather stations and radiation monitoring checkpoints. The way wildflowers and moss had begun to colonize the drifted soil on the roads, any large vehicle tracks should have been readily visible. Gennady didn't find any.

Despite this he was more circumspect the next day. Merrick might be right, there might well be someone here. Gennady had pictured Pripyat in black and white, as a kind of industrial dump. The place was actually like a wild garden—though as he explored on foot, he would often round a corner or step into an open lot and find the Geiger counter going nuts. The hotspots were treacherous, because there was no way to tell where they'd be.

A few years after the disaster, folk had started to trickle back into Pripyat. The nature of the evil was such that people saw their friends and family die no matter how far they ran. Better to go home than sit idle collecting coffin-money in some shanty town.

When the Release happened, all those who had returned died. After that, no one came.

He had to remind himself to check his watch. His first check-in with Merrick was half an hour late; the second two full hours. Gennady completely lost track of time while skirting the reactor property, which was separated from the town by marshy grassland. All manner of junk from two eras had been abandoned here. Green helicopters with red stars on them rusted next to remotely piloted halftracks with the U.N. logo and the red, white and blue flag of the Russian Republic. In one spot he found the remains of a wooden shed. The wood drooped over matted brown mounds that must once have been cardboard boxes. Thousands of clean white tubes—syringes, their needles rusted away—poked out of the mounds. The area was hot, and he didn't linger.

Everywhere he went he saw potential souvenirs, all undisturbed. Some were hot, others clean. The entire evidence of late-Soviet life was just lying about here. Gennady found it hard to believe a sizable group could spend any time in this open-air museum, and not pry into things at least a little. But it was all untouched.

He was a bit alarmed at the numbers on his dosimeter as he turned for home. Radiation sure accumulated quickly around here. He imagined little particles smashing his DNA. Here, there, everywhere in his body. It might be all right; he would probably be perfectly healthy later. It might not be all right.

A sound startled him out of his worry. The *meow* came again, and then a scrawny little white cat stepped gingerly onto the road.

"Well, hello." He knelt to pet it. The Geiger counter went wild. The cat butted against his hand, purring to rattle its ribs loose. It didn't occur to him that it was acting domesticated until a voice behind him said, "That's Varuschka."

Gennady looked up to see an old man emerge from behind a tall hedgerow. He appeared to be in his seventies, with a narrow hatchet-like face burned deep brown, and a few straggles of white hair. He wore soil-blackened overalls, and the hand he held out was black from digging. Gennady shook it anyway.

"Who the hell are you?" asked the old man abruptly.

Was this the extortionist? Well, it was too late to hide from him now. "Gennady Malianov."

"I'm Bogoliubov. I'm the custodian of Pripyat." Bogoliubov sized him up. "Just passing through, eh?"

"How do you know that?"

"The Geiger counter, the plastic on your shoes, the mask… Ain't that a bit uncomfortable?"

"Very, actually." Gennady scratched around it.

"Well what the hell are you wearing it for?" The old man grabbed a walking stick from somewhere behind the hedge. "You just shook hands with me. The dirt'll be hotter than anything you inhale."

"Perhaps I was not expecting to shake hands with anyone today."

Bogoliubov laughed drily. "Radiation's funny stuff. You know I had cancer when I came here? God damn fallout cured me. Seven years now. I can still piss a straight line."

He and Varuschka started walking, and Gennady fell in beside them. "Did you live here, before the disaster?" Bogoliubov shook his head. "Does anybody else live here?"

"No. We get visitors, Varuschka and me. But if I thought you were here to stay I wouldn't be talking to you. I'd have gone home for the rifle."

"Why's that?"

"Don't like neighbours." Seeing his expression, Bogoliubov laughed. "Don't worry, I like visitors. Just not neighbours. Haven't shot anyone in years."

Bogoliubov looked like a farmer, not an extortionist. "Had any other visitors lately?" Gennady asked him. He was sure it was an obviously leading question, but he'd never been good at talking to people. He left that up to other investigators.

"No, nobody. Unless you count the dragon." Bogoliubov gestured vaguely in the direction of the sarcophagus. "And I don't."

"The what?"

"I call it the dragon. Sounds crazy. I don't know what the hell it is. Lives in the sarcophagus. Only comes out at night."

"I see."

"Don't you take that tone with me." Bogoliubov shook his cane at Gennady. "There's more things in heaven and earth, you know. I *was* going to invite you to tea."

"I'm sorry. I am new here."

"Apology accepted." Bogoliubov laughed. "Hell, you'd have to do worse than laugh at me to make me uninvite you. I get so few guests."

"I wasn't—"

"So, why are you here? Not sightseeing, I assume."

They had arrived at a log dacha on the edge of the grassland. Bogoliubov kept some goats and chickens, and even had an apple tree in the back. Gennady's Geiger counter clicked at levels that would be dangerous after weeks, fatal in a year or two. He had been here seven years?

"I work for the University of Minsk," said Gennady. "In the medical school. I'm just doing an informal survey of the place, check for fire hazards near the sarcophagus, that sort of thing."

"So you don't work for the Trust." Bogoliubov spat. "Good thing. Bunch of meddling bureaucrats. Think they can have a job for life because the goddamn reactor will always be there. It was people like them made the disaster to begin with."

The inside of Bogoliubov's dacha was cozy and neatly kept. The old man began ramming twigs into the firebox of an iron stove. Gennady sat admiring the view, which included neither the sarcophagus nor the forlorn towers of the abandoned city.

"Why do you stay here?" he asked finally.

Bogoliubov paused for an instant. He shook his head and brought out some waterproof matches. "Because I can be alone here. Nothing complicated about it, really."

Gennady nodded.

"It isn't complicated to love a place, either." Bogoliubov set one match in the stove. In seconds the interior was a miniature inferno. He put a kettle on to boil.

"People die, you know. But places don't. Even with everything they did to this place, it hasn't died. I mean look at it. Beautiful. You like cities, Malianov?"

Gennady shook his head.

The old man nodded. "Of course not. If you were a city person, you'd run screaming from here. It'd prey on you. You'd start having nightmares. Or kill yourself. City people can't handle Pripyat. But you're a country person, aren't you?"

"I guess I am." It would be impossible to explain to the old man that he was neither a city nor a country person. Though he lived in a large and bustling city, Gennady spent most of his free time in the pristine, controllable environments of the Net.

Bogoliubov made some herbal tea. Gennady tested it with the Geiger before he sipped it, much to Bogoliubov's amusement. Gennady filled him in on Kiev politics and the usual machinations of the international community. After an hour or so of this, though, Gennady began to feel decidedly woozy. Had he caught too big a dose today? The idea made him panicky.

"Have to go," he said finally. He wanted to stand up, but he seemed to be losing touch with his body. And everything was happening in slow motion.

"Maybe you better wait for it to wear off," said Bogoliubov.

Minutes or hours later, Gennady heard himself say, "Wait for what to wear off?"

"Can't get real tea here," said the old man. "But marijuana grows like a weed. Makes a good brew, don't you think?"

So much for controlling his situation. Gennady's anxiety crested, broke in a moment of fury, and then he was laughing out loud. Bogoliubov joined in.

The walk back to his building seemed to take days. Gennady couldn't bring himself to check the computer for messages, and fell asleep before the sun set.

∞

Lisa shook her head as she sat down at her terminal. Why should she be so upset that he hadn't called? And yet she was—he owed her a little consideration. And what if he'd been hurt? She would have heard about it by now, since Gennady had introduced her to Merrick as a subcontractor. Merrick would have phoned. So he was ignoring her. Or something.

But she shouldn't be so upset. After all, they spoke on the phone, or met in the Net—that was the beginning and end of their relationship. True, they worked together well, both being investigators, albeit in different areas. She spoke to Gennady practically every day. Boyfriends came and went, but Gennady was always there for her.

But he never lets me be there for him, she thought as she jacked into the net and called him.

Though she didn't intend to, when he finally answered the first thing she said was, "You promised you'd call."

"You too? Merrick just chewed me out for yesterday." He seemed listless.

"Credit me with better motives than Merrick," she said. She wanted to pursue it, but knowing how testy he could be, just said, "What happened?"

"It's not like I'm having a picnic out here, you know. It's just not so easy to stay in touch as I thought." He looked like he hadn't slept well, or maybe had slept too well.

"Listen, I'm sorry," he said suddenly, and he sounded sincere. "I'm touched that you care so much about me."

"Of course I do, Gennady. We've been through a lot together." It was rare for him to admit he was wrong; somewhat mollified, she said, "I just need to know what's going on."

He sighed. "I think I have something for you." She perked up. Lisa loved it when they worked together as a team. He was the slow, plodding investigator, used to sifting through reams of photographs, old deeds and the like. She was the talker, the one who ferreted out people's secrets by talking with them. When they'd met, Gennady had been a shy insurance investigator unwilling to take any job where he had to interview people, and she had been a nosy hacker who get her hands dirty with field work. They made a perfect match, she often thought, because they were so fundamentally different.

"There's an old man who lives here," said Gennady. "Name's Bogoliubov. Has a dacha near the reactor."

"That's insane," she said.

Gennady merely shrugged. "That's where I was yesterday—talking to him. He says nobody's come through Pripyat in ages. Except for one guy."

"Oh?" She leaned forward eagerly.

"We had a long talk, Bogoliubov and me." Gennady half-smiled at some private joke. "He says he met a guy named Yevgeny Druschenko. Part-time employee of the Trust, or so he said." As he spoke Lisa was typing madly at her terminal. "He was a regular back when they still had funding to do groundwater studies here. The thing is, he's driven into town twice in the past year. Didn't tell Bogoliubov where he was going, but the old man says both times he headed for the sarcophagus with a truckload of stuff. Crates. Bogoliubov doesn't know where they ended up."

"Bingo!" Lisa made a triumphant fist. "He's listed, all right. But he's not on the payroll anymore."

"There's more." She looked at him, eyebrows raised. Gennady grinned. "You're going to love this part. Bogoliubov says it was right after Druschenko's first visit that the dragon appeared."

"Whoa. Dragon?"

"He doesn't know what else to call it. I don't think he believes it's supernatural. But he says something is *living* inside the sarcophagus. Been there for months now."

"That's ridiculous."

"I know. It's fatal just to walk past the thing."

Lisa scowled for a minute, then dismissed the issue with a wave of her hand. "Whatever. I'm going to trace this Druschenko. Are you through there now?"

"Not quite. Bogoliubov might be lying. I have to check the rest of the town, see if there's any signs of life. Should take a couple of days."

"Hmmf." She was sure he knew what she felt about that. "Okay. But keep in touch. I mean it this time."

He placed a hand on his heart solemnly. "I promise."

∞

It was hard. For the next several mornings Gennady awoke to find

Bogoliubov waiting for him downstairs. The old man had designated himself tour guide, and proceeded to drag Gennady through bramble, fen and buckled asphalt, ensuring he visited all the high points of the city.

There was a spot where two adjacent apartment blocks had collapsed together, forming a ten-storey arch under which Bogoliubov walked whistling. In another neighbourhood, the old man had restored several exquisite houses, and they paused to refresh themselves there by a spring that was miraculously clean of radiation.

What Bogoliubov saw here was nature cleansing a wound. Gennady could never completely forget the tragedy of this place; the signs of hasty abandonment were everywhere, and his imagination filled in vistas of buses and queues of people clutching what they could carry, joking nervously about what they were told would be a temporary evacuation. Thinking about it too long made him angry, and he didn't want to be angry in a place that had become so beautiful. Bogoliubov had found his own solution to that by forgetting that this was ever a place of Man.

Gennady was suspicious that the old man might be trying to distract him, so he made a point of going out on his own to explore as well. It was tiring, but he had to verify Bogoliubov's story before he could feel he had done his job. Calling Merrick or Lisa was becoming difficult because he was out so much, and so tired from walking—but as well, he found himself increasingly moving in a meditative state. He had to give himself a shake, practically learn to speak again, before he could make a call.

To combat this feeling he spent his evenings in the Net, listening to the thrum of humanity's great chorus. Even there, however, he felt more an observer. Maybe that was okay; he had always been like this, it was just cities and obligations that drove him out of his natural habits.

Then one night he awoke to the sound of engines.

It was pitch-dark and for a second he didn't know where he was. Gennady sat up and focussed on the lunar rectangle of the living room window. For a moment he heard nothing, then the grumble started up again. He thought he saw a flicker of light outside.

He staggered to the balcony where he had set up his good telescope. The sound was louder here. Like an idling train, more felt than heard. It seemed to slide around in the air, the way train sounds did when they were coming from kilometres distant.

Light broke around a distant street corner. Gennady swung the telescope around and nearly had it focussed when something large and black lurched through his visual field, and was gone again. When he looked up from the lens he saw no sign of it.

He took the stairs two at a time, flashlight beam dodging wildly ahead of him. When he got to the lobby he switched it off and stepped cautiously to the front doors. His heart was pounding.

Gennady watched for a while, then ventured out into the street. It wasn't hard to hide here; any second he could drop in the tall grass or step behind a stand of young trees. So he made his way in the direction of the sound.

It took ten minutes to reach the spot where he'd seen the light. He dropped to one knee at the side of a filling station, and poked his head around the corner. The street was empty.

The whole intersection had been overtaken with weeds and young birch trees. He puzzled over the sight for a minute, then stood and walked out into their midst. There was absolutely nowhere here that you could drive a truck without knocking over lots of plants. But nothing was disturbed.

It was silent here now. Gennady had never ventured this far in the dark; the great black slabs of the buildings were quite unnerving. Shielding the light with one hand, he used the flashlight to try to find some tracks.

There were none.

On impulse he unslung the Geiger counter and switched it on. It immediately began chattering. For a few minutes he criss-crossed the intersection, finding a definite line of higher radioactivity bisecting it. He crouched on that line, and moved along it like he was weeding a garden, holding the counter close to the ground.

As the chattering peaked he spotted a black divot in the ground. He shone the flashlight on it. It was a deep W-shaped mark, of the sort made by the feet of back-hoes and cranes. A few meters beyond it he found another. Both were incredibly hot.

A deep engine pulse sounded through the earth. It repeated, then rose to a bone-shaking thunder as two brilliant lights pinioned Gennady from the far end of the street.

He clicked off the flashlight but the thing was already coming at him. The ground shook as it began to gallop.

There was no time to even see what it was. Gennady fled through whipping underbrush and under low branches, trying to evade the uncannily accurate lamps that sought him out. He heard steel shriek and the thud of falling trees as it flung aside all the obstacles he tried to put between them.

Ahead a narrow alley made a black rectangle between two warehouses. He ran into it. It was choked with debris and weeds. "Damn." Light welled up behind him.

Both warehouses had doors and windows opening off the alley. One door was ajar. On a sudden inspiration he flicked on the flashlight and threw it hard through a window of the other building, then dove for the open door.

He heard the sound of concrete scraping as the thing shouldered its way between the buildings. The lights were intense, and the noise of its engines was awful. Then the lights went out, as it paused. He had the uncanny impression that it was looking for him.

Gennady stood in a totally empty concrete floored building. Much of the roof had gone, and in the dim light he could see a clear path to the front door.

Cinderblocks shuddered and crashed outside. It was knocking a hole in the other building. Gennady ran for the door and made it through. The windows of the other warehouse were lit up.

He ran up the street to his building, and when he got inside he pulled his bike into a back room and raced up the stairs. He could hear the thing roaring around the neighbourhood for what seemed like hours, and then the noise slowly faded into the distance, and he fell back on his bedroll, exhausted.

At dawn he packed up and by midmorning he had left Pripyat and the contaminated zone behind him.

∞

Merrick poured pepper vodka into a tall glass and handed it to Gennady. "Dosvedanya. We picked up Druschenko this morning."

Gennady wondered as he sipped how the vodka would react with the iodine pill he'd just taken. Traffic noises and the smell of deisel wafted through the open window of Merrick's Kiev office. Merrick tipped back his own drink, smiled brightly and went to sit behind the huge oak desk that dominated the room.

"I have to thank you, Gennady. We literally couldn't find anyone else who was willing to go in there on the ground." He shook his head. "People panic at the thought of radiation."

"Don't much like it myself." Gennady took another sip. "But you can detect and avoid it. Not so simple to do with the stuff that comes out of the smokestacks these days. Or gets by the filters at the water plant."

Merrick nodded. "So you were able to take all the right precautions."

Gennady thought of Bogoliubov's warm tea settling in his

stomach...and he had done other stupid things there too. But the doctors insisted his overall dosage was "acceptable." His odds for getting cancer had gone up as much as if he'd been chain-smoking for the past six months. Acceptable? How could one know?

"So that's that," said Merrick. "You found absolutely no evidence that anyone but Druschenko had visited the sarcophagus, right? Once we prove that it was him driving the RPV, we'll be able to close this file entirely. I think you deserve a bonus, Gennady, and I've almost got the board to agree."

"Well, thanks." RPV—they had decided the dragon must be one of the Remotely Piloted Vehicles that the Trust had used to build the new sarcophagus. Druschenko had taken some of the stockpiled parts and power supplies from a Trust warehouse, and apparently gotten one of the old lifters going. It was the only way he could open the sarcophagus and survive.

Merrick was happy. Lisa was ecstatic that he was out of Pripyat. It all seemed too easy to Gennady; maybe it was because they hadn't seen the thing. This morning he'd walked down to the ironworks to watch someone using a Chernobyl-model RPV near the kilns. It had looked like a truck with legs, and moved like a sloth. Nothing like the thing that had chased him across the city.

Anyway, he had his money. He chatted with Merrick for a while, then Gennady left to find a bank machine, and prove to himself he'd been paid. First order of business, a new suit. Then he was going to shop for one of those new interfaces for his system. Full virtual reality, like he'd been dreaming about for months.

The noise and turbulence of Kiev's streets hit him like a wall. People everywhere, but no one noticed anyone else in a city like this. He supposed most people drifted through the streets treating all these strangers around as no more than ghosts, but he couldn't do that. As he passed an old woman who was begging on the corner, he found himself noticing the laugh lines around her eyes that warred with the deeply scored lines of disappointment around her mouth; the meticulous stitchwork where she had repaired the sleeves of her cheap dress spoke of a dignity that must make her situation seem all the worse for her. He couldn't ignore her, but he couldn't help her either.

For a while he stood at a downtown intersection, staring over the sea of people. Above the grimy facades, a haze of coal smoke and exhaust banded the sky a yellow that matched the shade on the grimy tattered flags hanging from the street lamps.

Everywhere, he saw victims of the Release. Men and women with open sores or wearing the less visible scars of destitution and disappointment dawdled on the curbs, stared listlessly through shop windows at goods they would never be able to afford on their meagre pensions. No one looked at them.

He bought the interface instead of the suit, and the next day he didn't go out at all.

∞

He was nursing a crick in his neck, drinking some weak tea and preparing to go back into a huge international consensual-reality game he now had the equipment to play, when Lisa called.

"Look, Lisa, I've got new toys."

"Why am I not surprised. Have you been out at all since you got back?"

"No. I'm having fun."

"How are you going to meet a nice Ukrainian girl if you never go out?"

"Maybe I like English girls better."

"Oh yeah? Then fly to England. You just got paid."

"The Net is so much faster. And I have the right attachments now."

She laughed. "Toys. I see. You want the latest news on the case?"

He frowned. No, actually, he didn't think he did. But she lived for this sort of thing. "Sure," he said to indulge her.

"Druschenko says he was just the courier. Says he never drove the dragon at all. He's actually quite frantic—he claims he was paid to bring supplies in and do the initial hook up of a RPV, but that's all. Of course, he's made some mighty big purchases lately, and we can't trace the money and he won't tell us where it is. So it's a stalemate."

Gennady thought about Merrick's cheerful confidence the other day. "Did the Trust actually make the most recent payment to the extortionist?"

"No. They could hardly afford to, and anyway Druschenko—"

"Could not have acted alone."

"What?"

"Come on, Lisa. You said yourself you can't find the money. It went into the Net, right? That's your territory, it's not Druschenko's. He's a truck driver, not a hacker, for God's sake. Listen, have they put a Geiger counter on him?"

"Why..."

"Find out how hot he is. He had to have been piloting the RPV from nearby, unless he had a satellite link, and there too, he's just a truck driver, not James Bond. Find out how hot he is."

"Um. Maybe you have a point."

"And another thing. Has the Trust put some boats in the river to check for another radiation plume?"

"I don't know."

"We better find out. Because I'll bet you a case of vodka there's going to be another Release."

"Can I call you right back?"

"Certainly." He hung up, shaking his head. People who lived by Occam's Razor died young. That, he supposed, was why he got paid the big bucks.

∞

He spent most of the next week in the Net, venturing out for groceries and exercise. He smiled at a pretty clerk in the grocery store, and she smiled back, but he never knew what to say in such situations, where he couldn't hide behind an avatar's mask or simply disappear if he embarrassed himself; so he didn't talk to her.

In the platonic perfection of the Net, though, Gennady had dozens of friends and business connections. Between brief searches for new work, he participated in numerous events, both games and art pieces. Here he could be witty, and handsome. And there was no risk. But when he finally rolled into bed at night, there was no warm body there waiting for him, and at those times he felt deeply lonely.

In the morning the computer beckoned, and he would quickly forget the feeling.

Merrick interrupted him in the middle of a tank battle. In this game, Gennady was one of the British defending North Africa against the Desert Fox. The sensual qualities of his new interface were amazing; he could feel the heat, the grit of the sand, almost smell it. The whole effect was ruined when the priority one window opened in the middle of the air above his turret, and Merrick said, "Gennady, I've got a new job for you."

North Africa dissolved. Gennady realized his back hurt and his mouth was dry. "What is it?" he snapped.

"I wouldn't be calling if I didn't think you were the perfect man for the job. We need someone to make a very brief visit to Pripyat. Shouldn't take more than a day."

"Where's that bonus you promised me?"

"I was coming to that. The board's authorized me to pay you an additional twenty percent bonus for work already done. That's even if you turn down this contract."

"Ah. I see. So what is it you need?" He was interested, but he didn't want to appear too eager. Could lower the price that way.

"We want to make sure the sarcophagus is intact. We were going to do a helicopter inspection, but it's just possible Druschenko did some low level...well, to put it bluntly, got inside."

"Inside? What do you mean, inside?"

"There may be some explosives inside the sarcophagus. Now we don't want anybody going near it, physically. Have you ever piloted an RPV?"

"Not really. Done a lot of virtual reality sims, but that's not the same thing."

"Close enough. Anyway, we only need you to get the thing to the reactor site. We've got an explosives expert on call who'll take over once you get there and deactivate the bombs. If there are any."

"So he's coming with me?"

"Not exactly, no. He'll be riding in on a satellite link. You're to establish that link in Pripyat, drive the RPV to the reactor, and he'll jack in to do the actual assessment. Then you pull out. That's all there is to it."

"Why can't somebody pilot it in from outside the city?"

"It's only works on a short-range link. You'll have to get within two miles of the sarcophagus."

"Great. Just great. When do you want this to happen?"

"Immediately. I'm having your RPV flown in, it'll arrive tonight. Can you set out in the morning?"

"Depends on what you're willing to pay me."

"Double your last fee."

"Triple."

"Done."

Shit, he thought. *Should have gone for more*. "All right, Merrick, you've got yourself an RPV driver. For a day."

∞

Gennady debated whether to call Lisa. On the one hand, there was obviously more to this than Merrick was admitting. On the other, she would tell him not to go back to Pripyat. He wanted to avoid that particular conversation, so he didn't call.

Instead he took a cab down to a Trust warehouse at six o'clock to inspect his RPV. The warehouse was a tall anonymous metal-clad building; his now practised eye told him it might remain standing for twenty or thirty years if abandoned. Except that the roof would probably cave in...

"You Malianov?" The man was stocky, with the classic slab-like Russian face. He wiped his hands on an oily rag as he walked out to meet

Gennady. Gennady shook his hand, smiling as he remembered Bogoliubov, and they went in to inspect the unit.

"What the hell is that?" Whatever it was, it was not just a remotely piloted vehicle. Standing in a shaft of sunlight was an ostrich-like machine at least three meters tall. It sprouted cameras and mikes from all over, and sported two uncannily human arms at about shoulder level. Gennady's guide grinned and gave it a shove. It shuffled its feet a little, regaining balance.

"Military telepresence. Latest model." The man grabbed one of its hands. "We're borrowing it from the Americans. You like?"

"Why do we need this?"

"How the hell should I know? All I know is you're reconnoitering the sarcophagus with it. Right?"

Gennady nodded. He kept his face neutral, but inside he was fuming. Merrick was definitely not telling him everything.

That evening he went on a supply run downtown. He bought all the things he hadn't on his first trip out, including a lot more food. Very intentionally, he did not pause to ask himself why he was packing a month's worth of food for a two day trip.

He was sitting in the middle of the living room floor, packing and repacking, when Lisa phoned. He took it as a voice-only call; if she asked, he'd say he wasn't dressed or something.

"Remember what you said about how Druschenko would have to have had a satellite link to run the dragon?"

"Yeah." He hopped onto the arm of his couch. He was keyed up despite the lateness of the hour.

"Well, you got me thinking," she said. "And guess what? There's a connection. Not with Druschenko, though."

"Okay, I'll bite."

"Can you jack in? I'll have to do some show and tell here."

"Okay." He made sure the apartment cameras were off, then went into the Net. Lisa was there in full avatar—visible head to foot, in 3-D—grinning like the proverbial cat with the canary.

"So I thought, what if Druschenko did have a satellite link to the sarcophagus? And lo and behold, somebody does." She called up some windows that showed coordinates, meaningless to Gennady. "At least, there's traffic to some kind of transceiver there. I figured I had Druschenko right then—but the link's still live, and traffic goes way up at regular intervals. During the night, your time. So we're dealing with a night-hawk, I thought. Except he wouldn't have to be a night-hawk if he was calling from, say, North America."

"Wait, wait, you're getting way ahead of me. What's this traffic consist of? You intercepted it, didn't you?"

"Well, not exactly. It's heavily encrypted. Plus, once it's in the net it goes through a bunch of anonymous rerouters, gets split up and copies sent to null addresses, and so on. Untraceable from this end, at least so far."

"Ah, so if he's from North America, that narrows it down a bit. To only about half a billion possibilities."

"Ah, Gennady, you have so little faith. It's probably a telepresence link, right? That's your dragon. Nothing big was brought in, so it's got to be an adaptation of the existing Chernobyl designs. So whoever it is, they should be familiar with those designs, and they'd have to know there were still some RPV's in Pripyat, and they should have a connection to Druschenko. And—here's the topper—they had a lot of start-up capital to run this scam. Had to, with the satellite link, the souping-up of the RPV, and the missiles."

"Missiles? What missiles?"

"Haven't you checked the news lately? One of the Trust's helicopters crashed yesterday. It was doing a low-level pass over the sarcophagus, and wham! down it goes. Pilot was killed. An hour after the news was released I started seeing all sorts of traffic on my secure Interpol groups, police in Kiev and Brussels talking about ground-to-air misssiles."

"Oh, shit," he said.

"So anyway, I just looked for somebody involved in the original sarcophagus project, on the RPV side, who was American and rich. And it popped out at me."

Gennady was barely listening, but his attention returned when she brought up a window with a grainy photo of a thin-faced elderly man. It was hard to tell, but he appeared to be lying on a bed. His eyes were bright and hard, and they stared directly out at Gennady.

"Trevor Jaffrey. He got quite rich doing RPV's and telepresence about twenty years ago. The Chernobyl project was his biggest contract. A while after that he became a recluse, and began wasting his money on some pretty bizarre projects."

"Dragons?"

"Well, Jaffrey's a quadraplegic. He got rich through the Net, and he lived through it too. When I say he became a recluse, he already was, physically. He dropped out of Net society too, and spent all his time and money on physical avatars—telepresences. I've got access to a couple of them, because he had to sell them when he couldn't pay his bills. Want to see one?"

"What, now?"

"I've got a temporary pass. This one's being used as a theme park ride now. At one time Jaffrey must have spent all his free time in it. The mind boggles."

She had his entire attention now. "Okay. Show me."

"Here's the address, name and password. Just take a quick peek. I'll wait."

He entered the commands, and waited as a series of message windows indicated a truly prodigious data pipe opening between his little VR setup and some distant machine. Then the world went dark, and when it came back again he was underwater.

Gennady was standing on the ocean floor. All around were towers of coral, and rainbow fishes swam by in darting schools. The ocean was brilliant blue, the sunlight above shattered into thousands of crystal shards by the waves. He turned his head, and felt the water flow through his hair. It was warm, felt silky against his skin. He could breathe just fine, but he also felt completely submerged.

Gennady raised a hand. Something huge and metal lifted up, five steel fingers on its end. He waggled them—they moved.

This is not a simulation, he realized. Somewhere, in one of the Earth's seas, this machine was standing, and he was seeing through its eyes and hearing through its ears.

He took a step. He could walk, as easily as though he were on land.

Gennady knelt and ran his fingers through the fine white sand. He could actually feel it. Black Sea? More likely the Caribbean, if this Jaffrey was American.

It was achingly beautiful, and he wanted to stay. But Lisa was waiting. He logged out, and as he did caught a glimpse of a truly huge number in American dollars, which flashed *paid in full* then vanished.

Lisa's avatar was smiling, hands behind her back and bobbing on the balls of her feet. "Jaffrey can't pay his bills. And he's addicted to his telepresences. You should see the arctic one. He even had a lunar one for a while. See the common thread?"

"They're all places nobody goes. Or nobody can go," he said. He was starting to feel tired.

"Jaffrey hates people. And he's being driven out of his bodies, one after the other. So he turns in desperation to an old, reliable one—the Chernobyl RPV. Designed to survive working conditions there, and there's still parts, if he can pay off an old acquaintance from the project to bring them in."

"So he does, and he's got a new home." He nodded. "And a way of making more money. Extort the Trust."

"Exactly. Aren't I smart?"

"You, Lisaveta, are a genius." He blew her image a kiss. "So all we need to do is shut him down, and the crisis is over."

"Hmm. Well, no, not exactly. American law is different, and the Net connections aren't proven to go to him. We can't actually move on him until we can prove it's him doing it."

"Well, shut down the feed from the satellite, then."

"We were about to do that," she said with a scowl. "When we got a call from Merrick. Seems the extortionist contacted him just after the missile thing. Warned that he'd blow the sarcophagus if anybody cut the link or tried to get near the place."

"A dead-man switch?"

"Probably. So it's not so simple as it looks."

He closed his eyes and nodded.

"How about you?" she asked. "Anything new?"

"Oh, no, no. Not really. Same old thing, you know?"

∞

It was raining when he reached his apartment building. Gennady had driven the motorcycle in, leaving all his other supplies by the city gates. He wanted to try something.

The rain was actually a good thing; it made a good cover for him to work under. He parked his bike in the foyer, and hauled a heavy pack from the sidecar, then up twelve floors to the roof. Panting and cursing, he paused to rest under a fibreglass awning. The roof was overgrown with weeds. The sarcophagus was a distant grey dome in a pool of marshland.

He hooked up the satellite feed and aimed it. Then he unreeled a fibre-optic line down the stairs to the sixth floor, and headed for his old place.

Somebody had trashed it. Bogoliubov, it had to be. The piano had bullet holes in it, and there was shit smeared on the wall. The words "Stay away" were written in the stuff.

"Jesus." Gennady backed out of the room.

Scratching his stubble nervously, he shouldered his way into the next apartment. This one was empty except for some old stacking chairs, and had a water-damaged ceiling and one broken window. Radiation was higher than he would have found acceptable a week ago—but after he finished here he could find a better place. Then think what to do about Bogoliubov.

He secured the door and set up his generator and the rest of the computer equipment. He needed a repeater for the satellite signal, and he put that on the balcony. Then he jacked in, and connected to his RPV.

At first all he saw was dirt. Gennady raised his head, and saw the road into town, blurred by rain. He stood up, and felt himself rise to more than man-height. This was great! He flexed his arms, turned his torso back and forth, then reached to pick up his sacks of supplies.

It was a bit awkward using these new arms, but he got the hang of it after spilling some groceries and a satchel of music disks into the mud. When it was all hanging from his mantis-like limbs, he rose up again and trotted toward town.

The RPV drank gas to feed its fuel cells. Bogoliubov had shown Gennady some full tanks on the edge of town, enough to keep the thing going for months or years. Thinking of the old man, Gennady decided that as soon as they were done with Jaffrey, he would visit Bogoliubov with the RPV, and confiscate his rifle.

He jogged tirelessly through the rain until he came to his building. There he paused to hide the bike, in case the old man did come around today, then bumped his way into the stairwell and went up.

Gennady paused in front of the apartment door. He hadn't counted on the eeriness of this moment. He listened, hearing only the faint purr of the generator inside. Hesitantly, he reached to turn the knob with a steel hand, and eased the door open.

A man crouched on the floor near one wall. He was stocky and balding, in his late thirties. He was dressed in a teal shirt and green slacks. His eyes were closed, and small wires ran from his temples to a set of black boxes near the balcony door. He was rocking slowly back and forth.

Jesus, am I doing that? Gennady instantly cut the link. He blinked and looked up, to find the doorway blocked by a monstrous steel and crystal creature. Its rainbow-beaded lenses were aimed at him. Plastic bags swayed from its clenched fists. Gennady's heart started hammering, as though the thing had somehow snuck up on him.

Swearing, he hastily unloaded the supplies from its arms. After putting the stuff away he found himself reluctant to re-enter the living room. Under this low roof the RPV looked like a metal dinosaur ready to pounce. It must weight two hundred kilos at least. He'd have to remember that, and avoid marshy ground or rotten floors when he used it outside.

He linked to it again just long enough to park it down the hall. Then he shut the door and jammed a chair under the knob.

∞

The morning birds woke Gennady. For a long time he just lay there, drinking in the peace. In his half-awake state, he imagined an invisible shield around this small apartment, sheltering him from any sort of pain, aggravation or distraction. Of all places in the world, he had finally found the one where he could be fully, completely carefree. The hot spots of radiation could be mapped and avoided; he would deal with Bogoliubov in time; Jaffrey would not be a problem for long.

No one would ever evict him from this place. No one would come around asking after him solicitously. No noisy neighbours would move in. And yet, as long as he had fuel to run the generator, he could step into the outside world as freely as ever, live by alias in any or all of the thousands of worlds of the Net.

Be exactly who he wanted to be…

Feel at home at last.

But finally he had to rise, make himself a meagre breakfast and deal with the reality of the situation. His tenancy here was fragile. Everything would have to go perfectly for him to be able to take advantage of the opportunity he had been given.

First he phoned Merrick. "You never told me about the helicopter."

"Really? I'm sure I did." It was only a voice line; Gennady was sure Merrick wouldn't have been so glib if they'd been able to make eye contact.

Gennady would feel absolutely no guilt over stealing the RPV from him.

"Forget it, except let me say you are a bastard and I'll join the Nazis before I work for you after this," he said. "Now tell me what we're doing. And no more surprises or I walk."

Merrick let the insult pass. They set the itinerary and time for the reconnoitering of the sarcophagus. Gennady was to use the RPV's full set of sensors to ensure there were no tripwires or mines on the approach. Druschenko had denied knowledge of anything other than Jaffrey's RPV. Certainly hearing about the missiles beforehand would have been nice.

"You're to do the initial walking inspection this afternoon at 2:00. Is that enough time for you to familiarize yourself with the RPV?"

Gennady glanced at the apartment door. "No problem."

With everything set, Merrick rang off and Gennady, stretching, stepped onto the balcony to watch the morning sun glow off the sarcophagus. It was an oval dome made of interlocking concrete triangles. Rust stains spread down the diamonds here and there from the heavy stanchions that held it all together. Around the circumference of the thing, he knew, a thick wall was sunk all the way to bedrock, preventing seepage of the horrors within. It was supposed to last ten thousand years; like most people, Gennady assumed it would crumble in a century. Still, one had to be responsible to one's own time.

Humming, he groped for his coffee cup. Just as it reached his lips the computer said, "Lisaveta is calling you."

He burned his tongue.

"Damn damn damn. Is it voice or full-feed? Full-feed. Shit."

He jacked in. He hoped she would match his laconic tone as he said, "Hello, Lisa."

"You asshole."

He found it difficult to meet her gaze. "Are we going to get into something pointless here?"

"No. I'm going to talk and you're going to listen."

"I see."

"Why the hell didn't you tell me you were going back?"

"You'd have told me not to go. I didn't want an argument."

"So you don't respect me enough to argue with me?"

"What?" The idea made no sense to him. He just hadn't seen what good it would do to fight. And, just maybe, he *had* been afraid she might talk him out of it. But he would never admit that to her.

"Gennady. I'm not trying to run your life. If you want to throw it away that's your business. But I'm your friend. I care about you. I just...just want to *know*, that's all."

He frowned, staring out the window. Dozens of empty apartment windows stared back. For an instant he imagined dozens of other Gennadys, all looking out, none seeing the others.

"Maybe I don't want to be known," he said. "I'm tired of this world of snoops and gossips. Maybe I want to write my memoirs in a private language. Apparently that's not allowed."

"Pretty ironic for you to be tired of snoops," she said, "inasmuch as that's what you do for a living. And me too..." She blinked, then scowled even harder. "Are you referring to—"

"Look, I have to go now—"

"*That's* what this is about, isn't it? You just want to be able to hang up on anybody and everybody the instant you start feeling uncomfortable." Lisa looked incredulous. "Is that it? It is, isn't it. You want to have your cake and eat it. So you found a place where you can hide from everybody, just poke your head out whenever you need someone to talk to. Well, I'm not a TV, you know. I'm not going to let you just turn me on and off when it suits you.

"Keep your empty town and your empty life, then. I'll have none of it."

She hung up.

"Bitch!" He yanked off the headset and kicked the wall. No neighbours to complain—he kicked it again. "What the hell do you want from me?" He'd put a hole in the plasterboard. Dust swirled up, and he heard the Geiger counter buzz louder for a second.

"Oh, God." He slumped on the balcony, but when he raised his eyes all that met them was the vista of the sarcophagus, gleaming now like some giant larva on the banks of the river.

Unaccountably, Gennady found his eyes filling with tears.

How long has it been, he wondered in amazement, *since you cried?*

Years. He pinched the bridge of his nose, and blinked a few times. He needed to walk; yes, a long walk in the sun would bring him around…

He stopped at the door to the apartment. There was the plastic wrap he should use to cover his shoes. And the face mask. And beside that the Geiger counter.

A horrible feeling of being trapped stole over him. For a few minutes he stood there, biting his nails, staring at the peeling wallpaper. Then the anger returned, and he kicked the wall again.

"I'm right." To prove it, he sat down, jacked in, and called up the interface for the RPV.

∞

Gennady held his head high as he walked in the sun in a plaza where no human could set foot for the next six thousand years. He knelt and examined the gigantic wildflowers that grew in abundance here. They were *his*, in a way that nothing else had ever been nor could be outside this place. This must be how the old man felt, he marvelled—but Bogoliubov's armour was a deliberate refusal to believe the danger he was in. With the RPV, Gennady had no need for such illusions.

He didn't take every opportunity to explore. There would be plenty of time for that later, after he reported the accidental destruction of the RPV. For now, he just sauntered and enjoyed the day. His steel joints moved soundlessly, and he felt no fatigue or heat.

Beep. "Merrick here. Gennady, are you on line?"

"Yes. I'm here."

"Gennady, let me introduce Dentrane. You'll hand the RPV off to him when you get in position, and he'll take it from there. If we're lucky, we'll only need to do this once."

"Hello, Gennady," said Dentrane. He had a thick Estonian accent.

"Good to hear from you, Dentrane. Shall I walk us over to the sarcophagus and you can take a peek at what all the fuss is about?"

Dentrane laughed. "Delighted. Lead on."

Time to be 'all business' as Lisaveta would say. He jogged towards the river.

∞

"It's American law," Lisa was saying to Merrick. They had met in a neutral room in cyberspace. Merrick's avatar was bland as usual; Lisa had represented herself as a cyber-Medusa, with fibre-optic leads snaking from her hair to attach to a globe that floated before her. "When you're dealing with the Net, you've got both international and local laws to worry about," she explained. "We can't guarantee our trace of the paths to the satellite signal. We can't shut it down on the satellite end. And unless we have proof that it's Jaffrey doing this, we can't shut down it down at his end."

"So our hands are tied." Merrick's avatar was motionless, but she imagined him pacing. In a window next to him, the live feed from the RPV showed green foliage, then the looming concrete curve of the sarcophagus.

"You're going to have to trust me. We'll find a way to prove it's Jaffrey."

"I have sixteen military RPVs waiting in the river. The second I see a problem, Ms. MacDonald, they're going in. And if they go in, you have to shut down Jaffrey."

"I can't! And what if he's got a dead-man switch?"

"I'm relying on Dentrane to tell us if he does. And I'm relying on you to cut Jaffrey off when I order it."

She glared at the avatar. It must be ten times she'd told him she had no authority to do that. She knew how to, sure—but if they were wrong and Jaffrey wasn't the extortionist, she would be criminally liable. But Merrick didn't care about that.

He didn't seem to care about Gennady, either. And why should he? Gennady had chosen to plant himself right next to the sarcophagus. If it blew up he would have no one to blame but himself.

And that would be absolutely no consolation when she had to fly out to watch him die of radiation poisoning in some Soviet-vintage hospital ward. She had woken herself up last night with that scenario, and had lain awake wondering why she should do that for a man whom she knew only through the Net. But maybe it was precisely because their association was incomplete. Lisa knew he was as real a person as she; in a way they were close. But they would not have really met until she touched his hand, and she couldn't bear the thought of losing him before that happened.

Angrily she glanced at her ranks of numbers and documents, all of which pointed at Jaffrey, none conclusively. It all made her feel so helpless. She turned to watch the movement of the RPV instead.

The RPV had scaled the steep lower part of the sarcophagus, and now clambered hand over hand toward a red discoloration on one flank. With a start, Lisa realized there were some bulky objects sticking up there. The camera angle swerved and jittered, then the RPV paused long enough for her to get a good look. She heard Merrick swear just as she realized she was looking at tarpaulins, painted to resemble the concrete of the structure, that had been stretched over several green metal racks.

Then one of the tarps disappeared in a white cloud. The camera shook as everything vanished in a white haze. Then—static.

"What was that?"

"Holy mother of God," said Merrick. "He launched."

∞

Gennady froze. He had stepped onto the balcony to let Dentrane get on with his work. From here he had a magnificent view of the sarcophagus, so the contrail of the rocket was clearly visible. It rose straight up, an orange cut in the sky, then levelled off and headed straight at him. He just had time to blink and think, *I'm standing right next to the RPV signal repeater* before the contrail leapt forward faster than the eye could follow, and all the windows of the surrounding buildings flashed sun-bright.

The concussion was a sudden hammer blow, nothing like the roaring explosions he heard in movies or VR. He was on his back on the balcony, ears ringing, when he heard the *bang!* echo back from the other buildings, and could almost follow its course through the abandoned city as the rings of shocked air hit one neighbourhood after the next, and reported back.

A cascade of dust and grit obscured the view. It all came from overhead somewhere. He realized as he sat up that the explosion had occurred on the roof. That was where he'd set up the big dish necessary for Dentrane's data-feed.

The fear felt like cold spreading through his chest, down his arms. He leaned on the swaying balcony, watching for the second contrail that would signal the second rocket. The dish on the roof was the link to the

Net, yes; but it fed its signal down here to the transmitter that sat a meter to Gennady's left, and that transmitter was the control connection to the RPV. It was the only live beacon now.

Nothing happened. As the seconds passed, Gennady found himself paralyzed by indecision: in the time it took him to rise to his feet and turn, and take three steps, the rocket might be on him—and he had to see it if it came.

It did not. Gradually he became aware that his mouth was open, his throat hurting from a yell that hadn't made it from his lungs to his vocal chords. He fell back on his elbows, then shouted "Shit!" at a tenth the volume he thought he needed, and scrambled back into the apartment.

He was halfway down the stairs when the cell phone rang. He barked a laugh at the prosaic echo, the only sound now in this empty building other than his chattering foot-steps. He grabbed it from his belt. "What?"

"Gennady! Are you all right?"

"Yes, Lisa."

"Oh, thank God! Listen, you've got to get out of there—"

"Just leaving."

"I'm so glad."

"Fuck you." He hung up and jammed the phone back in his belt. It immediately rang again. Gennady stopped, cursed, grabbed it, almost pressed the receive button. Then he tossed it over the banister. After a second he heard it hit the landing below with a crack.

He ran past it into the lobby, and pulled out the bike. He started it, and paused to look around the sad, abandoned place he had almost lived in. His hand on the throttle was trembling.

The release could happen at any moment. There would be an explosion, who knew how big; he imagined chunks of concrete floating up in the air, exposing a deep red wound in the earth, the unhealing sore of Chernobyl. A cloud of dust would rise, he could watch it from outside. Quiet, subtle, it would turn its head toward Kiev, as it had years ago. Soon there would be more ghosts in the streets of the great city.

He would get away. Lisa would never speak to him, and he could never walk the avenues of Kiev again without picturing himself here. He could never look the survivors of the Release in the eye again. But he would have gotten away.

"Liar!"

The sound jolted him. Gennady looked up. Bogoliubov, the self-proclaimed custodian of Pripyat, stalked towards him across the courtyard, his black greatcoat flapping in the evening breeze.

"Liar," said the old man again.

"I'm not staying," Gennady shouted.

"You *lied* to me!"

Gennady took his hand off the throttle. "What?"

"You work for the Trust. Or is it the army! And to think I believed that story about you being a med student." Bogoliubov stopped directly in Gennady's path.

"Look, we haven't got time for this. There might be another release. We have to get out of here. Hop on."

Bogoliubov's eyes widened. "So you betrayed him, too. I'm not surprised." He spat in the dirt at Gennady's feet and turned away. "I'm not going anywhere with you."

"Wait!" Gennady popped the kickstand on the bike and caught up to the old man. "I'm sorry. I didn't mean to hurt you. I came here because of the dragon. How could I know you weren't involved?"

Bogoliubov whirled, scowling. He seemed to be groping for words. Finally, "Trust was a mistake," was all he said. As if the effort cost him greatly, he reached out and shoved Gennady hard in the chest. Then he walked rapidly away.

Gennady watched him go, then returned to the bike. His head was throbbing. He shut the bike down, and walked slowly back to the entrance of the apartment building. He stopped. He waited, staring at the sky. And then he went in.

∞

"Lisaveta, I'm linking to the RPV now."

"Gennady! What?" He smiled grimly at the transparent surprise in her voice. She who liked to Know, had been startled by him. Gennady had linked the cell-phone signal to the RPV interface. She would get voice, but no video this way.

He adjusted the headset. "Connecting now." He took a deep breath, and jabbed the *enter* key on his board.

Vision lurched. And then he was staring at a red tarpaulin, which was tangled up in the fallen spars of a green metal rack. Several long metal tubes stuck out of this, all aimed at the ground. A haze like exhaust from a bus hung over everything.

The missile rack shook. Gennady cautiously turned his head to see what might be causing the motion. Directly beside him was the black, rusted flank of a thing like a tank with legs. Several sets of arms dangled from its sloped front, and two of these were tearing the tough fabric of the tarp away from the collapsed rack.

"Gennady, talk to me!" He smiled to hear the concern in her voice. "Where are you?"

"Dentrane's out of the loop, so I've taken over the RPV. I've got it on the side of the sarcophagus."

"But where are you?"

"Lisa, listen. *Someone else is here*. Do you under-stand? There is another RPV, and it's trying to fix the missile rack."

"Jaffrey..."

"That his name? Whatever." The black dragon had nearly unravelled the tarp. If it succeeded in realigning the missile tubes, it would have a clear shot at the balcony where Gennady now sat.

"It's ignoring me. Thinks I've run away, I guess." He looked around, trying not to turn his head. There was nothing obvious to use as a weapon—but then his own RPV was a weapon, he recalled. Nothing compared to the hulking, grumbling thing next to him, but more than a match for—

—the missile tubes he pounced on. Gennady felt the whole structure go down under him, metal rending. He flailed about, scattering the tubes with loud banging blows, winding up on his asbestos backside looking up at the two spotlight eyes of the black RPV.

He switched on the outside speaker. "This isn't your private sandbox, you know."

Two huge arms shot out. He rolled out of the way. Metal screamed.

A deep roaring shook the whole side of the sarcophagus. He could see small spires of dust rise from the triangular concrete slabs. The dragon had leaped, and utterly smashed the place where he had just been.

Just ahead under the flapping square of another grey tarp Gennady saw a deep black opening in the side of the sarcophagus. "This your home?" he shouted as he clambered up to it.

"Stay away!" The voice was deep and carrying, utterly artificial.

"What was that?" Lisa was still with him.

"That would be your Jaffrey. He's pissed, as the Yankees would say."

"Why are you doing this?"

"Lisa, he's going to make a release. We both know it. Only a fool wouldn't realize there's a backup plan to me being here. If I fail, the men in the choppers come in, am I wrong? You and I know it. This guy knows it. Now he's got nothing to lose. He'll blow the top off the place."

"Merrick's ready to send the others in now. You just get out of there and let them handle it."

"No." The monster was close behind him as Gennady made it to the dark opening. "I can't avoid this one. You know it's true."

She might have said "Oh," and he did imagine a tone of sad resignation to whatever she did say, but he was too busy bashing his way into the bottom of a pit to make it out. Gennady rolled to a stop in a haze of static; his cameras adjusted to the dark in time for him to see a huge black square block the opening above, and fall at him.

"Shit!" He couldn't avoid it this time. Something heavy hit him as he staggered to his feet, flicking him into a wall as though he were made of balsa wood. He didn't actually feel the blow, but it was an impossibly quick motion like a speeded-up movie; sensation vanished from his right arm.

He managed to cartwheel out of the way of another piston blow. Gennady backed up several paces, and looked around.

This was sort of an antechamber to the remnants of one of the reactor rooms. Circles of light from the headlamp eyes of the dragon swooped and dove through an amazing tangle of twisted metal and broken cement under the low red girders of the sarcophagus' ceiling. Here were slabs of wall still painted institution green, next to charred metal pipes as thick as his body. The wreckage made a rough ring around a cleared area in the centre. And there, the thing he had never in his life expected to see, there was the open black mouth of the obscenity itself.

Jaffrey, if this was indeed he, had made a nest in the caldera of Reactor Four.

Gennady bounded across the space and up the rubble on the other side. He clutched at a cross-beam and pulled himself up on it while the dragon laboured to follow. When he reached with both arms, only one appeared and grasped the beam.

"Come down," said the dragon in its deep bass that rattled the very beams. Its bright eyes were fixed on him, only meters below.

"What, are you crazy?" he said, instantly regretting his choice of words.

The dragon sat back with a seismic thud. It turned its big black head, eerily like a bear's as it regarded him.

"I've been watching you," it said after a long minute.

Gennady backed away along the girder.

"When I was a boy," said the dragon of Pripyat, "I wrote a letter to God. And then I put the letter in a jar, and I buried it in the garden, as deep as I could reach. It never occurred to me that someone might dig it up one day. I thought, no one sees God. God is in the hidden places between the walls, behind us when we are looking the other way. But I have put this letter out of the world. Maybe God will pass by and read it."

"Gennady," said Lisa. "You have to find out who this is. We can't cut

Jaffrey's signal until we have proof that it's him. Can you hear me?"

"I watched you walking in the evenings," said the dragon. "You stared up at the windows the same way I do. You put your hands behind your back, head down, and traced the cracks in the pavement like a boy. You moved as one liberated from a curse."

"Shut up," said Gennady.

"Do you remember the first photos from the accident? Remember the image of this place's roof? Just a roof, obviously trashed by an explosion of some kind. But still, a roof, where you could stand and look out. Except you couldn't. No one could. That roof was the first place I had ever actually seen that had been removed from the world. A place no one could go or ever would go. To stand there for even a moment was death. Remember?"

"I was too young," said Gennady.

"Good," said Lisa. "We know he's old enough to remember 1986. Keep him talking."

Gennady scowled, wishing the RPV could convey the expression.

"Later I remembered that," said the dragon. "When I could no longer live as a person in the world of people. Remember the three men in the Bible who were cast in the belly of the furnace, and survived? Oh, I needed to do that. To live in the belly of the furnace. You know what I mean, don't you?"

Gennady crawled backward along the beam. The horrible thing was, he did know. He couldn't have explained it, but the dragon's words were striking him deeply, wounding him far more than its metal hands had.

"So look." The dragon gestured behind it at the pit. It had arranged some chairs and a table around the black calandria. A bottle on the table held a sprig of wildflowers. There was other furniture, Gennady now saw—filing cabinets, bookshelves, and yes, books everywhere. This monster had not merely visited this place; it lived here.

He saw another thing, as well. On the back of the dragon, under a cross of bent metal spars, was a small satellite dish. This spun and turned wildly to keep its focus on some distant point in the heavens.

"Lisa, he's linked directly to the dragon. No repeaters."

"That a problem?"

"Damn right it's a problem! I can't stop the thing by pulling any plugs."

"You and I have had the same ambition," the dragon said to Gennady. "To live in the invisible world, visit the place that can't be visited. Except that I was forced to it. You're healthy, you can walk. What made you come here?"

"Don't," said Gennady.

The searchlights found and pinned him again. "What hurt you?" asked the dragon.

Gennady hissed. "None of your business."

The dragon was now perfectly still. "Is it so strong in you that you can never admit to it? Tell me—if I were to say I will hunt your body down and kill you now unless you tell me why you came here—would you tell me?"

Gennady couldn't answer.

The dragon surged to its feet. "You don't even know what you have!" it roared. "You can walk. You can still make love—really, not just in some simulation. And you *dare* to come in here and try to take away the only thing I've got left?"

Gennady lost his grip on the beam and fell. A book-shelf shattered under him.

The dragon towered over him. "You can't live here," it said. "You're just a tourist."

He expected a blow that would shatter his connection, but it didn't come. Instead the monster stepped over him, making for the exit.

"I can run faster than your little motorbike," it said. Then it was gone, up the entrance shaft.

Gennady tried to rise. One of his legs was broken. One-legged, one-armed, there was no way he was getting out of here.

"Gennady," said Lisa. "What's happening?"

"He left," said Gennady. "He's gone to kill me."

"Break the link. Run for it. You can get to the motorcycle before he gets to you, can't you?"

"Maybe. That's not the point."

"What do you mean?"

He raised himself on his good elbow. "We haven't got our proof, and we don't know if there's a dead-man switch. Once he's done with me he's just going to come back here and tear the roof off. Are Merrick's commandos on their way?"

"Yes."

"Maybe they can stop him. But I wouldn't count on it."

"What are you saying?"

"I'm in his den. Maybe I can find what we need before he gets to me."

For a moment her breath laboured in his ear, forming no words. Gennady told himself that he, in contrast, felt nothing. He had lost, completely. It really didn't matter what he did now, so he might as well do the decent thing.

He bent to the task of inspecting the dragon's meagre treasure.

∞

"Talk to me," she said. Lisa sat hunched over her work table, out of the Net, one hand holding the wood as if to anchor herself. All her screens were live, feeding status checks from her hired hackers, Merrick's people, and all the archival material on Jaffrey that she could find.

"There's no bombs here," he said. His voice was flat. "But there's three portable generators and fuel drums. They're near entrance shaft. I guess dragon could blow them up. Wouldn't be much of an explosion, but fire would cause release, you know."

"What else is there? Anything that might tell us who this is?"

"Yes—filing cabinets." That was all he said for nearly a minute.

"What about them?" she asked finally.

"Just getting there—" Another pause. "Tipped them over," he said. "Looking...papers in the ashes. What the hell is this stuff?"

"Is it in English or Russian?"

"Both! Looks like records from the Release. Archival material. Photos."

"Are any of them of Jaffrey?"

"Lisa," he snapped, "it's dark, my connection's bad, and I only saw that one photo you showed me. How in God's name am I to know?"

"There must be something!"

"I'm sure there is," he said. "But I don't have time to find it now."

She glanced at the clock. The dragon had left five minutes ago. Was that enough time for it to get to Gennady's building?

"But we have to be sure!"

"I know you do," he said quietly. "I'll keep looking."

Lisa sat back. Everything seemed quiet and still to her suddenly; the deep night had swallowed the normal city noises. Her rooms were silent, and so were her screens. Gennady muttered faintly in her ear, that was all.

She never acted without certain knowledge. It was what she had built her life on. Lisa had always felt that, when a moment of awful decision came, she would be able to make the right choice because she always had all the facts. And now the moment was here. And she didn't *know*.

Gennady described what he saw as he turned over this, then that paper or book. He wasn't getting anywhere.

She switched to her U.S. line connection. The FBI man who had unluckily pulled the morning shift at NCSA Security sat up alertly as she rang through.

Lisa took a deep breath and said the words that might cost her career. "We've got our proof. It's Jaffrey, all right. Shut him down."

∞

Relief washed over Gennady when she told him. "So I'm safe."

Her voice was taut. "I've given the commands. It'll take some time."

"What? How much?"

"Seconds, minutes—you've got to get out of there now."

"Oh my God Lisa, I thought this would be instant."

Gennady felt the floor tremble under him. Nothing in the den of the sarcophagus had moved.

"Now!" She almost screamed it. "Get out now!"

He tore the link helmet off: *spang* of static and noise before reality came up around him. Sad wallpaper, mouldy carpet. And thunder in the building.

Gennady hesitated at the door, then stepped into the hallway. Light from inside lit the narrow space dimly—but it was too late to run over and turn out the lamp. From the direction of the stairwell came a deep vibration and a berserk roar such as he had only ever heard once, when he stood next to an old T35 tank that was revving up to climb an obstacle at a fair. Intermittent thuds shook the ceiling's dust onto Gennady's shoulders; he jerked with each angry impact.

Gennady shut the door, and then the end of the hall exploded. In the darkness he caught a confused impression of petalling plasterboard rushing at him, accompanied by a gasp of black dust. The noise drowned his hearing. Then Jaffrey's eyes blazed into life at ceiling level.

He was too big to fit in the hallway—big as a truck. So Jaffrey demolished the corridor as he came, simply scooping the walls aside with his square iron arms, wedging his flat body between floor and ceiling. The beams of his halogen eyes never wavered from pinioning Gennady as he came.

Into the apartment again. The dial on the Geiger counter was swinging wildly, but the clicking was lost now in thunder. The windows shattered spontaneously. Gennady put his hands over his ears and backed to the balcony door.

Jaffrey removed the wall. His eyes roved over the evidence of Gennady's plans—the extra food supplies, the elaborate computer set-up, the cleaning and filtering equipment. A deep and painful shame uncoiled within Gennady, and with that his fear turned to anger.

"Catch me if you can, you cripple!" he screamed. Gennady leapt onto the balcony, put one foot on the rail and, boosting himself up, grabbed the railing of the balcony one floor above. He pulled himself up without regard to the agony that shot through his shoulders.

Jaffrey burst through the wall below, and as Gennady kicked at the weather-locked door he felt the balcony under him undulate and tilt.

The door wouldn't budge. Jaffrey's two largest hands were clamped on the concrete pad of the balcony. With vicious jerks he worked it free of the wall.

Gennady hopped onto the railing. Cool night air ruffled past and he caught a glimpse of dark ground far below, and a receding vista of empty, black apartment towers. He meant to jump to the next balcony above, but the whole platform came loose as he tried. Flailing, he tried a sideways leap instead. His arms crashed down on the metal railing of the balcony next door.

He heard Jaffrey laugh. This platform was already loose, its bolts rusted to threads. As he pulled himself up Jaffrey tossed the other concrete pad into the night and reached for him.

He couldn't get over the rail in time, but Jaffrey missed, the cylinders of his fingers closing over the rail itself. Jaffrey pulled.

Gennady rolled over the top of the railing. As he landed on the swaying concrete he saw Jaffrey. The dragon was half outside, two big legs bracing him against the creaking lintel of the lower level. He was straining just to reach this far, and his fingers were now all tangled up in the bent metal posts of the railing.

Gennady grabbed the doorknob as the balcony began to give way. "Once more, you bastard," he shouted, and deliberately stepped within reach of the groping hand.

Jaffrey lunged, fingers gathering up the rest of the metal into a knot. The balcony's supports broke with a sound like gunshots, and it all fell out from under Gennady.

He held onto the doorknob, shouting as he saw the balcony fall, and Jaffrey try too late to let go. The bent metal held his black hand, and for a second he teetered on the edge of the verge. Then the walls he'd braced his feet against gave way, and the dragon of Pripyat fell into the night air and vanished briefly, to reappear in a bright orange flash as he hit the ground. Rolling concussions played again through the streets of the dead city.

The doorknob turned under Gennady's hand, and the door opened of its own accord—outward.

Trying to curse and laugh, hearing wild disbelief in his voice, he swung like a pendulum for long seconds, then got himself inside. He lay prone on some stranger's carpet, breathing the musty air and crying his relief.

Then he rose, feeling pain but no more emotion at all. Gennady left the apartment, and went downstairs to get on with his life.

∞

Lisa sat up all night, waiting for word. The commandos had gone in, and found the violated sarcophagus, and the body of the dragon. They had not found Gennady, but then they hadn't found his bike either.

When the FBI cut off Jaffrey's signal, the feed to the dragon had indeed stopped. They had entered his stronghold apartment minutes later, and arrested him in his bed.

So her career was safe. She didn't care; it was still the worst situation she could have imagined. For Gennady to be dead was one thing. For her not to know was intolerable. Lisa cried at four a.m., standing in her kitchen stirring hot milk, while the radio played something baroque and incongruously light. She stared through blurred eyes at the lights of the city, feeling more alone than she could have prepared herself for.

It was midmorning when Gennady called. Her loneliness didn't vanish with the sound of his voice. She started crying again when she heard him say her name. "You're really all right?"

"I'm fine. At a gas station near Kiev. Didn't feel like sticking around to be debriefed, you know. Sorry I lost the cell phone, I'd have called earlier." There was a hesitancy in his voice, like he wasn't telling her everything.

"Merrick says there was no release. Were you irradiated?"

"Not much. Ten packs or so, I guess." Despite herself she laughed at his terminology. She heard him clear his throat and waited. But he said nothing else.

She held the phone to her ear, and glanced around at her apartment. Empty, save for her. Lisa felt a sadness like exhaustion, a deep lowering through her throat and stomach. "You're just a voice," she said, not knowing her own meaning. "Just a voice on the phone."

"I know." She wiped at her eyes. How could he know what she meant, when she didn't?

"Look," he said, "I can't go on like this." His voice faded a bit with the vagaries of the line. "It's not working."

"What's not working, Gennady?"

"My—my whole life." She heard the hesitant intake of breath again. "I can't control anything. It's just…beyond me."

She was amazed. "But you did it. You got Jaffrey for us."

"Well, you know..." His voice held a self-conscious humour now. "It was your hand on the switch. I just kept him busy for you. It doesn't matter. I don't know what to do."

"What do you mean?"

"I can't just go back to Kiev. Sit around the flat. Jack into the Net. It's not enough."

"You don't have to," she said. "You have money now. I'll make sure Merrick comes clean."

"Yeah. You know...I've got enough for a vacation, I figure."

Lisa leaned back in her work chair. She toyed nervously with a strand of her hair. "Yeah? Where would you go?"

"Oh... Maybe London?"

She laughed. "Oh yes! Yes, please do."

"Ah." His shyness was such a new thing, and charming—but then, he wasn't falling back on the safety of the Net this time. "One condition?" he ventured.

"Yes?"

"Don't ask me too many questions."

For a second an old indignation took her. But she recognized it for the insecurity it was. "All right, Gennady. You tell me what you want to tell me. And I'll show you the city."

"And the Tower? I always wanted to see the Tower."

Again she laughed. "It figures. But we go only once, okay? No more castles for you after that. Promise?"

"Promise." ∞

The Energy of Slaves

∞ René Beaulieu ∞

translated by Yves Meynard

"I'M HERE TO TAKE CARE OF YOU." The voice of the Union representative is soothing, intended to reassure him. "They can't allow themselves the least discrepancy, the slightest irregularity. They're compelled to respect the Agreement." A fugitive gleam in his gaze, so indifferent until now. "You look rather old to me; perhaps we could have you put on the exemption list…"

"I haven't reached the limit yet." Gilbert Gilsen shakes his head sadly, resigned to his fate. "They pronounced me fit for another descent, right after I came out of the fridge and went through the checkup. According to them, I'm still in good health…"

"Too bad…" says the representative quietly; he seems a bit distressed, probably out of a sense of duty.

He looks down at the cabin's smooth floor, then stares pensively at the tip of his shined shoes, barely peeking out from beneath the arc of his swollen paunch.

Gilsen contemplates his wrinkled, parched hands, prematurely aged by his long stay inside the fridge; for all their claims, you never come out of it quite intact. Despite drugs and tranquillizers, his hands are shaking; they've been shaking ever since he woke up in one of the medblock's beds, ever since he realized they were in orbit and it was his turn again to descend. But these hands have to stop shaking. He will need them soon. His life will depend on their speed and precision.

"Do you have any special request? For instance, would you like a priest? We have a very good one aboard. Many Contractuals like this kind of comfort."

A priest… Maybe. The idea is tempting. Gilsen is intrigued: he's never seen a priest, except during the dominical holo-show, twenty minutes regularly interrupted by commercials from Monopoly companies or government propaganda, during which selected passages taken from a book are read. It's a beautiful book, with a gorgeous old-fashioned binding, all in ancient, polished leather, with bookmarks, gilded lettering and edges. Something solid and well-made. The kind of thing you don't see nowadays.

Sometimes, Gilsen likes to listen to the readings, but the "explanations" and "interpretations" always confuse things. They make it all sound just like the usual idiotic propaganda.

Although, now that he thinks of it, he can't really see how a priest might help him now. It would have been better if he'd been offered a maja cigarette, that might have quelled his trembling.

"No...no priest, thanks."

He hesitates to continue, to ask questions. He doesn't trust this too-round, too-cunning, too-friendly man. His long silence intrigues the other, who raises his head.

"You're worried about your family's future, about the insurance, isn't that right?" The representative is so proud to have figured it out. "Don't sweat it, man! Whatever happens to you, your family will receive the full indemnity as soon as possible. I'll see to it personally. But everything will go fine, have faith."

Gilsen is relieved to know that Helen and the kids will have enough to live on... If the Union takes care of it...

The representative smiles at him, a smile intended to be confident and reassuring, that reveals small, white, pointed teeth.

Some nights, in his single tiny room, suffocatingly hot, sunk at the bottom of the Planetary City, Level 1225, while he tossed on his bed, avidly seeking sleep but mostly forgetfulness, he would wonder what had to be feared most: the Government? The Order and its agents? Pseudocoms? The Resistance? The gangs of youths who prowled the artificial night along the black monoliths of the housing units? Those who lived on the lowest levels, the "Trash Can," splashing through chemical mud and the City's garbage, always ready to launch murderous raids against the levels above, or bloody and pitifully useless riots? His workmates, his neighbors, ready to denounce him, to report him for an imprudent word or gesture, hoping for a climb up a level, a two-room apartment, a position a trifle higher in the social hierarchy, or just an increase in their daily rations of food and maja? And the Union...

Jules Gerald had his ideas about all that; unfortunately, he didn't keep them to himself. Among the people Gilsen knew, Jules was the closest thing to a friend, as long as you assumed there still existed people who could fit that definition. He was a former synthetic food-preparation technician who'd taken a steep drop in both status and levels, and now worked with him in the power stations. But he still didn't walk straight enough;

he spoke too much, thought too much.

One doesn't get sealed inside a reaction chamber by accident. It is easy, though, to shove someone in then close the door. Not the first such "accident" to occur, nor the last. His lead-lined mechanic's suit hadn't protected him very long.

"Why are you under Contract?" the representative asks." The glimmer of interest has returned to his eyes. "I didn't have time to fully study your files."

Gilsen lifts his head. What would it change if he replied? Finally, he speaks of the illegal strike launched by the Union to accelerate negotiations in their industrial sector, so that their legitimate requests would be complied with; of the provocations, the incidents, the intervention of the Order's agents. He recites these formulas he has learned by rote, which have come to cover up a much simpler reality, transforming it into something he can no longer truly recognize. What really took place was this: some of the Workers were carted off, as an example for others; and he happened to be among them.

The representative's face is beaming now; this new perspective makes Gilsen worthy of his attention.

"In short, you sacrificed yourself for your fellow fighters." As if he'd had the choice whether or not to sacrifice himself! "Congratulations, Worker!" And this hateful word in the man's mouth, intended to be an honorific! "I'm proud of you. You're not some vulgar common-law criminal, you're a political prisoner, a martyr, an authentic proletarian hero!"

He looks as if he were giving a speech in front of an meeting, full of passion for the Cause. Is it Gilsen he's trying to convince or himself? As usual, it's all just grotesque. The man comes close and puts his hand on Gilsen's shoulder. The contact repulses Gilsen, but he tries not to let it show.

"How many descents in your Contract?" The other feigns solicitude, understanding. After all, that's what he's paid for.

"Two. I've already done the first."

"So this is the last stretch!" the representative continues in his hypocritical optimistic vein. His bracelet beeps shrilly, cutting him off. Annoyed, he shuts it off with a flick of his thumb.

"Sorry; I've got other obligations, I can't take care of you any longer." He pulls a pseudo-cigar out of his pocket and lights it casually, by tapping the end against the sole of his shoe. "A new contingent of Contractuals. I have to make sure that they've arrived in good shape; the military are so careless about these things..."

Let him go away, yes, let him leave!

The representative strides rapidly to the door, puffing huge clouds of opaque smoke, stops on the threshold for one last look back at Gilsen.

"Don't worry, it'll be over before you know it. Everything will go absolutely fine. Good luck, comrade Gilsen!"

Gilsen remains alone in the cabin, alone with his fear and his trembling hands. All that remains of the other man's visit is the reeking smoke already being dissipated by the ventilation system. Gilsen reflects bitterly that the man might have at least sneaked him a maja cigarette.

∞

He's been waiting an hour. He's almost come to hope they've forgotten him, when they come in, silently. In this place, you never hear what's going on outside the room you're in. Not even the ship's engines. It makes a change from the ceaseless racket, the dull beat of the City, its walls that let the neighbor's screams through, and the ceaseless roar of traffic. Everything is so perfectly soundproofed here, so shiny, so clean, so impersonal. There are five of them: a sergeant of the Order and four armed agents. Is Gilbert Gilsen so dangerous then?

The sergeant opens his mouth: "Sensors have located a deposit."

One of the agents, a youth with a slack-witted expression, is conspicuously playing with his holster flap. He's too nervous; he won't last long in active service. Gilsen rises to his feet; the others surround him and they leave the room.

Gilsen's mind tries to dispel his anxiety by dwelling on all sorts of insignificant details. The best thing would be to think of nothing, but he can't manage that. He's never managed it. His wardens form two perfect lines, their steps are in identical time. One, two, one, two. Security and order, security and order. He has trouble following them. He's always had trouble following them. Gleaming rooms and silvery corridors pass by, swept by the raw neon light. Metal and neons, that's all there is in this damned ship!

They take the immense passage that crosses the ship, wide as a ten-lane highway. Traffic is heavy; vehicles and pedestrians cross their paths, the activity of a perfectly policed anthill, like in the City. A miniature City. So that no one shall leave the artificial environment and the conditioning it maintains. It is the same anthill in fact, except that here it is better controlled, above all better organized. They turn into a wide passage, with a pair of large doors at the end of it. The descent room. A shiver flits back and forth along Gilsen's spine.

It looks like a gigantic train station: everywhere bustling machines, generators, repair and maintenance units swarming over ships and drills, cables, blinding lights and an awful din. Men, also. Working feverishly, arguing, shouting orders, running left and right. Mining engineers, technicians, mechanics, workers; and some agents standing here and there motionless like absurd posts, erected and forgotten. There are also other Contractuals, who will go down at the same time as him, and some foremen, recognizable by their immaculate white armbands; this sight triggers visceral hatred in Gilsen—yet part of this hate was carefully inculcated. As always the anthill's relentless efficiency, despite appearances. The drills wait in a line at one end of the room, a score of different models. Which will be his? Gilsen and the agents near a group of Techs and Engineers having an animated discussion. A man notices them. "You took your time! Get a move on! There's a lull down there, but we don't know how long it'll last."

They follow at his heels towards the drills. They detour around a submarine craft—a ray—which Gilsen identifies as the very one he piloted on his first descent. They stop in front of a kind of drill he's unfamiliar with; mechanics are busy all around it.

It looks like a concrete millstone about twenty meters in diameter, equipped with two pairs of enormous treads arranged in a square, which allow it to move freely in any direction. A steel cable, wide across as a man's torso, drops from a crane running on ceiling rails, loops through two large rings on top of the millstone and returns to the crane. A huge pipe is also linked to the millstone. The agents have stepped back. The Engineer grabs Gilsen by the arm.

"Ever piloted a millstone?"

"No, Engineer."

"Great." He motions to one of the agents. "Hey, you! Go tell one of the computer techs to meet me inside the stone."

He and Gilsen climb the ladder to a circular lock. Inside is a small cabin, furnished with glowing panels and controls; in the middle of it all, a seat from which every meter and indicator is visible, every lever and every button may be reached.

"Sit down," says the Engineer, pointing to the chair. As Gilsen obeys, he turns his back on him to fiddle with the controls. A smiling young man enters the cabin.

"I understand I'm needed here?"

The Engineer, without lifting his head, favors him with a grunt. The newcomer crosses his arms and waits, still smiling. When the Engineer deigns to turn towards him at last, the shadow of a satisfied expression wanders on his face: pride in a job well done.

"I'm handing him over to you. Give him full specs on the millstone, then plug him into the ship's computer for planetary characteristics and special instructions."

"Yeah, yeah, the usual routine." With a look of boredom on his face, the young man watches the Engineer leave; then he goes to a keyboard, types in some commands, makes a few adjustments, asks Gilsen for his medical card which he shoves into a slot. A few clicking noises, then the operator hands it back to Gilsen.

"Lie down, this won't take long," he says in a friendly tone. He buckles the belts that tie Gilsen to his seat. They are arranged so that only his head, arms and legs may move, and so he cannot undo them by himself.

The operator then opens a small storage compartment from which he takes out a helmet trailing long wires. "You know what this is?"

Gilsen nods: they call it a Teacher. No time for actual lessons, even summary ones, on piloting a millstone. They have no time to lose. They prefer to use a Teacher both as an interface to the computer and to fill the pilot with all available knowledge on relevant subjects. This machine is even more effective than implants, infinitely adaptable and reusable, always up-to-date. It can turn anybody into an expert and a veteran.

Gilsen looks at his hands: they're damp and shaking violently—yet this won't be too bad, just annoying, like an itch that can't be scratched. The operator is done with his connections and puts the helmet over Gilsen's head. "Ready?" he asks for form's sake.

Gilsen doesn't flinch. The other man depresses a lever and the world spins away into a brief burning, immediately replaced by an itch at the margins of what is left of his conscious brain.

In a few seconds, Gilsen assimilates everything about millstones: how they're built, how they work, how to pilot them. The memories, the competence, the experience of dozens of men and women pour into him. Gilsen becomes someone else, protean and infinitely complex, many yet one; the brain, the nerves, the reflexes of this artificial entity, this synthesis of many human beings, become Gilsen's own. Paradoxically, he remains himself at the same time; he is still Gilbert Gilsen, with his personal thoughts, memory and emotions. This is a feeling—more than that, a certainty—both strange and deep, as if he had inherited a double nature. Gilsen is at the same time the Engineer who designed the millstone, the Techs who built it, and all those who piloted it during tests and in the course of their work. He knows the millstone's weight to the nearest kilo—at least, it feels like that—the proportion of each individual metal in its alloy parts, the first name of each of its pilots; he could sketch a plan of it, draw up a costing sheet, call forth its rate of fuel consumption, belch out the favorite swearwords of the mechanics who raised its bulkheads, tightened its rivets and repaired various malfunctions…

A barely perceptible click, a vague shock: the ship's central computer takes over from the millstone's own comp, plugs into Gilsen's brain and fills his mind. A kind of screen lights up inside his head; the communication is both visual and auditory—the source is no more than a computer now, all emotion is lost—accelerated beyond reason and yet remaining fully understandable.

A-R*E*M*T* PILOT'S SUMMARY
...........No. 47682.........errata......... No. 4768522..FILE-253762............... LOCATION-NGCC 3548 - OFF FROM "HABERHAGEN" GLOBULAR CLUSTER......SYSTEM Y-445472 - CATALOG NAME "ATUKA-VLIL" - BLUE GIANT/YELLOW DWARF DOUBLE SYSTEM - POSSESSING 6 PLANETS - 4TH PLANET, "KAVAN-ARVIDA," OF CONSIDERABLE MINING VALUE...

A sudden stop. Then visual records taken by various probes are projected. The computer continues…

FILE 2537694562-d
"KAVAN-ARVIDA" - VENUSIAN TYPE, GANGLEN SUB-TYPE. DESCRIPTION: DIAMETER: 36,400 KM. - MASS: 5 - SCALE K - GRAVITY: 0.8g - TEMPERATURE: RANGING FROM -70°C (NIGHT) TO 120°C (DAY) - ATMOSPHERE: NITROGEN 64%, CHLORINE 34%, OTHERS 2% - PRESSURE: 2.8 ATMOSPHERES - ORBITAL PERIOD: 428 CITY-DAYS - DIURNAL PERIOD: 62 CITY-HOURS - NO TRACE OF LIFE BEYOND SINGLE-CELLED.

***

MINING REPORT: ABUNDANT LITHIUM, ORIDIUM, IRON, NICKEL, COPPER, ZINC - SIGNIFICANT AMOUNTS OF LEAD, ALUMINUM, URANIUM, SILVER. EXTRACTION DIFFICULT: CLIMATE FACTORS: IMPORTANT TEMPERATURE VARIATIONS, CONTINUOUS VIOLENT WINDS FROM 200 TO 250 KM/H WITH GUSTS OF 350 TO 400 KM/H; TOXIC ATMOSPHERE; SEISMIC INSTABILITIES, FREQUENT TREMORS.
EXTRACTION: USE OF "MILLSTONE"-TYPE DRILL RECOMMENDED.

***

PILOT'S SPECIAL INSTRUCTIONS: DESCEND ONTO A PROBABLE SITE - LOCATE DEPOSIT - ANCHOR - EXTRACT.
GOALS: EXTRACTION OF 70 TONS OF ORIDIUM FOR FACTORY-SHIP HOLD B - FIELD TEST OF IMPROVED "MILLSTONE" DRILL...................

It's over. The whole experience didn't last more than thirty seconds. The operator takes the helmet off Gilsen's head, stows everything away and leaves without a word. Two agents came in during the session. They now unbuckle the belts, help Gilsen put on a pilot's suit, then strap him in again. They leave, carefully sealing the airlock behind them.

Gilsen is alone now. His loud breathing batters at his eardrums, echoing from his helmet. Disquiet, anxiety; not really fear, not yet.

A crackling voice erupts in his earphones. "Worker Gilsen, can you hear me?"

"Loud and clear. Comm circuits functional." Unconsciously, Gilsen has adopted the calm, professional tone of pilots as well as their jargon.

"Prepare yourself for descent; we're transferring you into the well."

He stiffens in his seat; once again, he is surprised to feel only a slight swaying as the crane lifts the millstone's imposing mass. He checks the control panels: all LCD displays are green, every dial's indicator is at norm.

He's outside now. He feels the slow, regular swing of his craft, like a pendulum's. They're lowering him with the tractor beam. Gilsen waits; it's too early still. Finally, he activates the exterior cameras.

He tries to sense the evil wind of space, even though he knows it's only a legend. The men who work Outside have never heard it, no more than the voices and music they sometimes start to imagine when they have spent too many years exposed to vacuum. Gilsen waits a moment more, then lifts his gaze to the cold depths of space that fill his screens.

Space and its stars...stars City-dwellers never see because of the perpetually gray sky that crushes them, oppresses them, forces them to resign themselves to their life, their miserable state, to walk with their heads lowered, as if the City wasn't already heavy and depressing enough, from its very existence. People have long ceased to look at the low horizon, forever clogged by the accumulation of industrial exhaust, the result of the City's endless simmering and its slow rot. This other screen one can never pass through.

For the ordinary men and women of the City, the stars don't exist anymore. They can no longer see them, gaze at them, much less hope to rise towards them one day, tearing themselves free of the City's mud and mire.

These stars, despite the fear they also inspire—and at the same time, because of it—represent in a strange way what human beings yearn for in the end: they are like freedom, like happiness, like the person you've dreamed of in secret since childhood, knowing all too well that he or she does not really exist. The stars glitter far away, too far, beyond the horizon, enticing, fascinating, full of beauty and inaccessible promises.

For all its plasma-tachyon ships, humanity will never truly reach them. "The stars" are something more than titanic slow-detonating hydrogen bombs. Gilsen was very young when he *saw* them for the first time. It was on an old holo film that the Believers in Expansion showed to increase the ambient mysticism level amongst their telematic faithful, an old holo film blurred by time. And yet, he never forgot the stars, always pursued them. He even tried to sign up for the Fleet, but he was refused because his security coefficient was too low.

Sometimes, he'd let himself go and talked about it to Helen. And she understood him, or at least tried to understand. He was grateful. Helen… Could she make it alone, could she reject the temptation of the Voluntary Euthanasia Center? For the children, perhaps. She loves them so. Gilsen wanted to do so much more for her. He's never been able to tell her how much he loves her, far less show it.

A long moment of despair passes by, sinks away into the hungry abyss of the past. All that's left are the stars and the memory of a woman he loves. Their presence, her absence. The stars are here, simply, and Gilsen fills his eyes with them. He finds in them, for no reason he could name, a small measure of courage. Perhaps Helen will make it. And so, perhaps, will he. He doesn't know where the phrase comes from… "Wish upon a star."

Perhaps stars are no more than that in the end: hope, iridescent and fragile.

∞

Turbulence begins to be felt, the pendulum's swing increases: the millstone has entered the dense layers of the atmosphere. The earphones crackle once more. "Gilsen?"

Startled, he spits out in the mike: "I hear you! What is it?"

"Engineer Reeves here; we'd like you to test the drill's treads. Just routine."

The memories Gilsen has just acquired confirm this is indeed proper procedure. "Starting the program," he replies irritatedly. He takes the disk from its compartment and inserts into the reader.

"Wait for my signal, Gilsen. Ready… Go!"

Gilsen depresses the levers and listens to the machines waking up in the millstone's electromechanical depths. A soft but powerful purr, reliable and reassuring. The vibrations erase his perception of the craft's seesawing.

Crackling again: "All OK for us. Anything to report on your part?"

"Everything's running smoothly, Engineer."

"All right; next contact will come once you've landed. Over and out."

Gilsen raises the levers and watches greenish threads fill the observation screens, slowly blotting out the stars. The images swing back and forth, following the rhythm of the millstone sinking gradually into the atmosphere: a roiling, shapeless fog, viscous as an infection, slightly paler than the planet's surface, whose great curve is becoming visible. Impacts against the bulkheads. The wind. The constant swaying nauseates Gilsen.

Nothing left now but glaucous storms and typhoons of green dust, rising and falling. Enormous jolts toss the craft about. It is suddenly caught in an updraft, then falls brutally back down. Gilsen feels about to vomit. He switches the screens off. A heavy ball of ice is running through his clenched guts and he finds himself clutching the seat's armrests.

The descent drags on and on…

Another impact! Stronger… The surface! The now-useless tractor beam lets go. Despite his fear, thanks to his conditioning, Gilsen's hands immediately perform the necessary movements, as if they no longer belonged to him. Even though they're still trembling. The bulkheads are trembling also, under the terrible battering of the wind.

Yet the descent continues: the drill-anchors burst through the hardened crust but fail to catch. Gilsen activates probes, radar and sonar. Dammit! The millstone is in a lake of heavy dust; the treads slip and skid, futilely stirring up the sand where they keep sinking. Impartial, the wind alternately pushes the millstone down into the dust, then tries to tear it loose. Gilsen withdraws the drill-anchors, useless in this terrain. The vehicle has now sunk completely below the surface and keeps falling, slowly and silently, as if through molasses or thick oil. And at last comes contact with the solid bottom of the pit. The slope is not severe, and now the treads have traction. After about twenty minutes, the instruments announce the millstone has emerged into the open air with a sudden brief spitting of static. The wind batters once more at the craft.

A crackle, a barely audible voice trying to emerge from the interference. "Gilsen…hear me?" During his dive through the lake, the layer of electrically-charged dust had blocked all communications.

"Reading you."

"Targeting error...atmospheric perturbations...off course...locate you approximately two kilometers from the presumed deposit." Communications are slowly improving. "You'll have to go there by yourself...better hurry, the weather forecast for your sector is anything but good for the next few hours. Over and out."

Gilsen remains briefly motionless, then brings himself to orient the millstone towards the deposit, activate the detectors and the cameras. No point in moping; there is no time to lose.

∞

He is now running on a great eroded plateau. From time to time, he can see flattened mounds revealed by the sudden glare of lightning, through clouds raised by the constant gusts; they appear squashed, friable, strangely gnawed. The whole planet seems in their image: worn, bleak, maddening in its monotony. Near the center of the plateau, the detectors begin to glow pink, redden, then fall back into the pink. He's gone beyond the deposit. Assuming it is the one they wanted.

He turns the millstone around and begins the delicate task of pinpointing the site. Slowly, the millstone describes an ever-tightening spiral. Pink often, red sometimes, but still no crimson. The deposit must lie pretty far from the surface. Gilsen finally halts the millstone above the spot where he has detected the strongest concentrations.

With a single gesture from Gilsen, outside air rushes into the craft, is compressed inside tubes; pressure rises, reaches the limit. The man's gloved index finger mashes a button and the drill-anchors burst forth once more, with an abrupt jolt, ripping through the rock, corkscrewing into it, then, at the end of their tether, expelling a bundle of steel rods in a star pattern to serve as crampons. Flawless. The extraction drills now! They attack the granite, their vibrations lost amongst those born of the gale. Two more small levers to depress: one for the pumps that pull the shattered rock into the filtering chamber and expel the slag outside, the other for the tractor beam that sends the purified oridium through the flexible pipe to the ship.

Gilsen can do no more; it's all up to the millstone now.

The wind keeps roaring, deprived of its pound of flesh, its intensity rising with every passing moment. The shaking of the floor and the bulkheads threatens to dislocate Gilsen's bones and the thickness of his helmet fails to shield him from the screech and the moans of tortured concrete.

Debris spews out, the drills bury themselves deeper and deeper. At about fifty meters' depth, the readout lights glow crimson. The concentration is nearly twenty percent! The beam begins sending off the ore.

After a few minutes, he calls the ship. "Gilsen here! Acknowledge receipt of minerals."

"Acknowledged. Keep it going, just hold on."

Keep going, last a while longer… As if one could or would want to do anything else with one's life! Gilsen is nothing more than a machine, a machine that submits and performs, a machine that waits, listens, fears, its gaze riveted to a plastic ribbon slowly unwinding beneath a glass dial.

..............4T..............5T..............6T...............

Time passes, time that can never be grasped, never bent to one's will.

A harrowing shriek. Gilsen's seat topples violently, following the millstone's sudden lurch. He sweeps his worried gaze across the dials. One of the anchors has been torn off. Wind speed 320 km/h. Oridium:....48T... The millstone is shaken every which way. He calculates swiftly that another twenty minutes remain before he reaches the quota. Waiting, always waiting. Helpless.

A maddened giant attacks the millstone, dealing it thunderous blows from his club. The cabin vibrates like a bell. Suddenly, a terrible roar, another jolt: a second anchor, broken off like a twig.

Panic!

It won't hold, he won't have time. He doesn't want to die like this, alone, like a dog in its hole! Not like that! Not for that!

The radio!

"Engineer!" His voice quavers.

"I'm listening, Worker Gilsen."

"Pull me back up! Two of my anchors have gone."

"Wait a sec, you're at, let's see…fifty-six tons." Reevess voice is like collapsing styrofoam. "Show a little patience, it won't be long now."

"Pull me up, please!"

A moment of silence. The blows are deafening Gilsen.

"You signed a Contract; fulfill it!"

"Listen, I'll do anything, I'll do another descent if I must, but pull me up! *Pull me up!*"

"The Contract."

With a terrifying crash, something hurtles through the cabin and crushes into a bank of computers. One of the concrete and steel bulkheads now sports a gaping hole through which curls of green gas swirl in; across from the hole, a large boulder is lodged in a memory block, surrounded by smoke and electrical discharges. It has staved in the supposedly indestructible concrete carapace.

.......60T.......61T....... Gilsen dares not look at the wind speed indicator.

He must calm his terror, numb it. Wait, always wait. How long can it all hold? Don't ask questions, try not to think at all. He is surprised to find forgotten prayers coming to his lips, emerging from his past as a last bulwark against fear. He is drowning in feverish terror: he's hot and cold at the same time. He doesn't know who he is anymore, or why he's here. The only things that matters is waiting for the figure to appear on the dial.

To die, alone, like a dog.

Slowly, almost reluctantly, the 70 passes beneath the glass panel. Gilsen turns on the mike. "Gilsen here! I've fulfilled my Contract, you have what you wanted. Get me back up now!"

Silence.

"Engineer, can you hear me?" The storm and the lightning interfere with the commlink, but his instruments insist that the carrier wave is reaching the ship! "I'm done, Engineer! Pull me up!"

Nothing but the merciless battering of the wind and the millstone's creaks.

"Reeves!" Gilsen shouts. "I demand that you bring me back on board. I want to speak to my representative. Get me out of here, you fucking bastards!"

Rage and fear mix in him, his words jostle into each other, smother and die. Useless.

Silence.

A jolt stronger and more brutal than all the others lifts Gilsen from his seat; the straps dig into his belly, his breathing is cut off. Electricity snarls laughter in his earphones, the storm beats its drums, then a few short moments of true silence, heralding the imminent breakdown of the receiver and the unavoidable confrontation with reality...

Gilsen has never known anyone to come back after signing a Contract. Of course, what claims to be the news sometimes speaks of some common-law criminals who have been "cured," who have become honorable citizens of the City, perfectly integrated both socially and psychologically. They're shown talking about what they did, then viewers are treated to a glimpse of who they've become. But none of the faces Gilsen ever saw on the screen were those of people he had known... Gilsen looks at his hands; he can no longer tell if they're shaking or not. He gazes at their parched skin, its sick red hue. It has often been said that the preservation methods mining ships use for their human cargo are imperfect, that every year spent in the fridge is paid for dearly… He doesn't feel anything yet, but he's probably burned, like meat forgotten in the freezer. He's finished, ready for the trash. What a waste of human material! How much longer would he spend in constant pain, watching his body's decay? Better to end it quickly.

One last sarcastic crackle in his earphones and it's over.

Gilsen stays there, crushed, inert. He knows the storm is bearing down upon him and there is nothing to do. But once resignation has been reached, fear vanishes. He could stop the drilling, shut down the pumps and the beam that sends the minerals to the ship. A paltry vengeance. And what would be the use? The deeper the drills go, the longer the millstone will hold.

Worker Gilsen therefore continues with the job.

The storm screams in rage, redoubles its intensity. The millstone is filled with roiling gas. A huge shiver courses through the vehicle, then come two drawn-out, dreadful, sinister creaks, and everything topples over. The last anchors have come loose.

The world spins madly, a furious maelstrom, a vague, nebulous universe. Violent impacts, jolts, a great roar of crushed stone and the harrowing screech of twisted metal. Then…

Then, nothing, or almost nothing. Only the scream of the wind. But it's so soft and peaceful after the end of the world.

And Gilsen realizes he's still alive.

The lights have gone out. He feels dizzied, lost. Pain, dulled as if he'd already taken drugs against it, fills his chest. Broken ribs, probably. Also, the straps are sawing into his shoulders and belly, digging deep into his flesh despite his suit. He closes his eyes, shakes his head, opens them again.

It's clearer now. A very faint glow is coming through the hole and the cracks that run over the bulkhead. Everything is broken, upside-down; the millstone has flipped over. The cable and the pipe must have been torn off. Held by his straps, Gilsen looks at the ceiling now become floor.

∞

The wind's rage has died down somewhat, the storm has passed and the millstone has remained stable. Hours go by. Gilsen is ill. The blood has rushed to his head, and every heartbeat resonates inside his skull. He couldn't prevent himself from vomiting in his helmet; and the throat-searing reek makes him vomit again.

He can't do anything, he can't even unbuckle the straps, which fasten behind the seat, out of his reach. As always, he can only endure. He's still plugged into the millstone's stores, he has oxygen for a few days yet and the nutrient tubes at the side of his helmet will provide him with food and drink.

He wonders if they will try to locate the millstone and tractor it back. It has some value for them, more than he does, certainly. This is probably his only chance.

Hours? Days? He doesn't know. There have been other storms, much weaker. It is when the air begins to run out that he reaches a decision. The only one he has ever been allowed to make. This time, he won't wait; he will act.

He brings his hands to his helmet, and pulls it off. ∞

Extispicy

∞ David Nickle ∞

IT WAS TAIL-END OF A BLIZZARD, late afternoon, and the snow was piled in waist-high drifts at the shoulders of the highway. Three lanes became two, and where the road wasn't white, tires had exposed slick black ice underneath.

This time, I actually watched it happen.

∞

A northbound Cutlass was trying to make for the exit at Major MacKenzie Drive, but it was in the centre lane and the exit was at the far right. I couldn't tell if it was signalling, and evidently neither could the Jetta that was coming up on that right. The Jetta's front-end caught the Cutlass in the passenger-side rear door.

The two cars joined together like dancers and skidded along the highway in wide arcs and pirouettes. I stubbed out my cigarette on the windowsill and watched until they settled against the centre-lane drift. The police scanner at my side was still whistling and buzzing in happy oblivion. This one was *fresh*.

I ran downstairs.

My house is near the on-ramp—in my car, it's just a quick right onto Fir Spiralway, another right onto Major MacKenzie Drive, and then I'm on the highway. I can do it in under half a minute in good weather. But just then I didn't bother with the car; I don't think an accident had ever happened this close to home.

So on foot, it took me longer than I'd expected—about five minutes, all told. But when I got there, the police still hadn't arrived and other cars were taking turns wending their way through the tiny lane that remained to the right of the collision. I took a few shots from the overpass then made my way down through the hip-deep snow on the embankment for my close-ups. I wasn't expecting much; before I was finished up top, both drivers had climbed out of their cars and were shrugging at each other with that no-one-to-blame-but-the-weather nonchalance you see a lot of in Ontario winter fender-benders. As I crossed the embankment to the highway proper, the Cutlass driver had pulled some highway flares out of his trunk and begun to set them around the scene's perimeter. The Jetta driver, meanwhile, crouched in the lee of his car with his cellular phone.

The cars would both need a month or so in a body shop and maybe a wheel alignment, but that was probably it; certainly there were no dead, no injuries by which to order my investments. The Gods make you work for your prophecy, I remember thinking. And this one would have been too easy.

I took two more photographs and was about to leave when the Cutlass driver looked up. Our eyes met over the crackling fire of the flares.

Shit, I thought as I saw his face. *Emmet Rhouli.*

"Hey!" shouted Mr. Rhouli.

And he called my name.

∞

My solicitor's name is Charlie Evans, and he looks after me. I am his whiz-kid client, one of the few real-estate developers on his list that kept making him money, even through the dog-days of the early 1990s. "You and the Iranians," says Charlie when he sits in my kitchen drinking my scotch and shaking his head. "You've both got some kind of secret."

"The Iranians" are Emmet Rhouli and his son Lester. As practising members of the Baha'i faith, they wisely fled their homeland's choking fundamentalism in the '70s and brought their meagre fortune here to Canada. The Rhoulis are known to be fine, peace-loving gentlemen who have an uncanny knack for picking lucrative sites for their luxury condominiums. They make a fortune in real estate for themselves, and they pay a slightly smaller fortune in fees to Charlie and his pared-down firm.

That is the secret to which Charlie refers—the Rhoulis' and my own shared ability to draw profit and success from the driest of streams; and our knack for doing so in such times as these, when the Reichmanns and the Schneiders of the world are collapsing under the weight of their own precarious fortunes.

I don't know what the Rhoulis' secret is, although I long suspected that it draws from the inclusive theology of their religion, its delicate numerology: their nine-sided temples, the 27 Hands of Faith that rule them from Israel, their notion of final unity, an ultimate One.

Numbers from God.

"I have no secret," I say to Charlie, who answers with a perceptive "Bullshit."

Charlie has been in the business long enough to know that nobody does this well in real estate without secrets, without some kind of a guiding system. Of course he is right, but he is also discreet enough not to press me for the secrets of my own strategy.

Charlie looks after me. When I call him late on Labour Day Monday after I've souped the film from the Highway 400 pileup and spent some time with the pictures, he doesn't complain—just writes down my instructions in one of the legal pads he keeps by all his phones, reads them back to make sure he's heard me correctly and gets to work. On Tuesday he's setting the wheels in motion to acquire the properties and is already making calls to the local city councillor about rezonings and land-swaps and density allowances. By Thursday four, four-thirty tops, we've got the start of a deal. Charlie knows that side of the business in ways that I will never learn.

This is something to remember in our business: No matter how close you are to the on-ramp, no matter how clear your photographs and how good your math, a smart solicitor is worth his weight in gold. Charlie Evans is as smart as they come, and I don't know what I'd do without him.

As I stood staring at Emmet Rhouli crouched over the light of his signal flare, next to his ruined Cutlass, my camera a blunt object, clutched in my trembling hands, those were the words that scurried along my nerves:

I don't know what I'll do without him.

∞

I confess that I considered turning and running. He'd only seen me for a second, and if it ever came up in conversation with Charlie or anyone else later on I could probably deny ever being there. Charlie might have bought it—he *might* have—but Emmet Rhouli is a perceptive man. And I don't think I could have really convinced him that his eyes were playing tricks on him.

"Mr. Rhouli." I waved awkwardly, letting the Nikon drop to the end of its strap. A red sports car rumbled ingraciously between us, throwing up lumpy gouts of snow in its wake. There was a break in the traffic after that, and Mr. Rhouli beckoned me to cross.

"Come, sir! Join us while we await the police!" he shouted as I stepped nimbly across the dozen feet of icy road and into the protected semicircle of signal flares. "I've a thermos of coffee in the car, and perhaps—" He ducked his head into the open driver's door for an instant. "—yes, I have quite enough cups for the three of us."

What was I supposed to do? I stepped around the front of the Cutlass and shook Mr. Rhouli's hand. "I saw the crash from my window," I babbled, concocting my story as I went, "I wanted to make sure no one was injured."

To his credit, Mr. Rhouli did not so much as glance at my camera. He clapped me on the back and led me to the Cutlass' door. "Happily enough, your fears were unfounded," he said, bending to produce a stainless-steel thermos and a trio of matching Rhouli Group travel mugs. He motioned with one towards the Jetta driver, who nodded and smiled around his cellular. "Mr. Jenkins and I are quite unblemished. Except for our pride, eh Mr. Jenkins?"

Mr. Jenkins put his hand over the phone's mouthpiece and laughed. "And our insurance records," he said before returning to his own conversation.

"Quite so," said Mr. Rhouli, then turned to me and continued confidentially: "Although I believe it will be my record that suffers more than Mr. Jenkins'. If you saw the accident from your window, then you will have seen that it was I who cut into Mr. Jenkins' lane."

I shrugged. "On this kind of a night, I don't think the cops—the police, I mean—I don't think they'll lay any charges. I wouldn't worry."

Mr. Rhouli handed me a steaming cup of coffee. The same stock he served to ratepayer ladies in his office in Don Mills, it was very strong and very sweet.

"I'm not worried," he said. "We balance our fortunes in this lifetime. If my automobile insurers become uneasy and raise my rates a few hundred dollars, perhaps the Municipal Board will look more favourably on me the next time I am before them with an imperfectly-placed condominium tower. Who can ever say when it comes to the matter of our fate? Your meeting me here, for instance, is nothing if not a testament to unlikely fortune."

I raised my mug to his as we drank a toast to fate and unlikely fortune. After a moment, Mr. Jenkins switched off his cellular and tromped over to join us. He was in his late twenties, with sandy hair and a handsome jaw-line that chaffed against the collar of his woollen overcoat. When he sipped at the coffee Mr. Rhouli proffered, he made a face.

"I'm afraid the coffee is strong," said Mr. Rhouli. "But it will keep you warm, Mr. Jenkins."

"It'll keep me awake, that's for sure," said Mr. Jenkins. "Thanks. It's really very good."

Next, Mr. Rhouli made formal introductions. Mr. Jenkins' first name was Tom, and he worked as a sales representative for a personal computer chain in the city. Mr. Rhouli introduced me as a "home builder of great repute."

"We are in the same business, he and I," said Mr. Rhouli. "We make homes for people with too much money, yet it seems we can never get enough of that money to keep for ourselves."

I laughed along with the other two.

"I guess that's the way of it for everybody these days," said Mr. Jenkins, then looked at his watch. "I hope somebody gets here soon."

It was shortly after five o'clock, and the traffic was beginning to pick up. Where before there were gaps in the single clear lane that had been wide enough to walk through, now cars were pushing along at a steady clip of one every two or three seconds. I gnawed at my lip as I watched them pass. It would have been impossible to cross that road now without getting hit. Also, I didn't really want to be there when the police arrived—some of them knew me as a news photographer, rather than a real estate developer, and I wanted to keep it that way.

"More coffee?"

I accepted, but Mr. Jenkins shook his head. "Thanks but no," he said. "I'm going to wait this out inside my car if it's the same to you—this coat's like gauze when you get into a wind."

"As you wish," said Mr. Rhouli, and measured the thermos dregs between his cup and mine. We sipped at the coffee and watched the diminishing line of red tail-lights to the north as Mr. Jenkins trudged back to his car through the ankle-deep snow. The air was filled with thin snowflakes and car exhaust, and we spoke over the muffled din of struggling engines and splattering slush. In the distance, I could hear the truncate moan of a transport truck's horn.

"Tell me, my friend," said Mr. Rhouli then, "now that we are alone. Why do you bring a camera to an automobile accident?"

Behind us, the Jetta's door crunched open against the snow-drift, and I paused to consider.

I think if I'd had a moment longer, I would have told Emmet Rhouli something approximating the truth: it's a superstition of mine, like a businessman's lucky tie—the pictures bring me luck, and make my investments pay.

But before I could speak, the tractor trailer horn sounded again, much louder this time, and our shadows grew in front of us, fingers reaching forward to the night.

Mr. Rhouli realized what was happening an instant before I did. In a fluid motion, he threw his cup aside, grabbed my shoulder and dragged me over the snow-drift. We tumbled and I felt a sharp pain as my thigh hit the concrete abutment, but we made it over all the same. I landed on my back in soft, virgin snow and rolled down the small slope to the centre of the median.

I looked up in time to see most of it. The transport truck wasn't pulling anything, but it was going at least 50 kph when it ploughed into the back of the Jetta. The car crumpled onto itself, the supposedly shatterproof front windshield exploding outward in a cloud of glass-shards, and the roof over Mr. Jenkins' seat pressing down in a jagged fold-line. Mr. Rhouli's signal flares flew forward amid sparks from the rending metal and cresting waves of snow. The combined detritus of tractor trailer and Jetta enveloped Mr. Rhouli's Cutlass like a storm front.

The transport carried the entire mass of steel maybe thirty yards before it finally flipped onto its side. Miraculously, it did not catch fire—although several of the flares still burned, illuminating the falling snow in a halo around the jutting angles of the wreckage. The picture shuddered as a grey Topaz fishtailed into the sharp steel ruin of the trailer hitch, and again as another Volkswagen slid straight into the Topaz' passenger door.

Mr. Rhouli pushed himself to his feet in the deep snow. He stared blankly at the carnage, then shut his eyes. His hands formed into fists at his side, and they shook.

I got up too, but I didn't waste any time consoling Mr. Rhouli. I checked my Nikon and smiled: some snow had become wedged in the winder, and I would have to dust off the focus ring before I went to work, but fundamentally the machine was intact.

And I still had most of a roll of film left, with five more in pockets when that was done.

∞

Despite the trappings of my vocation, I am not religious, and the work that I do need not be interpreted as a fundamentally pious act.

Listen, how do you think I developed my system in the first place? It wasn't going to church or reading the Bible or freezing on some mountain top in Nepal with an old Hindu beggar, that I can tell you. Maybe there's a God in Heaven, maybe there's a whole pantheon of them up there, or maybe the universe is all just a big cold machine of which we are ineffectual and meaningless cogs. Frankly, I don't particularly care, because when you get down to it, the whole thing is math.

The math isn't easy, and I'm the first to admit that I wouldn't be able to duplicate even a tenth of the calculations that have gone into producing my templates: you've got your differential equations, your strange attractors, your multiple scaling patterns, and that's just to start. If you're not a mathematics PhD with a specialty in chaos theory and an unmonitored account on a Cray super computer, you might as well forget trying to work out the templates on your own.

My PhD's name is Ted Oliver. We were undergraduate contemporaries in British Columbia in the late 1970s—he studying math, me chasing an MBA. He didn't have many friends—in a way, that made him an ideal choice for my project—and for a time early on, I liked to think that Ted was my friend as well as my PhD.

But in 1986, seven months before Ted had produced the versions of the templates that now paper my basement walls, our association very nearly came to an end.

I was still living in Calgary when Ted called me. It was very late at night, and from the sound of his voice I guessed he'd been through at least a fifth of the single-malt scotch that I knew he preferred.

"Shouldn't you be at work, Ted?" He did most of his calculations for me after hours, when the Cray was free.

"Fuck you," he replied. "I'm not working for you any more, you shit-bastard."

"Are you all right, Ted? I couldn't quite make out—"

"You heard me, you fucker."

I let the silence go a heartbeat before replying: "Okay, I heard you. You're not working for me any more. I guess I'll just put a stop payment on all those post-dated checks, and that'll be that. Right?"

There was another pause. "Right," Ted finally drawled. "Don't want your money. It's dirty."

That stung, I have to admit. But I kept any reaction out of my voice. "I beg your pardon, Ted? Dirty? In what way?"

"You think I don't read the paper, watch the news?" There was a shuffling and banging in the background that I took to be Ted trying to stand up. "Witness Trust, asshole. Fucking Witness Trust!"

"You think we had something to do with that?"

Of course we had, in a peripheral way. On December 14, 1985—nine days before Witness chairman Alex Tobermore went into the hotel room in Montreal with the girl from the RCMP and spilled everything—I was at a pile-up on Highway 2.

It was very messy. A tractor-trailer had jack-knifed on a patch of ice and caught two cars, a station wagon and a pickup under its trailer before it scissored off into the median and tipped onto its side. Everything but the tractor-trailer itself was totalled, and six people died—two at the scene, the other four in hospital, the truck driver not among them. I came away with seventeen rolls of exposed film, and even before I souped them I could tell that this was going to be an auspicious scene indeed.

In fact, it saved my ass. With the help of some shrewd attorneys, I was able to divest every penny I had in Witness Trust, and with the help of friends who shall remain nameless, I managed to get inside the office and shred every document that might have tied me to some of the company's more questionable activities. If I'd had any less forewarning, I would have lost the opportunity to take either precaution. I would have been caught in the same net that the RCMP used to put Alex Tobermore and two members of his Board of Directors behind bars for the next fifteen years.

"People lost their homes," said Ted. "Pension funds—down the toilet! Millions of dollars… It makes me want to puke thinking I had a part in that."

I took a breath. "No Ted, you didn't have a part in the Witness Trust scam. We invested in the company," I told him, "just like everyone else, and we made a little bit of money, just like a lot of people."

"So why aren't you broke?" Ted asked. "Like the grandmothers and the young families and the other small-time investors who got screwed?"

"Because," I explained, "I invested wisely. And because of you, Ted, I knew enough to get out before it got ugly. The police were watching Tobermore like hawks. Don't you think that if I—if you and I—were involved in anything illegal, we would have heard from the police by now?"

That stopped Ted for a moment, and I thought I had him. But I should have known better. I should have known that Ted was worried about larger questions than whether he should be getting a good lawyer or just cutting his losses and hopping a jet for the south of France.

"I don't care if it's not illegal," he snapped back at me. "You can do the shittiest things in this country if you've got the money and the know-how, and it's all perfectly legal." He paused, and I heard the clinking of glass as he refilled his tumbler. "Do you know how much an old war bungalow is listing for in Vancouver this week? Two hundred and ninety-fucking-five thousand dollars."

I thought about asking if he were thinking about a move from the condo I bought him two years earlier, but kept it to myself.

Ted continued. "Ten years ago, you could have had the same house for fifty thousand. Twenty years ago—Christ, I don't know, twenty-five grand, maybe less."

"That was the time to buy," I commented.

"That's the point! Fucking speculators, you buy up millions of dollars in people's property, create an artificial shortage, flip your investment when the price climbs high enough, then start over again. You get rich, everybody else gets fucked."

"You're right, Ted."

"Of course I'm right. I'm glad you agree. Now I'll say it again, slowly: Fuck. You. I. Am. Out. Of. This."

"Hold on a second." Ted had been about to hang up, but I heard him pause, return the phone to his ear. "I wasn't finished. You're right about part of the equation. We get rich, and everybody else gets fucked. But we're not speculators. Not like Witness Trust, anyway. We know what's going to happen, Ted. We see the future, and we take advantage of that vision. But the future will unfold, whether we're there or not. We're not speculators, Ted—we *know*."

Ted didn't seem impressed with my reasoning at the time—he called me a lunatic and hung up the phone.

But I knew I had him all the same, and the next day he called me to apologize. After all, what was he going to do? I'd given him more money than he'd ever make at the university, true enough, but on top of that I'd shown him something even more valuable. Ted had seen the future, and had within his grasp—barely, albeit—a means to look even further ahead. My precognitive model is a tool, but it's also a narcotic. And since our discussion that night, I'd made certain that Ted didn't know enough about the system to use it effectively in either capacity.

∞

If you know how to read them, the lines and cuts on a dead driver's face can make you a million in a day.

I drop everything else when I see the fire-fighters' shoulders droop, when the new widow screams her husband's name in that way new widows have, when I hear a paramedic's voice go soft and the words, "we've lost him" or "no signs," or even a simple "Fuck. Fuck." I get as close as I can, as fast as I can.

And so it was with Mr. Jenkins, and the new wreck of his car.

The thin body-steel of the roof had sheared where it folded, and made an axe-blade to shatter the crown of Mr. Jenkins' skull. I crawled up to the hole where the windshield had been, moving gingerly to avoid the jagged stones of safety glass. A flare had landed to the front of the Jetta's wreck, so the car's interior was well-illuminated.

Mr. Jenkins' face was caught in a rictus of surprise, as though the gods had given him an instant of life as the steel pierced his brain, the barest of revelation. I propped myself against the hood of the Jetta and fired off maybe a dozen frames using only the flickering light of the flare. Icy breath cut swaths of rawness across the nerves in my throat, and from my lightheadedness I knew I'd begun to hyperventilate. But I didn't care—Mr. Jenkins' revelation was my fortune. I fished in my pocket for my flash, and slid it into the bracket on top of the Nikon. The next ten frames were agonizingly slow, as I waited each time for the battery to recharge. But I caught him.

Mr. Rhouli came around the front before I was finished.

"Are you all right?" he asked.

"Fine," I replied, "I am just fucking fine," and Mr. Rhouli said nothing more for a moment.

But he didn't retreat, either.

I pressed the release and started to rewind my film, and as I did so I turned to regard Mr. Rhouli. He sat on his haunches, median-snow sugar-frosted to the side of his coat. Our gazes met, for the second time that day. And for the second time, he made me want to bolt. I had gone too far, I thought; I had tipped my hand.

The tension released and the film made little whipping sounds as it sucked back into the depths of the canister. I opened the back of the camera.

"In Saudi Arabia," said Mr. Rhouli finally, "the King has a son. He is not the eldest son, and many in his father's court regard him as a layabout, a fool; not worthy of the crown. Yet it is he, not his older brothers, upon whom the King of Saudi Arabia chooses to heap his gifts. Do you know why this is?"

I shook my head. The film canister fell into the snow at my feet.

"A sorcerer told the old man, who is by every report very ill and not long for the world, that so long as he looks upon the face of his boy every morning, he will not die." Mr. Rhouli shifted, his eyes reflecting the sparkle of signal-flares. "A *sorcerer*," he repeated. "Can you imagine such a thing, my friend? Today, at the very end of the Twentieth Century, the age of science?"

I didn't answer. Mr. Rhouli motioned to my feet. "Here, take your film, before it becomes wet."

I felt my breathing slow, and my head begin to pound as the adrenaline rush began to abate. I reached down and scooped up the film, wiped the clots of slush away from the opening.

I pulled my gaze away from Mr. Rhouli's glittering eyes, and as I did so, it occurred to me:

All the signal flares were behind him. There was no fire between us or behind me that could have reflected itself back from those eyes.

The spark, if that's what it was, did not exist beyond the curve of Emmet Rhouli's deep, shining eyes.

It came from within.

"A sorcerer," he said again, and he laughed. "Such is foolishness, to listen to such superstitious rantings, would you not agree?

"And yet the king looks on his son every morning, and he does not die. And he is among the richest men in the world, and remains so—day upon day. And the sorcerer occupies a large suite of rooms in the king's palace, and is never far from his master's side."

I could hear sirens now, dopplering up from the south. If it weren't for Mr. Rhouli, the questions that were raised in the glitter of his eyes, I would have picked that moment to cut my losses and leave—those police that know me, know me as a freelance photojournalist, not a real estate developer.

But instead of fleeing, I pulled another roll of film out of my pocket and clicked it into place in the Nikon.

"All right, Emmet," I said. "Maybe it's time to come to the point."

"Maybe it is," said Mr. Rhouli softly. " 'All right,' indeed—here is your point."

He stood up, and I looked at him again. The signal flares made a crackling aura of fire over his shoulders.

"I was finally able to meet *your* sorcerer, my friend, just yesterday morning—at his condominium in Vancouver," said Mr. Rhouli. "And really, he was quite a sight; you should take better care of the things you make."

As I watched him there, standing with such ease in the face of the accident, the thought came to me:

Emmet Rhouli staged his accident. For my benefit. To draw me out.

"Not *staged*, not precisely that," said Mr. Rhouli, and I knew then with a chilling certainty that he was answering my unspoken thoughts. "Think instead that I *wished* it."

∞

I hid my camera under my coat and stood silent, face hidden in a fan of fingers, while Mr. Rhouli spoke with the police. He told them the story we'd agreed upon, more or less word for word.

Mr. Rhouli and I had been working at his office in Don Mills all afternoon, and were on our way back to my house— "Just over that rise," he told the police constable as a team of firefighters prepared to cut through the side of the transport's cab—for an early dinner.

He described the accident as it had occurred: a minor fender-bender brought about by the slick road conditions, made into tragedy when the transport slid out of control and ploughed into the Jetta. The constable only asked once if I would be able to corroborate this, apparently satisfied with Mr. Rhouli's answer.

"He is overwrought, my friend. Do not trouble him."

When the tow-truck arrived, Mr. Rhouli and I took our leave and trudged up the embankment to Major MacKenzie Drive; along the side of the road to Fir Spiralway; and my finally, along the winding curve of that street to the front walk of my house.

∞

"The basement," said Mr. Rhouli as we stood alone in the high front vestibule, dark but for a yellow square of light cast by a street lamp through the second-story window. "That's where you finally do it, isn't it?"

Ted had told him everything, he'd said, so there was no point in lying, trying to hide. He knew about the equations, the templates—Ted had even told him about Witness Trust and some of the other less-than-honourable dealings I'd been involved with during the 1980s.

"That's where I do most of the work," I said, my voice flat. "After the highway."

"I must see it."

I shrugged, and led him around the stairwell to the basement door. As we walked, I noted him peering through doorways and arches.

"Who was your builder?" he asked as I fumbled on my ring for the key to the basement door.

I told him.

"He has been known to cut corners," said Mr. Rhouli. "Although from what I understand, your specifications on this place would have been very exact; I am sure he has done an able job."

"I didn't ask," I said, and swung open my basement door. Light flooded through the opening, briefly filling the dim hollows of the ground-floor rooms.

The illumination was brief, however. I shut the door behind us and we began our descent into my workspace.

∞

Mr. Rhouli stood speechless at the base of the stairs, and I have to confess to feeling a father's twinge of pride as he gaped. The basement is the place I do the work that makes me rich, and there is an air of ritual about it that is impossible to ignore.

The largest part of the basement is a wide, papered chamber. I have inscribed my templates on that paper, using India Ink so that it does not fade over the years. In the centre of the room I have installed four slide projectors, aimed at right angles from one another and all fixed to the same rotating pedestal.

"The templates," said Mr. Rhouli finally, raising his hands to indicate the twisting mass of geometry on the west wall. They extended nearly twenty-five feet to the ceiling, angles and curves and polygons intertwining like vines as they climbed. "If I did not know better, I would count you as among the most ingenious madmen alive."

"But you know better."

Mr. Rhouli turned from the west wall to survey the diagrams on the north, east, south walls. "Yes," he finally replied. "I know your secret. It is why I came here."

Mr. Rhouli stepped toward the pedestal in the middle of the room, and flipped the on switch in the south-facing projector. A square of white light, not more than a dozen feet on a side, bounced off the wall.

"In Iran, there is a tradition of this kind of thing, you know; it is a part of our astrology.

"One word for it is *augury*. You take an animal, and with a knife you split its belly, and see the future in the little twists and turns of its viscera."

One by one, Mr. Rhouli turned the other switches, and the same white frames appeared on each of the walls. "I see you are careful; you do not keep the photographs in the projectors once you are finished with them."

"Why should I?"

"Quite right. They are the tales of futures past; they should become quite disposable very quickly, I would imagine."

"If you say so," I said. In fact, I keep all my slides in files—the more auspicious ones, in bank safety deposit boxes across the continent.

"No one really does augury any more; not for serious matters," said Mr. Rhouli. "But then, I don't think you do, either. You, my friend…" he stepped up to the east wall, his shadow at first immense against the paper. "…You practice that peculiar variant of entrail-reading called extispicy. As did the Etruscans."

"I don't read entrails."

Mr. Rhouli turned around, so that the focused beams of the projector caught his face. He didn't squint.

"The Etruscans," he continued, "had little faith that the intestines of a chicken, or a goat, chosen by a priest or maybe—if one were lucky—by an oracle, would contain any meaningful fate. So they waited until a lightning storm, and in the aftermath went wandering through the fields searching out those animals who had been struck dead by lightning.

Chosen by the Gods, yes? Very potent.

"And if they found a man in those fields—well. Therein a wise extispice might find divine providence, at its very purest."

I keep my basement cool, but I could feel myself starting to sweat. "So what do you want, Mr. Rhouli?" I said. "Do you want in on this?"

"It wouldn't do me any good," he replied, and looked away from the light for a moment before continuing.

"Tell me," he said finally. "Do you do your own photo finishing here?"

"I used to make prints," I replied. "Not any more. Now I just work with slide film—I develop it in behind there." I motioned to a doorway in the southwest corner.

"Of course." Mr. Rhouli stepped away from the projector and came back to the steps. "Then I shall leave you to it. From everything I understand, you will have quite an evening ahead of you."

"What—" I wasn't able to even finish my sentence before Mr. Rhouli brushed past me, and started to make his way up the stairs.

"I will let myself out," he called back over his shoulder. "I only wanted to see, before..."

And the door at the top of the steps swung open, and Mr. Rhouli was gone.

∞

I worked in fits.

First I souped the film, put it through the tanks and baths in the darkroom then paced the floor of my basement, jogged the stairs, showered and tried to eat, waiting for it to dry. I picked up the phone, the 911-rote of Charlie Evans' phone number running through my mind. Too soon to call Charlie, though. I set the phone down again.

When the film was dry, I went to it again. My hands shook inexplicably as I snipped the film into squares, slipped them into the slide-frames. By the time I arranged them into the proper order and set the carousels into the slide projectors, it was time to stop again. I was hyperventilating; it was as though the air in my basement had turned to sand. Once I began my interpretation, I told myself, I wouldn't be able to stop.

So I climbed the stairs from my basement, grabbed a coat from the rack by the door, and still in stocking feet stepped out onto the front veranda, to suck back some air. It was snowing again, and I stood for a moment in the falling white quiet. At that instant, I was sure that I wouldn't move from there. That I would stand still, in the perfect, silent present, and leave the future foretold by Mr. Jenkins' sacrifice below me.

But of course, I couldn't do that—I could never leave the future to itself—and eventually I went back to it.

The first quartet of slides, I remember taking down notes, running the variables through the equations, delineating the curves and twists. Then I repeated the process. As I always do. The next four, I plugged the numbers in directly, before writing anything down.

For the rest, I just looked.

Emmet Rhouli had laid out my future with such clarity that there was no room for doubt. The equations, I realized as I trembled alone in my cellar, were scarcely necessary to interpret the message he had written for me on the highway that day.

∞

I called Charlie Evans at home just after five a.m., and gave him what will be his final set of instructions from me. He is used to my calling at strange hours, but he seemed annoyed this time. I am not surprised; it is only a confirmation of my new fate.

The delineation of that fate was then projected on four walls in my basement. The forms and curves of the west wall nestled amid bent metal and furrowed ice; the 100 Rivers wending among the burst of shattered windscreen glass; and Mr. Jenkins' once-handsome face, his shattered dome of a skull, found a perfect match inside the 45th Form on the east wall. A *perfect* match.

Charlie wrote down my instructions and read them back to me. If they could all be summed up in a particular word, that word would be: DIVEST. By the end of today, I must have no money tied up in the Greater Toronto Area real estate market; my assets must all be liquid, and entirely portable.

I am not a religious man. When Mr. Rhouli tells me that fate is stronger in the guts of an animal that has been touched by God than it is in one that has been plucked from the barnyard, I listen because I am polite. I nod because I do not want to create a fuss.

But I look upon the future that has been laid out before me in the face of Mr. Jenkins, and I know that I have never seen the curve of tomorrow more clearly.

Through my entire career in real estate, I have always driven that curve; staying the course when it augurs well; turning off it when I see trouble ahead. It has never been within my power to warp it. Until yesterday, I had not thought it was in anyone's power. I had thought that vision—that augury—was as much as a man could do to order his future. As much as a God could, for that matter.

I do not think that Emmet Rhouli is a God. He is a gentleman, however. He has shown me the future; given me fair warning of his intentions—his *wishes*—for that future.

The seatbelt light has just flashed on, and as I look out the window of the 747 I can see an immense web of highways and roads reveal themselves far below, through the hot yellow paste of Mexico-City smog. Cars are still impossibly small, moving along that web like mites, baby spiders, their apparent speed diminished to a crawl by the incredible scale of the city that they have wrought.

Mr. Rhouli can have his future in Canadian real estate. I will take the highway. So long as I remember to read the signposts, I know it will never lead me astray. ∞

Afterward?

∞ Candas Jane Dorsey ∞

SO THERE YOU HAVE IT. Quite a package, isn't it? Starting with Clute's peripatetic sentences and roving through so *many* different landscapes. Can we say there is a Canadianness to the trip? To the landscapes? To the tone? To the intentions?

Do we have to?

It's a mature literature these days, certainly. That has its merits, including recognition in the international community, but it has its down side too: we can get a little complacent at times, and all the huskies on the team don't always pull together any more. In fact, we have the leisure at times to stop and snarl at each other, even take a nip of fur and flesh. How terrifically un-Canadian: which is to say, how terrifically un-nice. (I mean "we" collectively of course—you would *never* find the taste of fur in *my* mouth! That's my story, and I'm sticking to it.)

Which is to say, how human.

But you know, I *do* still find a difference between our work, even at its most commercial or esoteric, and that of the imperium to the south or any of the other domains of the English-writing (or translated-from-anywhere-else) world. It's an *average* difference, not a specific one. There are books and stories both in and out of our borders that can be compared point for point—but that's not the point. There is a ground we stand on to speak. The diversity of our speech is still assured. *That's* the point.

The point is that we are proud of the ground we stand on.

All over the world, people are united by artists' creative visions. In the original language or in translation, we often have more in common than we find difference. But the most powerful commonalties are narratives that begin locally and move, as the old writing rule will have it, "to the universal through the particular."

In speculative fiction, we have been familiar with that rule for a long time. Everyone (everyone who thinks about it for a moment anyway) knows that we aren't writing about the far future, the alternate past, the other world, the realm of magic—we are writing about *now*, and the internal date of our work is always the moment of its birth.

Speculative writing is the creation of a metaphor that explains for us our *now*—our particular reality—by invoking not the universal but the universe. Humans are inherently narrative creatures, perhaps because we are doomed to live sequentially in time, perhaps because we search for meaning, perhaps because we try to arrange the random universe into patterns that *make sense*. To the age-old metaphors which explain how and why the world works as it does—magic, fantasy, power, light and darkness—we have added the modern—science, technology, manufacturing, capitalism and spectator tourism—but it is all the same story.

The same story, and meant to answer the same questions: why does the world unfold as it does? What can we do about love and entropy? What means our history and to what purpose our future?

Are we closer to those answers in the north, or along the ribbon of settlement and railway, or in the concrete heat-sinks of our cities? No closer than anywhere else on the planet, but we are always close to the answers if we stay close to our hearts. And I don't know about you, but *my* heart lives here, where the summer days are long and the winter nights are short; where we have to spend calories on survival whether we like the idea ideologically or not; where we cope with economic and social and psychological effects of living next to the imperium like poor neighbours next to plutocrats—and where we spit the fur out of our mouths and stand together from time to time, appreciating our connections.

Clute said I was gonna give a you summary of the field, but you can do that yourselves. Just read. You had a good time with this book. Go read some more of our Canadian authors' books: some published at home, some by our big muscular cousins in New York and London and Paris.

Better still, read *all* the best books in the field. Then at the end of the year, count up. And I guarantee you—whether you're reading in English or French; whether you are interested in hard science, sociological exploration, fantasy, fear, escape, hard realities, love, war, redemption or all the rest of the possibilities: whatever your taste—you will find that in your count there are Canadian writers, Canadian books—the best the world has to offer, and our very best, from home.

Welcome home. ∞

∞ Biographies ∞

M. Arnott ("The Oceanographers" and "Chaff") lives in Toronto with one short-story writer, two cats, three banjos and several tons of books.

René Beaulieu ("The Energy of Slaves"), a librarian and documentarist as well as a writer, critic, and anthologist has also run a radio show and worked for a number of years in a SF bookstore. Winner of the Boréal Award (Best Book) for *Legendes de Virnie*, he was also a Finalist for the Grand Prix du Journal de Montréal [Dagon de Boreal] for short story *"Le Geai Bleu."* Rene founded the Boréal Awards in 1989, and is a current member of the board of the *Grand Prix de la SF Québécois*. He has published a number of story collections: *Légendes de Virnie*, *Le Préambule*, *Coll. Chroniques Du Futur*, 1981; *Les Voyageurs De La Nuit*, *Les Editions De L'A Venir*, 1997; and *Un Fantôme D'Amour*, Ashem Fictions, 1997. Of "The Energy of Slaves," René says: "Thinking about the French 'science-fiction politique,' what it used to be and especially what it might have been."

Jane Brierley (trans. "Umfrey's Head") lives in Montréal and has translated works of fiction, biography, history,and philosophy. She won the 1990 Governor General's Award for her translation of *Yellow-Wolf & Other Tales of the Saint-Laurence*, by the 19th century Canadian writer, Philippe-Joseph Aubert de Gaspé. She has translated several stories by Québécois writers for previous Tesseracts anthologies.

Peter Bloch-Hansen ("Why Starships Should Be Named for Moths") lives in Toronto, for which he apologizes, but that's where the work is as correspondent for *Starlog* magazine. Besides writing poems, stories, plays and filmscripts, Peter also acts and makes SF/F themed woodcarvings.

Sheryl Curtis (trans. "The Sea Below") lives with her husband, two sons and two cats in Montréal, where she works as a freelance translator of technical documents and corporate propaganda. She really prefers literary translation.

John Clute's ("Foreword") award-winning career as a superstar of Science Fiction criticism and scholarship has produced *The Encyclopedia of Science Fiction* (co-edited with Peter Nicholls) and *The Encyclopedia of Fantasy* (co-edited with Peter Grant). His extensive criticism in numerous publications is in part collected in *Strokes* and *Look at the Evidence*. As a Canadian living in London, England, and travelling, reading and collecting widely, he brings a truly international perspective to this year's anthology.

A resident of Vancouver, B.C., **A.M. Dellamonica** ("The Dark Hour") has previously worked as an actor, theatre technician, crisis worker, and guerrilla secretary. She is a member of the Fangs of God on-line writer's workshop. Her fiction has appeared in *Crank!*, *Realms of Fantasy*, and several other magazines and anthologies.

Cory Doctorow's ("Home Again, Home Again") fiction has appeared in *Asimov's*, *Science Fiction Age*, *Amazing Stories*, *Tesseracts7* and elsewhere. His non-fiction appears in *Wired*, *Sci Fi Entertainment*, *The New York Review of Science Fiction* and *2600*. More information is available at http://www.craphound.com.

Candas Jane Dorsey ("Afterward?") is a freelance writer and editor in Edmonton, Alberta, and the publisher of Tesseract Books. She co-edited *Tesseracts3* with Gerry Truscott and edited the 1994 WorldCon anthology issue of *Prairie Fire*. Her novel *Black Wine* (Tor, 1997) won the Crawford, Tiptree Award, and Aurora awards. Her other works include *Dark Earth Dreams*, *Machine Sex and other stories*, *Leaving Marks*, *Hardwired Angel* (now optioned for a film), two unpublished collections of short stories and the upcoming novel *A Paradigm of Earth*. Works in progress at present include a non-fiction collection of essays *Pornographic Culture: some thoughts about sex, gender, art and the politics of repression* and a mystery novel *The Adventures of Isabel*. She has two cats and timeshares a dog, a hedgehog and an otter.

Sandra Kasturi ("Games of Sea") lives and writes in Toronto, but often succumbs to the enchantment of Alberta. Her poetry has appeared in various magazines and anthologies (including *Tesseracts5* and *Tesseracts6*), and her first chapbook, *Carnaval Perpetuel* is forthcoming from Junction Books in September 1999. "Games of Sea" is "for Yves Meynard."

Susan A. Manchester ("Nightfall") has published in *The Georgia Review*, *Tranversions*, *Tickle Ace*, *Feminist Studies*, *Negative Capability*, and many other small presses and academic journals. She has an unpublished manuscript titled *A Wreath Cannot Satisfy the Dead*. She teaches English in Toronto and is a member of the Algonquin Square Table poetry group.

Sally McBride ("Speaking Sea") lives in Toronto. Her stories have appeared in *Asimov's*, *Northern Frights*, *F & SF*, *Realms of Fantasy*, *Tesseracts*, and others. With husband Dale Sproule, she published issues 1 to 11 of *TransVersions* magazine. Winner of an Aurora award for short fiction, Sally is currently at work on novels.

Yves Meynard ("Within the Mechanism"), born in 1964, holds a Ph.D. in Computer Science, lives in Montreal and earns his daily bread as a software developer. He has published eight books and over forty short stories, netting several awards in the process. His most recent novel is *The Book of Knights* (Tor Books).

David Nickle ("Extispicy") is a Toronto author and journalist. Along with Karl Schroeder, he co-wrote the novel *The Claus Effect*—based on their Aurora award-winning novelette "The Toy Mill." He's had stories published in all five *Northern*

Frights anthologies, *Tesseracts4* and *Tesseracts5*, *On Spec*, *The Year's Best Fantasy and Horror* and *TransVersions* among others. In 1997, he won the Horror Writers of America's Bram Stoker award for short fiction, for a collaboration with Edo van Belkom.

John Park ("Viking") works as a partner in a scientific consulting firm in Ottawa. His fiction has appeared in earlier volumes of *Tesseracts*, and in *Tomorrow SF*, *Cities in Space* and *Northern Stars*, among other publications, as well as in French and German translations. When he thinks on a grand scale, he suspects that "Viking" (a sequel to "Retrieval" in *Tesseracts2*) may be part of a 60-page trilogy.

Winner of the 1999 *Grand Prix de la science-fiction et du fantastique québécois*, **Francine Pelletier** ("The Sea Below") has published a number of short stories and science fiction novels. She is also known in Quebec as a writer of young adult sci-fi novels. "The Sea Below" was first published in the collection *Le temps des migrations*. Longueuil (QC), Éditions Le Préambule, 1987, pp. 55-88.

Ursula Pflug ("Gone With the Sea" and "Rice Lake") is an award-winning writer of genre and literary short fiction, publishing frequently in three countries. She has also had speculative narratives produced for stage and film. Currently, when not working on short stories, she writes commissioned historical theatre. "Gone With the Sea" is dedicated to "Michaela, both friend and relative, who still lives on the rainy, volcanic little mid-Pacific island of Kauai, in memory of a supremely surreal day, over twenty years ago now, that we spent navigating the mangrove swamps on Molokai by outrigger." About "Rice Lake," Ursula says, "No, I never had an affair with Yod, wonderful as he is." The story is dedicated to Martha and Gabriel: "Jill is based on my lifelong friend Martha Eleen. Martha, an artist and carpenter, has had her attendant care funding for her son, who requires labour-intensive 24 hour care, slashed by the current Ontario government. She has put together a lobby group to support her desire to keep her beautiful and unusual child at home, but as she and her supporters learn more, they become increasingly disturbed by their realization that we live in a society which neglects its most vulnerable. What can this say about our future?"

Karl Schroeder ("The Dragon of Pripyat") was born and raised in Brandon, Manitoba. He moved to Toronto in 1986 and has been working and writing there ever since. His first novel, written with David Nickle, is *The Claus Effect*, which is available from Tesseract Books. His second, *Ventus*, is being published by Tor Books and will be available in Spring, 2000. Karl is currently working on a new novel and a whole new universe to go with it.

Daniel Sernine ("Umfrey's Head") was born in 1955 in Montréal, where he now lives. Since 1978, he has become the most prolific and versatile Quebec writer of fantasy and science fiction. He has published thirty-two books in these genres for both adults and young readers, as well as a large number of stories in magazines, fanzines, anthologies, and collections of new short fiction in Quebec, France, and Belgium. He is the literary editor for Jeunesse Pop books for Mediaspaul, as well as editor-in-chief of *Lurelu*, a Quebec magazine devoted to children's literature, and has been associated with the magazine *Solaris* almost since its inception in 1974. His works have repeatedly garnered prizes, including the Prix Boréal, the Aurora Award, and the Prix Solaris. In 1992 he won the Prix 12/17 Montreeal/Brive for the juvenile novel *Le cercle de Khaleb*. He was twice winner of the Grand prix de la science-fiction et du fantastique québécois—in 1992 for his short story collectioins, *Boulevard des étoiles* and *À la recherche de Monsieur Goodtheim*, and in 1996 for his collected stories, *Sur la scène des siècles*, and his juvenile novels, *La traversée de l'apprenti sorcier* and *L'arc-en-cercle*. Three of his stories have appeared in English translation in earlier Tesseracts anthologies, and four of his juvenile novels were published in English by Black Moss Press. ("Umfrey's Head" first appeared in French in *Espaces imaginaires 2*, Trois-Rivières: Les Imaginoïdes, 1984, pp. 19-51.)

Sara Simmons ("The Edge of the World") lives in Toronto and is a member of the Cecil Street writers' workshop. During the summer she spends as much time as possible with her boat.

Hugh A.D. Spencer ("Strategic Dog Patterning") was inspired to apply for a writer's workshop established by Judith Merril after reading the first *Tesseracts* anthology. Since then his work has been twice nominated for SF Canada's Aurora Award, in 1992 for the short story "Why I Hunt Flying Saucers" and in 1996 as co-curator for *Out of this World*, the National Library of Canada's exhibition on Canadian SF. He was born in Saskatoon and currently lives in Toronto.

Jean-Louis Trudel ("Holes in the Night") is the author of two novels in French as well as fifteen young adult books and a number of short stories. He co-edited the *Tesseracts7* anthology (with Paula Johanson) and also finds time to translate, review, and work on a PhD in history. In English, he is the author of a handful of a short stories; this is his first published poem in either language. "Holes in the Night" is "For SK, to whom it comes naturally."

J. Michael Yates ("Smokestack in the Desert") is a west coast writer who has published numerous books which have been translated into numerous languages. Currently, he writes plays, scripts, stories, and poetry mostly for the web. ∞